COLD HORIZON

THE PATHWAY SERIES BOOK 2

KRISTY MCCAFFREY

A PATHWAY NOVEL

Praise for *Cold Horizon*

"Cold Horizon will grab you right out of the gate and keep you turning pages as fast as you can to keep up with the action and adventure and suspense! A spectacular story of determination, courage, and love." ~ Ann Charles, *USA Today Bestselling Author*

"Full of action, suspense and adventure. Loved this book!" ~ Rebecca Lyndsey, Author/Illustrator of the children's book *Into the Ocean*

"Blending romance, suspense, adventure, and action, it really was a great thrill ride of a book and one that I gladly recommend. Give *Cold Horizon* a try." ~ Jamie, *The Romance Studio*

"... danger, angst, and drama come to life brilliantly, with characters keenly portrayed and fully developed. A must read for any lover of adventure laced with spicy romance!" ~ FS Brown, *InD'tale Magazine*, a Crowned Heart review

"... this novel had me holding my breath! ... definitely recommend it!" ~ Jessica Belmont, *Author and Blogger*

"... dynamic and forbidding and full of vivid imagery ... a wild, emotional adventure, to the edge of the abyss and back." ~ Jane Hunt, *Author and Blogger*

"... the imagery was powerful, the characters strong, the setting authentic, and the climb so very exhilarating." ~ *Shalini's Books & Reviews*

2021 National Excellence in Romance Fiction Winner
2020 Carolyn Readers' Choice Awards Finalist
2020 RONE Awards – Second Runner Up Steamy Contemporary

Cover Design: K. McCaffrey LLC

Editor: Mimi The Grammar Chick – merrelli.wixsite.com/grammarchick

Proofreader: Diane Garland – yourworldkeeper.com

Author Photo: Katy McCaffrey – instagram.com/katymccaffreyphoto

E-book ISBN-13: 978-1-7331420-0-7

Print ISBN-13: 978-1-7331420-1-4

kmccaffrey.com

kristy@kristymccaffrey.com

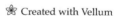 Created with Vellum

To my daughter Hannah ~
the mountains are calling.

I've long been fascinated by mountain climbing, although I'm not a climber myself. As an armchair enthusiast, I've read countless memoirs and followed the careers of many climbers over the years. Without question, I've always wanted to write a book set against the backdrop of the challenging environment of high-altitude mountaineering. I hope you'll enjoy this story about Ty and Lindsey as much as I enjoyed writing it. I've used many terms that are unique to the climbing community, so to help with any confusion I've included a glossary at the end of the book.

And now, I invite you into the world of high-altitude mountain climbing, filled with grueling work, endless suffering, and the ineffable glory of conquering the highest peaks in the world.

Kristy M.
xoxo

"Climbing is a conduit, a metaphorical plug that we can use to link ourselves
into powerful, life-altering forces—forces like passion, discipline, purity, nature, and the universe itself."
~ Steph Davis, *Women Who Dare: North America's Most Inspiring Women Climbers*

"Tho' much is taken, much abides; and though
We are not now that strength which in old days
Moved earth and heaven; that which we are, we are;
One equal temper of heroic hearts,
Made weak by time and fate, but strong in will
To strive, to seek, to find, and not to yield."
~ *Ulysses*, Lord Alfred Tennyson

"It's a savage mountain that wants to kill you."
~ George Bell, American climber after a failed K2 summit attempt in 1953

PROLOGUE

S ome people climb mountains. They just can't help themselves. It starts with the hills in the neighborhood when they're young but soon moves to the nearest, highest precipice. Climbing must be in my blood because my father, Robbie Coulson, was famous for his accomplishments in the mountains. I have memories of him but not many. He was never home. When I was nine, he died in the mountains he loved so much. The mountains he seemed to love more than my mom, more than my older sister, Alison, more than me. It only made sense then that I would climb, too. In my teens, I scrambled all over Yosemite and Colorado and Montana. Alison climbed as well, but we were very different—she so precise, so organized, so regimented. I climb because the dragon inside me can be appeased no other way. It pushes at my soul and I must feed it or I'll go mad. Alison suggested we climb the highest, coldest peaks on earth together, in honor of Robbie, in honor of the bloodline he bestowed upon us. In her mind, we were a force to be reckoned with, and fame and sponsorship soon followed. No matter, Alison handled all that. I got to climb, and that was all that counted, because in those moments the dragon is dormant, and I have peace.

But peace, like anything else in life, is an illusion....

Salt Lake City
January

Lindsey Coulson scanned the large convention room filled with vendors pushing everything from tents and sleeping bags to cutting-edge climbing gear and the latest in freeze-dried food. She generally kept it simple on expeditions—ramen noodles, hot chocolate, cheerios, peanut butter and saltines, and potato chips. Packaged tuna was good, too. Not too appetizing, any of it, but in high altitudes the appetite dwindled.

"Lindsey!"

Lindsey turned to see Mariah Blum grinning at her.

She smiled, hugging her friend. "It's great to see you." It had been over two years since she'd seen Mariah, or any of her climbing comrades for that matter. She relaxed a bit. Re-entering the arena that had been her world for so long had left her feeling ... nervous. What if she no longer belonged? What nagged more, though, was what if she no longer *wanted* to belong? It seemed as if her identity had always been intertwined with being a climber.

"I'm glad you came," Mariah said. "We've missed you."

"When you told me Athletica was having a mixer, how could I stay away?"

"You should talk to Amy. I'm sure they'd bring you back into sponsorship."

Lindsey nodded, not sure how to address that. She'd stopped climbing three years ago, the coffin that was now her mountaineering career facilitated by the disaster on Kangchenjunga, the third highest peak in the world, then nailed shut by the death of Alison on number two—K2—the following year.

"Thanks," she replied, "maybe I will."

"You'll climb again, Lindsey." Mariah looked at her with determination and compassion.

It was nice to be back among climbers. They were some of the most focused people she knew. In her academic life back at Berkeley, she immersed herself in DNA sequencing and genetic expression. Stimulating, but in a different way. While she still ran and hiked, camped and prowled the outdoors, she'd done no significant climbing during her grieving period. That's what she'd finally decided to call it. And perhaps it was time to be done with it.

"I have a question," Lindsey said. "Could you introduce me to Ty Galloway?"

An expression of surprise crossed Mariah's tan face. A few inches shorter than Lindsey, the woman's petite, fit frame belied a power-house free-climber. The dark-haired woman could out-climb Lindsey on an open face any day. Lindsey's strength, she'd come to learn once she'd started high-altitude climbing with Alison, was a strong, patient stride that had eventually brought her to some of the highest peaks in the world.

"You finally looking for a boyfriend?" Mariah asked.

Lindsey smiled and shook her head. "An expedition."

Mariah became serious. "K2?"

Lindsey nodded.

"All right." Her friend swung around and began searching the crowd. "I did just see him." She linked arms with Lindsey, guiding her from booth to booth.

Ty Galloway had been on Lindsey's mind this morning as she had gotten dressed. She was, in essence, pursuing an interview with the man and that desire had informed her choice of attire: black dress pants, flats, and a tan blouse. She'd secured her long blond hair in a loose bun at the nape of her neck and applied a minimum of makeup.

Mariah saw many people she knew, some Lindsey was acquainted with as well, but kept them moving forward. "There he is." She pointed to three men talking near a ski booth.

"Which one is he?" Lindsey asked.

"The totally hot one of course." Mariah laughed. "He's on the right."

Ty Galloway wore a dress shirt, dark slacks, and a tie. Tall with brown, short-cropped hair, she knew him by reputation only: he was a climber, but also a writer who frequently published in adventure magazines. She'd heard through the grapevine that he was mounting an expedition to K2 this June. Her decision to get to the second-highest mountain in the world at this late date had put her in a predicament. With no time to gain a permit or assemble her own team, she needed to beg her way onto someone else's trip, which was no easy feat. There was a Polish team going, as well as a group of German climbers, some of whom she was acquainted with, but Ty Galloway was preparing with a tiny American crew. That appealed to her immensely. She and Alison had always climbed in small groups, and Lindsey liked the autonomy. It meant more workload, but the benefit was a stronger likelihood of a summit. She had decided to approach Galloway first in her pursuit of getting to K2.

"Hello, Tyler," Mariah said.

"Mariah, good to see you." He leaned down and gave her a hug.

"I hope I'm not interrupting."

"Nah." He turned to the two other men. "I'll catch up with you later."

His companions were reabsorbed into the crowd.

"Ty, I'd like you to meet Lindsey—"

"Coulson." He held out his hand. "I know who you are. It's nice to meet you."

Lindsey grasped his palm, her hand engulfed in his larger one. "Same here."

"I think she wants to proposition you," Mariah said, "so I'll leave you both alone."

Lindsey frowned as her friend departed. Ty looked at her with a crooked smile and expectation in his blue-green eyes.

"I guess she's right," Lindsey said. "Can I buy you some coffee?"

"Of course. I like to be alert for a proposition."

They left the main convention floor, and Lindsey led him to the hotel restaurant accessible from the atrium. A hostess seated them.

Lindsey waved off the menu. "Hot tea, please."

"Black coffee," Ty added.

Once they were alone, Ty leaned back in his chair. "You've been off the radar for a while."

Lindsey silently agreed. "Look, I won't take too much of your time. I'm looking for a way to K2 this summer, and I've heard that you're going."

Ty nodded and smiled, then became serious. "David's on the team. I guess you're both looking for some closure."

"Since when?"

"I'm sorry—" Ty responded, clearly confused.

"Oh, no. I mean, when did David join your expedition?"

The announcement surprised Lindsey. Alison's fiancé, David Shaw, had been with her sister on K2 when she had died; however, Lindsey didn't have much contact with him anymore. It wasn't as if they'd been very close.

"It's recent. Do you have a problem with him?"

Did she? She dismissed the persistent notion that Shaw's influence over her sister may have contributed to Alison's death. "No."

"Let me do some checking, and I'll get back to you."

"Thanks. I'd appreciate it." Lindsey dug into her compact black purse and found a business card, replete with a University of California–Berkeley insignia. It had her address, email, and phone numbers. "You can reach me at any of these."

Ty took the card. "You're one of those climbers that actually works."

"It keeps me busy."

He looked at the business card again. "You're a chemist?"

Lindsey nodded as the waitress brought their drinks.

Ty added cream and sugar to his coffee. "I hated chemistry in high school."

"You must've been the only boy who did. There's nothing like mixing volatile substances that brings out the creativity in the male species."

Ty smiled. "I liked dissecting frogs more."

"That's biology."

"Maybe I should try that in my next life."

"I think you're already doing it," she said. "I read your recent piece about your climb in Peru. I liked the parts about the local plants and animals."

"Then I think you were one of five people who read it, including my mom." He took a sip of coffee. "Listen, I was really sorry about Alison. I've known David for a while and had a chance to meet her a few times."

"Thanks."

"She was very driven," he said.

"She was."

"I can understand why it would be hard to climb again. I have a sister. She's a pain in the ass, but I like her a lot. But don't ever tell her."

"Your secret's safe."

She soaked the tea bag in the cup of hot water, contemplating her next words. "I'd like to reassure you that I'm still a good climber. In case you have any reservations about me."

"No. You and Alison had a strong résumé in the mountains."

When she looked at him expectantly, he added, "I'm a writer. I generally keep tabs on most climbers of merit. If you're not opposed, I can probably swing help money-wise if you're willing to be written about."

"By you?"

"Probably. I can try to pitch a feature to Mountaineer Magazine. They might cover your costs, or at least part of them."

Lindsey hesitated. It wasn't as if this was a surprise—she and Alison had used such exposure in the past to their advantage—but it meant opening herself up, something she wasn't all that excited to do. Still, she'd barely be able to scrape the thousands of dollars needed for the expedition as it was. It would be stupid to turn it down.

"I'll think about it," she replied.

"Fair enough."

The waitress brought the check. Lindsey reached for her wallet, but Ty shook his head. He pulled a ten-dollar bill from his trouser pocket and dropped it on the table.

"But I invited you," she said.

"My treat. It's not every day I get to meet a famous climber."
Lindsey let out a half-laugh and stood. "You're not so obscure
yourself." Ty Galloway had climbed all over the world. She reached
out to shake his hand. "Thanks for talking to me."

As the contact ended, he asked, "Are you busy now?"

"Not really. Why?"

"My brother, Alec, is screening his latest documentary in the audi-
torium. It's sold out, but I could get you in if you're so inclined."

"What's it about?"

"His girlfriend freediving with great white sharks."

"That sounds intriguing."

"Don't say that to his face. He'll have you scuba diving in no time
flat."

"I take it you're not a diver," she said as they walked into the
sunny hotel lobby.

"I surf. That puts me close enough to sharks. I think he made this
film just to torment me."

She tried to keep pace with his long strides. "You don't have to
watch it."

"Of course I do. I can't let him think he's got the better of me. It's a
sibling thing."

Lindsey nodded, thinking of Alison. Her relationship with her
sister had been simple yet complicated, filled with love but also
competition, anger, and frequently, irritation. And now the final coda
of that bond was a gaping hole in Lindsey's heart, a grief so raw she
could hardly go near it.

She pushed the words past the sudden constriction in her throat. "I
get it."

CHAPTER 1

K 2 —*Karakoram Mountain Range, Pakistan*
27,230 feet —*Between Camp Four and the summit*
July 29

THICK, HEAVY SNOWFLAKES SWIRLED IN THE BEAM FROM LINDSEY'S headlamp. It was 8 p.m. and the weather was complete shit. Her elation at reaching the summit of K2 earlier in the day had dissipated as she struggled to get Elena Rossi off the mountain. How ironic that summitting was the easy part. Descending was always the true test of any climb.

Although Elena spoke English, she had reverted to her native Italian hours ago, and Lindsey had given up talking to her. At least they weren't alone. Ed "Ditch" Dittrich had helped belay Elena down some of the worst sections of the Traverse, the area above the Bottleneck, constituting the most dangerous area on K2. Lindsey was nearing her last reserves, and she suspected Ditch was, too.

Where was Ty?

He had lagged behind on their summit bid, having helped one of their other teammates, Billy Packer, back to Camp Four when the man couldn't go on. But then Ty had done an extraordinary push back to the summit. She and Ditch had passed him hours ago as they were descending, and he was closing in. Their exchange had been brief, and for one wild moment she had considered going back up with him.

But they were in the Death Zone, that area above 26,000 feet where all life was slowly dying, including them; exerting unnecessary energy was folly to the highest degree. So she and Ditch had resumed their descent while Galloway had pushed upward. He had no radio, so Lindsey didn't know if he'd made it or not.

In the ensuing hours, she had kept alive the hope that Ty would catch them, since their pace had slowed considerably while aiding Elena, whom they had found asleep on the snowfield leading to the summit.

It wasn't the first time Lindsey had been on a mountain with Elena and forced to deal with the woman's weak climbing skills, and it had crossed her mind more than once to leave her where she lay. But just when Lindsey was reaching her limit, Ditch would step in. Despite being almost twice Lindsey's age—and harboring his own resentment over a past relationship with Elena—he had proven why Ty relied on the man as a guide and mentor on this expedition. Ditch was steady, patient, and a world-class climber.

Lindsey stopped on the steep mountainside, anchored to the mountain with an ice axe in each hand and her boots, clad in spiky crampons, kicked into the icy terrain. In the glow of her headlamp, she spied the start of a fixed line.

She released a sigh of relief. They had reached the Bottleneck, so called because it was a narrow couloir, at times clogged with climbers. It was a dangerous three hundred-foot stretch of steep, slick, and unforgiving ice. It was also shadowed by a large serac from above, curved over them like the prow of a giant ship, and every climber passed as quickly as possible beneath it since pieces had been known to break off and come crashing down. This wasn't a place to dawdle.

But once they made it through this section, they would arrive at the relative safety of the shoulder where Camp Four was pitched.

She knew the fixed rope didn't traverse the entire Bottleneck— the Poles had placed it yesterday on the way to their summit bid and had only one hundred feet of rope on hand—but it was better than nothing. And they needed all the help they could get with Elena.

The wind blasted Lindsey, threatening to rip her off the mountain and throw her into the abyss far below.

It was blisteringly obvious that K2 wasn't going to give up her summit without a fight. Descending the Bottleneck in this shitstorm of low visibility was bad enough but having to guide an impaired Elena down was enough to give Lindsey sharp pangs of panic.

Had Alison been in this same spot, gripped with the same bone-deep fear?

Her sister had died on this mountain two years ago, likely not far from where Lindsey currently stood.

This won't be my fate.

Two climbers materialized behind them in the darkness. For a moment, Lindsey thought it was Tyler, but that elation was dashed when the first one spoke with a German accent. *Frieder.*

They came to Ditch first, but to her surprise didn't stop and instead climbed around him and Elena.

When they tried to do the same to Lindsey, she blocked them.

"Can you help us get Elena through the Bottleneck?" she asked.

Frieder stopped and said nothing, then finally shook his head and uttered one word, *"Nein."*

To Lindsey's shock, he said nothing more and climbed past her, hooking himself to the fixed rope.

What the hell?

When the second German, Volker, moved to do the same, she planted her axe in front of his face. "We need help with Elena."

Volker shook his head. "We are spent."

"So are we. If we leave her here, she'll die."

"Then she should not be here. Not our responsibility."

"Bullshit," Lindsey said. "It'll go faster with four of us."

Volker ignored her and climbed up a few feet to get past her. Then he went to the fixed rope, clipped on, and the swirling snow swallowed him up.

Stunned, Lindsey remained where she was, trying to quell her anger.

A loud snap filled the air, and then a rumble.

Shit!

"Hold on!" she yelled, facing the mountain and tucking her head, praying her helmet would fend off any blocks of ice.

She closed her eyes and held her breath, waiting as the roar grew. A cloud of snow and ice slammed into her, and she held tight to her ice axes to keep from being blown off the mountain.

But the avalanche hadn't hit them.

Trembling, she didn't move.

"Lindsey," Ditch said. "Where are the Germans?"

Her headlamp revealed the fixed rope to be still intact. Maybe the two shithead Germans were okay. She almost didn't care.

She swung her light back toward Ditch and Elena, trying to answer, but the words wouldn't come. Ditch had retrieved his radio. "David, come in."

In addition to Ty, Lindsey, and Ditch, their team had consisted of David Shaw and Billy Packer. Since Shaw had summited the day before with the Poles, a move that had irritated Lindsey, he had nonetheless stepped up to care for Packer at Camp Four until the rest of them could return to help.

"I'm here," Shaw replied.

"We think part of the serac broke off. Frieder and Volker might have gotten hit. Over."

"Copy that. I'll go out and look for them, but it's a white-out. Be careful. Over."

Ditch stowed the radio. "Is the fixed rope still there?" he asked Lindsey.

"It looks like it," she answered, her teeth chattering.

"You stay here with Elena," he said. "I'll go check."

Unable to move, all Lindsey could do was watch as he moved above her and soon disappeared into the snowstorm, just as the Germans had.

Ditch had hooked Elena to an ice screw before he had left them, so she was secure for the moment, allowing Lindsey to remain where she was and regroup.

She was shakier than she wanted to be.

The snow conditions were becoming untenable. It was too dark. A piece of the serac had just broken off, possibly killing Frieder and Volker. And if the two German men weren't dead, how would anyone find them? Was there anyone left at Camp Four besides David and Packer?

And now, as she waited for Ditch to return, she faced the fact that she might have to bivouac with Elena right here. Spending the night hanging off the side of K2 was a terrible idea, and one she wanted to avoid. Climbers joked that bivouac was French for "mistake." And Elena had certainly made a mistake as she'd tried to reach the summit earlier today, instead of turning around. Now, Lindsey was paying the price for the woman's piss-poor decision-making.

Knowing she needed to stop complaining, Lindsey switched to problem-solving mode, trying to corral her errant thoughts into something useful. Hours—no, it had been days—of oxygen deprivation was fast destroying her cognitive skills.

She had a bivy sac, but it was only meant for one person. There was no way she could secure it on this near vertical face, so they would need to ascend. But what if they got lost?

What about Ty? Was he still behind her? And wasn't the other American team also downclimbing from the summit? If she waited long enough, surely they would meet up with her and could help get Elena down. But it was already so late. They could be hunkered down, bivouacking despite the lunacy of sitting still and waiting out the storm. Waiting for sunrise.

Or they could be lost themselves.

Godfuckingdammit.

She really needed to get her and Elena down.

Now.

She gathered her courage and yanked an axe free and swung it into the icy slope with a loud thwunk, then kicked in a step with the sharp cramponed-toe of her right foot. Repeating this process, she carefully shuffled over to the start of the fixed rope. She gave a yank on the cord. To her horror, it released and flew back toward her.

Sucker punched, she gasped for air that wasn't there.

Please, God, no!

Where the hell was Ditch? Was he somewhere down below? Hurt, or dead?

If she left Elena, Lindsey knew she would never find the woman again. Not in this weather. Not in Elena's compromised state.

Elena would be Alison all over again, incoherent and lost, roaming the high reaches of K2 until death arrived and mercifully ended her suffering. And if she abandoned Ditch now, wouldn't it be a replay of when she had left Jim Shoop—family friend and her mentor—on Kangchenjunga? Her actions had led to his death. Hadn't they?

No, a voice echoed back to her. A familiar voice.

Lindsey swung her headlamp into the snowflakes whipping wildly around her. "Al?" she said, using her sister's nickname.

But there was nothing but wind and snow and darkness. Lindsey steadied herself.

Regroup. Focus.

She had to get Elena off this mountain.

She had rope in her pack—only a thin, fifty-foot length of nylon—but it would have to do. She went to work securing it between her and Elena, shortening the length, and then she did something unorthodox —she attached the longest part of the rope to the frayed end of what remained of the fixed rope. How would she deal with this when she and Elena had moved across the Bottleneck? She would cut it.

All of this was incredibly risky, but if Elena fell, Lindsey wasn't certain she could hold them both. Being connected to that ice screw might save their lives.

Yes, yes, it seemed plausible.

"Elena!" Lindsey yelled. "You'd better answer me in fucking English!"

The woman's response was barely audible, but at least she was still conscious. "What?"

"You've got to climb. I'll go first, and you follow. Face in. Make sure you kick your steps and get a solid purchase. Do you understand?"

Elena nodded, her bundled-up form illuminated in the glow from Lindsey's headlamp.

With everything secure, she inched her way horizontally out onto the steep face of the Bottleneck, sensing the large serac of ice above them. The very same serac that had already calved a large chunk.

Her heart pounded, and her muscles screamed for oxygen. The visibility was terrible. What if she went in the wrong direction?

Have faith. Just go.

"Lindsey!" A distant voice crept from the shadows.

Thinking she'd imagined it, she kept moving. At this altitude, climbers had been known to hallucinate. Lindsey vowed she wouldn't succumb. The voice she'd heard earlier, the one that had sounded so eerily like Alison's, was just a figment of her imagination.

"Lindsey!"

Galloway? She carefully looked behind her, but only Elena was there, creeping along behind her.

For a moment, her thoughts wandered. Was it the abominable snowman? The yeti, come to lure her to her death by pretending to be Tyler Galloway, a man she was pretty certain had snagged her heart despite her best efforts to treat him like every other guy she'd dated.

A figure slowly grew in shape behind Elena.

"Lindsey! It's me! It's Tyler!"

Relief swamped her. It *was* him.

A loud crack split the air.

"No!" Ty yelled, reaching for her, but he was too far away.

And then the thundering hooves of a thousand horses came crashing onto Lindsey.

∼

FOUR WEEKS EARLIER ...
   K2 Base Camp — 17,000 feet

. . .

15

"I DIDN'T SIGN UP FOR THIS SHIT." BILLY PACKER SHOOK HIS HEAD AND walked away from the group of climbers standing at the edge of the glacier. "And what the hell is that smell?"

Rotting flesh.

Lindsey stared at the body that had been discovered early that morning. The remnants of a yellow down suit covered a woman's torso, her hands and feet missing. She was also missing her head. Lindsey couldn't move as dread filled her.

Alison never had a yellow climbing suit.

But Lindsey hadn't climbed with her sister on that last fateful expedition that had claimed her life on this mountain. Maybe she had bought a new suit.

"I think it's Marie Broucet," said Frieder Berg, his English tinged with a German accent. "She disappeared two years ago. Volker," he said to one of the other men, "get your camera. We take photos then email to Gertie and see if she can notify family."

As the men dispersed, a woman touched Lindsey's arm. "It's not Alison," Brynn Galloway said quietly, her dark brown hair clipped away from her face, and her blue-green eyes—so similar to her brother's—filled with compassion.

Lindsey nodded, relief mixed with regret. A part of her hoped to find her sister, to lay her to rest properly, but a part also lived with the ignorant notion that without a body perhaps Alison still lived, somewhere, somehow. It made no sense, but the wish still lived deep inside. But Broucet had disappeared the same summer that Alison had. Her sister was somewhere on this mountain that cleansed it slopes regularly with avalanches, pushing perished climbers to the bottom where glacier movements ground bodies apart. This one aspect she had never shared with her mother, though Lainie Kincaid-Coulson was hardly uninformed about the cost of mountain climbing and the often gruesome aftermath.

It was a clear day and the perpetrator, K2, stood like a sentinel on Lindsey's left side. The locals had a more poetic name for the monolith: Chogori. But K2 was the moniker used in the climbing community, one that defined its remoteness and its savage simplicity with little fanfare. She craned her head to view the black rock dusted with snow, a perfect peak in shape, rising like a pyramid from the depths of the earth. Its relentless presence was both an omen and a siren's call, ever beckoning to the climbers who would dare its heights. Climb and you will find peace, it seemed to whisper. Perhaps it was true. If you survived, you could put the yearning to rest; if you died, the yearning was put to rest for you.

"Would you like some tea?" Brynn asked.

Lindsey nodded numbly and followed the woman along the broken trail back to the tents. The American expedition, led by Tyler, was situated off to the left. Ty, Brynn, and David had arrived two weeks prior. In addition to each individual tent, they had erected a mess tent with a cook stove and utensils, a table and stools, a laptop with internet connection, and a radio. They had hired a Balti porter to cook during the six weeks the expedition planned to stay at K2.

Lindsey had yet to see Galloway, as he and David had progressed to Camp One to lay fixed ropes and cache supplies. Brynn thought they would return the following day.

When Lindsey had spoken to David on the phone several months ago—the one and only time after Galloway had formally invited her to be a part of the team—he had assured her that Galloway was level-headed and one of the best climbers he knew. Ty wouldn't care that she was a woman. She hadn't thought he would. Brynn's presence at Base Camp now reinforced that notion, but David had thought it an important point to address.

It was yet another David Shaw irritation of many. What had Alison seen in the man? He was a strong climber, yes. He was handsome, but in a way that seemed to be only on the surface. Lindsey had always found him condescending with an ego that kept her radar on alert. And somehow, beneath it all, he just seemed desperate—for attention, for accolades, for being the best. Maybe that was the attraction for her sister. Alison and David had wanted the same thing: to make a name for themselves in climbing, to create a career around something they both loved. Alison's single-minded drive and ambition had found a compatible partner in David.

Lindsey couldn't deny that some of her bitterness toward David was simply that he had survived this mountain when Alison hadn't. It was so damned unfair. She knew mountains didn't pick favorites, that skill went hand in hand with luck, but that didn't make her feel more forgiving that David had lived, while her sister hadn't.

Two additional climbers rounded out the team—Billy Packer and Ed Dittrich. Lindsey hadn't climbed with either, but after the sixteen-hour bus trip from Islamabad to Skardu, followed by ten days of trekking from Skardu to Base Camp, she knew they were of the good sort.

Packer was a small, wiry man with long, crimpy black hair. His size had little to do with his strength. He was a fast climber who acclimated well to the thin air. This was his first crack at K2, although he had scrambled up many others including Everest, Lhotse, Cho Oyu, and most notably, Annapurna, a year prior to Lindsey's summit of the peak. It was the only one she'd made without Alison, who had turned back exhausted at 7000 meters. Packer's personality had blazed on the bus ride as loudly as the Pakistani music that had played continuously. He was funny, outgoing, and often inappropriate, cussing up a storm as the vehicle drove up and down precarious switchbacks through high mountain passes with the driver constantly blowing his horn. He'd taken to Lindsey immediately, eventually toning down the charm when he realized she wasn't interested in a quickie.

Ditch was older, much taller, and balding. Lindsey guessed he was in his fifties, and he had an extensive climbing résumé. He was known for being a careful and methodical climber, and had turned away from many summits due to bad weather—Everest, Gasherbrum II, and Nanga Parbat being the most notable. He'd done considerable climbing in Italy, Kyrgyzstan, and Chamonix, as well as lesser known mountains in the Himalaya. This would be his third attempt at K2. Besides him, only David had been here before; the rest of them were K2 virgins.

The dozens of Pakistani porters who had accompanied them during the trek, including the Pakistani Liaison Officer, Captain Jez, had departed shortly after arrival yesterday leaving the bulk of the unpacking to her, Packer, Brynn, and Ditch. It had taken the better part of the day to get everything organized, despite it being a small portion of the supplies. Brynn, Galloway, and David had already brought more than two-thirds of the gear with them.

Lindsey entered the mess tent behind Brynn.

"Habibe, some tea?" Brynn asked the cook. The young black-haired Balti smiled. He looked to be about twenty years old and had a limited use of English. He proceeded to heat water.

Lindsey sat across from Brynn and asked, "Are you planning to climb K2?" The addition of Brynn to the team had come at the last minute. With all the organizing the day before, they really hadn't had a chance to talk yet.

Brynn shook her head, her eyes the same color as Ty's. "No. I'm just here for a summer vacation."

Lindsey smiled. "I take it you're not a beach girl."

"Ty's been climbing a long time. When he invited me, I couldn't pass it up. It's an opportunity to see a mountain most people never do."

K2 was climbed less frequently than Everest. Not only was it a more difficult mountain, it required an arduous and dangerous hike just to reach Base Camp. The infrastructure that existed in the Himalaya—villages, porters, trekking companies, and the like—didn't exist in the Karakoram. And the starting point was Islamabad, an unsettling destination these days, unless an expedition was mounted from the other side. That required permission from the Chinese government, an almost impossible and headache-filled task. Most climbers opted to enter on the Pakistan side.

"Do you climb?" Lindsey asked.

"A little. Nothing like this."

"Maybe we can do some spelunking around here, if you like."

Brynn's gaze brightened, signaling her adventurous side. Lindsey hadn't expected to find a female to befriend on this expedition, and she was heartened not to be the lone girl on the team.

"It's awfully nice of you to come on a two-month campout," Lindsey said.

"Yeah, well, I like to keep an eye on Tyler. It goes back to an incident when we were kids."

"What happened?"

"Our uncle has a ranch near Telluride, Colorado, and when my brothers and I were young, we would spend part of our summers there. My dad called it boot camp, but Uncle Simon and Aunt Jen were pretty chill. They let us run around the wilderness like little rugrats. One day, when I was five years old and Ty was six, Uncle Simon was having a picnic. There were lots of people around, which I suppose is why Ty and I left all the noise and commotion and headed to a nearby meadow. We liked to play a game called explorers, where you pick a tree and walk off in different directions then return and report on anything interesting you found. Alec taught it to us, but he wasn't there this time. Ty walked off and didn't come back."

"That must've been frightening," Lindsey said.

"At first, I thought he was messing with me, so I sat down, angry, and waited for him. When Uncle Simon found me, a few hours had passed. I hadn't been afraid until I saw the look on his face, then I knew something bad must have happened. The police were called and a search party was sent out, but they didn't find him."

"Your parents must have been beside themselves."

"They were in California, so my Uncle Simon had to call and tell them. I remember wanting to talk to my mom, but she couldn't come to the phone. She was too distraught. My dad reassured me that it wasn't my fault, but of course I felt otherwise. Within hours, they flew to Telluride by private jet and joined in the search."

"But he was eventually found?"

"Eighteen hours later, he was picked up by a passerby on a dirt road who called the sheriff. He ended up walking about twenty miles in all. When he'd realized he was lost, he had been certain he could find his way back, so he took off walking."

Lindsey was stunned. "And he was only six years old when this happened?"

Brynn nodded. "He was a very confident child. After he was found, he was for the most part okay, but I remember that my mother could hardly pull off his shoes because his feet were so swollen and sore. But after a week they healed, and he was back traipsing around."

"And he still is."

A ghost of a smile flashed across Brynn's face. "He was called the 'Lost Boy of San Miguel' by the locals. I guess I still feel the need to keep an eye on him."

"That's understandable."

"Both my brothers are adventure junkies," Brynn said.

"I saw Alec's film about great whites."

"It's amazing, isn't it? He certainly met his match in Grace."

"How do your parents handle all this?"

Brynn laughed. "My dad was a big wave surfer and my mom was a climber. We grew up either in the ocean or on a mountain. You can't be a Galloway and sit on your ass."

"Aside from getting lost, it sounds like a great life."

Habibe set two plastic mugs before them filled with steaming sweet tea. Lindsey savored a swallow of the liquid as it warmed her throat and stomach.

"Wasn't your father a famous climber?" Brynn asked.

Lindsey nodded.

"You must've spent as much time outdoors as I did," she said.

"I think the drive for that came later. I was in high school the first time I went climbing."

"Well, I'll try not to be in anyone's way. I plan to take care of Base Camp for you guys." Brynn took a sip of tea. "Are you looking forward to going up?"

"Yes." It was the truth. Lindsey itched to push herself again, to hook herself to a mountain, to test her mettle while it tried everything to shake her off.

"Do you ever get scared?"

"I like to think I'm cautious, and hopefully that makes me a better climber." She hadn't been afraid, not initially, on Kangchenjunga. How stupid that had been to disregard her gut feeling, because it had made her ignore the subtle signs that always appeared when something was about to go wrong.

"I have to admit I was afraid just hiking in here to Base Camp," Brynn said. "I doubt I could make it up the mountain."

"You could. You just have to break it down into smaller steps."

"Do you mind me asking why you didn't come with Alison two years ago? Ty said you both always climbed together."

Lindsey sipped her drink, which had quickly gone from hot to tepid. "I didn't feel a desire for K2. It may sound strange, but when I anticipate climbing a mountain, I either feel something or I don't. And I didn't feel anything then. Maybe it had something to do with a climb from the previous year." She paused and stared at the brown liquid in her cup.

Brynn remained attentively quiet.

"We were climbing Kangchenjunga," Lindsey continued, "which is the third highest mountain. We'd had a terrible time with weather for weeks, but we thought we'd finally made it to the top. But we hadn't. The problem on Kanch is that there are four false summits. Alison and I both made the decision to go up again to get it right, despite being fairly worn out at that point. Another climber, Jimmy Shoop, decided to go with us. Shoop was an old family friend—he'd been my dad's best friend—and when Alison and I started high-altitude climbing he mentored us." Lindsey's throat closed suddenly and tears threatened. "The three of us decided to climb fast since we were already acclimated."

Lindsey suddenly felt Shoop, as if he were beside her, laughing and telling stories of her father. The tears came; she couldn't stop them. She impatiently brushed them aside.

"What happened?" Brynn asked quietly.

One reason Lindsey had been unafraid on Kanch during their summit bid was the fact that Jimmy had been with them. His presence had made her feel safe, the way a daughter should feel when climbing with her father. But Shoop wasn't her dad. Nonetheless, he'd come to occupy a place in her mind and in her heart that had been empty for years, maybe for Lindsey's entire life. Robbie Coulson simply hadn't filled her with enough memories that a father should. And it was

Shoop who had taught her and Alison how to climb the highest mountains in the world.

"I was stupid. I ignored the bad weather closing in. I ignored our slow pace. Near the top, I became separated from them, and I was forced to bivouac overnight."

"I know enough from Ty that people don't often survive that," Brynn said.

"Jimmy didn't." Her words caught in her throat. "He must've been worse off than Al and I had realized. It was probably edema, a swelling of the brain or lungs. On my descent I found Alison, but Shoop was gone. During the night he'd stumbled away, disoriented, and likely fell. We never found him."

During that long night, death had hovered around Lindsey, whispering in her ear sweet nothings and the promise of peace if she just took his hand and let him lead her away from the misery of the cold and the altitude. By morning, however, she'd shoved it back like an ex-lover who wouldn't stop stalking her.

But when it had become clear that they'd lost Shoop, she was sorry she had lived and he hadn't. Guilt continued to gnaw at her that she might have been able to help if she had gone to find him before it had been too late.

"I really didn't feel up for K2 after that," Lindsey added.

And now Alison was gone. The ever-present guilt over Shoop had shifted to her sister. If Lindsey had come to K2 two years ago, maybe Alison would still be alive.

"I decided to hike the Appalachian Trail with a friend instead," Lindsey continued. "That's where I was when the news came about Alison."

She downed the last of her tea.

A commotion outside the tent diverted their attention. Several climbers carried what remained of Broucet's body wrapped in a tent, headed toward the Gilkey Memorial. It was a trip Lindsey would soon make to honor Alison, but first she would wait for David. It was a concession for Al, not for him.

"Perhaps we should go, too," Brynn suggested.

Lindsey silently agreed. They rose and headed toward the rock cairn that commemorated the lives that K2 had laid claim to. Every climber knew they could easily be in the same position. All it took was bad luck and questionable decision-making while in the throes of hypoxia. But most climbers—and for most of Lindsey's climbing career this had included her—refused to believe it could ever happen to them.

CHAPTER 2

Tyler Galloway hoisted his pack onto his shoulders and secured the straps. It was before dawn and pitch-black outside except for the stars spread across the sky like a spilled bucket of sand. It took some doing to be completely cut off from civilization, but it was still possible, especially in a place as remote as the Karakoram Mountains.

It had been a dream for a long time to get here, harkening back to stories his mother would tell him when he was a boy of her climbing adventures. She had never made it to K2—and once she had married his father and begun having children, she had abandoned the drive for remote and dangerous endeavors—but she had often spoken of the mystique of this mountain that was so very different from Everest. For Ty's entire life, it had hung like a beacon in his mind, lighting the way to a goal he was hungry to conquer, a feat he could hold up to Jim Galloway's scrutiny. Ty was no different than any other son when it came to seeking approval from his dad.

The light from David Shaw's headlamp bobbed up and down as he readied himself for the hike from Advanced Base Camp, or ABC, back to Base Camp, a short trek that should take only two hours. They would arrive in time for a hot breakfast from Habibe.

David looked in Ty's direction, his face but a shadow beyond the light, and Tyler gave a nod. They began their journey off the glacier, the scraping of crampons acutely loud in the stillness of the night.

Brynn had radioed the day before that the remainder of the team had arrived—Packer, Ditch, and Lindsey. It would be good to assemble and map out their plan of attack. He and David had just spent two days fixing rope—sleeping one night at Camp One and the next at ABC—and while they'd spoken a little about Packer and Ditch, David had hardly mentioned Lindsey.

Tyler hadn't broached the subject, thinking that maybe it was a painful reminder of losing Lindsey's sister, Alison, but in truth Ty really hadn't wanted to swap stories with the man. A desire tugged at him to get to know Coulson directly, not from hearsay. Gossip had a way of inflating climbers into raging egomaniacs or heartless bastards or incompetent ninnies. None of it was ever true. Well, mostly.

That he harbored a secret admiration for Lindsey was beside the point. She was a good climber. That was it. And she had a nice smile.

Once they were past a stream of blue water that had broken through the glacier, Ty was able to walk beside David.

"Alison hated slogging through flows like that when we were here," David said.

"I don't blame her." Ty kept his face forward, so his headlamp illuminated the path ahead of him. He didn't want to fall into a hidden hole or even a crevasse.

"I always told her it was some of the purest water she would ever see. It was like being baptized by the earth."

"If it wasn't so cold, I'd say we shed our clothes and do our own version of a polar plunge." Since David had offered an opening, Ty added, "You okay?"

It had to be difficult coming back to the place where he had lost the love of his life.

David cleared his throat. "Yeah. It's strange, but sometimes I feel her."

"There's just no figuring out the mind of God."

David laughed, but it trailed off into something filled less with humor and more with sadness. "I wonder if Lindsey should be here."

"I'm assuming she considered that before she approached me."

The dark sky gave way to a tint of pink as sunrise approached.

"My experience with Lindsey was that she was a bit of a maverick when I climbed with her and Alison," David said.

"You're saying she always wanted to climb alone?"

"She never hung with the team."

"How often did you climb with her?"

"Twice," David said. "No, it was three times."

"That's not too many, Shaw. Maybe she just didn't want to share a tent with you and Alison. You probably couldn't keep your hands off each other," Ty teased, trying to lighten the mood.

David nodded. "Maybe."

Since Lindsey and Alison had always climbed together, it was likely that Lindsey had stepped back when David had become involved with her sister, becoming an inevitable third wheel. Or maybe Ty was completely off-base.

Ty had checked with David—as well as Ditch and Packer—before he'd invited Lindsey to come on board, and the three of them had agreed that Lindsey was a skilled mountaineer and would be an asset to the team.

"Are you having second thoughts about her?" Ty asked.

"You mean Lindsey?"

"Yes." Who else would he have meant?

David was silent for a moment as their crampons crunched along the icy path. Ty switched off his headlamp as there was now enough sunlight to see without it.

David released a heavy breath. "No. Sorry. I just didn't expect to feel so … heavy once I got here. Lindsey will be a reminder, that's all."

"This whole place is a reminder. Isn't that why you came? To put the ghosts to rest?"

He shook his head. "No. I came here to get this damned mountain off my checklist once and for all."

∼

LINDSEY AWOKE WITH A SPLITTING HEADACHE. SHE PULLED ON A FLEECE jacket and boots, brushed her blond hair into a ponytail, and headed to the mess tent with her mug in hand. Packer sat eating scrambled eggs and sipping coffee, while Ditch was on the computer.

"Good morning," Lindsey mumbled. "Is there any aspirin?"

Habibe produced two caplets and poured water into her cup. Lindsey thanked him, swallowed the medicine, then sat down.

"You better take it easy," Packer said around a mouthful of food. He pointed his fork at her. "Three years of no climbing—your acclimatization is shit. You should probably live here for a month before you even head up the mountain."

He spoke a measure of truth, but hell if she was going to sit for weeks and do nothing. "Don't worry about me. I start every climb with a headache."

Ditch looked over his shoulder at Packer. "I think she means you."

"Don't expect to follow me up the mountain," he replied to the older man, indignant.

"I won't. You break trail like a mouse. Look at you. You're no bigger than an eleven-year-old."

Packer made a face then grinned at her, his long wavy hair flowing from beneath the green knit hat he wore. "Small is good. Trust me."

She ignored the innuendo and took the plate of food Habibe offered. She did her best to eat the eggs and potatoes, knowing her lack of appetite was a sign of altitude sickness. She forced herself to drink a good amount of tea as well.

Brynn poked her head inside the tent. "Ty and David are coming in."

Packer stood. "Let's go greet the boss. It's hard to kiss ass when he's already up there fixin' ropes. How am I supposed to show him I'm the best climber here?"

"By climbing your ass off." Ditch logged off from his email. "There're no shortcuts."

As Packer left the tent, Habibe cleaned up the breakfast dishes, and Lindsey rubbed her forehead. She hoped the aspirin would kick in soon.

"You should take it easy," Ditch said. "It's been a while since you've climbed."

Lindsey silently agreed, but she didn't want to be treated like a child. Ditch's tone had been kind, not condescending, but a part of her chafed under his assessment. She had always felt a need to prove herself, some inward drive that propelled her to out-climb men who either tried to hit on her or talk shit about her.

"You ... okay?" Habibe said.

Lindsey stood and nodded.

"Choclit?" He held out a box of chocolate bars.

"Thanks." She took one and put it in the thigh pocket of her black cargo pants as she emerged into the sunny day. Before her stood the mountain that of late had been haunting her sleep. She pushed her sunglasses on as she scanned the Abruzzi Spur, the most traversed route on the mountain and considered the easiest. But easy was a misleading word for an 8000-meter peak. Her gaze followed the southeast ridge to an area known as House's Chimney, up higher to a dark rocky section known as the Black Pyramid, and higher to the Bottleneck, the site of many deaths. Beyond that, out of view, was the summit.

Where are you, Al?

Lindsey scanned the mountain, wondering where Alison's body might have taken refuge. Were there any climbers on the mountain today? She couldn't tell, couldn't see any tiny black specks creeping along the white spaces.

Lindsey closed her eyes and breathed in the cold air, breathed in the eternal promise of salvation that climbing offered. Within the pain and suffering, the mental anguish and physical toll, lay the assurance of renewal, of new life, of a moment so exquisite no words could describe it.

She loved to climb.

With immense relief the rush of that love filled her, an emotion she hadn't felt in such a long time. She thought she'd lost it, that connection, that spark that filled her spirit with such gladness and such familiarity. This was home for her. Thank God it hadn't abandoned her.

K2 stood in massive stillness, creating its own weather patterns, a mountain that gave peace but in the next breath took life. It was a relationship never to be reconciled. Maybe that was why climbers returned time and again, trying to understand, or maybe just reveling in the presence of their beloved once more.

A loud kraaah brought her attention back. A large black bird circled just beyond the tents, at the edge of the ice fall. Locals called them goraks, but Lindsey knew them to be giant ravens, present in the Himalaya as well as the Karakoram where they were known to scavenge the bodies of dead climbers.

Lindsey watched this one swoop and circle, clearly checking out the camp below, probably searching for booty. She looked for other birds since they usually flew in pairs or groups, but this one was alone.

"Charon," she said quietly, remembering her Greek mythology. Ferrier of the dead across the River Styx.

She picked her way past the German camp and the men who had disposed of Broucet's body the previous day. She nodded to Frieder, whom she had met on Everest several years ago, but she didn't stop to chat. He'd been a bit of a prick back then, and she had no desire to expend the energy to see whether that had changed. Three other men rounded out their team—Volker, Wolfgang, and Karl. At the moment their last names eluded her.

Further away was a Polish encampment, ten tents in all. She had spoken with her friend, Piotr, and he'd introduced her around. Some of the Poles were already on the mountain, climbing the south-south-east ridge. According to Brynn, two more teams were expected soon, but nothing was certain until porters and climbers appeared after the long trek from Skardu.

In the distance, two men approached from the tricky ice fall that lay at the base of the mountain; Brynn, Ditch, and Packer greeted them. Soon Lindsey caught up.

David gave her a hug as soon as he saw her, and she awkwardly accepted it.

"It's great to see you, Lindsey," he said.

"You too." He was much as she remembered, although a faint shadow seemed to haunt his features. Still, he appeared strong and tall, a man accustomed to hard work and a sense of control. Alison had found him irresistible during her time spent at Annapurna Base Camp. Isolation and a handsome face can confuse any woman. Lindsey's few mountain romances had never panned out into anything of merit—as much as she liked climbers, and male climbers were often muscular in physique and very easy on the eyes—it was usually the absence of common intellectual ground that left her wanting once they were back in civilization. And, in all honesty, male climbers lacked emotional maturity. Maybe it was something about that devil called pride that brought out the "king of the hill" mentality. After a while, it grew tiresome.

She turned to Galloway, who shook her hand. "How was your trek in?" he asked, pulling his sunglasses from his nose and letting them hang on the cord around his neck.

"Well, we lost a few porters in a crevasse, but we threw them some food before we abandoned them."

Galloway stopped, his blue-green eyes staring at her. "Seriously?"

She smiled and shook her head. "No. Sorry. It was fine."

He gave her an amused look of confusion and removed his fleece hat, running a hand through his short hair. "That's good. We're gonna need 'em on the way out."

She was glad to see him.

The thought caught her off-guard. This was a distraction she really didn't want. She pushed the tendrils of attraction aside, reminding herself it was just hormones. He likely had a girlfriend anyway. Male climbers usually had many.

As they walked back to camp, he started talking to Ditch.

David fell into step beside her as they trailed behind the other four, the helmet hanging from the center of his pack swinging back and forth.

"How's the mountain?" she asked.

David glanced at the white and silent sentinel. "Calm."

"What have you done so far?"

"We've got two tents at Camp One stocked with stoves, fuel, food for six days and extra rope. We left two sleeping bags, so we'll need to take up more."

"Did you fix all the ropes?"

"About a third done on the way to Camp One."

"Nice."

"The weather's been good, so no time to waste."

Lindsey silently agreed. The throbbing in her head was a dull ache now. "I may need a few days before heading up." She wished she didn't have to wait. To be considered a strong member of the team, she needed to help stock Camps One, Two, and Three, and fix ropes. But altitude sickness wasn't something to be taken lightly. She would be strong only if she gave her body time to acclimate, to begin generating the red blood cells that would increase the flow of oxygen to all parts of her body.

He squinted as if he were smiling, except the rest of his face bore little amusement and simply appeared strained. "Not adjusting as quickly as you used to?"

"I must be getting old."

"You are looking a bit decrepit." But the teasing fell flat.

Unease lingered on the edge of her psyche, reminding her why she had never cared for David Shaw—not when he was a new acquaintance after she and Alison had befriended him on Annapurna, not when Al had uncharacteristically drunk too much tequila one night and found herself in his tent on that same trip, and especially not when he and her sister had announced their engagement after knowing each other for only three months.

Lindsey slowed her pace, and soon David moved ahead of her.

Why had she come, knowing that David would be a climbing partner?

Her eyes shifted to Ty. Despite his yellow and black climbing suit, his tall physique was apparent. Her friend, Mariah—once she had learned that Lindsey would be on expedition with Galloway—had sent her links to write-ups and videos of his surfing days. He'd been much younger then, but he'd had a raw energy to him, and she'd wasted an entire afternoon glued to her computer screen, watching competition videos.

She liked to think she was levelheaded and not easily distracted by a handsome face and the potential of hot sex, so she had read some of his articles about his climbing endeavors. It had served only to make her like him more.

Had that been Alison's problem? Truthfully, her sister had had few boyfriends, and Shaw had certainly exuded a quiet magnetism. Lindsey really shouldn't fault Al for falling for him. Except that it had led her here. And here is where she would stay for eternity.

Lindsey blinked back tears and squared her shoulders.

No man would decide her fate. She wouldn't let Shaw keep her from the mountain. And she wouldn't let a distraction like Galloway —no matter how compelling—mess with her head.

She glanced at K2.

You're the only thing that matters.

CHAPTER 3

Ty spent most of the day resting in his tent, since he and David had worked hard the past few days. Now that the entire team was present, the expedition finally felt complete.

While Ty's mom had ignited his love of climbing, it was Ditch who had served as his mentor for the last seven years. Ty had met him in a climbing club based out of California when Ty was still in high school and spending most of his time surfing. When Ty was nineteen, Ditch had taken him on his first climb of Everest, which neither of them summited, but they had continued to climb together in the Dolomites, Kyrgyzstan, and Chamonix. He never would have considered a trip as big as K2 without Ditch on the team.

Packer was a good climber Ty had worked with before—they'd summited Everest and Lhotse within the span of a few days a few years after Ty's trip with Ditch. Although Packer was small in stature Ty was confident he would pull his weight, and the man's energy was always a boon.

He knew David through climbing circles, although they hadn't been on an expedition together. The rumor mill pegged David as a taskmaster and at times obsessively focused, but it was those very traits that Ty considered a positive addition to any team.

Bringing his sister, Brynn, hadn't really caused him any hesitation.

She had what it took to live in isolation for six weeks, to fend for herself, and to deal with big egos. He'd offered to bring Alec and his shark-lady girlfriend, Grace, but they had both decided they liked interacting with living creatures. Unfortunately, K2 had no life. It was barren, hostile, and unforgiving.

His mom had declined an invite as well. She was too old for such adventures, she said, cautioning Tyler to be careful and not break her heart by not coming home. In her older years, she had become less daring and more circumspect. Life was precious, especially her children's.

So when Lindsey had inquired about a spot on the team, Ty had the room.

Although they hadn't crossed paths until now, she'd been on his radar for some time. He was no different than any other male climber —attractive women in the sport always drew a second look. But his admiration had gone deeper than that. While she exhibited drive and ambition for the big climbs, she had a tendency for the offbeat. She liked to traverse the path less taken, and that appealed immensely to him.

David's assessment that she was a maverick could be a plus. It could also be a minus. But Ty considered his gut to be a reliable barometer when choosing teammates, so he wasn't going to waste time ruminating on what-ifs.

As dusk approached, the team met in the mess tent for dinner.

Ty sat at one end of the table, flanked by Ditch and Packer. David was at the other end, with Lindsey and Brynn on each side. Beside Brynn was the Pakistani Liaison Officer, Captain Juneid, a young man with black hair and bright eyes who was thrilled to be at Base Camp, admitting that he had hoped for this assignment since he'd dreamed of seeing the mountains as a boy. Unlike the other officer who had already departed, Juneid would remain at camp for the duration of the expedition, enforcing the rules of his government: no climbing unapproved routes, no team jumping, no climbing mountains not covered by the permit, no stealing any Pakistani military secrets. Ty hoped that the man's starry-eyed optimism wouldn't take a hit later when team dynamics invariably bent some of those rules; Ty had certainly experienced it time and again while in the mountains.

Habibe placed a large bowl of curried vegetables on the table—the aroma making Ty's mouth water—along with a generous helping of rice and a plate stacked high with fresh, hot flatbread.

"Chappatis," Habibe said, pointing at the bread.

Packer grabbed the rice spoon like a pouncing cat. "Habibe, if you were a woman, I'd marry you."

Habibe grinned, showing all his teeth. "I am already married."

Crisscrossing arms snaked to the center of the table as everyone grabbed food and water to drink.

"She hit the jackpot with you," Packer added, admiration in his voice as he started eating.

Once everyone was settled with their meal, Ty looked at the map he'd laid out on the table in front of him. "As everyone already knows, we're climbing the southeast ridge, which is the standard route known as the Abruzzi Spur. We'll keep it to four camps, as is the norm. How does the weather look, Ditch?"

The older man mixed his rice and vegetables together on his plate. "It's good. For now."

"We need to finish the fixed ropes to Camp One."

"If you'll wait two days, I'll go with you," Ditch replied, then took a bite of his dinner.

The new arrivals would need a chance to acclimate.

"I'll go, too," Packer said around a mouthful of food.

"Count me in," Lindsey added.

"Okay, great." Ty paused to feed his hunger before continuing. "We'll leave early July 5th. The Germans have agreed to share fixed ropes, and between all of us we should have it finished up to One by the end of the week. Then we'll figure out the next leg. Nothing will likely be fixed after Camp Three. From that point, we'll be climbing solo or roped together."

Packer tore off a piece of chappatis. "So, we've got Germans. Who else is joining us on our summer romp?"

"The Poles. You've probably already talked to them. They're

climbing a different route known as the Cesen line, which converges at Camp Four with the Abruzzi. There's a rumor that the Italians are also coming."

"What you're saying then," Packer said around the bread in his mouth, "is that after Camp Three, I'll actually have to climb."

"Are you a mountaineer or a tourist?" Ditch grabbed the salt shaker and sprinkled a generous amount on his dinner.

Ty laughed at Ditch. "The curry isn't enough?"

"The taste buds are the first to go in old age. You'll see. Just wait."

Packer wiped his mouth with the back of his sleeve. "Won't there be piña coladas at the summit?"

Ditch shook his head. "In your hallucinations."

It was a sobering statement. On the highest mountains in the world, delusions were not uncommon when climbing without supplemental oxygen. Sometimes they took on the absurd, sometimes the fearful. The most serious led climbers to their deaths.

"Never been plagued with 'em," Packer replied.

"My recommendation is to stash emergency oxygen cannisters at all three lower camps," Ditch said.

Ty reached for the water pitcher and filled his cup. "I agree, as long as everyone is willing to carry up tanks."

Ty didn't normally use supplemental oxygen while climbing. He wanted to scale a mountain on its own terms. And oxygen bottles could be damned heavy.

"If anyone has a problem with that, speak up now." No one answered, so Ty continued. "Lindsey, do you have a mask and regulator?"

She nodded. He had read about her climbs, and knew she didn't use oxygen, either, but she hadn't been in the mountains for a while. It was always good to have apparatus that fit perfectly, just in case.

"And so we're clear," Ty said, "when it comes time to decide on whether to summit, everyone will make up their own mind. Everyone has an equal shot."

"Right, boss." Packer stretched his lips into a wide smile. "Can I stay in my tent while you all get the mountain ready for me?"

"Bullshit," Ditch muttered under his breath, biting into a piece of flatbread.

Packer laughed in a high-pitched cackle.

"Packer, you can do what you want," Ty said, "but I won't be able to protect you from the rest of the team if you're a lazy ass."

Packer launched into a story of one such climber on a trip to Everest.

"The next year Galloway and I topped out on Everest, then ran up Lhotse in two days." Packer's wild-eyed gaze became uncharacteristically wistful over the memory. "It was a thing of beauty."

"I had trouble catching you," Galloway admitted.

Brynn pulled off her knit hat and pushed back the electrified flyaway strands from her face, tucking them behind her ear. "What's it like on Everest?"

"Crowded," Packer replied. "It's a goddamn circus at Base Camp. When we were there, there must've been hundreds of climbers. The noise and the trash. It's too much."

"What're you complaining about?" Ditch said. "You love being around people."

"Only certain ones."

"Have you summited Everest more than once?" Brynn asked Packer, sitting back in her canvas chair, her plate now empty.

"Two times." He held his fingers up in the peace sign. "Once with the boss." He nodded toward Ty. "And once with some bad-ass Russians."

"You know, those brain cells you lose at altitude never come back." Ditch drained the water in his cup.

"Yeah, I know. And those Russians had some vodka that probably killed the rest." Packer let out a big chuckle, then sighed. "But I do love my rectified corn-spirits."

"Isn't vodka made from grains?" Ditch asked.

"Whatever it's made from, it's an elixir from the gods." Packer stretched his arms above him. "Just wait. You'll be begging me for my stash."

Brynn glanced around the table. "Have you all been to Everest?"

"I've been once but didn't summit," Ditch answered. "Ty was with me and I didn't like the weather, but I'm glad he got it a few years later."

"Will you try again?"

"Maybe." Ditch crossed his arms. "It is Everest, after all, despite the hoopla that surrounds it now."

"It's amazing the characters that show up." Ty flicked away a few kernels of rice that had fallen on his map. "One year, some guy from Turkey decided he was going to carry his bicycle to the top."

"Did he?" Brynn asked.

"He got to the top but not with the bike." Ty shook his head. "He had to be rescued, otherwise he would've died. You get all levels of skill up there. It can lead to a lot of problems."

"Everest was my first 8000-meter summit," David said, running a hand through his short, dark hair. "I'm glad I did it first. I hear these days you can wait around for hours at the Hillary Step while trying to get to the top. The other peaks aren't as crowded."

"So you'll never go back?" Lindsey asked, stacking her plate on Brynn's now-empty one.

Packer snatched the last piece of chappatis. "Davy's trying to join the Fourteeners Club."

"What's that?" Brynn said.

Ty answered, "Climbers who've reached the summit of all fourteen peaks over 8000 meters. It's a small group, led by arguably the greatest mountaineer of all time—Reinhold Messner."

"Any chicks in this club?" Brynn asked pointedly.

"Yeah, a few," Ty answered. "Edurne Pasabán was the first, although one of her summits was with oxygen. Several years later Gerlinde Kaltenbrunner did all of them sans O2, although she and a Korean woman were in the running. The Korean's claim was disputed on her final climb. They said she never reached the summit of Kangchenjunga. She probably only thought she did."

"How do you know for sure?"

"Photos usually. And the word of the climber, along with descriptions they give of the route to the top. It's for that reason that most climbers on descent won't tell an ascending climber what the summit looks like. You gotta earn it."

Brynn looked at Lindsey. "Have you been to Everest?"

"Only once, but Alison and I did summit." She looked at Packer and smiled. "Then we ran up Lhotse."

He saluted her with his mug. "That's my girl. But didn't your dad die on a winter ascent?"

Lindsey gave a stiff nod.

"Robbie Coulson," Ty said. "One of the best climbers of his day."

"That takes balls." Approval rang in Packer's voice.

"Why in the world would anyone want to climb a mountain like Everest in the winter?" Brynn asked.

Ty folded up his map. "It's the last big prize, but winter ascents have always been considered suicide. Most 8000-meter peaks are best climbed either in May, like on Everest, or July or August in the Karakoram. Winter climbs are incredibly difficult, with the weather being the biggest problem. But in the '80s, the Poles knocked off several of 'em, proving it could be done. Lindsey's dad was the first American to make the attempt."

Packer swung his gaze to Lindsey. "Which mountain?"

"Manaslu," she replied. "But he disappeared."

Habibe cleared the dinner plates away, and everyone downed what was left in their mugs in anticipation of coffee.

"Do they know what happened?" Brynn asked.

Lindsey shook her head. "Contact was lost with both him and his partner at the same time."

"Wasn't he climbing with Carlos Gallo?" Ty asked.

"He did sometimes climb with Gallo but not on this one. He was with Rubén Ibarra."

"Yeah, now I remember." Ty held up his cup so Habibe could fill it with hot coffee, and everyone else did the same. "It was a huge loss."

"Let me guess," Packer said, leaning his elbows on the table and staring at Lindsey. "Your first 8000-meter climb was Manaslu."

Lindsey reached for the milk and nodded.

Packer waggled his eyebrows seductively. "Now I know what

makes you tick, Coulson." She gave him a questioning look, so he added, "Daddy issues."

Ty liked Packer, but he sensed the man was skirting precariously close to a wound that Lindsey undoubtedly wanted to keep private. She'd had it worse than most climbers, losing not just one family member but two.

"All the 8000-meter peaks have been conquered with winter ascents now, except for K2," Ty said, seeking to change the subject. "As usual, she's holding out. Here's another interesting fact—K2 is the site of the most famous belay in mountaineering history."

"I'm hoping to get a photo as we pass the spot," Packer said. "I'm gonna put it on my social media with hashtag 'BadAssBelay.'"

"Why is it so famous?" Brynn asked.

"One man held the force of six falling men," Ditch replied. "It was in 1953 and the summit of K2 had yet to be reached by anyone. The expedition—only the fifth one here—wouldn't reach it either. It was an American team led by a man named Charles Houston, an excellent and well-respected climber. They had made it quite high on the mountain when one of their teammates, a man named Art Gilkey, for whom the memorial here is named, became very ill. They had to bring him down in a makeshift stretcher, which is a very dangerous thing to do. At one point, each man slipped in fast succession, becoming entangled in the ropes. A young climber named Pete Schoening was at the end, and he held them all, saving their lives. It was an incredible feat, really. Unfortunately, later, they anchored Gilkey to the mountain while they set up a tent, and he disappeared, likely swept away by an avalanche."

Brynn took a sip of coffee from her mug. "Don't all of you find the death in these places unsettling?"

"You can't let it get to you," David said. "On Everest, some of the dead are still where they died. You walk right by them."

"One of the markers to the summit is Green Boots," Ditch said. "I think he was an Indian climber."

"They just freeze and are left there?" Captain Juneid asked, having remained silent during the meal.

"It's too dangerous to move them," Ditch replied. "It sounds unfeeling, but if they're dead, they don't need to get down the mountain."

"Sometimes climbers try to bring bodies down," Ty said quietly, glancing at Lindsey. Alison's body was somewhere on K2. "But most of the time it's all they can do to get themselves down safely."

"Well, if I freeze my ass to K2, I give everyone here the green light to leave me," Packer said. "I'd be happy to spend eternity here. Then everyone can pass me by, referring to the Packer marker."

Ditch smirked. "You mean they'd be saying 'The summit is just beyond the asshole blocking the route.'"

Packer let out a whoop. "I've been called worse."

Brynn's face took on an expression of concern. "I know climbing is addictive—I surfed for years, so I get the mentality—but really, why do you all do it?"

"It beats working," Packer said.

Ditch finished off his coffee. "Which I don't think you've ever done."

"If you're nice to me, I'll let you rope up with me."

"I think I'll rope with Lindsey."

Packer released an exaggerated sigh. "God, I hate it when there's a better climber on the team than me. I have to work so much harder. Wait a minute, why do you get to rope up with the lady?"

Lindsey looked at Brynn. "Are you sure you don't want to take up climbing?"

"Maybe I will. But I can see why you always climbed with your sister."

"You girls are too picky," Packer said.

"Just watch yourself," Ty cut in. "There'll be no messing around with my sister."

Glee filled Packer's face. "But Lindsey's fair game?"

"No." Lindsey answered at the same time as Ty.

He immediately regretted the force of his opposition, the hair rising on the back of his neck. The protectiveness for his sister didn't surprise him, but hell if he wanted anyone laying claim to Lindsey.

Shit. So much for keeping his feelings under the radar.

In the awkward aftermath, Lindsey stood. "I think I'll turn in."

Brynn also shot to her feet. "Me too. I'll walk with you."

"You girls watch out for those Polish dudes," Packer said, then flicked an amused glance at Ty. "They've got the look of love. And they've got a stash of Viagra."

Brynn tugged on her hat. "They do?"

"It's not for the usual reason," David said. "The drug's ability to increase blood flow can help with acclimating."

"But that doesn't mean it won't leave them rowdy," Packer added, snickering.

"We'll keep our distance." Lindsey avoided Ty's gaze, retrieving a flashlight from the pocket of her fleece and then giving a wave as she left the tent with his sister. "Goodnight."

Ditch grabbed a deck of cards. "Goodnight, ladies."

Packer directed a knowing wink at Ty. "Now we don't have to be on our best behavior. Time to break out the juice."

Ditch frowned as he laid out a game of solitaire. "That was your best behavior?"

Ty expelled a breath he hadn't been aware he'd been holding. "I'll take a shot of whatever you've got, Packer."

LINDSEY AWOKE EARLY, FEELING IMMENSELY BETTER. AFTER PULLING ON trail pants and a light jacket over her thermal underwear, she unzipped her tent. The sharp outline of K2's near-perfect pyramid greeted her, jutting upward into a bluebird sky.

"Good morning, beautiful," she murmured.

She rummaged around for her knit hat and tugged it on, her blond hair loose around her shoulders. Then she grabbed a nonfiction book about recent strides in DNA marking and transposons, along with her mug, and headed to the mess tent. She had plenty of other reading material on her e-reader if she decided her brain needed a break from work.

As she entered the mess tent, she stopped short. Galloway looked up, wearing a tan baseball cap emblazoned with GALLOWAY FILMS in black stitching.

"Good morning," he said.

"Morning."

"Would you like some coffee?"

"No. I'll just make tea, thanks." She moved past him to the stove. Habibe wasn't present, but water brewed in a kettle. She poured the hot liquid into her mug, added a tea bag, and then moved to the end of the table to sit.

"I'm not contagious."

She settled onto the folding chair. "You never know."

He smiled. "I usually have more success with the ladies."

She took a sip of her tea to test the hotness of the water. It scalded her lip. "If you say so." She set the brew back on the table.

"I met Alison a few times, after she and David got together."

Lindsey watched him.

"She was strong-willed and sharp," he continued. "I can see the resemblance between you both. She told me a story once about the two of you when you were younger and had started climbing hills outside of San Francisco—she miscalculated the belay and dropped you from a rock wall. She said you broke your pelvis."

Lindsey remembered the shock and the pain, and how she'd wet herself. And how angry she had been later because she hadn't been able to climb for nearly three months.

"She added that you never once complained." Ty's gaze softened. "And that you were tougher than she was—more daring, more of a risk-taker. She admired that and wished she was more like you."

Lindsey could hear the voice of her sister filtered through his deep timbre. She willed back the tears. "That isn't true," she said, her voice thick. "I just never liked the mainstream, the well-traveled routes. I've always liked being off on some rock face where no one else was."

"Yeah, me too," Ty replied. "I was really sorry when I heard she didn't make it off K2. I just wanted to tell you that."

Lindsey paused until she was certain her voice would work. "Thanks." She cleared her throat. "I appreciate it."

Ditch entered the tent with Habibe. Lindsey stood and reached for her tea and book.

"Can we talk later?" Ty asked. "Maybe this afternoon?" Was he regretting his decision to have her along?

"About the feature," he added.

She relaxed her shoulders. She wasn't normally so insecure in the mountains—it had been the one place where she had found strength and purpose—but of late she had begun to worry about her ability to climb.

"Okay." She nodded and left.

Once outside, she found a rock and sat for a while, but instead of reading she stared at K2. As her eyes followed the ridgeline on the right side, she imagined the route the team would take. For a moment, she entertained a vision of Alison slowly making her way to the top, and when a black speck appeared against a large white area, Lindsey's heart nearly stopped.

Al?

Logic told her it was likely a member of the Polish team.

A memory surfaced of her and Alison when they'd been just girls on vacation in Hawai'i. They had competed in a tide pool over who could hold their breath the longest.

Lindsey nurtured the fantasy that the black speck was Alison, still climbing, still trying to quiet the yearning to push against unseen boundaries. That young Alison who had stubbornly held her breath, forcing Lindsey far past her own reserves.

Since Alison's death, it had become clear to Lindsey that her sister had been the gatekeeper to the dragon, spurring the two of them into the fire of their ambitions while keeping a steady eye on what they could feasibly accomplish.

And ever present in Lindsey's mind was one question: How could she continue her passion of climbing without Al's unyielding guidance?

~

L~ATER~ ~THAT~ ~MORNING~ L~INDSEY~ ~TRAILED~ D~AVID~ ~TO~ ~THE~ G~ILKEY~ Memorial, Galloway behind her and Brynn, Ditch, and Packer following. Lindsey had thought to place the plaque for Alison quietly and discreetly, but they all had wanted to pay their respects. Threadbare scarves at the base of the eight-foot-high pile of rocks whipped in the wind, Buddhist offerings called *khatas*. Lindsey didn't understand the deeper meaning of them.

The collection of tin plates clanged a mournful tune in the wind, commemorating those who would spend eternity here, ranging as far back as 1939. The dates encompassed the months of June through August—the climbing season on K2. As Lindsey got close enough to read the names, she could see that many were famous within the mountain climbing community.

She brought a handkerchief to her nose to block the rancid smell that permeated the large cairn, her stomach roiling in protest. Many of the dead hadn't been recovered from K2, but of the ones who had been found, the remains had been placed beneath and around the memorial, as Marie Broucet had been a few days ago.

The memorial was both sacred and macabre, and Lindsey vowed to avoid it hereafter, and would instead remember Alison with a whisper of breath and a tear-filled prayer when she was alone in her tent.

Despite the wind, Lindsey felt a warm pressure around the marker. The mountain seemed to bear down on them, hovering like an icy stalker, its reach long and wide. This was the reality of K2: death.

David's face bore an ashen hue; Lindsey shifted her gaze so as not to stare at him.

With the collar of his jacket pulled over his chin and nose, Galloway gently took the plaque from Lindsey's left hand, along with the hammer and two bolts. The pinging echoed around them as he attached the memorial for her sister. The marker included a poem Alison had scratched out in her journal that had been recovered from her tent after her death.

Solemnly, Lindsey stared at the inscription, then looked at the mountain. Alison was up there, somewhere, her body preserved in its frozen state. It was unreal, almost ghastly to wrap her mind around, and the sadness uncoiled in her so swiftly she gasped to hold the tears back, but they spilled down her face anyway.

Alison Leigh Coulson
1990-2016
To meet the sage, old and wise
Who wore the mountain in disguise.
Escape the body and always soar,
Embracing freedom ever more.

CHAPTER 4

L indsey headed to the mess tent around 4 p.m. When she entered,
Galloway was alone. He stood and offered her a beer.

"You look like you could use it."

She nodded and took the can from him. She couldn't deny that she
had been on edge since she'd arrived, from finding Broucet's headless
body to seeing David again, and all the while thoughts of Alison
constantly flitting through her head.

Maybe that was why she suddenly honed her full attention on
Tyler Galloway. Last night, when Packer had made the remark about
chasing Lindsey, Ty's quick negative response had surprised her.
Maybe he liked her—then again, maybe he didn't—but she could sure
use the brief distraction of flirting with him.

His athletic frame was covered by a dark blue fleece pullover and
expedition pants. He had nice hands, large, with long fingers, no
doubt strong from years of climbing. Physically, he was everything she
preferred in a guy, but what really drew her were his eyes—sometimes
green, but today appearing bluer. They carried depth and understanding and connection to the places he had seen. Having read some
of his work, she had been drawn to his style, his insights, and his
humor.

And now she had to acknowledge that he easily jump-started her hormones.

Maybe she should invite him to her tent.

They could go at it like rabbits, and then she wouldn't have to think about her sister or her own concerns about climbing K2. Is this what male climbers did while on expeditions? Used sex to mask deeper problems, deeper concerns?

She pulled a packet of papers from her coat pocket and sat down, this time closer to him at his end of the table. "I did write down answers to all the questions you emailed me. Sorry I didn't get them to you sooner. It took me a little while to remember all the mountains I've climbed." She handed the stack to him.

"That's okay." He flattened the folded sheets on the table. "Thanks." He began reading through her notes. "It looks like you answered most of it." He flicked a glance at her. "I guess we didn't really need to meet."

"Except that you offered me a beer. That was worth it." She opened the can and took a swallow of the cold liquid. It definitely hit the spot. She just needed to relax. Hitting the sack with the boss wasn't the answer, and she knew better than that.

He grabbed a notebook and flipped to a page that already contained a stream of scribbles, and after glancing over them he looked at her. "I've got a few basic questions, if that's all right with you."

She lifted her beer in a mock salute. "Shoot."

"How old are you?"

"Twenty-six."

"Where were you born?"

"San Jose." She took another sip of beer.

"Where did you grow up?"

"San Jose until I was three, then we moved to Berkeley. My dad, as you know, loved to climb. My mom, too, but she spent more time working to support us until my dad became famous, at least in the climbing sense. After that, sponsorship helped to pay the bills."

Ty wrote in his notebook. "When did you start climbing?"

"In high school," she answered. "Alison hung out with a bunch of people who climbed for fun on the weekends. One day she and I went along. I was terrible, but I loved it. I couldn't wait to do more. I couldn't wait to get better than the boys."

Ty glanced at her, his blue-green eyes flashing amusement beneath the baseball cap he wore. "I think you achieved that." He returned to his notes before looking at her again. "Since we're alone I hope you don't mind, but I wanted to ask how you felt when Alison died, if you're up to talking about it."

His inquiry hit her with a jolt of unease. She had known that Galloway would question her about her older sister eventually, but an urge to bolt from the tent surged through her, to run out onto the frozen Baltoro glacier and never stop.

She took another drink, her breath rattling slightly against the can. "Okay."

"Did you wish you'd been here? You always climbed together but for this one trip you didn't come."

"I wonder every day that maybe she'd be alive if I'd been here." She paused. "I know David's your friend ...."

Ty narrowed his eyes. "You blame him?"

"No." But she wasn't entirely certain that was true. "Will you let me see your article before you submit it?"

"Of course. Are you worried I'll write something you don't like?"

"I'm worried that you'll slant this in a sensational way."

"Lindsey, I'll write the truth, but generally a narrative emerges, and the story will be shaped to it. I can't tell you right now what it will look like. I try to collect as much info as I can and piece it together later."

She dropped her gaze to the table and contemplated what to say next. She told herself that trusting Ty Galloway was stupid. But a part of her wanted to.

"All right, you asked how I felt when she died. At first, I was in shock. It couldn't possibly be true. Later, I was pissed at her for letting the mountain take her. And now, well, mostly I'm heartbroken because I miss her. I came here because I wanted to climb K2, but I also wanted a chance to say goodbye, personally."

Galloway scribbled more notes.

"Did David and Alison's engagement keep you away from K2 two years ago?"

Irritated, she slugged more beer. She didn't like the probing, but it was too late to hit reverse.

"We'd had a rough go of it on Kanch three years ago," she said. "That's why I didn't come to K2."

Ty watched her, his gaze hooded and contemplative. "I heard. Jim Shoop was one of the good ones, and a strong climber."

She silently agreed. As she searched for words to continue, the silence stretched longer than it should have, but Galloway waited.

"I'd never had that happen before," she said. "Losing someone close. Well, I did lose my dad, but I wasn't there with him when it occurred. With Shoop, it weighed on me that if I'd done something different, then maybe the outcome would've been different." She chewed on her lower lip. "It really shook me. I didn't know if I wanted to climb anymore. So, I didn't come to K2 with Alison. It was strange, to see her off on an expedition that I wouldn't be participating in, but she was excited to be with David, and for that reason I knew she could get along without me." Her throat constricted. "Guess I was wrong about that."

"The truth is," she added, "Alison's relationship with David did change ours somewhat, and that wasn't necessarily a bad thing. She was happy with him, and I was happy for her."

"But ...."

"David is a very," she searched for a diplomatic description, "self-assured climber. So was Al, for that matter. I was concerned that he might lead her into a scenario where she was in over her head, where her stubborn tenacity would backfire on her."

"Is that what you think happened?"

Lindsey shrugged. "I don't know." She gulped more beer. "You told me that Alison said she admired me, but the truth was that we had a good back and forth when it came to making climbing decisions.

She could prop me up when I was afraid, and I could cut through her pigheadedness. I'm not convinced that David had that ability. If anything, he may have simply ramped it up."

"But didn't she climb to the summit without him that morning?"

"Yes, that's what David said." Before she thought better of it, she added, "But is that really what happened?"

"You think he's lying?" Ty asked, clearly shocked by her words.

"No." Her shoulders sagged. "No, I don't. I just wish I'd been here. If I had been, then she wouldn't be dead."

The tension on Ty's face soon relaxed into a sympathetic gaze. "Regardless of the dynamic between her and David, she was a grown woman and an accomplished climber. You're taking on an awful lot of responsibility for this."

Was she? It had never occurred to her to guard the boundaries of her sister's aspirations while Alison had been alive. Why did it weigh on her now that Alison was gone?

"I suppose you're right." She set her empty beer can on the table. "This article is going to be too depressing for people to read, I think."

"I'll try to lighten it up." He looked at his notebook again. "Why don't you tell me how you prepare for a climb—physically, mentally, nutritionally."

She tucked a wisp of hair behind her ear, feeling slightly dizzy from the alcohol. "I run marathons, eat nothing but margarine, and climb the tree in my backyard with my ice axe three times a day."

"Alison never mentioned you were a comedian."

"And curiously enough, she never mentioned meeting you." She snapped her mouth shut. Mix a little beer with her simmering emotions over Alison, and she was a veritable volcano waiting to blow.

"Ouch," he teased before she could offer an apology. "You hurt my pride."

"Sorry," she said in a rush. "She was quite taken with David, and I think it made other men invisible to her."

"He does have that effect."

"You playing for both teams?" To her horror, her voice had taken on a desperate plea.

He chuckled. "No."

Good grief. She needed to leave before she jammed her foot clear down her throat.

He closed his notebook and stacked his papers. "I'll look through what you gave me and see what else I might need. I think Habibe needs to get in here to make dinner."

Relieved that she could escape, she stood.

"Hey, Lindsey."

"Yeah?" She turned back to look at him.

"David's a good climber," he said, "but if you have any problems, let me know. It'll be off the record, I promise."

The tension in her gut relaxed. "Thanks."

She exited the mess tent and made her way along the rocky pathway to her own tent.

Why had Alison never mentioned Ty Galloway? He was a man who was hardly invisible.

～

"You did a great job with the mac and cheese," Tyler said to Habibe as the cook cleared away the dirty plates and forks. "I do love comfort food." While traveling was in Ty's blood, homesickness still tended to blindside him. There was nothing like sleeping in his own bed with his chocolate Labrador snuggled beside him, nothing like a beer and good friends at a local hangout in San Francisco, nothing like a pretty girl.

On that thought, Ty's gaze shifted to Lindsey, bookending the table opposite him with Packer and Brynn on either side of her.

She was troubled about David, and while Ty didn't know exactly what had happened on K2 two years ago, he hadn't heard any stories that implicated Shaw in being overbearing to the woman he had planned to marry.

Maybe he should ask Shaw about it at some point. Thankfully, the mood during dinner had been friendly, and Lindsey didn't appear to be harboring a grudge. Or maybe she was simply good at hiding it.

"Are you still studying chemistry at Berkeley?" David asked her.

She nodded, waving off the bottle of vodka Packer was offering around. "I'm more on the research end now as I go for my Ph.D. It's definitely given me more latitude with my schedule."

"You can't actually have a real job and be a climber," Packer said, handing the liquor to David who passed it to Ty.

Ty added a dash to his mug and gave the bottle to Ditch, who poured a generous helping into his own cup.

"Spoken like a man who doesn't like to work," Ditch responded, giving Juneid the vodka.

"And what do you do in your normal life?" Packer asked the older man.

"I sell insurance."

Packer released a whoop. "Excellent. Can we all get covered while we're here?"

"No. Mountain climbers are extremely uninsurable." Ditch looked at Lindsey. "What kind of research do you do?"

"I study junk DNA."

"I was born with junk?" Packer exclaimed. "That explains everything."

Amusement beamed on Lindsey's face, and Ty decided she should smile more often.

"Ninety-seven percent of your DNA is junk."

"No shit?" Packer took a big swill from his mug. "God must've been drinking the day he made those spirally little strands."

"Actually, it was us who didn't understand what was going on. We called it junk because it didn't appear to do anything. It was believed it was just extra baggage from eons of evolution—every virus and bacteria that we've ever merged with."

Packer released a loud belch. "Apologies. But Lindsey, you're making me a little sick."

"Genetics isn't for the faint of heart. Life is a complicated process that prospers ever so briefly before the inevitable death throes set in."

Packer leaned close to her. "I'm guessing Halloween is your favorite holiday."

She laughed, the gleam in her eyes encompassing her whole face. It was clear she enjoyed her work.

"So what's the purpose of junk DNA?" Ty asked.

"It's the birthplace of transposons, but we like to call them jumping genes. We think they're responsible for mutation and evolution."

Packer knocked back the contents of his mug and reached for the vodka now sitting at the center of the table. "Zombie kangaroo genes. Now we're getting somewhere."

"That's not a bad image," Lindsey said. "We're still not exactly sure what triggers it—and there's maybe hundreds of thousands of ways this can happen—but jumping genes basically insert themselves into other genes, especially when an organism is stressed."

"Like us?" Ditch asked.

"I'm not stressed," Packer countered. "Why do you think I bring the hooch?"

"Exposure to harsh environments can trigger a change in a person's DNA. Sometimes it's beneficial, sometimes it's not. The ultimate goal of all genetic research is to sequence each individual's genome, since we're all different. How your genes react to medications and the food you eat is as varied as the number of humans on earth."

Packer chuckled. "So the more vodka I drink, the more vodka I can drink."

"You're just looking for an excuse to be a lush," Ditch said.

Lindsey held out her mug so Habibe could add hot water from the kettle. "The triggers tend to be of the more life-threatening kind," she said.

Packer raised an eyebrow. "If I can't drink vodka, I *will* die."

Ditch shook his head and said, "God help us if we run out before we can summit."

Lindsey popped a teabag into her cup. "Another project I've worked on is the origin of DNA."

Packer whistled. "It was either God or aliens."

"Believe it or not, some of my associates and I have had conversations about that," she replied. "Our genetic code carries our evolution, including everything our ancestors have ever experienced from plagues to parasites to fending off predators."

"Humanity's encyclopedia," Ditch said. "So what are we made of?"

"It's thought that RNA—ribonucleic acid—came first out of the primordial goo of a volatile early earth, and that DNA became a kind of backup hard copy, in case something went wrong in the RNA."

"All right, my head's starting to hurt." Packer scratched the whiskers on his cheek. "You females are too smart these days, using your brains and climbing mountains, too. Next thing you know, you're not going to need us."

"Then we'd better make ourselves irresistible," Ty said with a laugh.

"Done." Packer grinned as he unscrewed the lid on the vodka and added more to his cup.

Ty looked at Lindsey. "At least you and Brynn have each other if you get bored with us."

"And what's your area of expertise?" Packer asked Brynn.

"Sumerian culture. I'm an archaeologist."

"Ah, numerology." Packer's speech held the slightest slur. "My favorite is sixty-nine."

"I think you need a hearing aid," Ditch said with mock disgust. "She said archaeologist, not numerologist."

Everyone laughed.

"Where did the Sumerians live?" David asked Brynn.

"In Mesopotamia, known today as Iraq, about five thousand years ago."

"Well, you girls don't take the easy way, do you?" Packer said, a hint of admiration in his voice. "'Cause I sure as hell wouldn't go to Iraq."

"I've only been there once," Brynn said. "I spend most of my time in Istanbul, analyzing tablets at the museum. I've brought some books along if you're interested in reading more about it."

Packer snickered. "You really don't know me. I gave up reading years ago."

"Then I'll get you a documentary."

"Look," Packer said, "I appreciate what you girls are trying to do, studying the past and making the world a better place and all that, but honestly, what's wrong in enjoying the moment, the here and now. What's wrong with just climbing a mountain?"

"Aren't you ever driven to achieve something?" David asked.

Packer took a bigger drink this time. "Of course. My goal is to achieve happiness. I'm happiest when I'm in the mountains. I'm only driven to make enough money to get here."

"I'm happiest in the mountains, too," Lindsey replied.

"You sound like Ty," Brynn said.

His sister cast a knowing look at him. He frowned back. He hadn't admitted that he liked Lindsey beyond anything as a colleague, but Brynn seemed to have other ideas.

Lindsey glanced his way, and he readjusted his baseball cap. "Everything's better outdoors," he said. The unintended innuendo filled the tent, but thankfully David jumped in before Packer could put his personal spin on it.

"Becoming a professional climber isn't impossible. I've managed it the last few years."

"That's because you're good-looking," Packer said.

Ditch reached for the vodka. "Behave yourself. Ty told us no passes at team members."

"He was talkin' about the women. Davy here is fair game."

Ditch moved the liquor out of Packer's line-of-sight, and Ty silently thanked the man.

"But seriously," Packer said, his gaze landing on David, "don't you have to jump through hoops to keep your sponsorship?"

"Some. But don't we all jump through hoops in our life for something?"

"Can you pick the mountains you want to climb?" Packer asked.

"Sure. But some make more of a statement than others."

"My point exactly. I wanna climb whatever I want, when I want. I don't want people in an office telling me what to do."

"Then that kind of climbing probably isn't for you."

"But I'm still a climber." Packer held his hands up. "And you're a pretty boy jumping through hoops."

The atmosphere became as chilly as outside the tent. Despite Packer's considerable climbing skills, he tended to be a loose cannon when it came to interpersonal interactions. David was similar in that his stubbornness could also grate.

Different strokes, as Ty's dad always said.

There's no right or wrong way, but you damned well better pick one *way.*

Lindsey broke the standoff by scooting her chair back. "I think I'll turn in."

Ty grabbed the opportunity. "I'll walk with you."

"What about strip poker?" Packer asked as Brynn and David came to their feet.

"Maybe another time," Brynn said.

"Is that a promise?"

Brynn smiled and patted his shoulder. "No, Packer."

"Your ability to clear a room is astounding," Ditch said.

"One of my many skills. Are there any women in the Polish camp?"

Packer's voice faded as Ty flicked on a large flashlight and entered the cold dark night.

He lit the path as Lindsey fell in step beside him, Brynn and David following. K2 loomed large to their left, but with uneven rock and ice underfoot, Ty had to give his attention to the ground. David and Brynn said goodnight and ducked into each of their respective tents, the yellow domes glowing once they switched on a lamp. Ty continued walking with Lindsey despite passing his own abode.

"I guess you didn't like the neighborhood," he said, referring to the fact that her tent was thirty yards away from any of the others.

"Just in case you all talk in your sleep."

"I'll just have to make a point to yell then."

"Only if you've got contraband Oreos."

"I'm not likely to share those." He panned the light from right to left. "Did you build rock cairns around your tent?" Several small pillars of stones created a ten-foot perimeter around her K2 home.

"I did. I like to set a boundary."

"To counter trespassing?"

"Kind of."

They stopped at her doorway, and with her hands jammed into her jacket pockets, she glanced at the miniature monoliths she'd built. "I guess you could say it's a superstition from studying genetics. It's at the edge where everything happens—growth and chaos and evolution. When I demarcate my environment, it seems to soothe me, giving me a sanctuary, a place to rest from all the inherent disorder that awaits. As perfect a specimen as K2 is, we both know the mountain is a shitstorm of uncertainty."

"You're right. Does your boundary technique work?"

She laughed. "Sometimes. My dad always built cairns. I suppose I really do it so I can keep him close when I'm in the mountains." Craning her neck, she looked at the glittering night sky. "He also liked constellations. His favorite was Orion the Hunter, although it isn't visible right now. It'll show up again in August."

Ty clicked off the flashlight so they could see better.

"When Orion is visible, it's the easiest way to tell direction," she said.

"How so?"

"Orion sits at the equator and always rises in the east and sets in the west. The three stars just below his belt represent his sword, and it acts like a compass needle. Depending on how high the constellation is in the sky, the sword will point either to the east, south, or west. If you know the general time of night, you can quickly use it to orient yourself."

Ty smiled. "I didn't know that."

"For weeks after my dad disappeared on Manaslu, I was sure he'd find his way home. I reasoned that since it was wintertime, he'd be able to see Orion and could use it to navigate."

"How old were you?"

"Nine. I was too young and too hopeful."

"You have a lot of reasons to hate climbing. I'm glad you're here."

"Me too." She pointed upward. "Do you see those three bright stars?"

"Yep."

"That's the Summer Triangle. When it gets to its highest point, it forms an arrow pointing south. I just wanted to leave you with something practical in case you get lost walking random women to their tents."

Was she flirting? Unsure, he played it safe and said, "I'll keep it in mind since walking women to their tents is my specialty." He flashed a friendly grin, then flicked on his flashlight to illuminate her tent.

She unzipped the entrance, crawled inside, and gave a wave. "'Night, Galloway."

"Goodnight, Lindsey."

As he navigated the uneven path to his tent, he debated turning around and … what? Ask her to watch a movie on his laptop?

He stayed the course until he was tucked into his own version of home-away-from-home. He could handle his attraction to Lindsey. There was no reason to upset the balance of the team. There was much work to do and many grueling days ahead, and he couldn't jeopardize all the time, money, and logistics that had gone into this expedition just because he liked a girl.

But Lindsey was no ordinary girl.

And maybe that was the biggest reason why he held himself in check.

CHAPTER 5

The next morning dawned clear. As Lindsey emerged from her tent, she smiled and soaked up the warmth of the sun on her face. As always, K2 stared right back at her, its fluffy white contours revealing streaks of black rock beneath.

Charon appeared, flapping his wings in a flurry as he landed several yards away and watched her.

"Sorry, no food." She feared feeding him would only encourage him to scavenge her tent. As it was, he still might do just that. Peeking back inside, she double-checked that no food—granola bars or crackers—was out and about but was secured in the small plastic container she kept on hand. She exited and zipped her tent.

Charon released a stream of *kraas* aimed at her.

"We don't always get what we want," she muttered under her breath, giving a wave to her avian buddy.

She donned sunglasses and pulled a knit hat down over her ears, her braided blond hair trailing between her shoulder blades.

Everyone was cheery in the mess tent when she entered.

"There's nothing like sunshine to make you want to howl at the sky." Packer grinned at her.

Lindsey laughed, surprised by his good humor considering he was likely nursing a dreadful hangover. His love of vodka surely had contributed to the burgeoning scuffle last night with David. Apparently, she wasn't the only one with a prickly relationship with Shaw.

Ty and Ditch soon appeared followed by Brynn. David had left earlier in the morning to take a load to Advanced Base Camp. Captain Juneid, who was spending much of his time with the two liaison officers embedded with the other teams, also stopped in. Everyone drank coffee and tea and ate eggs and fried potatoes.

Since today was another rest day, Ty planned to do some writing and get caught up on blog posts and correspondence. Ditch and Packer decided to take additional loads to ABC as David had. Lindsey thought to do that as well, but Brynn asked to go climbing. When Captain Juneid also expressed interest, Ty gave them his blessing, and Lindsey thought it might be okay to take a fun day. It would help her acclimatization and perhaps her confidence as well. The captain retrieved his equipment, and they located a spare harness and extra rope for Brynn, then the three of them set off midmorning.

They walked several hundred yards down the glacier and spent the afternoon scaling 30 to 50-foot ice walls. With crampons and ice axes, they went up and down several times. Lindsey enjoyed it, her muscles opening up from the exertion and her heart pumping. She was feeling good—clear-headed with no headaches, an appetite that was steadily increasing, and urine that was clear, an indication that she was hydrating.

Brynn and the captain took to the climbing. The captain's English was adequate, and Lindsey found him to be polite and focused. He spoke of his wife and young son in Islamabad, and she could tell he missed them very much. Brynn had a natural athleticism to her, and while she'd done only minimal bouldering, she adapted to the techniques required of ice climbing quickly.

Several hours later, tired from their endeavors, they gathered their gear and supplies and began the return hike, roped together for safety —Lindsey first then Juneid then Brynn. After thirty minutes of uphill trekking, Lindsey caught sight of Base Camp. As she stepped forward, the ice moved, the earth groaning in response. Lindsey acknowledged her anxiety with little fanfare, since the glacier moved with regularity. But in the next moment, she lost her footing and fell to her knees.

She kicked the toe of her crampons into the ground as she searched for a firm purchase, chancing a quick glance behind her as she stood. Brynn had her arms out trying to balance, and suddenly she disappeared, releasing a scream that instantly went mute.

Oh shit!

Brynn had fallen into a crevasse.

Lindsey threw herself onto the ground, jamming the pick of her axe into the ice, and pressed hard onto the adze, jerking to a halt.

Over her shoulder, she caught sight of Juneid's frantic struggles not to follow Brynn into the abyss.

"Arrest! Arrest!" she yelled to him. "Use your axe! Brace your feet!"

Scraping along the ground on his belly, he finally stopped.

"Shit!" She shouldn't have tied the ropes so short. Both she and Juneid easily could have gone into the crevasse with Brynn. As it was, he was awfully damned close to the edge.

"Juneid, I need to stand up," she yelled. "Are you secure enough to hold Brynn?"

"I think so," he said in a rush.

"I need you to be sure."

"Yes." Then with more conviction, "Yes, I can hold her."

Carefully, she pushed back and moved to her knees, slowly shifting to a standing position, ready to throw herself back to the icy ground if Juneid slipped.

"Are you good?" she asked.

"Yes," came his muffled response.

Lindsey attached a friction knot to the rope and started prusiking —sliding the hitch—toward Juneid, keeping slack out of the line. At the same time, she used the end of her axe to probe for any other crevasses. She passed Juneid, and with a heaving thrust she jammed her axe into the ground to make an anchor. Then she attached a single runner girth hitch around the axe, prusik-hitched her hero loop onto the rope, and attached them together with a carabiner.

Placing her foot in front of the anchor to protect it, she said, "Juneid, you can stand now."

With great care, he rose to his feet.

"Brynn?" she yelled.

"Yes," came her response, soft and weak.

She was alive. Lindsey sagged with relief. "Are you hurt?"

"My knee and ankle, but I'm on a ledge."

"Okay, hang tight."

She met Juneid's worried gaze. Setting up a pulley system was too complicated to explain to him, so she retrieved her radio from her pack.

"Lindsey to Base Camp, over."

Nothing.

"This is Lindsey. Base Camp, come in now, over."

She tried not to sound panicked but feared she was failing.

"This is Ty. Go ahead, Lindsey."

"We need help. Brynn has fallen into a crevasse. She's conscious and stable, for now."

"What's your location?"

"Southeast of Base Camp, maybe three hundred yards."

"Hang on. Be right there."

Only then did Lindsey take a moment to catch her breath.

Ty and David came rushing toward her with as much speed as they could muster considering they were trying to choose their path carefully. They both had coiled rope slung across them and Ty carried a pack.

"I've got an anchor," she said to them. "I need you to rig a pulley."

Ty swiftly transferred the rope attached to Juneid to himself—effectively anchoring himself directly to Brynn—while David pulled out a double-runner and set a second anchor, then attached the runner to Brynn's rope. With that complete, he secured a line between him and Juneid. They didn't need to risk another mishap, and it was a toss-up between who had the least experience—Brynn or the captain.

Lindsey attached a pulley device behind her prusik, then secured it by folding the rope into a figure-eight knot. They now had the start of a Z-pulley system. Ty set to work going closer to the crevasse and set another anchor with his axe, adding a second pulley to the setup. He also jammed his pack underneath the rope so that it didn't bite into the ice.

"Brynn, it's Ty."

"I'm here," came her shaky response.

"Get ready. We're gonna haul you out."

"Okay."

Ty backtracked to Lindsey and removed the backup figure-eight knot, so the rope could now slide. With David's help, the three of them started to drag the zigzagging line back, bringing Brynn out.

When the pulley devices were almost on top of each other, Lindsey prusiked back to the edge of the crevasse and reset the rope. With two more tugs Brynn was free. She crested the edge and they pulled her completely clear before Lindsey moved to her.

"You okay?"

"Yes," Brynn said with a nervous laugh. "Scared the shit out of me, though."

"Can you stand?"

Brynn pushed herself up, visibly shivering, and Lindsey helped her until they reached Ty. She limped a bit but otherwise appeared more shaken than injured.

Ty had unhooked himself from the rescue setup and now attached a rope between him and Brynn.

"You go ahead," Lindsey said. "I'll clean up the gear."

When Brynn faltered, Ty and David lifted her between them.

Ty glanced over his shoulder. "Don't linger, Linds."

Juneid helped her coil the ropes and retrieve the axes, then they made their way back to camp.

THAT EVENING LINDSEY SAT ACROSS FROM BRYNN IN THE MESS TENT, THE woman's color finally looking better. Ditch had wrapped Brynn's ankle, and while it was twisted, she wasn't completely immobile.

Once dinner was finished, the men departed to visit with a new encampment of Italians that had arrived earlier that day. Lindsey did a crossword puzzle while Brynn settled into a book about the Egyptian god, Thoth.

Brynn glanced up. "Did I almost die today?"

Lindsey met her gaze and wanted to shake her head, but that would've been a lie.

In answer to Lindsey's silence, Brynn said with a shaky laugh, "I think I'll just sit in my tent for the next six weeks."

"I don't think you're the type of person to do that."

Tears sprang to Brynn's eyes. "I'm not usually. I've chased after my brothers all my life, even surfing the big waves because I wanted my dad to think I was as tough as Ty and Alec. But this ...," her voice trailed off. "This shook me."

"It'll pass. Just give it a few days."

"What if we hadn't been roped together?" Brynn asked.

"But we were," Lindsey replied gently.

"My God, I can't believe how this is getting to me."

"Don't be too hard on yourself."

"You're so calm. It's impressive."

While panic had jolted Lindsey when Brynn had disappeared right before her eyes, it had eased quickly into a calm acceptance of how to deal with the rescue, her training and experience in the mountains kicking in.

She held tight to the knowledge that she still had the ability to function under pressure. This had worried her, nagging in the back of her mind. Would she crumble when the going got dicey? Would she be unable to make decisions?

"You're calm too," Lindsey said. "You're not fooling me."

"Oh hell." Brynn laughed, brushing away the tears. "I'm sticking to the climbing wall in the gym."

"Maybe next time Ty should go with you."

As if on cue, Galloway entered the tent with David, Ditch, and Packer following. They all took seats and poured coffee from the pot at the center of the table.

"I sure as hell hope this is decaf," Packer said. "I need to get some sleep tonight."

"It is," Lindsey replied. "I told Habibe to always make decaf in the evening."

"So, Brynn," Packer said, sitting beside her. "You gotta tell us all the gory details of your fall into the abyss. That's how you shake it off, dear. You look Death in the face and say 'Fuck you!'"

Packer's bluntness appeared to ease the strain on Brynn's face. She huffed a derisive laugh.

"Yeah, fuck you, Death," she said, running both hands through her loose brown hair, pushing it away from her face. "You got any of that vodka handy?"

"You betcha." He pulled a bottle from his coat pocket.

"Seriously, you walk around with that?" David asked.

"It has healing properties. You never know when it's needed." He poured a bit into Brynn's empty mug. She toasted him and took a swallow, closing her eyes as it slid down her throat.

"Gimme some of that." Ty pushed his cup toward Packer. "I'm beginning to question bringing my sister here."

Packer poured the liquid. "Anyone else? It wouldn't hurt to toast Brynn. She's seen the innards of the glacier and lived to tell the tale. I think it means you have the gift now."

"What gift?" Brynn asked.

"The gift of the mountain. If you close your eyes you can hear her. She didn't want you today, so she spit you back out. But she may try to speak with you again. Just make certain it's on your own terms."

"No more excursions too far from camp," Ty said. "Always go with someone and always go with gear." He downed the alcohol in his mug. "Lindsey, thanks for what you did."

Lindsey voiced what had been bugging her through dinner. "The ropes should've been longer."

Ty shook his head. "You did it right. I always short rope if there's crevasses."

"There are many opinions about how long the ropes should be," Ditch said, shuffling a deck of cards.

"That hole was deep," Ty said quietly, but everyone had stopped talking to listen. "If the ropes were longer Brynn might have gotten wedged. Falls like that have killed people."

"Is Juneid ever going to come out of his tent?" Lindsey asked.

The captain had retreated after the incident, and no one had seen him since.

"I checked on him." David pulled off his fleece hat and scratched his head. "He'll be fine. Nothing a good night's sleep won't fix."

Ty's gaze locked with Lindsey's. "Thanks again."

The worry and fear were evident in his eyes. He could've lost his sister as easily as she'd lost hers.

Not sure how to respond to the rawness in the exchange, she changed the subject. "How are the Italians?"

Ty sat back in his chair. "Getting organized. There's six of them. They'll probably head up in a day or two. I told them they could use our fixed ropes."

"Will they pony up?" Packer asked. Generally, if a team used another team's fixed lines, they paid a toll of sorts.

"I'm not sure," Ty responded. "I didn't want to make a federal case."

"We'd better get some raviolis or somethin' out of it." Packer tucked the flask of vodka back into his jacket.

"One of them—a woman—says she knows you." Ty said to Lindsey. "Elena Rossi?"

Lindsey suppressed a grimace. "Yeah, I know Elena."

"She looked hot," Packer said. "Maybe you can put in a good word for me."

Lindsey made a noncommittal sound with a slight roll of her eyes. Elena was trouble from start to finish, and Lindsey damned well didn't want to climb with her.

"We'll head out at three a.m.," Ty said. "Everybody better get some sleep."

"Brynn, you can bunk with me tonight if you like," Lindsey offered.

Brynn silently agreed.

"That's a good idea," Ty said. "I don't think she should be alone. Lindsey, come get me if you need anything." He shifted his attention to the group. "Who wants to fix ropes and who wants to carry?"

"I'll fix," Ditch said, keeping his eye on his game of solitaire.

Packer sighed. "And I shall fix too."

David dug into a bag of peanuts. "I'm on the ropes as well."

"All right," Ty said, "then Lindsey and I will carry a load to Camp One."

"I'm gonna bunk at One for the night," David said.

Ditch and Packer decided to see how they felt before determining to stay higher or return to either Advanced Base Camp or Base Camp, to which Lindsey also agreed.

Ty glanced at Brynn, then Lindsey and said, "I'll check in with Brynn before I choose my sleeping option."

His innocuous comment made her cheeks heat, as if he were deciding whether to bunk with her or not. She cleared her throat and stood, her intention to help Brynn move a few things from her tent.

Everyone followed suit and departed to their respective homes except Ty, who helped transfer Brynn's sleeping bag and pad to Lindsey's tent.

Lindsey felt as awkward as a middle schooler around him, bumping into him and avoiding eye contact. When he finally bid them goodnight, Lindsey was both relieved and frustrated. But girl talk with Brynn was out of the question. As Ty's sister, it was too much a conflict of interest.

Lindsey zipped herself into her sleeping bag. "You don't have a headache, do you?"

"No," Brynn replied. "I'm just tired from this long day. Have you ever fallen like that?"

"Yes. Maybe Packer is right—you've been initiated."

"By the mountain?"

"Maybe. Maybe we all need to be tested, to prove we're worthy to be here."

Brynn paused, then said, "My dreams have been very vivid since I arrived."

"That happens when I'm in the mountains, too." Lindsey's dreams of Alison had been steadily increasing now that she was hunkered down at K2's doorstep. Sleep was proving to be a portal in which to spend time with her sister once again, igniting both joy and deep grief.

"It usually fades after a week or two," Lindsey said. "Maybe that's how long it takes us to get in sync with the energy of a place."

"I guess I should've waited and gone climbing later when K2 doesn't want to eat me alive."

"Then we will, because you'll need to do it again."

"You mean climb?" Brynn groaned. "I know what you're saying. I spent my childhood facing down my fears while being harassed by two brothers." She released a pent-up breath. "A part of me can already feel it."

"Feel what?"

"The desire to try again."

Lindsey knew full well of what Brynn spoke. It was that push from the inside, of knowing that you could have done better, that you *needed* to do better. It had nothing to do with the mountain and everything to do with the dragon.

CHAPTER 6

Ty made his way to the mess tent in the dark, his headlamp lighting the way. He deposited his pack at the entrance and went inside. It was only a few hours past midnight, but Habibe was awake to make a quick breakfast for the team before they headed out.

Still groggy, Ty yawned and settled his tall frame into a folding chair, gratefully accepting a cup of coffee.

Ditch stepped inside. "Damn."

"What's wrong?" Ty asked.

"I just lost a bet with Packer." Ditch took a seat. "He said I'd never beat you here, and it would seem he was right."

Ty leaned back as Habibe put out fresh chappatis, butter and jam, and Ditch didn't waste time digging into the simple fare.

"You know I don't like sitting around when there's work to be done," Ty said, reaching for the cream and sugar.

"Mountain climbing is an odd dichotomy, requiring days of laziness matched with the ultimate workout at twenty thousand feet. But you've always been restless. Have you heard back yet?"

Ditch was referring to the editor-in-chief position at Mountaineer Magazine that was opening up in the fall. Something had compelled Ty to apply for it.

"Not yet," Ty said.

"If they offer it to you, are you going to take it?"

"To be honest I don't know. That's the million-dollar question."

"I'm sure the thought of being tied to a desk is enough to give you a case of hives, but it would be a good opportunity for you."

Ty raised an eyebrow. "Have you been talking to my mom?"

Ditch filled his cup with steaming coffee from a carafe Habibe had set on the table. "I do enjoy talking shop with your mother," he replied, referring to Lily Galloway's modest but diverse climbing career, "but it was actually your dad."

Ty nodded, knowing where this was going. As one of the original big-wave surfers and a Silicon Valley software engineer who hit it big when social media exploded, Big Jim Galloway embodied both adventurous spirit and ambitious drive. *Conquering the wilderness is to be applauded,* he would say, *but don't live like a pauper.*

At twenty-six, Ty had certainly spent stretches of his life precariously close to the existence of a vagabond. While he could always crash at his mom and dad's place in Palo Alto, or their house in Telluride, Colorado, or their small apartment in New York City, he prided himself on not being a beggar. But freelance writing didn't pay much, and spending chunks of time on extended expeditions—and disappearing from the world, one of his favorite pastimes—hadn't helped his bank account. For several years, he'd supplemented his income with guide jobs in the mountains.

"I expected you to give me all the reasons why I should retain a life of dirtbagging."

"Don't compromise your soul, Tyler, but what about a wife, children?"

Ty laughed. "That's definitely my mom talking."

"If I have one regret, that's it. My wife left me before we could have kids. I understand the drive to climb, but it doesn't keep you warm at night or fill your home with laughter and joy."

"Since when did you become so maudlin?"

Ditch sipped his coffee and sighed. "I've been thinking—this might be my last climb."

Surprise sliced through Ty. "Really? I had no idea you were thinking of retiring. Did you even want to come to K2?"

Ditch sat with his back ramrod straight, his movements precise with little wasted effort. He climbed much the same way. "I did. K2 has always been on my mind, as you know. And if I was to go out with a bang, then being here with you is the way to do it."

Tyler paused and watched him. "I'm not sure I'm ready for this."

"A last climb with me, or your own domestication?" Ditch removed his Penn State knit hat and scratched his balding head. "I apologize. Maybe I should have waited until the expedition was over, but it seemed right to tell you now."

"Why?"

"Because I don't want you to lean on me when we get up there. You're a good climber, Ty. A world-class one, in fact. You've got the skills, the drive, and the heart. I know you'll make good decisions."

"Stop, Ditch. You're gonna make me cry."

"How's Brynn?" he asked, shifting the conversation. He had never been one to sink too deeply into sentiment.

"Good, I think. She's tough."

"I know."

"Tougher than me."

Ditch laughed. "She always was. But the fall rattled her."

"Probably," Ty conceded. "I'd send her back to Islamabad, but I know she wouldn't go. And I don't want her hiking out alone."

"I think Lindsey is glad to have another female around. Elena doesn't count."

"I'm getting the feeling you don't like the Italian woman, either."

"I'd rather avoid her."

His implication dawned on Ty. "You've slept with her?"

It wasn't often that Ty encountered a speechless Ditch, but his silence was confirmation enough.

"Damn." Ty sat forward. "I had no idea you were a Romeo."

Ditch huffed. "I'm not. Lydia didn't divorce me because I played around. I was just *never around*. Elena was a momentary lapse of judgment that occurred right after Lydia and I had split. A moment of weakness, I suppose. There are never many women in the hills."

Ty nodded. "I know."

"And I'm not quite as eye-catching as you. The ladies usually pass me by. Elena was interested, and that made *me* interested."

"You don't have to make excuses. And you think I'm eye-catching?"

Ditch gave a derisive snort. "With so many mountains to climb, it's rather ironic how often I cross paths with her."

"Maybe she wants a second chance with you."

Ditch chuckled. "Not me. But maybe you."

Ty laughed, a genuine response that released the tension of talking about the trajectory of their lives, and reached for the carafe. As he poured more coffee, he murmured, "Elena's not my type."

Ditch drained the last of the liquid in his mug. "I know. And that leads me to my last bit of advice."

"For the whole trip?"

"Don't be a smart ass." Ditch sobered. "It's about Lindsey."

Ty fiddled with his mug and waited.

"I've seen the way you look at her."

Ty narrowed his gaze. "How do I look at her?"

"The same way I looked at Elena, at least in the beginning."

"What are you trying to say? I thought you were gonna stop treating me like a boy."

"I am." Ditch's gaze softened. "I like Lindsey. I can completely understand what you see in her. And maybe she could be the one. You could have it all with her—a climbing partner, a wife, a family. There's no doubt that she's a catch. But fooling around on expedition puts undue stress on the team, and you. Believe me, I know. I'm just preaching caution. This climb is important to you, and I don't want to see you screw it up over a woman."

Ty cocked an eyebrow. "Are you saying you don't want an invitation to the wedding?"

Ditch shook his head. "You Galloways are so bloody stubborn."

Ty grinned broadly and leaned back in his chair.

Packer appeared, his face puffy with sleep and his hair mussed. "What's so danged funny? Because it's sure not the time of day. Habibe?" He waved toward the cook. "I'll have flapjacks and eggs benedict, please."

∿

AT 3 A.M., LINDSEY FOLLOWED TY, DAVID, DITCH, AND PACKER IN THE dark to ABC. Her entire world narrowed to a six-foot swath of ice illuminated by her headlamp, the only sound the steady scrape of crampons.

As they neared the base of the mountain, the snow turned soft, and in some places, she sank to her knees. The final insult was periodically breaking through snow bridges into pools of ice water. Thankfully her double-insulated boots and gaiters kept the chill at bay.

After a few hours, they reached the two tents that staked their team's claim at ABC. They reorganized their gear, mostly removing food items and replacing them with oxygen tanks. Packer, Ditch, and David also added extra rope and snow pickets.

They were soon headed upward, carefully making their way past giant chunks of ice that had avalanched from higher up.

It felt good to finally be ascending.

As Lindsey exited the field of frozen boulders—the headlamps producing dancing balls of light in the darkness—she clipped her jumar onto the fixed ropes that Ty and David had laid. The weather was clear, revealing a dense smattering of stars, and Lindsey felt strong. She steadily placed crampons into the snow and inched her way up the incline, moving her ascender along the safety rope and soon settling into a routine: step, step, pause and breathe; step, step, pause and breathe. The five of them thinned out along the path and in her solitude, Lindsey focused on the rhythm of her movements.

At the end of the fixed ropes, everyone stopped to hydrate, and Lindsey ate a granola bar while watching a thin sliver of pink in the distance, heralding the coming of the sun.

Soon, she and Ty continued upward, attaching a safety rope

between them since Packer, Ditch, and David were staying behind to continue anchoring and attaching the fixed rope.

By late morning, the two of them reached Camp One. Breathing heavily but feeling good despite the long workout, Lindsey checked her altimeter: 20,500 feet. She paused to take in the view. White-covered peaks buffered them in every direction and a winding valley curved below, cut by the movement of the Godwin-Austen glacier and resembling a frozen river.

"It's not a big area," Ty said, referring to the location of the camp, "but it's relatively secure. According to Ditch, it has little history of avalanche danger."

The two tents that Galloway and David had previously erected sat together, as did two other tents belonging to the Germans. With little discussion, Lindsey set to work digging out a snow ledge with a small shovel, and Ty helped her. They erected a third tent, and Lindsey put her gear inside.

"Do you mind if I take a nap?" Ty asked.

With me?

Her tongue-tied expression must have given her away, because he released a self-conscious laugh and added, "Not in your tent."

"Good, because I'm not tired," she said in a rush.

His forehead furrowed, as if he wasn't sure of her meaning. Did he think she had just made a pass at him?

Had she?

She cleared her throat. "No problem," she said. "I'll just keep the home fires going."

Stop talking, Lindsey.

She grabbed a Bunsen burner and concentrated on setting it up outside her tent since it was a sunny day. "Leave me your water bottle and I'll refill it for you," she said without looking at him, feeling like a schoolgirl embarrassed around the boy she was crushing on.

"I'd appreciate it."

A neoprene bottle appeared over her shoulder, which she took from him. The crunch of snow followed by muffled shuffling in his tent signaled that she was now alone. Within minutes, faint snoring drifted back to her.

Galloway must have been exhausted.

Settling into a routine of chipping chunks of icy snow, melting them in the pan, and then pouring the liquid into their bottles, she enjoyed the next two hours of solitude and sunshine, her nerves around Galloway subsiding.

The glaciers that cut the valleys below could be plainly seen, a river of ice moving through the landscape. From her viewpoint, Broad Peak was visible as well as Gasherbrum I and Gasherbrum II. She hadn't climbed any of these monoliths, and she wondered if she would ever return to try.

Fluffy, white clouds began to hover on the horizon of the Karakoram Range.

Did you sit where I am, Al? Did you gaze out at the body of the earth and drink up its stark beauty?

But Lindsey knew the answer. Alison, for all her affinity for being outside, propelling herself at what nature had made, had never appreciated it truly. At least, that's how it had seemed to Lindsey. Alison had approached climbing mountains as if it were a job. There were goals to reach, details to organize, contingency plans to consider. Alison had been methodical, and she'd had a great eye for detail. It wasn't a bad way to climb; she had always been prepared. But no matter how ready a climber strived to be, there was always that unknown aspect, an intangible, hard-to-quantify realm that lived side-by-side with the order most humans craved.

Lindsey often had felt that Alison hadn't heeded her intuition, her instincts, enough. That gut feeling that whispered its presence whether you wanted to hear it or not. Alison didn't work to fine-tune it, never closed her eyes and allowed an experience to flow through her instead of striving to conquer. Their mother had said once that Lindsey was right-brain, while Alison was left.

What was Daddy? Lindsey had asked their mother at the time.

Her mother had smiled—not a sad, grief-filled gesture, but rather with a twinkle in her eye as if remembering a delicious secret. Gently stroking Lindsey's cheek, she'd said, "He was both, a perfect balance of you and Alison."

Then why was he gone? Had he battled the dragon and lost?

It was a question that had haunted Lindsey her entire life, a question with no answer.

In the beginning, she had climbed for the sheer passion of it. For the angst, the anger, the struggle, the bliss. In the mountains, there could be no room for past regrets and future worries, there could be only now. It was these moments of clarity that continued to lure her back, because as much as she tried, she couldn't find it back home, in the land of the living, with cars, and people, and grocery stores, and bills, and television. Sometimes in the lab, after working endless hours on a hypothesis and finally reaching an epiphany ... she came close. But nothing could mimic time in the mountains.

Under Alison's tutelage, her drive had become more focused, but had Lindsey failed to return the favor? Should she have helped her sister engage her senses more, to embrace a little bit more fear? Would it have kept her alive?

Another question with no answer.

Lindsey hung her head and closed her eyes.

I miss you, Al.

All those moments she had lost with Alison. All those milestones that Alison wouldn't experience—marriage, children, old age.

The earthquake of grief grew, a fearful rumbling that Lindsey instinctively scrambled to suppress. She waited, unmoving, until it subsided.

Alison would have been a great mom—so organized, so regimented, so focused.

Lindsey could have been an aunt to those inevitably precocious kids.

Now it would never be.

Will I have children?

She surely owed it to her mother, who already had lost so much— first a husband, then a daughter. Lainie Coulson was an only child. Her parents—Lindsey's grandparents—were deceased, as were

Robbie Coulson's mother and father. There were cousins on Robbie's side, but Lindsey wasn't close to them.

And when Lainie passed, Lindsey would be very much alone.

Ty appeared at the entrance to his tent, squinting, his hair angled in sleep-smashed directions.

Shaking off her dark mood, Lindsey asked, "How did you sleep?"

"Good," he replied and yawned.

She stood and walked the few steps to where he sat, then handed over his now-full water bottle.

"You're spoiling me," he said.

"Don't tell the others." She moved back to her perch near the stove. "Everyone will want me to melt their snow."

She grimaced inwardly. Why did everything she say around Galloway of late drip with sexual overtones?

She busied herself with cleaning up her K2 kitchen. "I'm going back to Base Camp."

"Me too. I don't want to leave Brynn on her own tonight."

"She'll need to go climbing again."

Irritation flashed in his eyes. "Says who?"

"You have to ask?" She met his gaze head on, the dragon within stirring to life. "If she wasn't your sister, what would you tell her to do?"

Still trying to shake off sleep, he muttered, "You're really annoying sometimes."

The comment brought a smile to her face. Alison had often said the very same thing.

LINDSEY FOLLOWED TY AS THEY DESCENDED TO ADVANCED BASE CAMP, where they met up with David, Ditch, and Packer who all decided to remain the night and rise early the next morning to finish fixing rope to Camp One. Ty took a brief break, but the nap must have energized him, so Lindsey had to scramble to catch him as he trekked clear back to Base Camp. They made it just in time to eat with Brynn in the mess tent.

Lindsey ladled lentil soup onto a bowl of rice, then sat at the table across from Brynn. "Anything eventful today?"

"You mean aside from complete isolation from civilization? I see many long days ahead of me, but I did chat with the Italians."

Ty set a bowl filled twice as high with food on the table and took a seat beside Lindsey. "If anybody hassles you, tell Juneid."

Brynn gave a mock salute. "Yes, sir."

He reached past Lindsey and grabbed the pitcher of water, filling his cup. "I know you think I'm being bossy, but there's usually far fewer women on these expeditions than men. You're a rare commodity, and they'll sniff you out."

Lindsey's gaze locked with Brynn's, and they both scrunched their faces in disgust.

"Is that what you do on expeditions?" Lindsey questioned, curious about his technique.

"No, of course not. I'm one of those rare males who never chases women."

Brynn burst out laughing. "God, you're so full of crap."

"That's just your opinion. Besides, you're not one to talk. Remember that motocross guy you dated? He was mental." Ty shoveled a heaping spoonful of lentils and rice into his mouth.

Brynn exhaled a deep breath. "Yeah, well, back then I was determined to defy Dad, since he was always hovering over my love life. The crazies were the only ones who would actually come to the house and face him. But you're trying to misdirect the conversation, Tyler. Let's get back to the topic at hand." She looked at Lindsey. "Don't you think Ty is like every other male of the species?"

Not really. "I pass on answering. I don't want to get kicked off the team." And she really didn't want to hear about any other women he may have pursued in the past.

Ty gave her a sidelong glance. "Smart lady."

"All right, let's move on to the next interesting topic then. I met

Elena." Brynn paused, then added, "I get the feeling she doesn't like you."

"Me?" Ty asked. "What's not to like about me?"

"No," Brynn reprimanded. "Not you. Lindsey."

Lindsey stirred the food in her bowl, trying to loosen the giant rice clump with the juicier lentil stew. "It's a long story."

"C'mon," Brynn said, "I need to know if I should sabotage her tent while you're all on the mountain."

Lindsey smiled. The thought had merit. "It was several years ago," she said. "Alison and I were climbing Cerro Torre in Argentina with two other climbers. Elena was also there, with a man named Paolo something. I think he was her boyfriend, or maybe not. I've heard rumors over the years that she sleeps with everyone she climbs with."

Tyler made a noncommittal sound. Lindsey waited for him to elaborate, but he continued eating.

Brynn arched an eyebrow. "A climbing prostitute?"

"Something like that. The problem at the time was that she wasn't a very good climber. I was young and didn't have much experience either at tackling something as big and remote as Cerro Torre, but I did have a lot of Yosemite time under my belt, so I wasn't completely inept. Anyway, one afternoon she was roped above us with Paolo. He slipped and fell about thirty feet. I remember Alison started cussing up a storm because he almost hit us. She had a long fuse, but when it went, watch out. Alison blew right past Elena to overtake the lead, telling her in no uncertain terms that they were to stay behind us. We managed to summit, but Elena and Paolo—while they continued to climb—never did. We didn't speak with them again, so I can't say why they didn't, and frankly, none of us really cared at the time. We figured that was the end of it.

"Three weeks later Elena complained to the Alpine Climbing Club about us, saying that we interfered with her climb, which was complete bullshit. Every year since, I've heard from other climbers how incompetent she is, how she gets into scrapes and blames others."

"How is it that she's still climbing then?" Brynn asked. "Why would anyone let her on their team?"

Lindsey glanced at Ty. "Men still succumb to sex. It's my only guess."

"Hey, not me," Ty answered.

Brynn smirked.

"Maybe she's become a better climber over the years," Lindsey continued. "At least, I hope so, but I'm not willing to stake my life on it. And if I can avoid her on this mountain, I will."

Brynn shifted her focus to her brother. "And what about you, Ty? Will you avoid her?"

He pushed to his feet. "I feel a trap coming on, so I think I'll turn in."

"Coward," Brynn muttered under her breath.

"Will you be okay here for the next few days?" He deposited his spoon and empty dinner bowl into a wash bin. "I think all of us are gonna stay at Advanced Camp."

Brynn tugged her ponytail tighter. "Yes, I'll be fine. I survived the crevasse to live another day."

"I'll check in on the radio each evening at six." Ty reached the mess tent opening and looked at Lindsey. "I'll see you at three a.m."

"It's a date."

Lindsey immediately busied herself with scooping the last of her food from her bowl, while Ty zipped up his coat. What the hell was wrong with her? After condemning Elena's romantic entanglements in the mountains, it appeared on the surface that she was no better.

She hadn't been feeling overly flustered by Galloway's presence in her life in the months leading up to the expedition, but now he rattled her.

Damn.

Before he left, he looked back one more time. "It's a deal, Coulson. But I get to pick the second date."

Lindsey glanced up in surprise, her heated face surely glowing a bright red, and he gifted her with a partial smile and a glint of amusement. Then he turned and was gone.

An awkward silence ensued between her and Brynn.

"He likes you, you know," Brynn finally said, her voice low.

Lindsey lifted her gaze to the other woman. "It's a bad idea to get involved with team members," she said.

Brynn's face softened. "You're not like Elena."

Lindsey pushed her nearly-empty bowl aside.

"You're not," Brynn insisted in a sterner tone. "And Tyler thinks very highly of you."

"He does?"

"Yes. I think the bigger question here is—are you gonna let Tyler sleep his way to the top of the mountain via the famous and esteemed Lindsey Coulson?"

Lindsey laughed.

"I'm serious," Brynn continued. "From what I've been hearing in Base Camp, you're better than a lot of these guys. You've got the pick of the boy-toy litter."

Lindsey finished the water in her cup. "Sex just complicates things. I like your brother, and I don't want to mess up our climbing relationship."

"Aha. You do like him."

Lindsey crossed her arms and watched the other woman in silence.

Brynn threw her arms up. "Okay, okay, you win. If he asks me if you asked about him, I'll say no."

"But I haven't asked you about him, have I?" She had to concede, though, that perhaps she had, in roundabout ways. "Would he ever question you about such a thing?"

"Maybe. I don't know. Probably not. He's never confided in me much about his girlfriends in the past."

It was time to change the subject. "You can stay in my tent again tonight if you're still feeling out of sorts," Lindsey said.

"No, I think I'll be all right, but thanks for the offer. Plus, you're getting up early; I'd like to skip the alarm. I'm learning that if I stay in my sleeping bag until midday, then it's not so cold when I get up."

"We'll be back in about three or four days, depending on weather and how we feel. You'll have to keep me updated on the gossip in camp."

"Actually, I'm content to keep to myself," Brynn said. "I just said that other stuff to irritate Ty. But if I hear anything, you'll be the first to know."

Lindsey said goodnight and headed to her tent, holding her head-lamp in her hand to light the way. She'd accomplished a full day of climbing, and although it wouldn't be the most difficult part of the mountain, she was feeling immensely satisfied over this small accom-plishment.

The next several weeks would be filled with climbing high and sleeping low, carrying load after load to each successive camp, returning to Base Camp for rest periods, all so that when—if—a weather window appeared, they could shoot to the summit and back down before K2 could get her icy tentacles into them.

Steal your way up the mountain, Shoop had liked to say.

Incognito was more how Lindsey viewed it. Don't be flashy like an alkali or an acid, be more like a neutral salt.

The blood in her veins thrummed.

She couldn't wait to get started.

CHAPTER 7

Tyler trudged upward along a well-worn path carrying a pack filled with nothing but heavy oxygen tanks. For three days he and his team had been ferrying supplies between Advanced Base and Camp One. Eventually much of this gear—fuel, food, additional tents, oxygen, and rope—would be carried to higher camps. The rope was now fixed to Camp One, and the Germans had fixed most of the rope to Camp Two at 22,000 feet, so both teams would be making a concerted push higher up the mountain very soon.

Brynn had reported that another team had arrived consisting of four Americans and a Norwegian, and Packer had grumbled loudly when it was revealed to be all men. Since Packer had been unable to secure a romantic rendezvous with the women currently in camp, he was hoping for a new opportunity.

Ty was partnered with Lindsey again, something Packer also grumbled about, but it had become clear in the past few days that Ditch could handle Packer's temperament the best. And Ty sensed that Lindsey avoided David whenever possible, so Ty had taken it upon himself to keep Lindsey close.

Yeah, that's what he told himself.

On this sunny afternoon, she was about twenty yards behind him with her own heavily-laden pack.

He stopped to look behind him and was surprised to see that a climber in red had passed Lindsey's blue-clad form and was almost upon him. Since he had been slowed considerably from the load he carried, he waited to let the person pass. Besides, he wanted to close the gap between him and Lindsey.

The climber pulled down a neck gaiter, revealing a feminine outline. It had to be Elena Rossi.

She smiled and held out a gloved hand. "Tyler Galloway?" she asked in English tinged with an Italian accent.

He shook her hand, although it was more of a mitten slap, and nodded.

"We were not properly introduced the other day," she continued. "I'm Elena. I've heard great things about you."

I can't say the same. "Welcome to K2," he replied. "Is it your first time?"

She pushed her goggles onto her orange helmet. The glare of the sun off the snow was intense, causing her to squint. Ty left his dark sunglasses in place, shielding his eyes.

"Yes," she replied. "First time here. We shall have to meet in Base Camp and share stories. It's always fun to visit with Americans. You all are like cowboys."

He chuckled. "I suppose."

He unhooked his jumar from the safety line and stepped to the side.

"You can pass me," he said. "I'm waiting on Lindsey."

"It is good to see her climbing again. I thought it was over for her when her sister died."

"I'm sure she just needed a break."

Elena took a step forward, placing herself close to Ty. "I have heard that she is here to search for the body. You should be careful. This could jeopardize your team."

Ty wanted to step back further, but that would place him too far from the fixed rope, so he stared down at the woman. "Thanks for your input, Ms. Rossi."

She gave a nod and a friendly smile, then moved her goggles back into place. "See you at Camp One."

When she finally moved past him, Ty hooked his jumar on the rope again and waited for Lindsey.

"Did you have a nice chat with Elena?" she asked once she was near, breathing heavily.

Not once had Lindsey balked at the hard work of climbing with a small team with no high-altitude porters.

"She told me to watch out for you," he answered honestly.

Lindsey's jaw tensed, and her lips pressed into a thin line as she gave a shake of her head. There was no doubt that she was pissed. He wondered if his climbing watch would show a barometric pressure shift surrounding her, and he was impressed when Lindsey didn't release a tirade of cuss words.

Instead, she said, "I don't think I should pass you. I'll just slow you down."

"You're going to let me follow her? I'd prefer a buffer. I'll let you lead." He unhooked his jumar again.

He was glad to see a grin grace her lips as she ascended.

"I'd follow you over her any day." The last bit he muttered under his breath as he returned to the rhythm of climbing.

THAT NIGHT, TY BUNKED IN A TENT WITH DITCH AT CAMP ONE, WHILE Lindsey was alone next door. Time to change that.

Ty pulled the hood of his jacket onto his head. "I'm going to ask Lindsey to join us."

"It would be the neighborly thing to do," Ditch said as he sorted through packets of freeze-dried food.

"Try to clean up the place, would you?" Ty scooted to the front of the tent and unzipped the doorway, then crawled out into the blustery cold and braced himself against the wind. As night descended, an eerie isolation had encompassed them.

"Lindsey," Ty yelled. "Can I come in?"

"Yeah, help yourself," came her muffled response.

He unzipped the opening of her tent and got himself inside as quickly as he could, securing the entrance behind him. He remained in the vestibule, so he wouldn't get snow from his boots all over her tent. He was also careful not to bump into the burner hanging from the tent ceiling that she was using to melt snow. It was easy to have a mishap in a very flammable tent.

"How are you doing?" he asked.

Sitting atop her sleeping bag, she rubbed her wool-clad feet. "I'm a little tired and sore, but otherwise I feel good."

"You sound surprised."

She jammed her fingers into her ponytail and scratched her head. "I guess I was a little worried. You never really know how you'll do until you're on the mountain doing it." She hugged her knees toward her chest.

"Wanna share a candy bar for dinner?" He pulled off his gloves and retrieved the treat from his coat pocket.

"Maybe we should split it three ways. Ditch might be hungry."

"He's already eaten. He had half a Pop-Tart."

Ty unwrapped the candy bar, twisted it in half—exposing peanuts resting in a hardened nougat center—and handed a piece to her.

"Thanks."

"You're welcome to hang out in our spacious accommodations," Ty said. "Ditch likes to play Hearts, and it's no fun with two."

She shut off the stove and donned her mitten to carefully remove the pan filled with hot water. "Well, as you can see, I am quite busy." Holding her water bottle between her feet, she carefully poured the liquid into it.

"If you join us then at least we'll have an excuse to say no to Elena."

Lindsey's head snapped up. "Did she try to get in your tent?"

Regretting his words, Ty said, "No, sorry. I was just kidding." But he thought he detected a tinge of jealousy in her voice, and he liked it.

He couldn't tell if the flush on her cheeks was from the cold or from her sudden outburst, but either way she looked too damned enticing.

"All right, I'm heading back," he said, conceding defeat in his efforts to be neighborly.

"Wait. I'll go with you. It's kind of lonely in here by myself."

"You could invite Elena over for a slumber party."

"Bite your tongue."

Once she secured the lid on her water bottle, she reached past him for her boots, bumping into him. A charged atmosphere settled around them as it became impossible for Ty not to touch her in such a confined space.

Ditch had encouraged Ty to dial it back where Lindsey was concerned, and yet at the same time he had cautioned Ty against ending up old and alone.

Ty released a laugh, easing the tension sparking between him and the woman who was affecting him far more than he'd ever anticipated.

"What's so funny?" Lindsey asked, zipping her jacket.

"I was thinking about a passage from Alice in Wonderland. 'It's no use going back to yesterday, because I was a different person then.'"

Lindsey smiled. "'We're all mad here,'" she said, quoting another line from Alice with a gleam in her eye.

Ty leaned close. "'You must be, or you wouldn't have come....'"

TIME FELL AWAY, AND LINDSEY WAS SURE TY WAS GOING TO KISS HER. SHE didn't move, waiting for the inevitable, anticipating it. Wanting it. But he remained a gentleman and eased back from crossing the barrier they would be unable to retain once it was breached. A mixture of relief and disappointment filled her.

She grabbed her helmet and strapped it on, since rock fall could happen anytime day or night.

Tyler Galloway would be no quick fling. And if she was being honest, she wasn't ready to let her heart become entangled in something with so much potential for bliss and angst.

He would be a huge complication.

She switched on her headlamp.

As Ty exited her tent, a flash of irritation cut through her at the thought of Elena getting her claws into him.

If anyone's going to make bacon with him, it's gonna be me.

So much for hanging back and playing it safe.

He leaned back inside and grabbed her gloved hand to help her stand, two puffy pillows trying to make contact, and was forced to slip his other hand under her shoulder to haul her up and out. Once clear, the wind slammed into her, and she braced hard to remain upright. Ty released her, and they trudged to the other tent. The soft glow from two additional tents rose from the featureless white terrain like gumdrops in whipped cream—the humble abodes of Elena and the Italians. Ty stepped aside to let Lindsey enter first, and she crawled into the cramped and cozy man cave.

"Close the door," Ditch grumbled. "You're letting all the heat out."

Lindsey settled further in while Ty zipped the entrance shut.

"Thanks for inviting me," she said. "Where are the hors d'oeuvres?"

Ditch dug around in a pocket in his pack and produced a bag of crackers.

"They aren't crushed," she said. "Amazing." She removed her helmet but left her parka on. The thin tent walls did little to stave off the cold. She dug out a fleece hat from a pocket and pulled it over her braided hair until it covered her ears.

"Ditch seems to have the touch with food," Ty said.

"Wait." Ditch fished around in his pack again. He produced a baggy filled with individually wrapped pieces of cheese.

"Wow," Lindsey said, impressed. "Now all we need is some wine."

"The Italians might have some," Ditch said.

Lindsey made a derisive sound. "It's not worth it to go over and find out."

Ty removed his jacket, still bundled up in a turtleneck covered by a dark gray fleece pullover. In the tight quarters, they all huddled together, and his leg touched hers. He produced a deck of cards and removed the two of diamonds.

"Are you married, Ditch?" Lindsey asked, picking up the cards Ty dealt.

"I was. She divorced me a few years back."

"I'm sorry."

He shrugged. "It gave me more time in the mountains."

"It can be hard on those around you with being away so much," she said. "Do you have any children?"

"We never did." He laid down the two of clubs, beginning the game. "Sometimes I regret that. If you want kids, don't wait."

Lindsey played a club from her hand. "I suppose you're right." All it took was the right guy. She avoided looking at Ty, worried that he might somehow see the stark need that he'd somehow unleashed in her.

Ty won the trick and started the next set, throwing down the eight of clubs.

"How is it that the Italians are your enemy?" Ditch asked, throwing down his play.

Lindsey won the trick and scooped up the three cards, then started the next set with the king of diamonds. "Word travels quickly."

"You're just a better climber than Elena," Ditch said. "She was present when I was at Nanga Parbat, and she was a piece of work. Nanga is called the maneater, and I think Elena took it to heart. I realize that some females become upset if they can't stand side by side with men in these endeavors, but I hate to say that women like her make the case for banning girls from the mountains." He tossed out the queen of spades.

Lindsey didn't speak, surprised both by Ditch's judgment of women climbers and by his bold move in the game.

Ty whistled and glanced up, amusement in his gaze. "Shit, Ditch, tell us how you really feel."

"She was involved in three separate incidents of climbers getting into trouble. I never reached the summit, and my one consolation was that she didn't, either. I wouldn't trust any rope she tied, any belay she offered."

While Lindsey didn't find it difficult to believe this assessment of Elena, it was in stark contrast to how Ditch had treated Lindsey up to this point in the expedition. And suddenly she knew—Ditch had slept with Rossi. Time to change the subject.

Ty played a low diamond, forcing Lindsey to win the trick and take the dreaded queen of spades, costing her thirteen points.

"So, we're heading down tomorrow?" she asked, changing her strategy. She laid down the ace of hearts, intending to gather all the hearts and beat Ditch and Ty.

"The lady isn't going down without a fight," Ty said. "And yes, we'll descend in the morning. It looks like some weather is coming, so I'll give everybody a few days off before we start pushing to Camp Two."

Lindsey collected her win and played another high card in the hearts suit. "I was thinking of heading up to House's Chimney in the morning," she said. "I'm curious to see what it's all about."

House's Chimney was a band of rock with vertical smears of ice about five hundred feet wide. It was approximately fifteen hundred feet above them.

"I'm game. How about you, Ditch?" Ty said, then made a disapproving grumble when Lindsey took yet another trick filled with hearts.

"Let's start early. I'm not sitting around here with Elena."

Three more tricks, and Lindsey had the game.

"Rematch, boys?" she asked.

Both Ty and Ditch laughed.

"Let's make it interesting," Ditch said. "Winner gets shotgun at House's Chimney."

~

THE NEXT MORNING LINDSEY AWOKE TO HER WATCH ALARM AT 3 A.M., THE wind having quieted during the night. She rose and used a funnel to relieve herself into a bottle marked with a skull and bones, then quickly donned her gear, craving warmth. She opened her tent just enough to scoop snow into a silver pan, then unhooked the stove from its ceiling perch, placing it in the vestibule to vent the gas, and fired it up. Once she had melted water, she added it to her mug and mixed in dry oatmeal, powdered milk, and walnuts. Heating more snow, she added an English Breakfast tea bag and drank it directly from the pan.

Ty and Ditch didn't want to head out until 4 a.m., so she took time to gather her thoughts and enjoy an unrushed routine. It was important to stay fed, hydrated, and as well-rested as possible, although she wasn't sleeping deeply. The high altitude promoted a certain amount of restlessness.

She stowed the gear that would remain in the tent and emptied anything extraneous from her pack, then she laced her boots and unzipped the tent to attach her gators and crampons. Standing, she hoisted her pack onto her back, looking toward the lightening sky in the east. Ty and Ditch soon appeared.

"You ready?" Ty asked.

She nodded as she buckled her helmet beneath her chin.

The Germans had fixed ropes, so they decided to use them, although Ty suggested they still rope up. Didn't hurt to have a back-up just in case. They climbed slowly for several hours through a mix of snow and rock. At House's Chimney, a spider web of ropes greeted them. Many were old, some new.

The wind was picking up and the sky had darkened with cloud cover.

Ty scanned the situation. "I hate to say it, but I think we should turn back."

"I still get my shotgun, though." Lindsey had to yell, mummified as she was with a face mask, goggles, and parka hood pulled over her helmet.

Thick snowflakes began to blanket them.

Ditch pulled the radio from a pocket in his climbing suit and contacted Base Camp to let them know their status.

"Thank God you called in," Brynn said. "The Italians have an injured team member, over."

"Where, over?" Ditch asked.

"They were at Camp One. We thought you were with them. One of them was hit by a falling rock and he's down and having trouble breathing. Can you assist, over?"

"Yes," Ditch answered. "We're currently at the bottom of House's Chimney, but we're heading down now. Give us one hour, over."

"I'll let them know, over."

Without further talk, the three of them descended. When they came to Camp One and the cluster of tents, one of the Italians approached. Lindsey thought his name was Fabrizio. "It's Aldo," he said. "He is in much pain. We need to move him down, but it is just Elena and I."

"I have medical training." Ditch removed his pack. "Let me have a look at him."

Fabrizio told Elena to exit the tent. As she did, her ashen face brightened. "Eddie. Thank you so much." Ignoring her, Ditch entered the tent on his hands and knees.

Lindsey pulled her face mask down as Ty asked Elena, "What happened?"

"A large rock hit Aldo on the shoulder," she replied. "He fell and would not stand again. He complains of the pain."

Snowfall danced and swirled around them, getting thicker.

Ditch's head popped out of the tent entrance. "His shoulder is dislocated. Ty and Lindsey, I need some help. Grab a pole."

Lindsey dropped her pack and retrieved her trekking pole buckled to the side. She and Ty crawled into the tent. Aldo was conscious but panting heavily and clearly in pain.

"I know it's tight in here," Ditch said. "Lindsey, squeeze on the other side."

When she was in position, he grabbed the pole, holding it across Aldo's upper body, and Lindsey took hold of the opposite end.

"Ty, I need you to raise Aldo's right arm and tie his wrist to the pole with this rope." Ditch tossed a coiled pile of nylon to him.

Ty unwound the rope and pressed in, all three of them now huddled tightly around Aldo. When Ty reached for the man's arm, Aldo screamed in agony.

"Unfortunately, my morphine is back at Base Camp," Ditch said, his voice tight. "Just do it."

Ty's eyes widened and a muscle in his cheek flexed as he gave an uncertain nod. He took Aldo's arm again, raised it up ninety degrees as the man's howling blasted them all, and Ty swiftly anchored Aldo's wrist to the pole.

Ditch levelled his gaze at Lindsey. "Raise the bar up now."

Bracing her end on her own shoulder, Lindsey rose up onto her knees, trying to ignore Aldo's protests. It was all in Italian, but begging was begging in any language.

Lindsey felt a pop.

Aldo quieted, tears streaming down his face.

"Good job," Ditch said.

Ty quickly removed the rope and pole, and Lindsey followed him back outside, her heart pounding.

"We need to get him down," Ditch's voice trailed after them. "But I don't think he can walk."

Lindsey took a deep breath, trying to calm her rattled nerves. "I'll get one of the extra tents. We can use it to carry him."

Ty nodded, then said, "Leave anything unnecessary so our packs are as light as they can be." He looked at Elena and Fabrizio. "Are you both able to descend?"

Their heads bobbed in agreement, both appearing shell-shocked.

Slowly, everyone went to work. It took an hour but finally they were on their way with Fabrizio, Ty and Ditch guiding Aldo's tightly-wrapped body with ropes attached. Elena was in front, using the fixed rope to find their way in what was now a whiteout. Even with her three-year hiatus, Lindsey suspected she was stronger than Elena, so she positioned herself in the rear, ready to catch Aldo if he slipped.

"I'll switch with one of you if you get tired," she had said to Ty before they began their slow and tedious descent.

It took three hours to get the injured man to ABC since they made frequent stops to catch their breath, sip water, and give fluid to Aldo. As they approached ABC, they were met by three other Italians and David and Packer, who took over transporting Aldo. By nightfall, they had reached Base Camp.

Ditch headed to the Italians' camp with his patient as Lindsey followed Ty to their mess tent. She dumped her pack at the entrance and stepped inside, and Habibe and Brynn greeted them.

"How is he?" Brynn asked.

"Not sure." Ty pulled off his mittens and pushed back his parka hood, having removed his helmet during the one mile walk from ABC. He rubbed his hands on his face.

Lindsey took a seat as Habibe handed her and Ty two steaming cups of hot cocoa.

"Thank you." She wrapped her fingers around the mug for warmth. For one long moment, she savored the sweet beverage, sipping it over and over. Now that she had stopped moving, exhaustion consumed her, and she considered laying her head on the table and going to sleep.

Brynn set her book aside. "I have to admit, I was glad it wasn't any of you."

Ty leaned back in his chair and sighed. "Luck of the draw."

David and Packer joined them.

"Three cheers for the A-Team," Packer said with a flourish, sniffing the cup of cocoa that Habibe handed him. "There's no booze in it but thank you."

David accepted his in silence as Ditch entered and took a seat. "I think Aldo will be okay. I gave him some ibuprofen. He just needs to rest now."

"I can't believe you popped his shoulder back," Ty said.

Packer started poking around in the food bins stacked along the tent wall. "Oh hell," he groused. "Do we not have any marshmallows?"

Ignoring him, Ditch said, "While it's usually not wise to reduce a shoulder in a situation like that, mostly because nerves and blood vessels can be damaged, he was in too much pain. It was all I could come up with on such short notice, but luckily the traction worked. Thanks for your help." His gaze included Lindsey and she nodded.

"Holy shit!" Packer cried, startling everyone. "I owe someone my firstborn."

Ditch looked over his shoulder, his weariness apparent. "How did your parents ever hide Christmas presents and Easter baskets from you?"

Packer reverently picked up a blue packet, staring at it like a besotted lover.

"What is it?" Lindsey asked.

"Kendal mint cakes," Ditch replied. "They were supposed to be a surprise for our summit push."

"I've never heard of them."

"Neither have I," Brynn added.

Ditch stood and replaced the lid on the food bin, shooing Packer away. "In Britain, they're an outdoor staple. Sir Edmund Hillary ate one when he became the first man to summit Everest. Shackleton took them when he went to Antarctica in the early 1900s."

Packer scurried to the other side of the table with the one he stole and sat beside Lindsey. "If you've never had one, then you've never known Heaven on earth."

She frowned. "They can't be that good."

Every male in the tent besides Habibe quietly refuted her statement.

"You have no idea," David murmured.

"It's hard to eat just one," Ty added under his breath.

Packer carefully tore open the packet and broke off one of the rectangles of the white confection, then split it further before handing a piece each to Lindsey and Brynn.

"Gee, don't give me too much," Lindsey said, not trying to hide her sarcasm.

Under the intense scrutiny of all the males, she and Brynn put the tiny portions in their mouths. Lindsey expected it to be like a peppermint patty but was surprised by the granular yet creamy texture and the smooth melding of sugar and mint. Her fatigue seemed to melt away.

Brynn's expression of enlightenment must have been reflected on Lindsey's face as well, because Packer grinned with smug satisfaction. "Well?"

"I think I need one more piece to be sure."

Packer released a peal of laughter. "Not for a million bucks."

CHAPTER 8

Despite the exertion of the previous day, Ty awoke early and walked over to the recently-arrived American encampment, ducking his head into their mess tent.

"Hey, Galloway!" Dan Beck greeted him with his usual dark shaggy hair and wide grin.

Ty shook his hand. "I had no doubt you'd be up early. Some things never change." He and Beck had spent several seasons guiding together on Mt. Rainier, as well as a handful of trips to Denali.

"First to rise always gets the best food." Beck motioned for Ty to sit.

A Pakistani cook poured Ty a cup of coffee.

Ty settled into a plastic chair and drank it black. He needed the kick. "I was surprised to hear you were on your way in."

"I scrambled, baby, but I made it." Beck chuckled. "Where there's a will, there's a way. We're not in Kansas anymore, Toto."

The cook set two plates down piled with scrambled eggs, potatoes, and bacon. Tyler's stomach rumbled and he grabbed a fork. "You're not kidding about the food." He added salt and pepper and started digging in. "And you could've come in with my team."

"I knew you wanted to go small. So I went small too. How much rope is laid?"

"We're pushing toward Camp Two. The Germans and the Italians are helping."

Beck nodded. "Sounds good. We'll lend a hand where we can. We brought in fifty thousand feet of rope."

Ty laughed. "Yeah, right." Beck was a cheap bastard who climbed with only the essentials. "Who made it in with you?"

"Artie's here. He'll be happy to see you."

Ty had climbed with Artie Gillespie in Alaska.

"And there's Jasper Jones and Stan Ingerman. Dan Jordan bailed out a few weeks ago, so at the last minute, Artie recruited a Norwegian named Anders Fiske."

Ty shook his head. "I don't know him."

Beck's expression turned to annoyed amusement. "Let me know what you think of him. I think his middle name is BFE."

"Translation?"

"Big Fucking Ego," Beck answered, keeping his voice low. "His climbing suit is a checkerboard of corporate sponsors. He claims he's a celebrity in his country. Big whoop. We'll see how he climbs."

Ty chuckled.

"I hear you've got Lindsey Coulson," Beck said.

"I do. And I'm not trading her for your Norwegian."

Beck ran a hand through his hair and grinned. "Don't make any hasty decisions, man. I'm always open for negotiation. Did I hear right that Brynnie is here too?"

Ty nodded.

"I'll come by and say hi. I always did have a crush on your sister."

"I'm pretty sure if she wouldn't date you three years ago, it's still a no go."

Beck sighed. "You're probably right, but a man can dream, can't he?" He sobered. "Ingerman was here when Alison Coulson died."

"I know, but on a different team."

"How's David?"

Ty drained the last of his coffee. "He doesn't talk about it. Can't say I blame him."

"You think he and Lindsey are gonna be okay?"

"Since when did you become a nursemaid?"

Beck leaned his chair back. "Haven't you figured it out yet?"

"What's that?"

"When you're in charge you're part cheerleader and part psychologist."

"I thought the most important requirement was total hard-ass."

Beck wadded a rag on the table and threw it at Ty. "You're a prick, Galloway."

Catching the cloth, Ty laughed and threw it back. "You better be nice to me or else I won't invite you over for dinner."

"Such a sweet-talker. You can expect me for happy hour."

LINDSEY ARRIVED LATE TO DINNER, HAVING FALLEN ASLEEP WHILE reading her book. She halted at the entrance, surprised to see the mess tent packed with more testosterone than usual. The pungent aroma of cinnamon and cloves wafted from the cooking area as Habibe hustled over pots and pans, and her mouth watered in anticipation. At least she hadn't missed any food yet. Her eyes sought out Brynn and found her crammed between Packer on one side and an unknown man with a handsome face beneath a dark mop of hair on the other.

Across the tent, Ty laughed at something said by his neighbor, then his gaze locked with hers. She stared, caught in the headlights of his thousand-watt smile. He tilted his head, indicating for her to come sit beside him. She broke free of her trance and scooted past several male backsides before making her way to Galloway. He grabbed a canvas stool and pushed it toward the man sitting beside him.

"Out of the chair, Artie," Ty said.

The man stood and said, "You must be Lindsey."

He extended his hand and Lindsey shook it, craning her neck to look up at him. He had an Irish look to him with red hair, a long face, and a genial smile. He offered his vacated chair to her and settled onto the stool, and she was soon wedged between him and Ty. When her knees began bumping up against various legs, she angled herself slightly toward Galloway.

She didn't want this Artie to get the wrong idea.

But she wasn't averse to Ty getting the wrong idea.

"Beer?" Ty asked her.

She nodded, and he passed her one.

She shifted her attention to the men around the table interspersed with their own team members as Ty introduced her to Dan Beck—the man chatting up Brynn—and, on the far side of him, Jasper Jones, sporting one hell of a beard. He raised a beer can to her and Lindsey smiled. Stories had circulated of JJ and his penchant for pushing through terrible conditions and succeeding. His nickname in climbing circles was Moses.

At the end of the table talking with Ditch was Anders Fiske— blond-haired and blue-eyed, his strong jawline pegging his obvious Scandinavian lineage—and Stan Ingerman. The second name caught Lindsey's attention. She'd never met the man, but he'd been on K2 when Alison had died. He was sitting quietly while the others talked and laughed and shared climbing stories, his demeanor somewhat retracted from the group dynamics, his complexion looking a bit gray against his light brown hair.

Maybe she could speak to him at some point in the days, maybe weeks, to come.

But did she want to?

She drank more beer and sank into the energy of the group, letting herself get swept into it, not wanting to dwell on the one person who was missing. The one person who would always be missing from Lindsey's life.

Habibe began passing around plates of rice and cooked vegetables.

"What's the skinny on the climbing scene in California, Lindsey?" Beck asked.

"I actually went to Colorado to get my sea legs back." She bumped arms with Ty as they both started eating.

"Why did you need to get sea legs?" Fiske asked from across the table, his gaze fixated on her.

While Lindsey had no desire to vent her past amongst everyone—she suspected the others knew her story anyway—she also didn't like the glint in Fiske's eye, as if he were pissing a circle around her to stake his claim. She'd seen it before. Men like him didn't respond well to no.

JJ spoke up, his tone compassionate. "Lindsey lost her sister here two years ago."

Fiske gave a nod of understanding. "I am sorry for you."

She silently acknowledged the exchange, then turned to Dan Beck. "I went to Longs Peak earlier this summer."

"Excellent climbing," he replied.

"Where in Colorado is Longs Peak?" Fiske asked.

"Outside Boulder," Ty answered.

"I've never been there. I've always wanted to visit the United States. Maybe you can be my tour guide, Lindsey."

"Just let me know when you're coming," Ty cut in. "I know plenty of climbers who'd be happy to hold your hand."

Fiske narrowed his eyes and scooped a spoonful of rice into his mouth.

Warmth spread in Lindsey's belly from Ty's obvious effort to shut down Fiske's pass.

"It's been about five years since I was at Longs Peak," Beck said. "How was it?"

Lindsey wiped her mouth with the back of her hand. "Reassuring."

The look in Beck's eyes told her he understood her meaning. "You never really lose it," he said. "It's like riding a fucking bike."

"A bike at a hundred miles an hour straight down to hell," Packer said, adding a cackle at the end for good measure.

Lindsey gave him a good-natured frown.

Packer pointed his fork at her and asked, "Who was your partner?"

She hesitated, expecting censure. "I climbed alone."

A moment of silence ensued. Longs Peak was as dangerous as any other mountain. She'd even gone as far as to free climb it one day. If she'd fallen, there would have been no help.

"Still a maverick," David said under his breath without looking at her.

Before she could dwell on the meaning of the comment, Packer exclaimed as if she'd won the lottery, "No shit?"

"Yeah, shit," she replied, her spine stiffening as she prepared to stand up for herself. These men weren't her father, and her actual father was dead. Lindsey had been on her own for a long time. "I didn't want to conform to anyone else's schedule. I needed to find my own rhythm."

Packer gave her a roguish wink. "I know what you mean. It's a special thing when you figure out your bump and grind."

"Get your face out of your pants, Packer," Ditch said.

"Believe me, it's not *my* pants I'm trying to get into."

Ditch leaned back in his chair. "Neither is anybody else."

As several conversations started up, Lindsey turned to Ty. "Are you gonna grill me too?" she asked for his ears only.

He looked at her, sitting so close that she drank in the full vibrant color of his blue-green eyes. She knew he understood her question, referring to David's subtle and derogatory comment.

With a slight shake of his head, he said, "Nah." He paused, then leaned closer. "Believe me, I understand. It just would've been a shame if something had happened to you after I'd worked so hard to get you on the team."

She nudged his leg with hers. "I didn't know you cared."

"I care about everybody on the team." He resumed his focus on his dinner, but he did return the nudge.

Lindsey awoke to heavy snowfall. When she visited Aldo to check on his progress after the rock fall, which thankfully was improving each day, Fabrizio uttered, *"Il tempo é merda!"*

Packer, who had accompanied her, replied, "Yeah, the weather here *is* crap." It was a sentiment she suspected they would utter many times during their stay.

The snow continued, stretching from hours into days.

She spent her time sleeping, doing crossword puzzles, and listening to music on her iPod. Afternoons often found her in the mess tent with Brynn and Packer, engaging in spirited discussions ranging from the meaning of life, the existence of God, and the proper way to make an omelet. She wouldn't have suspected that Packer could cook anything, but he demonstrated a knack in the kitchen, preparing none other than an upside-down pineapple cake using canned fruit. A deal was struck that he was the backup cook if Habibe ever took ill.

In the evenings Ty had movie nights, playing DVDs on his laptop. Afterwards she, Brynn, Ty, and David would play Scrabble. She took a fair amount of grief over playing words like "amoeba," "guanine," and "ribose."

"I dispute that," David had said when she played "allele." "That looks made up."

"It's a variant form of a given gene," Lindsey answered. "A mutation."

"Use it in a sentence."

"Packer is an allele." She managed to say it with a straight face.

David worked hard to maintain his seriousness, but the sides of his mouth nevertheless twitched.

"I'll give it to her," Brynn said.

Ty grinned. "Me too."

David had sighed, accepting defeat.

Around dinnertime, members from the other teams would visit. She enjoyed catching up with Piotr and two of the other Polish climbers, Janusz and Lech, but when Elena and Fabrizio made an appearance, Lindsey bugged out at the first opportunity.

Then there was the American team. She genuinely liked Beck, Artie, and JJ, but Ingerman hadn't come around since that first night, and Fiske had come around too much. The Norwegian, who she had learned had been invited to fill a last-minute spot vacated by another climber, spoke too highly of his accomplishments in the mountains, annoying Lindsey, and if she had to guess, everyone else.

Fiske appeared more and more frequently in their mess tent, and while he gave equal attention to both her and Brynn, Lindsey soon felt him crowding her.

"We've got company every damned night," Packer complained over a lunch of macaroni and cheese, which Lindsey was enjoying immensely. The creamy mixture was hitting the spot.

"I thought you liked all the chitchat," David said, studying a map of K2 with Ty.

"I am a sociable guy, but I don't want to run out of liquor. We can't keep entertaining this much."

"So what are you saying?" David asked. "Should we put out a sign that says we're not home?"

"No, but Brynn and Lindsey should stop bathing or something. They're like honey, drawing all the males in."

Lindsey glanced up from her lunch. "I hate to break it to you, Packer, but I haven't bathed in over three weeks."

Ty flashed her a quick grin causing her stomach to do a flip-flop. Damn. Talk about honey.

"Me either," Brynn seconded.

Sitting beside her, Packer made a face of disgust. "Maybe you could just crank up the rudeness."

She and Brynn glared at him.

"What I meant was," he continued, trying to lighten his tone, "perhaps you could hone your rudeness toward other climbers."

Brynn eyed him with an air of disdain and said slowly, "So you're saying that we're rude."

"Not to me, of course."

Lindsey grabbed a warm chappatis from a basket at the center of the table and took a bite. "What about Elena?" she asked around her food. "We're not the only women in camp."

"True." Packer nodded, his expression becoming contemplative. "But while you girls would just be disappointed in me sexually, Elena would probably cut my balls off while I was sleeping."

Brynn choked on her food, drawing a concerned look from Ty. Packer gave her several whacks between her shoulder blades. From his position at the computer, Ditch glanced over his shoulder. "And finally, you speak the truth."

Brynn had regained herself, trying not to laugh.

"I'm just a boy," Packer waxed, "looking for a girl."

"What if Brynn and I spread the word that we're lesbians?" Lindsey asked. "Would that drive all the men away?"

Packer's eyes widened in anticipation. "Wait, what?" He shifted his gaze from one to the other. "Is this true? Don't tease me, ladies." A sly grin took shape at the corner of his mouth.

Before Lindsey could grunt out her disapproval, Fiske peeked his head inside. "Am I interrupting?" he asked.

Packer must have noticed Lindsey's look of defeat, because when she looked across the table at him, he silently mouthed the word in obvious delight, "Lesbian."

She suppressed a chuckle. Would such an admission even work on a man like Fiske?

"No," Ty said. "Come on in."

Anders entered and took a seat beside Lindsey. She began shoveling what was left of her macaroni into her mouth so she could leave.

Leaning close to her, Anders said, "That looks delicious." He was doing this more and more, trying to touch her in subtle ways. At first it was an annoyance, now it just angered her. He invaded her space, and she'd given no indication of reciprocal interest. It had quickly gone from flattering to creepy. No, scratch that. It had never been flattering, only creepy.

He wasn't the first climber to make a pass at her—she and Alison often had been the target of vigorous wooing—but most men, when a boundary was laid down, backed off.

It wasn't until Ty looked up that she realized in an effort to avert her attention from Fiske, she'd been staring at Galloway. Embarrassed, she returned to finishing her lunch.

"I'm gonna go build a snow-woman," Packer said, standing. "Habibe, you got anything I can use for tits?"

Habibe shook his head, clearly confused by what Packer was requesting.

"I'll help," Lindsey mumbled around her full mouth, trying to swallow the last of her meal. She stood, handed the plastic plate to Habibe, and made her escape. She pulled on gloves as she and Packer headed into the whiteout.

"It was gettin' too crowded in there," he said.

"Yep."

"You know I was just kidding about the snow-woman." Packer stopped to look up at her. "You're not sweet on me, are you? Must have been all that talk of my lack of sexual prowess."

Lindsey smiled. "Out of all the men here at camp, you're one of the few I like."

He grabbed his chest. "Be still my heart." He walked away, waving her off. "You're not so bad yourself, Coulson."

After visiting the latrine tent, she made her way to her tent, but was unfortunately cut off by Fiske.

"Lindsey, would you like to join me later?"

"No thanks." She tried to keep her voice light, her mood cheery.

"You might want to reconsider." His English was good, with only a slight hint of an accent. "I've got great music and a bottle of scotch."

Panic stirred in her chest. That didn't sound like a good idea at all.

"I appreciate the invitation," she said, "but I'm just here to climb." She tried to sound casual, as if she didn't really understand what his offer implied.

Flurries of snow swirled around them. Lindsey pulled the hood of her parka over her head.

"Hey, Linds," Ty said, exiting the mess tent about twenty feet away. "Can I talk to you?"

Relieved, she said, "Yes."

She moved toward him, unsure if Fiske would follow, but she didn't dare glance back. He would likely interpret it as a come-hither look.

When she reached Ty, he smiled and looked over her shoulder. "You don't mind if I borrow her, do you?"

Fiske must have been right behind her.

Then Ty did something that surprised her; he put an arm around her shoulders, a clear and obvious possessive move. Her heart pounded at Galloway's proximity. Frozen in place, she stared at the top of his down jacket, unsure what to do.

"Just giving her a choice," Fiske said from behind.

"That's nice of you, but I think we'll be fine." While Galloway's words sounded polite there was an edge to his voice, an unmistakable warning in the tone.

As Fiske walked away, Ty moved closer. "That guy's an ass," he said under his breath, then removed his arm, finally putting a little space between them. "Sorry. I thought you could use some help."

"Thanks." She stared at her snow boots, guessing her face would make a nice heater to ward off the chill in the air if the spike in her internal temperature was any indication.

"Maybe I should kiss you, just to make sure he stays away."

Her eyes snapped to his. Did he mean it? She wasn't sure.

A nervous laugh escaped her mouth.

"I'm just kidding," he said. "I'm sure you can take care of yourself. Not sure why I got all territorial right then. I feel like I should look after you sometimes."

"I appreciate it." She searched desperately for something to say, but her mind was blank.

"I guess I should go check on Packer," Ty said. "And make sure his snowman isn't too pornographic."

She blurted the first thing she could think of. "What's the movie for tonight?"

"I don't know. Do you wanna choose?"

"Okay."

"The DVDs are in my tent. Wanna have a look?"

"Okay."

She followed Ty to his tent, the path covered with snow. He unzipped the door and crawled inside, shuffling through piles of books and clothes then gesturing for her to enter. She brushed snow from her jacket and hood and crawled inside on her knees.

"Sorry, it's a little messy," he said, sitting on his sleeping bag and reaching for a bag in the corner.

She settled on the opposite side, trying to minimize how much snow she dispersed all over his things. While he rummaged through a bag, she glanced at his accommodations. It smelled of worn clothes and mild body odor, distinctly Galloway, and it wasn't altogether unpleasant. A lantern sat atop a plastic bin, alongside an iPad with headphones attached. Notepads and several books were strewn about. She pushed them around to read the titles. Ernest Shackleton. Roald Amundsen. The conquest of the South Pole.

"Are you planning a trip?" she asked.

"Yeah, I am. I've always wanted to go to Antarctica. I'm a fan of remote locales. I guess you could say I love getting lost."

"The Lost Boy of San Miguel."

Ty laughed. "Brynn told you about that?"

"It's an extraordinary story. What compelled you to walk so far? You were so young, you must've been terrified."

"I don't recall being afraid, but I do remember thinking that my dad wouldn't be proud if I simply sat down and gave up, so I kept going."

"And going," she added. "I guess we all don't want to disappoint our fathers." She picked up another book. Tennyson. "Is he any good?"

"Do you like poetry?"

"Not really."

"Well, Tennyson is the man, especially in places like this. Sometimes it's the only thing that inspires me when I'm tired and don't want to crawl out of my sleeping bag."

"Sleeping bag-itis. Happens to me frequently." In the ensuing lull in the conversation, Lindsey realized it may have sounded as if she was inviting him into hers. Not that she didn't want to … "What's your favorite Tennyson quote?"

He stopped searching inside the duffle and thought for a minute. "Well, it's probably 'To strive, to seek, to find, and not to yield.' But his most famous is probably one you've heard, ''Tis better to have loved and lost than never to have loved at all.' I lean on that when I think of friends who didn't make it."

"Sometimes I can't reconcile Alison's death, as if it's not real. And yet I could so easily die in the same way."

Ty retrieved a canvas case and opened it. "You can't dwell on it. It messes with your equilibrium. But I have to admit this mountain carries a bigger aura of death than I've felt in other places."

"As much as I try not to be, sometimes I'm afraid," she said quietly, the space between her and Ty crackling with awareness. Was she scared of the mountain? Was she scared of facing the well of grief in her heart from losing Alison? Or was she scared of him? She suspected it was all three. So much for the hear-me-roar woman she aspired to be.

"What have you got?" she asked, happy to change the subject.

He handed her the goods and she started flipping through the plastic pages that held the DVDs. Ty had eclectic taste: *Surf's Up, A Beautiful Mind, The Matrix, Sherlock Holmes, Cast Away, City Slickers, Armageddon, Pitch Black.*

"You like a lot of science fiction," she said.

"I do. I have *Star Wars* but *Empire* is by far the best. I've also got *Raiders of the Lost Ark* for Brynn. I always imagine her as a female Indiana Jones."

"You should go on an expedition with her in the jungle somewhere," she said. "It was awfully great of her to come here with you. This is hardly a vacation destination."

"You're right. I guess I owe her."

Lindsey flipped another page. "*Top Gun?* Really?"

"That's a great movie," he responded. "When I was a kid I wanted to be a fighter pilot. Iceman was such a cool call sign. Where's your next destination?"

"There's always the usual suspects—Makalu, Cho Oyu, Dhaulagiri—but I'm intrigued by Badrinath. It's in the Indian Himalaya. It would be nice to climb and not worry about records and blogs and press, to simply explore instead."

"I hear you."

"Maybe I'll see if I can tag along with Brynn into the jungle," she said. "That sounds fun, too."

"Just so long as there's no Norwegian dudes out there."

"I'm questioning how I ever survived the many Base Camps I've lived in without your protection."

"I'm available whenever you need me."

"Thanks." She turned her attention back to the movies before she was tempted to take him up on the offer. "Why do you have *Out of Africa*? That seems like a chick flick."

"I have a weakness for Meryl Streep."

Lindsey smiled. "I liked the movie where she was a river guide. I can't remember the name, but Kevin Bacon played the bad guy."

"*The River Wild.*"

"Yeah, that's it."

"What's your favorite movie?" he asked.

Lindsey thought for a moment. "When I was eleven I remember seeing *Contact*."

"Great film," Ty murmured.

"It was after my dad had been gone for a few years. Jodie Foster's character also loses her father. It really got to me. I guess I've always harbored a secret hope that one day I might be able to contact him, somehow, like she did with her dad when she visited the aliens. I sometimes think he's near when I climb. I can almost feel him, looking over my shoulder, watching my handiwork."

Ty's gaze was a mixture of compassion and contemplation. And desire. There was no mistaking it.

She flicked her eyes back to the book of DVDs. "How about *Galaxy Quest*?"

"Great choice. Why don't you keep it and bring it to dinner later?"

He was giving her an out, and she took it. She slid the disc from the plastic pocket and scooted toward the tent entrance. "See you then," she said, not looking back.

Ty's voice trailed after her. "Bye, Jodie."

As she hustled back to her tent, she ducked her head to keep snowflakes from landing on her eyelashes.

Why didn't she just go for it with Galloway? What was she so afraid of?

The answer hit loud and clear.

She had lost nearly everyone she loved in the mountains. If she kept her heart far away from Tyler, then she would never have to endure the gut-wrenching and soul-searing pain of possibly losing him, too.

CHAPTER 9

L indsey awoke the following morning to a sunny and clear day,
but at breakfast everyone agreed no climbing. With all the fresh
snow the risk of avalanche was too high. Lindsey and Brynn took
advantage, as did many of the men, to wash out clothing, laying items
on rocks and tents to dry.

Chairs were moved outside the mess tent to enjoy the outdoors,
and members of the other teams could be seen milling about. Lindsey
donned sunglasses and left her hair down, tucking it behind her ears.
A light blue fleece pullover proved to be enough warmth. Ditch
hooked up speakers to his iPod and Taylor Swift filled the air.

Lindsey sat beside Brynn in the two most comfortable canvas
chairs.

"What is that noise?" Packer asked, joining them. "Who put that
saccharine music on?"

"I happen to like Taylor Swift," Ditch replied, unpacking a blue
plastic barrel filled with rope.

"Ugh, shoot me now. Does anybody have anything useful to a
mountain climber's psyche? The Eagles, the Stones. For God's sake,
I'll even listen to Fleetwood Mac." Packer released a loud sigh.
"Ladies, calm yourselves. I plan to work on my tan."

Lindsey cracked an eye open in time to see Packer remove his shirt. He was short but fit. As he wrestled with a chair to keep it from wobbling on the rocky ground, she smiled, leaned back and closed her eyes again. She'd rather see Ty's naked chest.

"I've got something Packer might like," the man on her mind said from behind.

She resisted the urge to peek at Galloway and confirm the current state of his clothing. Some of the males in the other camps were already parading around shirtless, revealing the lean and muscular builds common with climbers. She hoped Fiske wouldn't feel compelled to showcase his physique in front of her, and quickly pushed away that dark cloud of thought. It was too beautiful a day to waste on the likes of him.

Ditch's music stopped and Boston's "More Than A Feeling" started up.

"That's more like it," Packer said. "I can't be my manly self without proper tunes."

Brynn chuckled.

"You ladies can put on your bikinis any time you'd like," he added.

Lindsey turned to him and said, "If you don't use sunscreen, you're going to regret it."

"Sunscreen is for pussies."

Lindsey went back to enjoying the sun warming her face. "If you say so."

The sound of bags unzipping and the clinking of metal on metal signaled Ty's intention of reorganizing gear. She stood to help.

"Ah," Packer uttered. "She's leaving to get ready for the swimsuit portion of the competition."

"Bikinis are too heavy," Lindsey answered. "I couldn't afford the weight in my pack."

"Then just go naked, ladies." Packer fluffed his thinning hair. "You won't hear me complain."

Ty grinned at her. "I think I'd be scarred for life if my sister paraded around like that."

"I heard that," Brynn said.

Lindsey held her disappointment at bay that Ty's broad shoulders were covered with a worn, navy blue t-shirt sporting "Iceland" on the front. The Galloway Films baseball cap he often wore shadowed his face and the beginnings of a beard.

Despite all the testosterone in camp, and the sometimes-annoying he-man mentality that went along with it, Lindsey liked men, especially fit and athletic ones. She especially liked Galloway's brand of male.

"Need help?" she asked him.

"Sure. Ditch is pulling the remaining rope we have stashed, so I wanted to take an inventory."

She began sorting through the stacks of coiled rope that Ditch had piled onto the ground.

David was conspicuously absent. Again. If it were any other guy, she would guess he was having a love affair with Elena, but Shaw hadn't even chased Brynn.

"David seems really chummy with the Polish team," she remarked.

"Yeah," Ty said, sorting through piles of carabiners. "I think he's picking their brains about their route." They were on the south-southeast line, otherwise called the Cesen Route; the other teams, including theirs, were on the Abruzzi Spur.

"Do you think it's easier?"

"No," Ty replied. "Nothing on this mountain is gonna be easy."

"Ditch, when you were here before, how was it?" she asked.

He had emptied the barrel and now rested a hand on the rim as he caught his breath. "The weather is temperamental, the campsites are few and crowded, and as you've seen with Aldo, falling rock is a constant battle. The most technical climbing won't be until we reach the top, when we'll be at our worst physically."

"Just say it Ditch," Packer said from where he sunned himself. "K2 is a mofo."

Ditch grimaced. "I prefer a relentless foe."

"Yep, hoe, she's that, too."

Ditch half rolled his eyes along with a dismissive smile. "And don't forget about the wind. You know what happened to Hargreaves."

Lindsey knew. Alison Hargreaves, a British mountaineer, had been blown off the top after summiting when freakishly high winds had suddenly hit. That was in 1995.

"Why did you come back?" she asked.

"Ty's an amazing climber and a careful mountaineer, but I wanted to make sure he did it right on this one."

"I love you too, Ditch," Ty said, his tone mocking but filled with warmth.

Lindsey grabbed another coil of rope. "He's lucky to have you."

"Thanks," they both replied.

"The mountain never stops pushing," Ditch added, dragging the empty barrel over to the mess tent where it would sit until the trek out.

Lindsey pointed at a pile of baggies filled with something yellow and squishy. "What's that?"

Ty stood and moved beside her. "Bags of butter."

She scrunched her face and glanced up at him, startled by his gaze. The blue of his shirt made his eyes more indigo than green on this bright morning.

"I got the idea from a friend who went to the South Pole. I figured you'd appreciate it, seeing how you love margarine and all." His eyes danced with amusement.

"Not a bad idea," Ditch said. "It's a fast way for each of us to ingest a large number of calories."

Ty added in a low voice just for her, "I'll make sure you get extra." Then he moved away and returned to squatting over piles of gear.

She remained where she was, trying to keep her demeanor nonchalant as a jolt of nervous energy coursed through her.

"You can't expect a woman to eat bags of butter," Brynn said, her voice edged with mock outrage.

"Oh hell, you girls eat more junk then you let on," Packer said. "Don't be afraid to have some curves."

Still trying to collect her thoughts, Lindsey glanced up at K2, the mountain looking quiet and serene with its fresh dusting of pearly white snow.

A loud snap cracked in the air, followed by a rumbling sound.

"Avalanche!" The yell came from somewhere in Base Camp.

Everyone took off running, not out of fear but rather curiosity. About thirty feet from camp they all stopped, Ty beside her. He must have been behind her the entire time. Snow slid down a couloir, building in momentum, and finally stopped in a puff of fluffy clouds at the base of the mountain. Everyone stared, spellbound, some using binoculars. Then, a strong gust hit them, the aftermath of nature's spectacle.

"A caress from the Savage Mountain," Packer murmured.

If the wind didn't kill you, or the intense cold, or the lack of oxygen, then there was always an avalanche.

IN THE LATE AFTERNOON LINDSEY STRIPPED DOWN TO A LONG-SLEEVED shirt and picked her way among the rocks and icy patches a short distance from Base Camp, making certain to avoid areas known for crevices.

It felt good to get a little alone time to recharge the batteries.

Base Camp was located at 17,000 feet, already higher than the highest peaks in the Rocky Mountains, and the terrain was barren and desolate. The air was so thin that nothing grew, and despite that life was all but choked out, something in the stark beauty called to her.

She sat on a large boulder, but she wouldn't last long before her rear end got too cold. She wondered what Alison's day had looked like before her death. Had it been like this one? Had she and David gotten along? Had they made love? Had she been happy? Or just tired. Had she tried too hard to make the summit when she should have turned back sooner?

Lindsey rested her chin on bent knees. A big, black bird landed in a flutter nearby.

Charon.

He cawed loudly and watched her. The feathers on his sleek body, dark as night, shimmered despite the late-day shadows.

He was magnificent.

A blissful smile reached her lips. Charon was a testament that life went on, that even in the harshest environments creatures found a way to live, to thrive even.

She wondered if he'd found anything to eat, if he'd ever dined on a dead body. Did he hang around to befriend her, or to size her up as a possible meal? She suspected she wasn't very meaty.

Where did he sleep? With whom did he mate? Maybe Charon was a female.

Her backside finally became too cold, so she stood and walked a bit before returning to camp. She stopped at her tent to grab a water bottle and a light jacket, and then made her way to the mess tent for dinner. Fiske approached with Beck and Artie.

She sighed. It would be another long evening, and she'd best accept that she would need to eat quickly and escape to her tent.

She waved to them then ducked inside. The enticing aroma that had been lingering around camp now hit her full force—Habibe was vigorously stirring a pan filled with sizzling onions and vegetables. If her nose was correct, there was plenty of garlic, too.

Ty and David both sat at the table, amazingly still wearing t-shirts despite that the setting sun had brought a sharp chill to the air.

"How was your walk?" Ty asked.

"Good, thanks," she replied. "We're about to have company."

Ty indicated the empty chair beside him and with gratitude she took it. A few seconds later Fiske and the two Americans appeared.

"We come not bearing gifts," Beck said.

"Typical." Ty sank back in his chair. "I suppose you want beer while you're here."

Beck sat on a stool while the others also gathered at the table. "Of course."

Ditch stood and dispersed cans to everyone. Lindsey cracked hers open and took a long drink.

"Can we head up tomorrow?" she asked, weary of all this sitting around.

Ty nodded. "Yep. It's a go. All the teams are gonna push to Camp Two."

"We'll stop at One and start setting up," Beck said. "Then we'll start sleeping around."

"You're a slut, Beck," David said, stretching and rolling his shoulders.

"I can't help it. Galloway, where's your sister?"

"Bug off, Beck."

But Lindsey didn't sense any heat in Ty's response. From what she had witnessed so far, Dan Beck and Ty were good friends.

"Lindsey," Artie asked, "how do you put up with these yoyos?"

"I take the lead," she answered. "Then I don't have to listen to them."

They all let out a holler.

Everyone moved to a second beer.

Fiske looked at her. "Lindsey, you do not have to put up tents at the higher camps. You can bunk in mine."

"Bullshit." Ty dragged the word out under cover of a cough.

"That's all right," she answered. "I've already promised Ditch I'd sleep with him."

With raised eyebrows, everyone turned to stare at the older man, still standing near Habibe. "What can I say?" He shrugged. "I'm a catch in these parts."

Artie grinned, his red hair pushed back from his face. "Lucky Ditch."

❧

LINDSEY SAT IN HER TENT WITH BRYNN. AFTER DINNER, THEY BOTH HAD decided to leave the boys to their fun, since Beck, Artie, and Fiske had seemed inclined to stay for a while.

Brynn grabbed her camera to show Lindsey the photos she'd taken over the past few weeks, including the trek in with David and Ty.

"It's too bad you can't climb up the mountain with us," Lindsey said. "You could get some great shots."

"Ty's a good photographer, better than me. I'm sure he'll be documenting it."

"You going to be all right while we're gone?" Lindsey asked, referring to their departure in the morning. "If it goes well, we probably won't be Back to base for five or six days."

"Well, I have to admit that while hanging out at K2 Base Camp is a dream come true that not many people get to experience, it's incredibly boring too. But Juneid is here, and Habibe. Now that he's feeling a little better, Aldo invited me to play cards with him."

"He seems like a decent guy," Lindsey replied. "Unlike Fiske. He's starting to creep me out."

"I agree. Have you ever been worried about being attacked or forced while you're on an expedition like this?"

"A little. It would be stupid to think it couldn't happen. This place is more isolated than Everest, and there's far fewer climbers that come to the Karakoram. You trekked in, so you know how hard it is to even get here. I do have an ice axe, though."

Brynn gave a nervous laugh. "That could be messy."

"Does Beck bother you?"

Brynn shook her head. "Gosh, no. He's a good friend of Ty's. If we were gonna hook up, it would've already happened."

"The guys on our team are solid." As soon as Lindsey said it, she knew it to be true. Even David. "They wouldn't tolerate excessive harassment. And Fiske is going with us, so you won't be stuck with him."

"That's not so lucky for you, though. I've got some pepper spray."

"Really?"

"A Christmas present from Ty."

Lindsey laughed.

"Kind of a joke," Brynn said, then sobered. "Kind of not. Want to borrow it?"

Lindsey shook her head. "I'll be fine. And if some asshat down here tries something, then radio us. We'll come right down."

People sometimes behaved in strange ways when cut off from civilization and living at high altitude. Violence was rare but it did happen.

Brynn nodded. "Will you keep an eye on Tyler?"

"From the unwanted attention of other males?" Lindsey handed the camera back to her, and Brynn flipped the power button to off.

"Yes, of course. But it's more that I worry about him being up there." She indicated the mountain with a tilt of her head. "I worry about all of you."

"I know," Lindsey answered quietly. To break the somber mood and appease her own curiosity, she asked, "So how many girlfriends are pining away for Ty at the moment?"

"Hmm. I think zero. The last girl I met was named Megan, or maybe it was Mary. I can't remember now. She was nice. She worked at a magazine he was dealing with. But he's away so much, it's hard to keep up with relationships."

"I'm sure it is."

"Are you involved with anyone? Besides Anders Fiske." The last was said with a tone of sarcasm.

Lindsey groaned. "No, and I hope he gets diarrhea. Then he'd be stuck in his tent for a while."

Brynn laughed, then said, "I can remember Tyler talking about you several times in the past few years, about you and Alison and your climbs. I asked him once who he'd like to profile that he hadn't yet. He named you."

"Really? Why didn't he ever contact me?"

Brynn shrugged. "I don't know. But when he told me about this trip, he said it would be better for me because you were going. That way I wouldn't have to be the only woman in the group. He said he thought you and I would get along really well."

"I think he was right."

"He seemed really honored that you wanted to climb with him."

Lindsey didn't know what to say. There were many good climbers, many great ones. She never considered that she stood at the top of any heap.

"God, you're making me sound so impressive. I'd better tell my friends how great I am." Lindsey covered her face with her hands for a moment, indulging her embarrassment, then pushed her hair back from her face. "I'm just grateful that Ty brought me along."

"I hope after this is over that we can stay in touch."

"Yes, definitely."

"But if you and Ty have a steamy romance, I'll pass on hearing the details. He is my brother, after all."

Lindsey responded with a smile.

Getting involved with Ty wasn't on her to-do list, and yet she couldn't help but feel that she was headed toward it.

CHAPTER 10

Ty didn't wake Brynn before the team headed out at 4 a.m., not seeing any reason to disturb her. David was in the lead, followed by Ditch, then Packer, then Lindsey. Ty took up the rear as they set out through the ice fall to Advanced Camp.

Beck and his team were also assembling and were likely not far behind. Lindsey had conferred with the Germans and relayed that Frieder, Karl, and Volker were setting out today as well, intending to push for a summit bid the day after tomorrow, but Wolfgang Schroeder was staying in Base Camp, wracked with terrible bouts of coughing.

As if it wasn't crowded enough, the Italians were climbing, too.

After such a long stretch of blizzards and snow, all the teams were determined not to waste a potentially good weather window.

Bobbing headlamps became spread out along the path and vertically up the mountain.

Ty's pack was heavy with supplies, as was everyone else's. The next several days would consist of moving much of the gear banked at Camp One to Camps Two and Three.

The wind gusted as Ty settled into pushing through deep snow as first light broke the horizon. They rotated who was at the lead, since breaking trail was arduous work. By mid-morning the five of them arrived at Camp One. They stopped to eat and hydrate, then continued upward.

The mountain became steeper, and the recent snowfall was evident in a loaded couloir, the narrow gully filled to the brim with freshly fallen snow. Navigating a tricky traverse over mixed terrain, they came once again to House's Chimney and its forty-degree slope.

"You still have shotgun privileges," Ty reminded Lindsey, but she shook her head.

"I concede my spot. You go."

She had just finished leading the last section and was no doubt tired.

Ty had to dig out the fixed rope laid by the Germans. "It seems a bit thin," he said.

"I agree." Ditch retrieved rope from his pack. "We'll lay a new line. You up for the job?"

"Yep."

The route was a fissure filled with hard ice and a thick coating of new snow. With Ditch belaying him, it took time to set new anchors, but soon everyone followed, keeping their heads down as loose rocks and small chunks of ice periodically banged off their helmets.

By late afternoon, sweating under the bright sun, Ty crested a slope and came upon Camp Two, sitting at 22,166 feet, two new yellow tents in residence—likely belonging to the Germans—along with a grave-yard of wrecked ones.

Lindsey came to stand beside him, huffing to catch her breath, and they took in the scene, alongside Ditch and Packer.

The aura of death in the air was palpable, clinging to the crevices and rock faces, to foot-deep snow and swirling ice crystals. Only David seemed immune, busying himself with scoping out a spot for two tents.

"It looks like a goddamned morgue," Packer muttered.

Ditch removed his pack. "It just appears that way. The wind and the snow are hell on gear here. Much of it gets left behind."

Using small shovels, everyone helped clear two ledges. As soon as the tents were up, they crawled inside—Lindsey opting to bunk with Ty and David while Ditch and Packer took the other tent.

As Ty scooted to the side, Lindsey and David bumped into each other.

"I was thinking that we could have a ladies' tent and a men's one," Lindsey said.

"I'm not bunking with Packer," David said, retrieving a Bunsen burner from his pack. "And you're not playing the chick card here. You're gonna have to suffer with the rest of us."

They all sat upright, and David put his stove in the small vestibule off to the side. Lindsey also pulled out a stove and hung it from the ceiling.

The higher they went, the longer it would take to melt and heat water.

In anticipation of dinner, Ty dug into his pack. "I have noodle soup," he said, holding a food packet, then produced a second one. "Or, I have noodle soup."

"I'll have noodle," Lindsey answered.

Ty grabbed his stove to contribute to the water supply.

David pulled a map covered with handwritten scribbles from a pocket inside his down suit.

Lindsey peeked around his shoulder. "Alison never told me what a note-taker you are."

"I just like to keep things straight."

"We should head back to Camp One to sleep," Lindsey said, as if sensing that David wanted to rally on.

"Too crowded here?" Ty asked.

"I do have my own place there," she remarked. "Just trying to take care of myself. Rest is important."

Ty stirred the slush of ice melting in his pan with his finger. "A deep sleep is nigh impossible at this altitude."

"That's why we should forge ahead as quickly as we can," David said. "Before our bodies start breaking down. The longer we stay, the weaker we become."

"When I first started high-altitude climbing," Lindsey said, "I didn't take very good care of myself. I'd lose too much weight, my hair would start falling out, and I often stopped having a menstrual cycle."

David refolded his map. "That's too much information, Coulson."

"So," she continued, as if David hadn't spoken, "I now work with a nutritionist to organize a regiment of supplements. Did you know that drinking nothing but glacier water was a big culprit? It's devoid of natural minerals."

"That might explain Packer's early baldness," David said dryly. "But you're right. We need to stay as healthy as possible for as long as possible to make the summit a probability." Then he added, "Tomorrow we should push to Camp Three."

Ty nodded. "Let's hope the weather agrees."

David prepared the first batch of noodle soup and handed it to Lindsey.

"Thanks." She took the pot with gloved hands since it was hot. Not bothering with a spoon, she gingerly sipped the hot liquid then started sucking the noodles down. Then she offered up the pan of melted snow from her stove for the next round of soup.

"Are you and Stan Ingerman friends?" Lindsey asked David.

"Not really."

"But he was at Camp Four with you and Alison and Freddy Myerson the night before she disappeared."

"He was," David answered. "But at some point, he left. We were all getting sick. He was the worst of us. I didn't see him again after that, at least until he showed up in our mess tent last week."

She looked at Ty. "Do you know him?"

"A little," he replied. "I've never climbed with him, though." He made a third batch of soup.

Lindsey leaned out the doorway and scooped more snow into her now empty pan, then placed it atop her hanging burner.

"How's Myerson?" she asked.

"Good, I guess," David answered.

Ty sensed the tension coming off Lindsey. David and Freddy Myerson had lost three members of their team the day Alison had died—Alison, Cameron Gant, and George Davis. The men had been young and fairly inexperienced. The entire tragedy had been heartbreaking.

From what Ty had read and heard from others, David's whole team had been at Camp Four, but he and Myerson hadn't been feeling well, so Alison had left for the summit around 2 a.m. with Gant and Davis. Later that day, bad weather descended. Initially, they'd had radio contact with Alison. She had told them she and the two younger men were abandoning the summit and coming down, but later all communication was lost. David and Freddy, despite suffering from altitude sickness, had left to search for them, but the weather forced them back to Camp Four.

They had assumed that Alison and the two men were stranded, and they had hoped they would survive a bivouac above the Bottleneck during the night. The following day, David and Freddy tried to go up again but didn't get far with heavy snow and high winds hampering their progress. At that point, they learned an avalanche near Camp Three had killed two Russian climbers. During this time, David had tried desperately to raise Alison on the radio, but there had been no response.

With David's condition deteriorating, Freddy forced him to descend, knowing if he didn't that Shaw likely would die. It already had been three days since they had lost contact with Alison; there was little hope that she, Gant, or Davis were still alive.

"Will he ever come back to K2?" Lindsey asked.

David shrugged again, still refusing to look at her. "How should I know."

Lindsey tended to her pot of melting snow.

A charged silence followed. Time to step around the wound that clearly still existed for the two of them. "We'd best head down," Ty said.

They started unloading the contents of their packs to leave inside the tent, then they refilled their water bottles with the latest batch of melted liquid. Ty added lemonade mix to his, since he was getting tired of the blandness of nothing but water.

"Ditch," Ty yelled. "You and Packer ready?"

"Hold on," came Ditch's muffled response. "I have to wake up Packer."

In a short time, all five began the descent to Camp One, which thankfully went faster than the upward climb.

∾

THAT NIGHT LINDSEY SETTLED INTO HER OWN TENT AT CAMP ONE, SINCE they had three in position at this elevation. Several of the Italian team also stayed, but the Americans descended to ABC. Everyone was tired, and after eating and melting water they all crashed.

The next morning dawned windy and overcast, and by the time Lindsey was up and moving a light snow had begun to fall.

Ty was out of his tent and looked to be assessing the conditions, but they couldn't really see past the ledge where everyone currently resided.

"What do you say?" he asked her.

"I say we go."

He gave a nod. "I was thinking the same. I radioed Brynn. The weather should clear in a few hours."

Packer crawled out of his tent and stretched his arms above his head, the wrinkles on his red climbing suit noticeable. "I love the smell of napalm in the morning."

"We're not at war," Ty said.

"You sure about that? It's always a battle to the top." Packer shifted his gaze to Lindsey. "Good morning, gorgeous. When's breakfast?"

Lindsey laughed and crawled back into her tent to load her pack with supplies, Packer's voice drifting to her, "I'll have strawberry crepes with a tall glass of freshly squeezed orange juice...."

She loaded an oxygen bottle, an extra tent, a sleeping bag, packets of soup, hot chocolate, and Pop-Tarts, and they all set out.

Three hours later they came to Camp Two, rested briefly, and switched out more supplies. Ty got on the radio with the Germans, then relayed what he'd learned.

"Frieder says we can use their fixed rope up to Three, but I don't know. If it's like what was at House's Chimney, then we may have to lay down something new. Make sure we have enough line with us."

Everyone agreed. As they left Camp Two, they came immediately upon the obstacle known as the Black Pyramid, a thousand-foot section of vertical rock and ice, and one of the most technically challenging areas of K2 after the Bottleneck.

Snow continued to whip around them, and Lindsey fought to brace herself against the wind, the heavy pack throwing off her balance. She adjusted her balaclava to cover any cracks on her face where the arctic air could infiltrate and double-checked that her goggles were snug on her nose. She cinched her hood tight over her helmet to protect her neck from the biting cold. A check of her watch revealed the temperature: minus ten degrees Fahrenheit.

A spiderweb of old ropes greeted them, dangling and flapping in the wind. She waited while Ty searched for the fixed line the Germans had laid. Choosing wrong could lead to a fatal fall, since many of the ropes were old and likely no longer properly anchored. If Ty couldn't find the German's handiwork, or if he deemed the line too thin, then they would use the ice screws and pitons with them to lay a new rope. She hoped that wouldn't be the case, since it would be time-consuming, not to mention energy-draining.

But Ty was the leader. It would be his call.

He signaled that he'd found the German's rope. "It should work," he said, as they gathered around.

"You still owe me a shotgun," she said. "I'm calling it in."

"It's still a risk," Ty responded. "I'll go first. David will belay me in case the fixed rope isn't stable."

"I'm lighter," she said. "You should let me go."

"Actually, I'm pretty sure I weigh less than you, Coulson," Packer cut in. "I just didn't want to say anything and have you get all depressed about being fat."

"Are you volunteering to go first, then?" Ditch asked him.

"Nah. I'm better as a middleman."

"Well?" Lindsey said, looking at Ty.

He paused, then gave a nod. "But leave your pack here."

"Why?" she asked. "Is one of you going to carry two packs up?"

"She's right," Ditch said.

"I can do it," she added.

Ty appeared to regroup quickly. "Right. I'll belay you, but I want to set another anchor first."

While he and David started discussing options for ice screw placement, Packer gave a nudge to Lindsey. "You got O2 in that pack of yours?"

"Of course."

"Why don't you hand it over?"

Lindsey raised her voice, so they could all hear her. "While I appreciate all of you looking out for me, I'm not playing the chick card, so leave it alone."

"Right on," Packer said. "You are woman. Hear you roar."

He raised a hand to high-five her, and for a split-second she thought to ignore him. But his earnest gesture broke her stoic resolve, and her bristly backbone relaxed of its own accord.

She hit Packer with a gloved fist pump.

"Hand me your camera, Galloway," Packer continued. "I'm gonna get this on film."

Galloway shrugged out of his pack, retrieved a small but complicated-looking camera, and handed it to Packer, then went to work setting up a belay station.

Surprised, Lindsey asked Ty, "Aren't you going to show him how to use it?"

"He knows," he replied, uncoiling rope while David inched up the face of the ice wall about five feet using an ice axe and his crampons.

"Packer's actually won photo awards," Ditch commented.

Lindsey swung her gaze to the shorter climber. He shrugged and said, "What can I say. I do have a marketable skill or two."

David pulled an ice screw from his harness belt and with the built-in lever he rotated it into a slab of ice, then added a second one about two feet beside it. He attached a sling then ran the end of the fixed rope through the carabiner at the end. He also ran a second redundant belay from a spare ice axe.

Lindsey sighed. "You two are a couple of Hardy Boys," she said to Ty.

"Don't mock the process," he teased. "We'll catch you if you fall." He pulled off his mittens and started tying the rope into the front of her harness, giving a general tug to the apparatus and bringing her body closer to him. He was checking to make sure it was secure. Climbers had fallen to their death when a buckle was loose or not closed correctly. She grinned but he couldn't see it, so she returned the gesture with a tug on his harness, her gloved hand fumbling and making the gesture awkward.

Through his goggles, his eyes crinkled then he turned away.

At least the heatwave of embarrassment briefly warmed her feet, which had been steadily going numb for the last several hours.

She was like a Tyler Galloway groupie, because surely there was a collection of women who waited for the lanky mountain climber with the soul of a poet to return from his far-flung adventures, despite Brynn's pronouncement that he didn't have a girlfriend.

Once Ty had her secured, she took hold of the ice axes hanging from each of her wrists and gave a nod. He stepped back and got himself hooked up for the belay.

She moved to the start of the Black Pyramid and glanced upward. Mixed rock and ice on a steep, vertical incline greeted her. This would take a while.

"On belay," she said.

"Belay on," Ty replied. "Climbing."

She planted an ice axe. "Climb up."

It was slow-going and by late afternoon they were only halfway to Camp Three. Everyone agreed to return to Two to sleep. Luckily, they were able to rappel down quickly what they'd spent hours climbing.

Lindsey regretted that her pack had been so heavy. She should have left some of it in Camp Two. Now she'd be carrying it again tomorrow when they attempted to push back up to Three. The Black Pyramid had been more challenging than she had anticipated.

When they arrived at Camp Two, Ty pulled a bivy tent from his pack.

"This was supposed to be for Three, but you can set up house here," he said to her.

The gesture buoyed her flagging energy, and they managed to squeeze it in near the two tents that had been erected already for the team. It was starting to get crowded on the mountain.

"You can have dinner with us if you like," he added, nodding toward the tent he and David would share.

"Great," she replied. "I'll bring dessert."

"If you come early, I'll give you first pick of our freeze-dried options."

That night the three of them dined on lasagna and chicken fettuccini followed by a shared chocolate bar courtesy of Lindsey. They swapped climbing stories about places like Cerro Torre, the Eiger, and Half Dome.

When Lindsey wrapped herself into her sleeping bag inside the coffin-like bivy sac, she decided to take a melatonin pill, and it soon helped her to fall asleep. When she awoke it was a surprise that she had managed to slumber for several hours without waking, and she felt somewhat rested.

The Black Pyramid dominated the following day. While Ty and David relaxed their diligence on belaying—trusting the fixed ropes that the Germans had set—they still roped together in certain sections. Lindsey felt popular, because by the time they had reached the top of the Pyramid, she'd been roped to each of the men in turn. Or perhaps, in case she fell, they wanted to be able to brag that they'd saved her.

Try as she might to attach the machismo mentality to her teammates, however, it was becoming clear why Ty had invited them into his circle. Even David. He was strong, agile, with a discerning eye for the terrain. Ditch was solid with an extra sense for the weather. Packer was fast, and as long as he had energy, he generally led most pitches.

Galloway didn't push himself into the limelight, instead remaining content to let the team work as a unit.

During the long day, Lindsey ruminated over this, and she found herself warming to the group dynamic, feeling somewhat humbled. She'd secretly harbored the idea that as they neared the summit, she would push past any of them if need be and grab the peak on her own terms. She didn't want to come this far and be denied a chance to top out, not if she were feeling strong.

Despite the slow, upward movement and the unrelenting weather, Lindsey had taken great joy in the day's accomplishments; although, she suspected they were all pushing hard to keep the Italians from passing them.

During the ascent, rock fall had periodically rained down, and the trickle of stones ricocheting below reminded her that she was vertical, that gravity was very much in abundance around her. Alongside this stark reality, however, was an almost mystical window into another world in which time and space had fallen away. She wasn't in Pakistan, in the Karakoram Mountains; she was inside her mind, a place filled with purpose and strength as she merged with the mountain, inch by inch.

When she finally alighted onto a wide ledge in the late afternoon, the clouds had cleared, and blue sky revealed itself. They were just above the Black Pyramid at 24,000 feet, the location of Camp Three. Two yellow tents stood a lonely vigil, surrounded by a thick pile of snow, an ominous reminder that this camp was prone to avalanche and was frequently wiped out.

Lindsey glanced around, her lips and nostrils freezing as each breath she took lacked the precious oxygen to which her body was accustomed. She took a moment to calm herself, so as not to succumb to the panic that would have her gasping for air as if she were drowning. She could use O2, but like an alcoholic taking just one drink, it would never be enough. Cycling on and off oxygen would actually wreak more havoc on her system than simply staying off it.

Wispy clouds raced past the mountain above, revealing a K2 of simple grace and beauty. But if Alison had managed to survive in this place, it wouldn't have been for long. Was her sister perfectly preserved in an icy tomb somewhere?

What if I find her?

Three men in colorful down suits emerged from the tents, as a dizzying wave of nausea accosted her.

Frieder Berg opened his arms wide. "You have made it. It is good to see you all." He shook Ty's hand then David's after they each unshouldered their packs. "And you have brought clear weather."

"It was the least we could do," Ty replied.

Volker and Karl approached, both bearded and looking haggard.

"You should make camp near us," Karl said.

Ty agreed.

"Have you been up higher?" Lindsey asked, setting her own pack onto the ground, her discomfort thankfully having passed.

"Not yet," Frieder answered. "We will try for Camp Four tomorrow, then summit the following day."

"There's been a lot of snow."

"Yes," he said, nodding. "But we will see how it is higher up. Maybe the summit will happen."

"I hope so," she replied.

Packer hiked into camp, Ditch behind him, and released his pack. "I'm beat. You boys got any lagers?"

Frieder laughed. *"Nein, wir haben es im Basislager gelassen."*

Packer shook his head. "I'm guessing that's a no. Looks like it's tea and soup again."

Pulling a shovel from her gear, Lindsey said, "He says it's in Base Camp."

"Oh yeah?" A gleam flashed in Packer's eyes, despite his weary expression. "You think they've got any schnitzels, too?"

Since much of what Packer said was rhetorical, Lindsey didn't bother to answer and instead went to work with the others in digging out an area for two tents and another bivy sac for herself. Soon the Italians arrived—five of them, including Elena—and they got to work on their own tent assemblage. Everyone was too busy and tired to engage in much conversation.

Because it was late in the day, the teams agreed they would sleep at Camp Three.

Lindsey joined Ty and David in their tent once again for about an hour to eat and melt snow before retiring to her private accommodations.

"Do you have a knife?" Ty asked as she prepared to leave after a dinner of ramen noodles and miniature chocolate chip cookies.

She nodded.

"Wear it around your neck."

"Yes, sir."

Avalanches were so common here that climbers needed any advantage they could get. If she became buried in snow, she could use the knife to fight her way free from the nylon of the tent as well as the snow.

She suspected she wouldn't sleep well tonight.

CHAPTER 11

"Let's take Mom somewhere for Christmas," Alison said as she moved upward, jamming her fingers into a narrow crack and smearing chalk as she went. Lindsey belayed her from below, positioned on a tiny ledge as her gaze rested on the rich red colors of the sandstone inches from her nose.

They had been practicing all week on different parts of Moonlight Buttress, arguably one of the best sandstone big walls in the world, located in Zion National Park. Today they were finally tackling their big goal—free the route from base to summit.

"Where?" Lindsey asked, releasing a bit of rope as Alison climbed higher, fatigue pressing on her from a bad night's sleep as anxiety had held her hostage.

"How about Hawai'i?"

"I think it reminds her too much of Dad. If you're thinking beach, then let's just go to Mexico."

The nuts, cams, and carabiners on Alison's harness rack jangled from her hips as she shifted. Lindsey didn't like that setup and instead preferred a gear sling, running from one shoulder to under the opposite arm, a preference that put her in the minority of climbers, and Alison loved to hound her about it.

On a climb that required a full rack, Lindsey didn't like the weight of all that gear around her waist. Alison liked to point out that the top-heavy distribution of the gear sling was a full-on nuisance as it shifted while climbing, getting stuck on the harness and chalk bag.

Shush, you two, their mom would say. *You each should do what you like.*

They did, but that never stopped Alison from expressing her displeasure over Lindsey's setup.

Alison made good time on a steep 12+ lieback corner, emptying her rack as she went. As Lindsey prepared to follow, she imagined herself as a spider, her limbs strong, her muscles honed into lithe, contoured lines. Moonlight was all finger crack climbing, and upon arriving Lindsey had loved the security of it over the face-climbing of Yosemite. But today's endeavor had filled her with a flurry of self-doubt. Halfway up the pitch, she stopped to grab a breath. *Okay,* she conceded, *it's scary as shit.*

"Don't be a wuss, Linc," Alison's voice echoed down to her, using her nickname for Lindsey, a combination of Lindsey and Coulson. "I'll give you the jacket."

"That's an empty promise," Lindsey muttered. In high school, their mom had given Alison a faded bomber jacket that belonged to their dad, with patches sewn on from his various climbs. Lindsey coveted it more than she cared to admit. The one and only time she'd borrowed it, Alison had found out and now kept it hidden, periodically dangling it to motivate—and torment—her little sister.

"I could leave you up here, you know," Lindsey added.

"You can do this in any old climbing gym. Quit psyching yourself out."

"Shut up, you hag."

"I heard that."

Lindsey glanced at her weather-worn hands, her fingers wrapped in slightly filthy and fraying tape, and steeled herself. Jamming her nerves down, she sent the pitch and came level with Alison. "How do you do it, Al?" she asked, no longer caring if her pride was showing chinks.

"What?"

"Control your fear."

"I don't give it any space to live in my head. Period."

"It's not that easy."

"Of course it is. We have Robbie Coulson's genes."

Lindsey awoke with a start, the sound of Alison's voice still ringing in her ears. The tent compressed and shuddered as the wind howled.

The dream had felt so real, and Lindsey squeezed her eyes shut from the emotion clawing up her chest to her throat, ready to choke her.

Truth be told, that climb had terrified her, and until that moment she hadn't truly appreciated Alison's cold-hearted approach to climbing. She'd simply assumed that her sister had learned to navigate the dragon that both lured and breathed fire from within, always threatening to annihilate if not handled with care. But that climb had showed Lindsey that Alison was somehow immune, that her determination and drive lived on a different plane, a place Lindsey had always instinctively stayed away from. It just didn't seem like the right way to climb.

Before her death, Alison had been determined to climb full-time, to use her exploits and mini-celebrity to support herself with sponsorship and endorsement deals. The two of them already had a small income from promotional interests, but it was hardly enough to abandon a real job. Alison had studied to be a nurse, but found the structure too inhibiting for all the climbing she had desired to accomplish.

Lindsey had understood her sister's frustration. Pursuing her own studies and a research position at the university had forced her to juggle commitments. She generally climbed in the summers and on holidays. When she trekked in the Himalaya, she'd had to take several spring semesters off, delaying the completion of first her bachelor's degree and then her master's by more than two years.

But to become a full-time climber bothered Lindsey on some level. Their father had been one, and while his name was spoken with great respect, Lindsey had lived the hardships firsthand of family life without him, without the semblance of a normal existence filled with regular hours, regular meals, and holidays and birthdays to be counted on.

It was an ambivalence that left Lindsey feeling both guilty when she climbed and claustrophobic from the monotony of daily life.

There was no answer, no easy reconciliation.

But always the wild regions called to Lindsey. Always the dragon whispered in her ear.

We have Robbie Coulson's genes.

Is that why neither she nor Alison could stay away from the mountains? In studying genetics, Lindsey knew that while genes played a part, it was the activation of them that truly brought out their full potential in an organism. If she had never set foot on an 8000-meter peak, would she have been content to live her life at the safety of sea level? Would Alison be alive today? Were Robbie's genes less a blessing and more of a curse?

Lindsey burrowed deeper into her sleeping bag to stay warm. As she drifted back to sleep, her thoughts turned to her dad's jacket. Since Alison's death, it had gone missing. A thorough—and heartbreaking—clearing out of her sister's apartment and its belongings had turned up nothing.

Around 4 a.m., she dragged herself up and in the cramped quarters of the bivy tent she made hot chocolate before venturing over to Ty and David's. As soon as she left the cocoon of her shelter, the terrible weather revealed itself. Whiteout conditions, high winds, snow piled high. Carefully, she trudged over to their tent.

"It doesn't look good," she said to Ty when he unzipped the doorway, still looking half-asleep. Did he have vivid dreams of dead people as she did?

"Okay. Maybe we should stay here for the time being. I'll radio Brynn for a weather report."

Lindsey nodded and returned to her tent, crawling back into her sleeping bag. No sense wasting a chance to rest. She half-hoped, half-dreaded that Alison would visit her again.

~

On the evening of the second day of being pinned at Camp Three from high winds and heavy snowfall, Ty decided that spending all his time with Shaw was ludicrous when there was a pretty girl the next tent over, so he carefully made his way through the blustery conditions to her doorstep.

Thoughts of being buried alive were never far from his mind. He and the others—the Germans and the Italians were stuck too—had already shoveled the white stuff several times to keep the weather from overwhelming the tents. And there was the ever-present fear of avalanche. No one had slept much.

Brynn had put a call in with the meteorologist they had hired out of England to keep them updated and the consensus was that the storm would break on July 22nd, at which time all the climbers would descend. All they had to do was be patient.

Ty came to Lindsey's bivy tent, glowing yellow from the lamp inside. "Hey, Linds, you home?"

She unzipped the entrance. "The Germans invited me over for tea, but they can wait. Quick, get in here."

He removed his crampons then crawled inside. She quickly shut the door.

"Lucky you, receiving invites," he said.

She brushed past him in insulated pants and a wool pullover as she crawled to the far end of the narrow shelter to give him room, which wasn't much.

"What can I say, I'm popular," she said, climbing back into her sleeping bag. "But now you've given me a chance to stay in. We can make popcorn and watch a movie."

He pulled off his fleece cap and scratched a hand through his hair that had become longer as the summer wore on. "I wish. My electronics are all dead."

"Mine too." She placed a folded fleece jacket beside her and patted it. "We can lie here and stare at the tent ceiling together. It'll be riveting, I promise."

He settled in beside her, shoulder to shoulder. "Anything new since I saw you last?"

"You mean you missed the group hike around the mountain earlier?"

"The one with all the Kodak moments?"

"You're never gonna make it in the magazine world if you keep missing the group shots. I did melt snow for two hours, and I have a nice canteen filled with hot chocolate. Want some?"

"Yeah, that sounds great."

She pulled the container from inside her sleeping bag and handed it to him.

Leaning on his elbow, he unscrewed the lid and took several gulps, then gave it back to her. "That hits the spot."

He reclined on his back once again, and they both stared at the thin nylon fabric above them, flexing and flattening from the wind.

"You and David getting on each other's nerves?" she asked.

"He is a bit moody."

"Aren't all climbers moody?"

"I suppose."

"Is he thinking about Alison?"

"Maybe. He's not very chatty about that." He glanced at her. "How are you doing?"

"I think about her a lot. I think about our early days of rock climbing. Isn't it always the case that you realize too late how great a time you had?"

"Yeah. I saw a picture of you once, in a climbing magazine. You were in Utah, surrounded by red rock, clad in gear, chalk on your hands and knees, and clearly happy after a good pitch. What I liked most was your smile. You looked content and satisfied and completely in your element. To me, it was a perfect shot, because it captured everything I like about climbing." *What I like about you.*

Lindsey turned to him, making him acutely aware of how gushing that response had been.

He shrugged, trying to feign nonchalance. "Not that I've thought much about that photo."

She shot him an amused look, then said, "I know the one you're talking about. Alison took it in Zion. That happy smile, though, came at the end of a stressful week on Moonlight Buttress." She returned her gaze to the ceiling, doing its best to protect them from the wrath of K2. "What else do you do besides climb?"

"There's my Meryl Streep addiction."

She scrunched her face and scoffed. "You're picking brains over beauty?"

"Meryl Streep is very beautiful. And you kind of remind me of her."

Neither of them made eye contact, so Ty kept going. "I'm a simple guy who lives in the Bay area near my folks. Since I'm frequently away from home, it makes it easier for them to watch my dog. Her name is Meryl, and she's a chocolate lab."

"You named your dog after Meryl Streep?"

"Well, if it's any consolation my mom calls her Muck because she likes to traipse through the mud and occasionally roll in deer poop."

"Sounds lovely."

"Maybe you can come meet her sometime."

"Your mom or Muck?"

"Both," he replied. "And my dad's a lone wolf like you."

She threw him a quizzical look. "Thanks, I think."

"Lindsey Coulson, Chemist," he said. "What's that like?"

"I have to contribute to the world in some way. Climbing is so self-centric."

"Are you one of those 'I-feel-guilty-climbing' climbers?"

"Kind of, I guess. Maybe it's because my mom was a single parent raising Alison and me. I decided that I would try to make something of myself." She pressed her lips together, then released a huff. "But it's hard to shake the climbing bug. It's like a burr under the skin, an irritation that only goes away when I'm in the mountains. No matter how I wish it were otherwise, I'm just like my dad—a climbing bum."

"Sometimes it's hard not to be one."

"True. There were a few summers that Alison and I lived out of our car, but my mom wanted us to have more. She pushed us both to go to college and helped us get scholarships. I recently started work on my Ph.D."

"At least you're starting with something small," he teased.

"It's not any different than climbing a mountain. It's one small step after another, and then finally you're there at the top, or at the end of a degree, or discovering how life started on Earth. Maybe RNA was zapped into being with the thunderbolt and lightning action, or maybe it began on Mars."

"Don't tell me that Packer's right. Are we all Martians then?"

"Maybe. Last year I worked on a project that tried to create RNA in the lab, but to do that there are two things needed: minerals containing borate and molybdate. But borate is found only in deserts after large seas have evaporated. Four billion years ago there were no such deserts on Earth. Molybdate needs oxygen to form, but early Earth doesn't seem to have had any."

"Is that why you like to hang out on mountaintops with no oxygen?"

"Just trying to put myself into Earth's shoes."

"Did these minerals exist on Mars?" he asked.

"Evidence is mounting that they might just have."

"Is it really so important to understand how we came to be here on Earth?"

"I think so," she replied. "If for no other reason than curiosity. I sometimes think that's why I climb—just plain curiosity about what's out there, what I can do, what's possible. I guess that's what I like about chemistry, and science in general. What's the point of being here if we don't try to learn more about ourselves, to push our understanding to a new level, whether it be personal or scientific?"

"The higher purpose climber."

"It'll be on my epitaph."

"And then there're those climbers that just want the record, just want to know they're the best, and are constantly in a state of needing to prove it."

"Or the ones who live at the edge because life has thrown too many curveballs. I've wondered sometimes if that isn't me." She rolled her head and looked at him. "What is it for you? Are you a tree-hugger or a masochist?"

He laughed. "I guess I'm one of your 'curious' specimens. I try to make a living off my outdoor exploits, but I don't generally choose the places, they choose me. I see where I'm drawn, what locale naturally pulls me in. I think it drives my mom crazy."

"Because she never knows where you'll be?"

"I suppose."

"Why did you want to come here?"

"K2 has a reputation for being a bitch of a mountain. I think I was always curious about that. And then things started to line up. Ditch wanted to go. I had a break in my schedule. Then you chased me down at that convention."

"I didn't chase you."

"You sure?" He arched an eyebrow in her direction. "I was flattered. You could be with the Germans right now."

Her lips stretched into a smile, distracting him. "Never. Frieder's a bit of a douche. I was gonna beg the Poles if you had said no."

"Then I'm forever grateful you begged me. Truth is I wanted to meet you."

"I think you're just cold and want to get in my sleeping bag."

He pushed back onto an elbow and debated whether he should kiss her. "It is cold over here without a pad." He referred to the fact that her sleeping bag was atop an insulated pad. Where Ty was lying, he was essentially in contact with the frigid ground beneath him. "But I should probably leave before it gets too late."

Lindsey caught his gaze for a moment, her brown eyes holding him captive. "It probably doesn't work this high."

"What?" But he had some idea to what she referred.

She laughed and shook her head, giving him a playful push. "You'd better leave before things get out of hand."

For a moment he indulged watching her, then reluctantly scooted toward the entrance and strapped on his crampons. As he exited the cozy tent and Lindsey's enticingly warm body, he looked back over his shoulder and said, "If you ever want to have sex at 24,100 feet, I'm your guy."

Still bundled in her sleeping bag, she released a bark of laughter and covered her face with both hands, clearly embarrassed.

He stepped into the swirling snow, bracing against the wind. He grabbed hold of the rope they had rigged between the tents so that no one would get lost trying to move between them. When he turned to secure the entrance, Lindsey waved at him, still grinning.

"See you in the morning," she said.

"You too."

As soon as he crawled back into his own sleeping bag, David's restless form beside him, Tyler had to wonder why he hadn't stayed with her. If he was reading her signals correctly, she was open to it.

But Lindsey was different.

He didn't want to screw things up.

He also wasn't entirely sure the one-eyed monster would work at this altitude.

And of one thing he was certain—he had no intention of disappointing her the first time they were together.

CHAPTER 12

L indsey awoke on the third morning feeling groggy. As she sat upright, the top of her head smashed into the low ceiling of the bivy tent, and she frowned. Where was she? Her pack lay near the entrance ... she'd been in surroundings like this many times before.

It was so cold, and her head was swimming, barely able to contain a thought.

She rubbed her forehead and struggled for a deep breath.

K2.

Now she remembered. She'd been at Camp Three for three days now. It was a long time to be at this altitude.

She stared at her stove. First things first. She needed to eat except she wasn't hungry.

That's normal.

She needed sustenance anyway. As if she were outside her body and watching someone else, her hands gathered snow into a pot and she lit the stove. She glanced at her watch. 5 a.m.

She watched the melting snow, then glanced at her watch again. 5:50 a.m.

Huh.

It hadn't seemed like that much time had passed.

She added a tea bag to the water and started eating a blueberry

Pop-Tart with methodical precision, breaking it into perfect bite-size pieces and popping them in her mouth. The sugar greatly improved her spirits, and she washed her breakfast down with the tea straight from the pan.

"Linds." Tyler's voice came to her, triggering a fluttering in her stomach as a memory arose of them chatting last night, of him all but offering her sex. Or was it her? Maybe she had imagined the whole thing.

"Come in," she said, quickly licking her fingers so she could pat her hair, making sure she didn't look like Animal from the Muppets.

He unzipped the entrance and crouched. "Good morning."

Blue sky framed Galloway's dark profile, making him appear remote and mysterious and entirely too attractive.

"Good morning." She all but gushed the greeting, swooning a little as if she were tipsy. What the hell was wrong with her? Her giddiness was way over the top. She never acted this way around guys.

"The storm is over?" she asked, dismayed that she couldn't seem to remove the grin from her face.

"Yes. Are you okay?"

"I'm dandy."

He hesitated before saying, "We're gonna head down, since the threat of avalanche is too high after so much snowfall. We'll establish Camp Four later."

"What about Frieder? Are they going for the summit?"

"No. From the tone of the German chatter coming from their tents, I'm thinking they're arguing about what to do, but it would be crazy to continue. Let me know when you're ready."

She nodded. He closed her tent and left her alone again. She gave a shake of her head, attempting to reboot her brain. *It has to be the altitude.*

Happy to finally have a task—descending to Base Camp—she set to work. Leaving the bags of butter that Ty had her haul up for future meals, she suited up, donning boots, helmet, crampons, and then her backpack, which was mostly empty. She must still have been in slow motion, because by the time she was ready to leave,

Ditch and Packer had already departed, as had the Germans and most of the Italians.

"I'm sorry," she said to Ty. "I didn't realize I was holding you up."

"It's okay." He hoisted his pack onto his shoulders. "Shaw was slow too."

"We've been high for too long," David muttered.

Elena and Fabrizio were moving about, and Lindsey tried to remain upbeat about the prospect of climbing with the woman, since the two Italians were clearly getting ready to descend as well. Maybe Lindsey could ask Ty to wait a bit, but they had a long day ahead and needed to get started.

Her earlier euphoria had given way to a headache that had started pulsing behind her eyes. Trying to ignore it, she paused to take in the expansive view. An endless array of peaks, whiter than usual, filled the horizon. The world was crisp and new, the sun a small, shining dot in a sky as blue as a swimming pool. Lindsey had to imagine the warmth it could offer, because no rays of sunshine had reached them as yet.

She attempted an invigorating inhale of fresh mountain air, but instead it was like dragging ice cubes through her nose, and her lungs struggled for oxygen that wasn't there. With one final sweep, she enjoyed the abundance of mountains surrounding them, a mythical, almost unreal collection of snow-covered summits and the frozen river at the bottom carved by glacier movement.

Ty, covered in a yellow and black climbing suit, motioned for her to precede him. David, clad in a blue suit, was already at the top of the Black Pyramid. He hooked onto the fixed rope, faced the mountain, then disappeared.

Ty stepped in front of her and gently pulled at her harness, doing a safety check on her once again. She didn't bother to suppress the smile that crept on her face since the balaclava hid it. Despite the exhaustion pressing on her, she'd already checked her gear three times.

Giving a reciprocal tug on his harness, she eyed the buckle. All good.

Carefully she kneeled and clipped her harness to the fixed rope with a figure-eight device and then eased herself over the edge. The memory muscle of rappelling kicked in, and she began her descent.

Suddenly, Ty released a guttural roar. She glanced up just as Elena's red clad body careened toward her. Lindsey scrambled to move, but it was too late—the woman slammed into her and with a jerk, they snapped to a stop.

Stunned, Lindsey hung upside down with her back to the mountain, struggling to hold Elena against her chest since the other woman likely wasn't tied on—to anything. Lindsey's descender had snapped off the fixed rope and was dangling in her face. Her backup clip must have caught her, but how long would it hold?

"Elena," she said, trying to get her attention.

"Here," she replied, her head near Lindsey's.

Good, she was conscious.

"Before I can let you go, you've got to get hooked to the rope."

Elena flailed and a wave of dizziness hit Lindsey, her stomach boiling.

Oh no.

"Hold on," Ty yelled.

"Don't move," Lindsey ground out between her teeth. "Wait for Ty."

"I'm below you." David's voice echoed beside her ear.

"I'll get Elena," Ty said, now closer.

The woman was yanked from Lindsey's grasp. From below, David pushed Lindsey's shoulders as Ty leaned down and took hold of her harness as well, but rather than attach her to the fixed line, he hooked himself directly to her. A wave of nausea hit as she shifted upright; she had no time to offer a warning and barely got her balaclava free before she lost her breakfast.

Twisting downhill, she vomited, barely missing David.

"Sonovabitch," he bellowed.

Coughing, a second wave of convulsions overtook her, the bluish contents of her stomach splattered across the white snow.

"Lindsey, take it easy," Ty said, his voice calm and soothing.

She hung off the rope, praying the queasiness would pass. This wasn't the place to be sick.

"David, we need to get her down." The icy change in Ty's tone signaled the urgency of the situation.

With her insides empty, she no longer expelled food, but she had started shaking and her headache felt like an axe between her eyes. "My head hurts."

David propped her up from below. "You need to get down. Can you do it?"

"I could go back up." It would be so much easier if she simply returned to Camp Three.

"No," Ty and David said at the same time. Why were their voices so loud and stern?

"Fabrizio," Ty yelled. "Get down here and help Elena."

The Italian soon got Elena situated on the fixed rope above Ty.

Galloway clambered closer to Lindsey. "Can you climb on your own?" he asked her.

Despite the goggles, she could tell he was worried. She nodded. Of course she could climb. What other option was there?

"David, I'm keeping her hooked to me," Ty said. "Climb farther down so she doesn't hit you if she falls."

Another wave of dizziness swept over her. *This is annoying.* She didn't usually succumb to sickness while on a climb.

Ty yanked and reattached her descender to the fixed rope.

Just back down and slide it along the fixed rope.

Slowly she began to move. When she came to a belay station where she had to unhook and re-hook the belay device, her mind blanked on how to do it. Ty climbed closer and performed the action for her. It was sweet. But even covered in his puffy climbing suit she could tell that his body was taut, his actions hurried. In fact he seemed angry.

I should be able to do this myself.

Lindsey tried and tried, but she couldn't seem to get past her own confusion.

When they made it off the Black Pyramid, she turned and began to trudge through the snow down the mountain. Ty appeared in front of her.

How'd he get out in front of her so fast?

He tied her to both him and David, putting her in the middle. Shaw went first, and Galloway brought up the rear, periodically tugging on the rope, slowing Lindsey's forward motion. After the tenth time he'd done it—or was it the fiftieth?—Lindsey glared back at him in irritation, but she didn't have the energy to berate him, so she had to hope that her steel-edged gaze was enough. He gave no acknowledgment of her pissed-off signal, so she continued to trudge forward, grumbling to herself about the man's overbearing attitude about safety. She was perfectly capable of getting down on her own. She didn't need him to leash her like a dog, and her only satisfaction was the dressing down she planned for him once they were within talking distance.

When they finally reached Camp Two, she quickly abandoned her lofty goal of explaining to Galloway that she damned well knew how to climb. Instead, she went straight to her tent, dropped her pack on the ground, and collapsed inside on the sleeping bag.

Galloway was talking—God, was he yelling again?—and wouldn't shut up.

Suddenly Ditch hovered right at her face. "How're you doing, Lindsey?"

She closed her eyes, a sharp retort on her lips, but she bit it back. "I just need to rest."

"We think you might have a concussion. Do you remember Elena hitting you?"

"Yes, of course. I don't have amnesia."

"You might also have altitude sickness."

Sweet Jesus. She was on an expedition with a bunch of mother hens. "I'm fine. I just need some sleep."

"You can't stay here." Ditch's voice was stern, serious. "We need to get you all the way to Base. We'll remain long enough for you to drink something."

He forced her to sit upright and offered her a water bottle. As soon as she drank, her body revolted. She spewed the fluid all over herself.

"Lindsey dear," Ditch said, "we need to go now."

∼

IT TOOK ALL DAY TO GET LINDSEY BACK TO BASE CAMP. TY KNEW IT WAS fortunate that she was still able to walk, because bringing Aldo down had been fraught with danger. Moving an incapacitated climber was one of the most dangerous activities in high-altitude climbing.

While Ty had insisted on roping behind her, ready to catch her if she fell and slid, his reserves soon became taxed. Ditch insisted they all take turns in this position, rotating every hour until they were down. At times Lindsey was cognizant, but then she would slide into incoherence, as evidenced by some bizarre babbling.

"Is it edema?" Ty had asked Ditch at one point.

"Maybe." Ditch must have seen the concern on Ty's face because he reached out and clasped Ty's shoulder. "Getting her down should clear it up. I think the fall knocked the wind out of her, and we know how that can escalate in a place like this. She just needs some rest."

Fabrizio and Elena had gone ahead, so Ty didn't know if the Italian woman was suffering any after-effects from her fall, but he was feeling little sympathy for her. The damned woman had clipped onto the wrong rope before descending.

At last they came to Camp One. Ty threw off his pack, grabbed hold of Lindsey, and eased her to sit down on it.

She tried to stand. "Let me lie down in the tent."

"No." He stopped her from standing. "I know you're tired, but you can't sleep." *We'll never get you back to a standing position.*

David handed over his flask of water, and Ty gave it to her. She held it between her gloved hands and simply stared at it.

Shit.

Ty pulled off his gloves, took the bottle from her, undid the cap, and forced her to drink. While Ditch, Packer, and David retrieved food and fired up the stoves to melt snow, Ty got as much water into Lindsey as he could.

Finally, she pushed the container away. "I have to pee, you know," she grumbled.

Ty paused. She'd been in his sights since the accident, so she hadn't done her business all day.

"How do you want to do it?" he asked.

It was easy enough for the guys to urinate into a bottle inside a tent, but he suspected that Lindsey would struggle in the confining space. And worse, she would probably fall asleep as soon as she finished before he could get to her.

She'd need to do her business outside, and it wasn't the lack of privacy that concerned him as much as her safety. One misstep and she could fall off the mountain.

"David, can you help me?" he asked. "Ditch and Packer, you need to look away and give Lindsey some privacy."

"Ah," Packer replied. "You'll be making the outdoor loo. Here comes some yellow snow."

Ty helped Lindsey to stand.

David got on the other side of her. "I'll unhook her harness."

"I'll just go over here," she mumbled, trying to leave them.

"Wait." Ty grabbed hold of her arm. There was no safe place on this ledge, especially with Lindsey in such a confused state.

"Let me set an anchor," David said. He planted two ice axes and ran a sling between them, then secured a rope and brought it back to Lindsey.

"*Come on already*," she said, her teeth chattering as she shifted her feet back and forth.

David stepped forward and looped the cord under her armpits, then tied a knot. He gave a test tug. "You're good."

"You want me to unzip you?" Ty asked.

"Yes." Her unenthusiastic response was no surprise, since Ty would hardly welcome such intimate help. He leaned down and released the up-and-under zipper until it was open.

"I can do the rest," she said.

Ty turned his back and stepped away.

As he joined the others, Ditch said, "I think she's becoming more cognizant. The drop in altitude is helping."

"Will she be all right?" Ty asked.

Ditch nodded. "But one of us will need to keep an eye on her through the night."

"Who wants to bet a G-note that'll be Galloway?" Packer said, dumping a packet of purple drink mix into his water bottle. He secured the lid and gave it a good shake.

David ripped open a gel packet. "If you're saying I'll win a thousand dollars if Tyler sleeps in Lindsey's tent, then I'll take that bet." He squeezed the contents into his mouth.

A low rumble of laughter saved Ty the effort of rebutting the claim, which would likely be a lie. Being witness to her deteriorating health and behavior had filled him with panic. He'd definitely be keeping an eye on her.

"I'm done." Lindsey's weary voice floated back to them.

Ty moved quickly back to her position and helped her secure her climbing suit, while David removed the rope that would have stopped her had she lost her balance.

"God, this is humiliating," she mumbled as the men treated her like a ragdoll.

"We won't tell," David said, then left them, coiling up the rope.

"All that's missing is me naked without my homework."

Color had returned to her face and for the first time all day, hope sprung a leak in Tyler's chest, and he allowed the barest hint of a grin to reach his mouth.

She's gonna be all right.

Before he thought better of it, he cupped her cheek with his left hand. In her eyes he saw shock, probably because he was making the gesture in full view of the other team members. But they all knew. Lindsey was important to him.

He gave a slight caress with his thumb before withdrawing, and then he stepped aside so she could precede him back to where the others stood waiting.

CHAPTER 13

Lindsey had never been so happy to see her tent at Base Camp. Darkness descended as Ty pulled off her pack and she crawled inside. He came in right after her and switched on the battery-powered light she kept near her bed, then he helped remove her boots.

Despite her pounding headache and overwhelming fatigue, she could still recall the look he'd given her after he had gently touched her face earlier. If she didn't feel so rotten, perhaps she would consider a similar romantic overture, but accompanying that excitement was also apprehension.

"I'm not going to sleep with you, Ty," she blurted.

"That was quick. You didn't even give me a chance to buy you dinner and win you over with intelligent small talk."

He unzipped her suit and she rolled back and forth as he extracted her from it.

"What on earth is intelligent small talk?" she asked as she lifted her hips so he could remove the bulky outwear.

He stuffed it into a corner of the tent. "It's where we connect on an existential level."

He motioned for her to put her legs inside her sleeping bag, which she did.

"Does such a technique actually work for you?"

He smiled, tucking her in as if she were a child. "I don't know. Is it?"

Maybe.

She stared into eyes filled with a wicked gleam of amusement. "I'm not such a bad guy."

"I never said you were."

"If you're going to tell me you secretly like Fiske, then there's only one thing I can do."

"What's that?"

"I'll have to challenge him to a duel."

"You know he'd fight dirty."

"Don't count me out yet, Linds."

She couldn't suppress a pleased grin. Why did it make her happy that he'd fight for her?

Ty squeezed her shoulder. "Don't go to sleep. I'll be right back."

The memory of that simple touch lingered as she waited for him, keeping at bay the utter exhaustion threatening to overtake her.

Finally, footsteps signaled his return. He entered her tent with two thermoses. "Hot chocolate and broth," he said. "Try to get this down."

She sat up and obeyed, and thankfully the liquids remained in her stomach. As much as she wanted to keep talking to him, she could hardly keep her eyes open. "I really need to sleep, Ty," she said, then asked, "How's Elena?"

"David talked to Fabrizio. She's fine. She hooked onto the wrong rope."

"And the moral to that story is don't climb below Elena."

"You were right about her."

Weariness showed on Ty's face, along the grim edges of his mouth. Lindsey reached up and tried to smooth out the wrinkles, his whiskers poking her fingers.

"You should get some rest," she said. "You look like Elena hit you, too."

His face remained impassive as he watched her.

"Thanks for not leaving me," she added, her voice thick with emotion.

"No chance of that."

She cracked a smile, trying to lighten the mood. "Quit being a moody climber."

As she let her hand fall away from him, he clasped it, his fingers cool to the touch, filled with a gentle strength. How would it feel to have those hands on her, touching and exploring?

"I'll let you sleep for a bit," he said, "but I'll be back to check on you."

He released her hand and reached for the thermoses as she burrowed into her sleeping bag, then he set them on the plastic container that she used as a table.

"You have a key," she said, "so just let yourself in." She closed her eyes, relieved to sleep at long last.

Quietly Ty departed.

She awoke later to find Ty in her tent again, the lamp back on.

"What time is it?" she asked, groaning as she moved. Stiffness had set in and every muscle in her body screamed in hot protest.

"Around eleven p.m." He handed her another cup of hot chocolate.

Leaning on an elbow she dutifully drank.

"How do you feel?"

"Like Elena pummeled me with bricks." She handed the cup back to him, then grabbed a nylon cinch sack near her bed and pulled out a journal, grimacing from the effort. "I wanted to show you something."

She flipped a few pages then handed the book to Ty.

He smiled and studied the photo of her at Moonlight Buttress, the one he had mentioned that he liked. "Yeah, this is the one. You look really good."

"Better than I do now?"

Gratitude showed in his eyes. "You're alive. That's always the best look."

She lay back on the pillowcase stuffed with clothes. "I was never going to die. Everyone is being overly dramatic."

"Better safe than sorry." He flipped through the book, pages affixed with newspaper and magazine articles, photos, notes from expeditions, funny stories. "This is a great memento."

It was. The book meant everything to her. It was her life, a life intimately shared with Alison—sister, comrade, taskmaster.

"I don't normally travel with it, but for some reason I felt compelled to bring it here."

He carefully set the journal beside her bed. "You should try to sleep again." He leaned down and kissed her on the forehead. "But I'll be back at two a.m. for another check."

Her body reacted to Ty's overture with a flush of desire and need. He exited her tent and secured the door, and the sound of his footfalls faded as he went to his own tent. If she called him back, would he make good on the promise of that kiss? For a moment, she wanted nothing more than to lose herself in him.

Spasms of pain reminded her she was in no shape for a bedroom romp.

It was silly to fool herself, however. Ty would be so much more than sex, and she was beginning to not care.

She should stay away from him.

She really should.

Because she was pretty sure falling in love with Tyler Galloway would be so very easy. And if she really gave it any thought, she was already halfway there.

THE NEXT MORNING, LINDSEY FELT AWFUL. BRYNN STOPPED IN TO BRING her oatmeal and a cup of tea, and she confirmed Lindsey's fever.

Ty's 2 a.m. visit was hazy, but Lindsey recalled him talking with her in the dark, smoothing her hair from her face. He'd kissed her forehead again. She may have leaned into him; he may have held her. She wasn't quite sure now. But he'd aroused her yet again, that was certain, if her sexy, restless dreams of him during the hours before dawn were any indication.

"She's got a fever," Brynn said to her brother as he entered the tent. "I'll get some ibuprofen," she added and left.

Ty crawled in beside her. "Do you feel like throwing up?"

"No, just achy all over and my head hurts."

"Okay, then you need to eat the oatmeal and keep your fluids up."

Despite the fog that filled Lindsey's mind, she was certain of one thing—she didn't want to be sick around a man she wanted to romance. "You don't have to stay," she said. "You might catch it."

"Yeah, well, I'm the only one willing to brave the quarantined area. Except for Brynn, but after she brings the ibuprofen I'm telling her to stay away. You're right, no one else should get sick."

"But what about you?"

His eyes, a beckoning shade of blue, rested on her. The baseball cap added to his boyish charm and the stubble on his cheeks just made him more damned compelling. "I'm willing to brave the virus."

"You're crazy and you know it." An urge to cry welled up inside her. It was likely the effect of the illness, lowering not just her immune system but her emotional defenses as well, but she was overcome with gratitude that Ty wanted to stay with her.

"Well, I do have an ulterior motive. I've been wanting to do a Meryl Streep marathon. Now you'll be forced to join me."

"No *Sophie's Choice* please."

"We'll start with a comedy then. Maybe *Death Becomes Her*?"

For the remainder of the day Ty stayed in her tent, and they watched movies on his laptop. This was such a rare thing for her, to lie around and do nothing. If she hadn't been so sick, she would have been disgusted by her own laziness, would have been disconcerted for Ty to see her in such a state of idleness, but she really couldn't summon the energy to care. The movies passed the time and hanging out with Ty was a treat that under other circumstances would not have occurred. They were at the base of K2, the second highest mountain in the world, behaving like unmotivated teenagers. If this were a date—Lindsey wasn't quite sure, but she suspected it was—it was the most unusual one she'd ever had.

In late afternoon, Ty left to get caught up on email on the computer in the mess tent then to fetch soup for her. The evening plan was to watch *Out of Africa* after he recharged the battery on his laptop using one of the solar chargers.

Lindsey decided it was time she brushed her teeth.

After taking care of her personal hygiene, she sat outside. The fresh air, the ibuprofen, and getting cleaned up had made her feel better. Climbers milled around in the other camps and the aroma of cooking food occasionally wafted her way.

She sipped a sports drink that Ty had insisted she consume; he was right, she needed to keep her body hydrated and flush with sugars and electrolytes, especially now that she was fighting off a virus.

The incessant coughing that generally overtook Base Camps could now be heard from other climbers in the surrounding tents. While not necessarily a sign of illness, it could lead to one, and the longer they stayed at altitude, the worse it could get.

Lindsey needed to take care of herself, especially after this bout of sickness. The body simply couldn't recover properly at this elevation. But she could still climb with less reserves—she'd done it before.

A sharp crack resounded, and an avalanche roared down the mountain, the reverberations rattling inside Lindsey's chest. That was the fifth one today. K2 was shedding her wintry coat after the last bout of storms, and she wasn't being coy or quiet about it.

Despite feeling weary, Lindsey wasn't ready to abandon the climb. She simply needed to rest, to be patient, to be ready when the time came. It would be soon. She could feel it. A window would open and when it did she needed to be prepared physically, but more importantly, mentally. A mountain like this offered few chances to scale it. Previous years had borne this out when no summits had been attained.

Don't count me out yet.

A large raven circled overhead. Lindsey smiled at her avian friend, wondering if it was Charon.

"That bird is a pest," came a voice from behind her.

Fiske.

Her moment of rest and relaxation abruptly ended.

He stopped beside her, wearing sunglasses, a knit hat, and a bright metallic blue puffy down jacket. "I hear you are ill," he said, removing his eyewear.

"Just the flu."

Could she skirt around him and escape to her tent? He'd probably follow her. And she wasn't done enjoying a break outside. She'd be damned if Fiske would ruin that. So much for her rock-cairn boundary doing its job.

"I have Echinacea tea. You should drink some. It will make you strong."

"I'm fine. We have medicine. Thanks."

"Lindsey." The way he said her name popped a red flag in her mind, and she could swear she heard an accompanying notification ding very similar to her cell phone. She scanned for anyone nearby, but they were remarkably alone. Maybe she should have put her tent closer to the others after all.

Fiske sat beside her, and she shifted to create distance, however small, but then he draped his arm across her shoulders and pulled her against him.

"You could climb with me."

She tensed, her heart rate ramping up. "Why?" She refused to look at him.

He leaned close, his breath hot against her skin and smelling of smoked meat. "We could have a good time. All the Americans tell me you are a great climber."

She shot to her feet, repulsed by his nearness, and stepped away from him. "Thanks, but I'll climb with my own team." She crossed her arms. "And besides, it goes against the rules of the permits."

"You know that is not strict. Not now. It is everyone to themselves."

"Are you having trouble with your team?"

"There are too many leaders. I am a very strong climber, and I don't need them. Together, you and I could move very fast. I know you want to get to the top, to honor your sister. And I have an entire country expecting my success. I will not be denied that which I go after." He stood and moved toward her.

She countered swiftly with a side-step. "I don't want to be rude, Fiske, but get lost."

At least he stopped.

"American girls are so independent. It is very refreshing."

The knot in Lindsey's stomach threatened to release whatever food she'd managed to keep down since breakfast. It was getting dark. She zipped her fleece to her neck to ward off the chilly air.

A glance at Fiske made her stomach clench again. For a moment, his eyes gleamed with ... determination. Or was it malice? Her shivering increased.

"I have Norwegian ale. Come see me when you feel better."

She didn't answer but willed herself to hold his gaze, refusing to let him have the satisfaction of intimidating her.

He turned and walked away.

Beneath a ragged breath, she said, "Oh I will, you piece of shit, and I'll bring a pair of sharpened crampons with me."

She detested men like him, whose overblown egos were allowed free reign in a place as remote as K2. She had felt far safer on Everest, where the sheer volume of climbers and support staff greatly diluted the impact that one blowhard could have on a mountain and the women in residence.

Until now, Fiske had simply been an uncomfortable irritation, a borderline bully that she could dodge. As she returned to her tent, it was clear that she had to make sure she was never alone with him again.

Fiske was dangerous.

CHAPTER 14

"Tell the missus we miss her, Mr. Coulson," Packer said with a smirk as Ty left the mess tent with warm chappatis bread wrapped in a cloth, a jar of peanut butter, and a knife.

"Smart ass," Ty uttered under his breath. Packer's hearty chuckle followed Ty as he picked out the path to Lindsey's tent with the light beaming from his headlamp.

He was spending so much time with Lindsey that the others had urged him to move in with her. He soon learned they had an ulterior motive—they wanted to convert his tent into a game room.

"Drinks and poker, 24/7," Packer had said.

The night sky was clear, a thousand points of light against the dark canopy, and K2 glowed like a nightlight with its snowy attire. As he neared Lindsey's tent, she opened the entrance.

"Hurry, it's cold," she said.

He passed the food items to her and crawled inside, zipping the door closed. The glow of the interior camp light illuminated everything they did, their silhouettes visible to the rest of the camp if anyone decided to spy on them. Not that Ty was making moves on Lindsey.

Aside from lustful imaginings, he'd been a perfect gentleman while she recovered from her illness.

But considering the fair amount of ribbing thrown his way whenever he talked to Beck, or the Poles—not to mention Packer's running monologue on Tyler's whipped status—everyone in the small Base Camp village assumed he was getting it, and frequently.

He'd considered staying away—Brynn could easily play nursemaid in his stead—but until Lindsey asked him to leave her alone, he'd take the crumbs of attention she threw his way.

She sat on her sleeping bag with legs crossed, wearing thick black leggings, wool socks, and a snug gray thermal, her hair in a loose braid resting across one shoulder.

She was the prettiest girl in camp, and he tried not to stare.

Who was he kidding? She was the prettiest girl, period. When he'd met her face-to-face for the first time in January in Salt Lake City, he'd had to force himself not to gawk at her even then. From that first encounter, the air had sparked and crackled, as if the molecules in the universe couldn't contain themselves around the force of nature that was Lindsey Coulson.

Chemistry.

Lindsey had spoken of the search for the origins of DNA.

Until he'd met her, he hadn't realized what he'd been searching for. And it was a woman with no makeup and bright eyes—a blessing after her illness, after her scare on the mountain—and he had the feeling that he could easily follow her around the world in a bid never to be far from her.

Is this what it was like for his parents? Lily and Jim Galloway had a bond that had always amused Ty, but he'd never given it much thought until now. Until Lindsey.

She smeared peanut butter onto a piece of bread and savored the first bite.

"This is great," she said around a full mouth. "Thank you for the comfort food."

He pushed his Lindsey-admiration-club into the basement. "At least your appetite is back. The Germans are planning to head out tomorrow for a summit try. Piotr and his team are thinking about the day after."

"Do you think it's safe?"

Ty shrugged. "That's the million-dollar question. Unfortunately, the forecast is iffy."

"What's your plan?" She licked her fingers and stuffed more chappatis in her mouth.

"Bring you peanut butter sandwiches and loaf around watching movies."

She shook her head. "You don't have to wait for me."

"I know." But he would. "Are you sure you want to go back up?" Maybe she was done and simply hadn't voiced it aloud.

Her eyes widened. "Of course I'm going back up. I'm not sure what happened up there with Elena, but I've never had trouble with edema before. I don't think that was it. It was just altitude sickness, that's all. And now that I've rested, I should be more acclimated."

"Maybe you should wait a few more days."

She stopped eating, her demeanor developing an edge. "What do the others think?"

"Ditch is cautious, Packer's a wise-ass, and I get the feeling David won't leave this mountain until he's conquered it. But they all agree that you should be with us."

The fight in her appeared to dissolve. "Really?"

"You seem surprised."

"I guess I am, a little. This is a strange team you've put together, Ty."

"The magic of the mountains. Beck and Artie said their team would like to climb with us, too."

Lindsey released a barely audible huff.

"Fiske?" he asked. There was no missing the way the man looked at Lindsey, and it irritated the hell out of Ty. He'd never been the jealous type, but the Norwegian had changed that with more than one possessive eye-sweep of Lindsey.

"It's okay, nothing I can't handle. Just promise that I won't end up in a tent with him at Camp Four. I'd rather hook myself to a rock and sleep outside."

Seeking to keep the edge out of his own voice, he said in a light tone, "Maybe we can set up a decoy—bring an inflatable doll and let him snuggle up to it. He'd probably never notice the difference."

Lindsey laughed, her approval reaching her eyes. "That high up she'd probably deflate."

"Would serve him right."

She wiped peanut butter from her mouth and took a drink of water. "You're quite the chef," she said.

"Back in the real world I make a pretty good lasagna. I'll cook for you sometime."

Her smile never faltered, and he liked that he could make her happy.

"You realize that all of the time you've been spending in my tent has likely ruined my reputation," she said.

"No, it's ruined mine. I've always been known for being celibate on expeditions."

"I doubt that."

"I can't imagine what it's like being a woman in the mountain climbing community," he said. "You must get hit on all the time."

She shrugged. "Some are worse than others. This isn't part of the magazine feature, is it?"

"I've been considering a sidebar on the sex life of a woman mountaineer."

Her expression took on a restrained look. "Do you want to include that I'm on birth control not because I look forward to mountain romances, but because rape in remote foreign locations is a very real possibility?"

"I'm on birth control for the same reason."

She gifted him a bashful smirk and dropped her gaze, her cheeks a nice rosy hue. The tent was small, and he wanted her. He'd wanted her all along.

"I promise that if we have a romance, I'll leave it out of the article," he teased.

"That's reassuring. You're not going to write one of those tell-all books one day about the exploits of Anders Fiske and Elena Rossi?"

"Never say never. And wouldn't the two of them make a darling couple?"

"I wouldn't wish Fiske on anyone, not even Elena, but at least if they were focused on each other, they'd leave the rest of us alone to actually climb the mountain."

"Is that why you dance around me?" he prodded.

"Huh?"

"Are you afraid that my irresistible magnetism will distract you from climbing?"

She laughed, biting her lip and giving a slight roll of her eyes. "You got that about right," she replied under her breath.

He sobered. "I'm not Fiske. If you want me to leave, I will."

Her eyes flicked to his. "You're nothing like that asshat. It's just that ... you make me nervous."

"In a good or a bad way?"

She held his gaze. "Both. I think you might be more than I can handle."

"I'm flattered, but you're wrong. I'm pretty sure you could handle anything thrown at you."

"Now you're flattering *me*. This could get complicated."

He moved closer. "I know. And I've decided that I don't care."

She leaned past him and clicked off the light. "No reason to give everyone a show."

Anticipation flooded him, but he held it in check. He'd often thought of this moment, and he didn't want to rush it.

He lifted his hand and brushed aside strands of hair that had escaped her braid. As his vision adjusted to the dark and the shadows revealed her face mere inches from his, he was struck again by her beauty, by the combination of grit and vulnerability that he often saw in her eyes, by the feminine contours of her cheeks, her lips, her neck, and more. Her athletic frame was tempered with curves that hit all the right spots in what he liked in a woman.

But it was more than that.

Lindsey Coulson filled a corner of the world that was uniquely her own. And he was gripped with a longing to inhabit that place with her. Being on the outside looking in was never going to cut it. Not with her.

His fingers trailed along her cheek. She trembled slightly, and he hoped it was from his touch and not the chill in the air.

Very gently, he kissed her, then kissed her again. He rubbed his nose against hers, enjoying the intimate contact.

It felt like he'd been waiting for Lindsey his entire life.

She scooted forward so he could gain better access to her mouth, slanting her lips against his, giving him a taste of the remnants of her peanut butter meal. Her hand tugged at his neck and her arm hooked around him. He pulled her close and deepened the kiss, his tongue plunging into her mouth, and his body shuddered with need, escalating like wildfire.

He wanted nothing more than to bury himself inside her.

He stopped and leaned his forehead against hers, holding the sides of her head with both of his hands. "We can do as much or as little as you want," he whispered against her mouth. "I know you still don't feel well."

She expelled a breath and a chuckle at the same time. "You're not gonna leave me hanging, are you? I expect to see you naked, Galloway."

"That can be arranged."

She kissed him, hard and demanding, her mouth hungry. That was all the invitation he needed. His arms encircled her, and he brought her against him, letting his hands roam down her backside. He cupped her butt and she shifted her legs to straddle him, sliding along him until her pelvis nestled perfectly against him.

His mouth possessed hers as he buried his fingers in her hair. He broke away and trailed his lips along her neck as he slid his hands beneath the bottom of her shirt and ran his palms along her back.

She tugged at his clothing, so he let go of her long enough to pull the fleece and long-sleeved shirt over his head. As soon as he was bare chested, her hands began to explore him in earnest, but his patience had fled. He pulled her thick shirts—he wasn't sure if there were two or three of them—off her. The glow of a yellow sports bra greeted him, but before he could decide how to handle it, she shed it herself.

Despite the darkness, her breasts were round, full, perfect. He cupped them with his hands and nibbled along her collarbone with his lips. Her fingers raked through his already disheveled hair, holding her to him.

He replaced his hands with his mouth, suckling one nipple while his arms wrapped around her, holding her in place. She responded by grinding against him, and although he had big plans to extend this foreplay, he was too damned close.

He pushed her onto her back and stripped the thick leggings and socks from her, grabbing her panties in the process. Now she was fully naked. He ran a hand along her thigh, enjoying the feel of her smooth skin, his gaze drinking in every inch of her.

He kissed her stomach and then the undersides of her breasts as her fingers dug painfully into his hair.

"Ty," she whispered, her voice strangled. "Don't wait."

He still wore his snow boots and knew he didn't have time to get them off, so with a frantic tug he undid his trail pants and pushed what remained of his clothing as far down as his calves, then he covered Lindsey with his body, trying to warm her cooled skin. They should get into the sleeping bag, but that would have to wait until they were done.

She widened her legs and kissed him, deep, wet, hot, arousing him to a flashpoint. He entered her in one push, her body slick and ready. She locked her legs below his buttocks, tightening around him, and he rocked against her, each thrust stronger than the last. Only when her back arched and she pulsed against him did he let go of the precarious hold on his own need, releasing it like an avalanche, long and intense. For a moment, he forgot where he was, his attention solely on Lindsey.

~

"YOU STILL ALIVE?" TY WHISPERED AGAINST HER CHEEK.

Lindsey sighed. God, that had been good. "Barely."

It had been a long time since she'd felt the delicious sensation of longing and hunger. She kept him in place atop her, inside her. He felt so right. She decided she could stay this way for a long time, surrounded by the faint citrus aroma of his hair, the compelling smell of his skin, and the erotic musk of making love with him. It had all come together into a perfect storm of male sexiness and satisfaction.

"Are you always this good?" she murmured.

He raised his head and gave her a thorough and drugging kiss. "I released the Kraken for you. I don't normally do that."

She smiled. "I approve. But you should know I'm pretty certain I'm going to need more than one attempt by your Kraken."

"I'll give it to you on one condition."

She shifted her hips and his resulting groan sent a fresh wave of desire through her abdomen, pooling at the point of their connection.

"Anything," she said, her voice breathless.

"Let me take my boots off first."

CHAPTER 15

L indsey sat in the mess tent with Brynn. They'd eaten breakfast and now chatted over tea. The men had departed under cover of a light snowfall. The Germans and Poles had delayed their departure to the summit, so several of them, along with Ty, David, Ditch, and Packer, had decided to hike to Base Camp at Broad Peak, K2's next-door neighbor and the twelfth-highest mountain in the world. Lindsey would've gone, but she hadn't had much sleep and she was still recovering from her sickness, so it seemed wise to relax, although relax was a relative term. Her body practically hummed from her night with Ty.

She'd never considered herself a woman who needed sex, who craved it, who was practically starved for it. It had always been a pleasant, interesting pastime, and sometimes not so pleasant.

But with Ty it was something altogether different.

Still bewildered by the experience, one thought went through her head—he'd been thorough. Not just physically, although God knew her body responded just thinking about him, but something more. He stirred in her the same pull that brought her again and again to the mountains. A deep-rooted connection that grounded her.

He would have kissed her goodbye this morning—she could see the intention in his eyes as they'd gathered in the mess tent with the others—but he hadn't. No reason to make it awkward for the rest of the team.

"So, I'd ask you how it was," Brynn finally said, "but he's my brother, so I really don't want to know."

"Hmm?"

"Snap out of it," Brynn scolded.

Lindsey brought her focus back to the mess tent. "Sorry." Then, realizing that maybe she hadn't been upholding her end of their female friendship, she asked, "Are you with anyone?"

"Do you mean here?"

"No. Why? Are you and Packer in love?"

Brynn laughed. "No. And no, I don't currently have a boyfriend. I tend to pick guys that are a little … edgy. That doesn't translate into *long term*."

Lindsey stared at her tea mug and sighed. "I hear you. Expedition romances don't last either."

"Your sister's did," Brynn said quietly, then added, "and Ty has it bad for you."

Happiness spread through Lindsey like warm brownies.

Brynn's brows wrinkled together. "You look surprised."

"I was just thinking about brownies."

"With fudge?" Brynn asked, hope lighting her face.

"And chocolate chips."

They both released a moan of contentment.

After a moment of silence, Brynn said, "I started surfing competitively when I was seven, but I took a beating for a while from the other kids, and not just in the water. Ty was only a year older, but he was so much better than me. Between him and Alec, he's the more athletic and the more daring."

"Hold on," Lindsey said, holding up a hand. "Alec films great white sharks. That's pretty daring in my book."

Brynn grinned, nodding. She leaned back in her chair and crossed her arms over her puffy lavender coat. "Well, that's true, but when it came to surfing Tyler was always closer to the edge of his abilities than Alec ever wanted to be. When I was struggling, Ty took me under his wing and started training me himself. My dad was tough on us, and Ty always seemed to look out for me, always giving me pep talks, always pushing me to do better. I love both my brothers, but Ty is … special."

"So what you're saying is …," Lindsey prompted.

"It's difficult to find someone worth all the effort, someone that you're willing to go through the relationship bullshit with." Brynn drained the last of the tea from her cup. "But Ty's your guy, the one you can get all gaga for and uproot your life for."

"Whoa. Slow down. You're all but planning the wedding."

Brynn cast an assessing look Lindsey's way. "I've seen him with other girls, and he's never looked at them the way he looks at you. And I think you like him just as much."

"Okay, you're probably right, but can we talk about something else?"

Brynn shrugged. "Sure."

Lindsey's feelings for Galloway were definitely in a league of their own, but she didn't want to dwell on it right now.

"Hey, do you have a paperback I can read?" Brynn asked. "I can only circle the camp so many times to stave off boredom."

"I do. I'll give it to you on one condition."

"If it's a double-date with Packer and Ty, I must decline."

Lindsey shook her head. "No. Ty told me that Stan Ingerman wasn't going with them today. Would you come with me to pay him a visit?"

"An excursion." Brynn's face brightened. "Let's go."

They both stood, zipped up their jackets, and pulled on hats and gloves then carefully picked their way through the rocks to the American team's encampment. Ingerman sat inside the mess tent wearing a ball cap over his brown hair.

"Knock, knock," Lindsey said.

He glanced up from a pile of papers he was studying, dark circles prominent under his eyes. "Come in," he replied. "You girls didn't go to Broad Peak?"

"Nah. Can we join you for a bit?"

Ingerman nodded, so Lindsey pulled out a chair and took a seat at the end of the long table. Brynn settled across from her. "We wanted to take it easy today," she added.

"Want some coffee?"

"Sure. That would be great."

The mess tent was much like theirs with a cook stove in the back and a laptop sitting on a makeshift desk in the corner, a box of tissues and a plate covered in crumbs beside it.

Ingerman grabbed two insulated mugs and poured coffee from a thermos.

"I've been sick," Lindsey added. "I'm trying to rest for when we go up again. How high have you gone?"

"I've made it to Camp Two. I've been under the weather, as well. Can't seem to shake it. Always frustrating after coming this far." He settled back in his chair and crossed his arms. "But I'm guessing you didn't come here to talk about our climb. You came to talk about Alison's."

"I'm curious to hear your side of the story," she said.

"I doubt I could add more than you probably already know."

"Can I ask how it affected you?"

"It's a terrible blow when something like that happens. It makes you question everything, wondering why them and not you."

"But you decided to come back to K2," Brynn said, voicing a statement and not a question.

"I'm no different than anyone here. I still want to get to the top."

"Why do you think Alison died?" Lindsey asked.

Ingerman stared at her, his gaze as droopy as a St. Bernard, then he looked away as if he knew something but hesitated to speak. Lindsey had wondered why there had been so little commentary from him after the tragedy, but he'd been in very bad shape when he'd left K2 that summer two years ago.

But, now, he was back, and if she didn't at least try to speak with him then regret would hound her in the days to come. With most everyone away from camp, the golden ticket of opportunity had landed in her lap. Still, trepidation had gripped her, so she'd asked Brynn to accompany her to gain a little moral support.

Ingerman swung his gaze back to her. "You really want my opinion?"

Lindsey gave a curt bob of her chin.

"Her head wasn't in the right place."

Lindsey frowned. "Why do you say that?"

"She and David were fighting."

This was news. In the few emails that Alison had sent while she'd been here, her sister had never mentioned any issues with her fiancé.

"Do you mean minor disagreements that most couples have?" Brynn asked.

"Of course they argued from time to time," Ingerman said, "and I certainly wasn't with them all the time, so I don't claim to know everything happening between them. But at Camp Four the night before the summit push, they had a heated fight in their tent."

"About what?" Lindsey asked.

"I don't really remember. Look, it was honestly none of my business. The day she went for the summit, I was very ill, and I began to descend in the afternoon. It wasn't until later that I heard what had happened."

"And what had you heard?"

"That Alison and those two young pups on their team, Gant and Davis—despite a bad weather report—had left for the summit early in the morning before dawn, but David and Freddy weren't with them."

"Why weren't they with them?" Brynn asked.

"David said he hadn't been feeling well," Lindsey said, reiterating David's story that he'd told her after he'd returned to the States, "and Freddy had agreed to stay back with him."

Ingerman palmed his face and shook his head, saying, "I can't figure out why Alison would have gone to the summit with two very inexperienced climbers over the two on her team that *were* experienced, and especially with the threat of a storm coming."

"Are you saying that because she and David had fought, she'd refused to climb with him?" Lindsey asked.

"Or maybe he refused to climb with *her*," Ingerman said, his voice quiet. He paused, then said, "I don't know if I should share something with you."

A sick feeling formed in Lindsey's stomach. Did she need to know any of this? Alison was dead. For one fleeting minute, the urge to get up and leave nearly overtook her.

"Tell me what?" Her voice was barely a whisper.

"On the day that David and Freddy finally descended, the weather had cleared. I had the scope on the mountain, and above the Bottleneck I saw something ..."

A cold chill swept through Lindsey. "What are you saying?"

"I saw a climber in a bright blue suit."

Lindsey was stunned. Alison had owned a bright blue climbing suit.

Brynn's quiet voice sliced into the tension-filled air. "I don't understand."

"He's saying that Alison was still alive as David left the mountain," Lindsay said, her voice rising with each syllable. "How? At that point, she'd been missing above 24,000 feet for three days. She'd had no tent, very little gear, and no oxygen. She'd been completely exposed to the weather. No climber could survive that."

"Maybe by some miracle she did," Ingerman said.

"Why didn't you tell anyone?" she demanded. "Right then. Why didn't you try to get a rescue party up there?"

Ingerman released a heavy breath. "I wasn't entirely sure that what I'd seen was...." He hesitated, then added quietly, "... real. The doctor in camp said I had edema. I was feeling a little better since coming down to Base but not much. And as soon as I saw that blue speck, it fell. It fell far. Everyone in camp was reeling from the bad weather and the avalanche at Camp Three. All of us were sick. David and Freddy had stayed too high for too long searching for her and the other two members of their team. They looked like death walking when they finally came into camp. What good would it have done to tell them, to tell anyone? There was no hope for her, Lindsey. And if any climbers had gone back up, they would've likely died, too."

Shock filled her.

If she'd been here, she might have prevented *all* of this. It wasn't like her sister to make a rash decision, to go for a dangerous summit under questionable conditions, with teammates that were unproven.

Why, Al? Why would you make such a reckless choice?

Alison's error in judging the weather conditions had cost her life, but shouldn't David have stopped her?

Lindsey couldn't help but feel that some of this was his fault, and her shock was quickly turning to outrage.

BY DINNER THE MEN HAD RETURNED. AS TY MOVED PAST LINDSEY TO take a seat, he dragged her hat down, covering her face. She pulled it off and glowered at him as she smoothed her flyaway hair back into place, then shifted the knit cap once again to its previous position.

"How's it going at Broad Peak?" she asked.

"Good." Ty sat at the end of the table near her. "No summits yet."

"How many climbers?"

"About twelve or thirteen. Three are already gone. One guy broke his wrist; the other two reached their limit and left."

"How'd he break a wrist?" Brynn asked.

"The old-fashioned way," Packer answered from his position at the opposite end of the table. "He punched his teammate because they couldn't agree on how many camps to set up."

"No," David said. "He slipped on a rock face."

"C'mon," Packer moaned. "We need some drama for those blogs everyone's gonna write once we're off the mountain."

"You shouldn't lie," Ditch said.

Habibe began serving dinner: rice, vegetables and boiled eggs.

Packer sighed loudly. "I really could use a steak. What happened to that yak that came in with us?"

"The cooks and porters will eat it," Ty said. "If you need protein, open a can of tuna."

"You have someone cooking for you," Ditch said to Packer, "and you're complaining?"

"I know." Packer shook his head. "Go figure." He proceeded to dig into his meal.

Ty turned to Lindsey and asked, "What did you do today?"

"Brynn and I visited with Ingerman."

David poured water from a pitcher into his mug. "He's been hanging back. Is he sick?"

"He said he was," Brynn answered. "He looks worn down."

As they ate, talk turned to other topics. Frustrated by her conversation with Ingerman, Lindsey wanted to ask David about it but held back. The mess tent wasn't the best place to hash out the death of her sister.

Ty's hand found her knee under the table. He squeezed then stroked, igniting a slow burning fire inside her belly; she looked up for a second to give him a quick smile. He soon proved to be a huge distraction, but one that she welcomed. Ty was the only thing that could pull her thoughts from Alison.

After dinner, Packer dug out a bottle of vodka.

Not paying attention to how much she imbibed—Ty's proximity had her thinking about all the things they would do later in the dark confines of her tent—a sense of boldness bloomed inside her.

Her attention landed on David. "Were you and Alison fighting before she died?"

The atmosphere inside the tent became hushed.

"Why would you say that?" David asked. "Because Ingerman told you?"

"He said she wasn't herself."

David looked away, a muscle in his jaw flexing. "She was exhausted," he said. "We all were."

Ty clasped Lindsey's hand and gave it a quick squeeze. When she glanced at him, he gave a slight shake of his head.

Okay. He didn't want her making a scene in front of everyone. It was bad for team morale. She knew that. And maybe she was being a tad spiteful; maybe she wanted to corner David.

"You're saying that in her fatigued state, she made a mistake?"

Irritation crossed David's face, and he turned his gaze on her. "I know you're looking for someone to blame, Lindsey. Do you want to blame me? Then go ahead. It won't change the fact that she's not here."

"Why didn't you go to the summit with her?"

The air exploded in anger around David. "You don't think I play that day over and over in my head?" he demanded. "Goddammit, Lindsey, I didn't want her to die."

"Neither did I!" she flung back. Her eyes burned with unshed tears, and her throat tightened as if a snake had coiled around it. Ty reached over and clasped her arm, murmuring something to her, but she couldn't understand him as anger and grief roared in her ears.

"You don't get it, do you?" David said, his body taut and his voice on edge. "She was acting like *you*."

Lindsey stilled, and Ty removed his hand. "What do you mean?" she asked.

"Both Freddy and I weren't feeling well. I asked her to wait two hours for us, but she refused. Gant and Davis left with her, but she didn't climb with them. She'd turned off her radio. She'd gone all lone-wolf on me."

"Al would never do that. She always got on me when *I* did that."

David didn't answer, and the others had taken to staring at their mugs.

Then David sighed, and his voice broke when he spoke. "We *had* fought, if you must know. It really wasn't anyone's business—" he paused "—but she wanted to break off the engagement."

"What?" Despite Ingerman telling her about the fighting, Lindsey was stunned that it had gotten that bad. "Why?"

David shook his head and rubbed a palm down his face. "Frankly, I'm surprised that you never knew any of this. I figured she must've confided in you." He expelled a deep breath. "We couldn't agree about children."

Lindsey's head was beginning to pound. "I don't understand. You didn't want kids?"

"Not me. Her." He hesitated before continuing, "Not many people know, but I grew up in foster care. My mom got pregnant as a teen and my father was nowhere to be found, so she gave me up. I bounced around a lot in my youth."

"No shit, Shaw?" Packer said. "I'm sorry, man."

"Yeah, well that's why I don't talk about it. I'm not looking for sympathy. My youth was no cakewalk, but one thing I've always wanted was a family, a real one. I knew that Alison wanted to focus on her career, but I assumed eventually she'd settle down, have babies—I couldn't really believe the woman I loved wouldn't want that. Not if I wanted it."

"But she didn't?" Lindsey asked, shocked that Alison had never shared any of these concerns with her.

"No. She didn't. I really thought she would change her mind, but she was adamant about it, and it all came crashing down on us while we were here. I had no intention of letting her go to the summit, but she'd decided that I was holding her back." He released a hollow laugh. "She said we'd deal with this when we got back to the States. In the meantime, she was gonna climb the fucking mountain with or without me."

"Why didn't you ever tell me any of this?" Lindsey asked.

David pinned her with a stupefied look. "I honestly thought you knew. Since you never said anything, I assumed you didn't want to talk about it. She blamed it all on your dad, his death, and his selfish regard for his climbing passion. I guess she decided early on that she'd be just like him. I assumed you were the same." The razor-sharp flash in his eyes brought her up short as if he'd cut her.

Was she like her dad?

But Lindsey hadn't checked out of life because of it, hadn't decided that her whole world would be nothing but climbing and the accompanying ambition that went with it.

Alison was the one who had powered through any fear she might have had as if it never existed in the first place. If Lindsey took chances, it was always on her own terms, when the dragon was sleeping. Alison had never been that discerning. Is that what Robbie had truly been like?

Lindsey's head was swimming.

Ty urged her to stand. "Come on, Linds. You should go lie down." She let him guide her to the tent entrance.

David swore under his breath. "Lindsey, I'm so damned sorry. You don't think I miss her? You don't think I feel guilt over her death? I should have let the children thing go, but I was hurt, and I was angry."

Lindsey turned back to him. Should she tell David that Ingerman had possibly seen Alison wandering around on the mountain? That when David had descended, she very likely had still been alive?

For the first time since she had met him, her heart thawed for David Shaw, flooding her with compassion for everything he'd gone through.

She couldn't tell him.

At this point, it would be cruel. Heartless, in fact.

He couldn't have saved Alison. None of them could. Her sister's stubbornness and lack of respect for the dragon had been her undoing.

The truth of her family bloodline chilled Lindsey more thoroughly than the blast of cold K2 air as Ty grabbed her hand and led her along the rocky path toward her tent.

Did ice run through all Coulson veins? Were she and Alison as hard-hearted and selfish as their father had been? Was Alison right to avoid having children, to spare them the same life that she and Lindsey had been forced to deal with, only to embrace it as adults?

She silently railed at Alison. *Why didn't you tell me any of this?*

As she and Ty walked, snow fell in a soft wave over them. A cold, hollow space grew within her. She and Alison had been close, and yet she suddenly felt a wide chasm in the relationship that had always defined her.

What else didn't you tell me? What other wounds and anguish did you bury?

Ty led her to her tent, and she crawled inside.

As she lay on her bed it came, the tidal wave of grief that she'd kept locked up for two long years. The dam broke with a crashing virulence that left her reeling, a swirling whirlpool of tears, heartache, loss, anger, and bewildering sadness.

Ty took her into his arms, talking to her, soothing her, but the words couldn't penetrate the unrecognizable sobs and wails pouring out of her.

Alison was gone.

She was truly gone.

CHAPTER 16

A t 3 a.m., Ty entered the mess tent. David sat alone at the table, while Habibe was busy in the background.

Ty took a seat. "Good morning." He grabbed an empty mug at the center of the table and poured hot coffee from a carafe.

David met his gaze. "Morning. How's Lindsey?"

Ty added extra cream and sugar, seeking the coffee version of a comfort meal. "She had a rough night."

He'd held her while she'd sobbed, feeling helpless in the face of her grief. Eventually, they had both slept, but she'd been restless. When he slipped out of her tent an hour ago, she was finally in a sound sleep, and he hadn't had the heart to wake her. But now he wasn't sure what to do. Should he let her climb today? They had a window of clear weather and needed to go, but if her head wasn't in the right place.... Two years ago, Alison's head hadn't been in the right place.

David sighed. "I really thought she knew about my problems with Alison. Lindsey seems to think I'm a cold-hearted robot, but I still feel a tremendous amount of guilt."

"Have you thought about seeing someone?"

David raised an eyebrow. "You mean a shrink?"

Ty shrugged. "Maybe it would help."

"Isn't that why we climb? To bury our feelings and avoid life issues? That had definitely been a problem between me and Alison."

"I think you're being too hard on yourself."

"I have the reputation of being a hard-ass, and to be honest, I've always kind of liked it."

"Well, according to Packer you're just a pretty boy."

Habibe placed a plate of eggs and potatoes in front of each of them. Ty grabbed a bottle of ketchup and squeezed a generous portion onto his.

"No, that's you," David said. "For some reason Alison made the assumption that I wouldn't really want to settle down, but the truth was that I did. I was ready to be a full-fledged member of society for her."

"Really?"

"I would've done anything for her." David ran a hand across his face. "I shouldn't have let her leave the tent."

"If you'd gone with her, you might both be dead now," Ty said quietly.

David's gaze was bleak. "There've been days when I've wished for that."

Concern filled Ty. Was David in the right head space to climb?

"Look, Ty. I'm not trying to drag you down. I'm good now. I can do this. And I wouldn't have brought any of this up if Lindsey hadn't said something last night."

"Maybe it helps to talk about it. We're all going up there together." Ty flicked his chin in the direction of K2. "We're gonna need each other."

"You don't have to worry about me." David narrowed his eyes. "But you *are* worried about Lindsey."

Ty couldn't finish his breakfast and pushed it away. "Do I bench her?"

David surprised him by laughing, lightening the somber mood that had settled around them.

"I know that Lindsey and I have never been great chums," David said, "but she's a helluva climber. She and Alison definitely inherited a genetic gift from their dad. If you're gonna be with her, then don't ever underestimate the Coulson determination. Learn from my mistakes. You have no say in whether she climbs or not, and you're a fool if you ever thought you did."

Outside the tent, the voices of Packer and Ditch signaled their imminent arrival.

"Thanks for the advice."

A stark agony revealed itself in David's eyes. "And don't waste one minute you have with her."

LINDSEY AWOKE AND IMMEDIATELY WANTED TO SUCCUMB TO HER grogginess and go back to sleep, but someone was unzipping her tent.

She recognized the shadowy outline. Galloway.

Reaching for him, she said, "I didn't hear you leave."

"It's my superpower." He secured the entrance and then reclined beside her, pulling her into his arms. "I'm as quiet as a church mouse."

She buried her face against his neck, inhaling the familiar scent of him, her nose warming his cold skin. "I'm sorry about last night."

"Don't be." He kissed the top of her head.

"What time is it?"

"Three-thirty."

"Since it's still dark out, I'm guessing it's not three-thirty in the afternoon."

"Did you get some rest?"

She nodded. "Where were you?"

"Getting things together. We're gonna head up."

"Really?"

"The weather broke. We can't delay."

She paused, then said, "Are you angry with me?"

"About what?"

"About last night. About me talking to Ingerman."

"No, of course not." He rubbed a thumb along her cheek. "But I'm concerned about you."

"You don't think I should climb," she said flatly, rolling onto her back and breaking the contact with him.

He rose onto an elbow. "Linds, I can't tell you what to do. Look, if it's any consolation, I just said the same thing to David."

"And what did he say?"

"He's climbing."

She stared up at the ceiling of her tent. "What do the others think?"

The silence stretched before he finally said, "They're worried—not about your climbing skills—but about you."

"I'm not a fragile snowflake," she said quietly.

"No. You're not."

Lindsey lay in silence, then glanced at Ty and asked, "What do you think?"

She didn't just want to know his thoughts about the climb—she wanted to know what he thought about her, about them, because his strong presence now occupied every empty space inside her that had been revealed during the night.

"I think you're in pain and I'm sorry for that, but you're a good climber, and good climbers can get past setbacks. And you've never struck me as someone who asks for permission to do anything."

"Are you trying to butter me up so you can get in my sleeping bag?" she asked, trying to ease the tension between them.

He leaned close. "Is it working?"

"Maybe."

He kissed her, but it was sweet and chaste, nothing like the heat from the other night. She wanted more but knew they didn't have time.

He lifted the edge of her sleeping bag and pretended to peek at her. "Just checking."

"For what?"

"In case you were naked."

His mouth found hers again, and this time the kiss was filled with fire and need and hunger. With his breath heating the chilled air around her mouth, he said, "If you keep kissing me like that, we'll never get out of here."

"You're an impossible distraction." A perfect distraction.

"That's what all the girls say."

Reluctantly, she sat up, and gave him one more quick kiss. "I'll be along in a few minutes," she said.

He moved to leave. "Time to climb this mountain, Coulson."

"Yes, sir."

Without further discussion, he left her tent.

Lindsey turned on the lamp and began organizing her gear. Her pack was mostly ready—she'd sorted items the day before—but she did a last check. Fifty feet of rope, ice screws, food, extra mittens and batteries and crampons, axes, trekking poles, and a basic first-aid kit that included an anesthetic eyedrop in case of snow-blindness and Dexedrine, a stimulant drug to be used only as a last resort. In a small zippered side-pocket she placed her super- stitions. She usually only carried two—a butterfly necklace her father had given her shortly before his death when she was eight years old, and a tiny brown turtle figurine from her mother. She'd always imagined they spoke of transformation and freedom, but also of patience and boundaries, all traits needed to succeed in the mountains. But she had added one more item before she'd left the U.S.—a laminated photo of her and Alison from atop Manaslu, the final resting place of their dad. Her dreams had been fulfilled with her sister at her side, and for that she would always be grateful. Selfish or not, this was her passion. A passion she had shared with Alison.

She added more layers of clothing, brushed her hair and teeth, and checked her gear one last time, attaching her climbing helmet to her pack. Departing her tent, she secured it closed. If all went well, the next time she returned, it would be after reaching the summit. She made her way to the mess tent. Everyone had gathered, even Brynn, along with Juneid and Habibe, who offered her a plate of eggs, which she declined.

"Are you ready?" Packer said to her, his tone challenging, but Lindsey was glad he broke the ice.

"Yes. You can count on me."

Brynn reached out and touched her arm, the gesture a silent sign of support.

David flicked a glance at her, and Lindsey acknowledged him with a nod. They didn't speak, and maybe it was best.

Ty moved past her and gave her shoulder a squeeze.

Ditch handed her a granola bar. "Eat something."

She took the food, then unwrapped the bar and ate. Habibe handed her a steaming cup of coffee, and while the others finished checking and buckling their packs, she downed half of it.

"Let's get this party started," Packer exclaimed. "I'm ready to kick some serious K2 ass."

Anticipation began to march a steady beat in her chest, and a smile tugged at her lips.

"I saw that," Packer said, pointing at her. "As long as you're smiling, you're gonna be all right."

"Thanks." And she meant it.

"Now, everyone out of my way, goddammit." Packer pushed out of the tent. "I call shotgun."

Lindsey let the men on her team depart, then she set the mug of coffee on the table. She looked at Brynn, Juneid, and Habibe.

"*Allah Haafiz,*" Habibe said with a nod. *May Allah protect you.*

Brynn smiled. "Good luck."

"Godspeed," Juneid added.

Lindsey squared her shoulders. "See you on the other side."

As Lindsey trailed behind the men, light from each man's headlamp bobbing in the cold stillness, a dark shadow caught her eye.

A gorak landed nearby, watching.

Charon.

Lindsey followed him out of the corner of her eye, since looking directly would shine her headlamp upon him and likely scare him off.

In a place of cold stark beauty, Charon represented death but also a pulsating life force. Perhaps that was why he frequently visited—he wanted to be near other living creatures. It was only natural to seek warmth when the world appeared to be a scary, formidable place.

As she moved away and soon lost sight of him, she set her sights on the climb to come. The goal was to push all the way to Camp Three today. The following day would be spent climbing to 26,000 feet to establish Camp Four, then in the early morning the day after they would set out for the summit. Today was July 25th; if all went well, in 48 hours they would be standing atop K2.

CHAPTER 17

Bobbing lights ahead of and behind them alerted Lindsey that other teams had already begun to move out as well—the Germans, the Italians, and the other American team would be accompanying them on the Abruzzi route. The Poles would converge at Camp Four via the Cesen route, making it possible that a large crowd could attempt the summit at the same time. It would be a veritable party up there.

The next two hours were spent in knee-deep snow and sludgy ice, Lindsey's boot occasionally breaking through snow bridges into thigh-deep pools of blue ice water. As they came to a small ice fall, they all roped together, David leading, then Packer, Lindsey, Ty and Ditch. The sky began to lighten and by the time they reached Camp One, sunlight bathed them. They stopped for a brief rest.

Lindsey smiled when Ty produced flat bread coated with peanut butter and offered half to her.

Beck, Artie, JJ, and Fiske caught up to them.

Ty rose to greet the men, but Lindsey remained sitting on a chunk of ice, watching over the stove she'd fired up to melt snow. David moved to sit beside her.

"There isn't a day that goes by that I don't regret letting Alison leave the tent," he said quietly.

Shadows lined his face, and sadness lingered in his eyes. David wasn't a man prone to elaborate displays of emotion—that much Alison had shared with her.

Lindsey fiddled with the pot on her burner. "I'm sorry for my outburst last night."

"I believed I had time with her, that despite our disagreement we could get through it once we'd climbed this mountain and could have a serious talk about where we were going."

Lindsey looked at him, sensing a shift in his tone. "But you knew it was over?"

"I think I did," he murmured. "The night we fought, a very small part of me had a feeling we were done. I didn't want it, but sometimes you know. I wish I'd had the chance to talk to her, to tell her that no matter what, I didn't regret anything. If the last two years without her has taught me anything, it's that I'm not angry at her anymore for not wanting the life that I did. I only wish I could've told her that."

His voice caught and he cleared his throat, turning away, but not before Lindsey saw the sheen in his eyes. She grabbed his mitten-covered hand, her fingers nimble in her black glove liners, and squeezed. He returned the gesture.

Then it was over and they each resumed the task of melting snow.

Ty settled beside her as Beck and Fiske dropped their packs nearby and retrieved a stove from the tent they had pitched days before.

"The Germans and the Italians are ahead?" Fiske asked, scooping snow into a pan.

"I think so," Ty replied. "Not sure who exactly."

"Where's Ingerman?" Lindsey asked Beck, ignoring Fiske.

"We think he has pneumonia. Once he regains enough strength, he's heading back to Skardu."

"I'm sorry to hear it."

"That's nothing to take a chance with," David said.

"I know," Beck replied. "It sucks to be sick out here."

Lindsey poured her melted water into Ty's bottle and handed it to him.

"Thanks," he said.

She scooped more snow into the pan and set it atop the stove. Ty was all business with her, giving no indication that they were more than friends. A few times she had to stop herself from touching him, or leaning into him, or standing too close. Not that there was any big reason to keep it a secret. Still, she was tempted to kiss Galloway in full view of Fiske if only to get the jerk off her case.

"Ty, you still planning to go to the South Pole?" Beck asked.

"Maybe. It depends on my schedule." He drank from his water bottle, flinching from the hot liquid. "You wanna go?"

"I'm interested. Let me know when/if you settle on a date. Maybe you should come too, Lindsey."

"Why's that?" she asked.

"It's the last great frontier. A real feather in any explorer's cap."

"I thought space was the last frontier," Packer said from his spot just outside their circle.

Beck ripped open the wrapper on a candy bar. "We're nearly in space on this mountain."

Packer laughed. "That's for damned sure."

Fiske took a bite of a power bar. "Mountains are more difficult," he said around the food in his mouth. "The South Pole is just dragging a sled for miles."

"It's all about the mind, Fiske." Beck broke off a piece of chocolate and popped it in his mouth. "Seeing if you have the mental capacity to do it."

Was it Lindsey's imagination, or did Beck's voice hold a hint of sarcasm?

If Fiske noticed, he gave no indication, and said, "I think it a waste of time. Climbing has better goals. Will you climb while you are there?"

Ty shook his head. "No. It would be a trek across ice."

Beck's attention shifted to her. "So, what do you think?"

If for no other reason than to irritate Fiske, she answered, "I've always wanted to visit Antarctica."

Ty gave her a sidelong glance, a wicked gleam in his eyes. "Then you should come."

She smiled and looked away before she did a happy jig over the open invitation.

Packer moved to stand beside her and said, "But please, by all that's holy, don't go near any strange creatures and try to study their DNA. We all know what happened in 'The Thing.'"

"Because that was a completely true story," Ditch said in a dry tone.

"Did you know that the dot on an 'i' is called a tittle?" Packer chuckled.

"Do you get whiplash?"

"From what?"

"Your ADD," Ditch said.

Lindsey looked over her shoulder at Packer. "That movie wasn't really that farfetched. The alien functioned like a virus, infecting its host and taking over. Viruses like to jump around, and we humans are ripe for the picking because we like to take a lot of risks. We eat things we probably shouldn't, and we poke around in places where maybe we should stay away."

Packer's eyes widened. "Like here?"

Lindsey smiled. "We do like to push those boundaries. It's evolution, baby."

"All right, Lindsey-baby, you lead, I'll follow."

Lindsey dumped the snow that hadn't yet melted from the pan, shut off the stove, and packed up her gear. When she stood, Fiske angled in front of Packer to move behind her.

"Hey, Norsky. No cut-zies." And on that comment, Packer scrambled behind her, giving her a wink, and muttered for her ears only, "A virus of the human variety."

$\sim$

THE DAY REMAINED CLEAR AND CHILLY, BUT AS THE SUN WARMED THE mountain—warm being a relative term as Ty lost feeling in his exposed cheeks—the rocky face of House's Chimney loosened, raining down chunks on the climbers who had the misfortune to be in the middle or end of the pack. And Ty was one of those, having switched spots with Packer. While he was grateful that Packer had moved quickly to keep Fiske at bay, Ty had decided he would protect Lindsey's back, especially after witnessing the calculating looks in the Norwegian's eyes when he watched her.

So Ty had switched places with Packer, who was leading up ahead. He hoped that some of the rockfall smattering his helmet was bouncing straight onto Fiske.

At Camp Two they again rested for about forty-five minutes. Lindsey opened a packet of tuna and crackers which Ty declined to share—the fishy smell was a bit too much for him—and instead opted for beef jerky, while Packer slurped on a disgusting-looking green concoction.

"What in God's name are you drinking?" Lindsey asked, making a face.

Packer swallowed and smacked his lips. "You want some, don't you?"

Lindsey scrunched her nose. "Ugh. No."

"I have trouble eating up here, so I carry super-power drinks," Packer said.

"Is that what those vendors told you when they gave you a free case?" Ditch asked. "You know they want you to advertise it for them."

"You're right," he exclaimed. "Captain Galloway, come take a photo of me with it. Maybe they'll put me in a commercial."

Ty grabbed his camera and snapped several pictures as Packer acted first coy then serious, finally deciding he should remove his helmet so that everyone would know it was him. Once they were finished, Ty photographed the camp and the team members, snagging several of Lindsey. He didn't want to seem obvious, so he made sure he photographed everyone equally. She gifted him a ghost of a smile and blew a quick, silent kiss his way before anyone noticed.

Cloud cover soon blanketed the mountain and the wind picked up as they pushed to Camp Three. Up and up they went, clipping and unclipping from the fixed ropes, monkeys in winter as they traversed the Black Pyramid. Snow crystals blew shards against any exposed skin, so Ty tugged his balaclava over his face, neck, and ears, and secured his hood over his climbing helmet to block the wind further, as did everyone else. It was slow going and they didn't reach Three until nearly dusk.

Thankfully, their camp was still intact, with the three tents visible amidst the snow swirling in violent gusts around them.

Ty wanted nothing more than to bunk with Lindsey, but that would require too much explaining. As everyone dropped their packs to gain shelter quickly, Ty asked her, "Will you be okay on your own?"

She nodded.

"If you're not, come get me," he added.

Buried beneath her clothing and gear, he couldn't get a read on her, but she gave his shoulder a friendly tap then went to her tent. He watched and waited until she was tucked inside. It would be a long evening with the girl of his dreams a few feet from him yet inaccessible. It was cold as shit, so fooling around would have been out of the question anyway. Still, he craved being with her, whether she was naked or not.

Beck appeared, and Ty caught him before the rest of his team made it into camp.

"What's your setup?" Ty asked.

Beck tugged down his neck gaiter. "Whaddya mean?"

"Lindsey's on her own." He nodded toward one of the tents. "I don't want Fiske getting any ideas."

"I hear you. I'll bunk with the sonovabitch and trip him if he tries to leave. You got any medicine? Maybe we could drug him."

"Don't tempt me. Thanks, I owe you one."

"What've you got to barter?"

"Bags of butter."

Beck laughed loudly. "That's disgusting shit. I'll take two."

"Done."

Ty retrieved the booty and gave it to Beck, then retired to his tent with Shaw to melt snow and try to sleep.

It seemed as if he'd just bedded down when he awoke abruptly.

Was someone yelling?

He sat upright, a voice carrying in the wind that sounded a lot like Elena.

David stirred. "What is it?"

"Something's wrong." He didn't relish leaving the warmth of his sleeping bag and struggling into his climbing suit and boots, but he did it anyway.

David swore from the cold blast of air when Ty opened their tent. In his haste, he didn't bother to secure it. He slipped his headlamp onto his head and turned it on, bracing himself against the wind so not to slip. It was dangerous traipsing around a high camp in the dark.

He went to Lindsey's tent, but it was empty and the entrance was open.

He continued toward the sound of voices. Lindsey was leaving the Italians' tent as Ditch was entering.

"What happened?" Ty asked.

"It's Salvatore." In the glow of his headlamp, her pinched face was hard to miss. "He's not breathing. I started CPR but Ditch has taken over."

Ty reached out to her, offering support, then moved past her to help Ditch. But as soon as he came inside the tent, it was clear that Salvatore Gallo was dead.

～

"THERE IS NOTHING MORE TO BE DONE," FISKE SAID, HIS FACE AN impassive mask. "We keep climbing."

Dawn began a slow creep into the world of darkness, and Lindsey tried to overcome the grogginess of a restless night with Elena in her tent.

Sal had likely died from cerebral edema. Ty had already contacted Brynn on the radio to have her relay the news to Sal's family in Italy. Now, everyone in Camp Three was huddled together to discuss options.

Lindsey swept her gaze from the tents to the gray horizon beyond, the wind having died down and the eerie stillness heightening the strange atmosphere. She had hardly known Sal, but that didn't make his death any less shocking.

"We can bring his body back on descent," Artie said.

Dan Beck and Ditch agreed.

"That is a foolish idea," Fiske rebutted, but everyone ignored him.

"It wasn't supposed to happen like this," Elena wailed, her voice pitched with panic.

Appearing shell-shocked, Fabrizio shifted his stance. "I'm not certain we should continue."

Agitation pushed at Lindsey. She'd questioned Elena during the night. Had Sal shown signs of his condition? Why hadn't they gone back down if he was clearly struggling? But Elena claimed there had been no symptoms; Sal had been fine. He simply went to sleep and never woke up.

But as much as she hated to admit it, Fiske was right. There wasn't anything more to be done, and they'd come too far to abandon their ascent now. Furthermore, it was foolhardy to try and bring Sal's body down. They'd brought down Aldo, but he'd still been alive. Trying to descend with Sal was an unnecessary risk to all of them.

She didn't voice her thoughts. Shoop had remained on Kangchenjunga; Alison was still here on K2. Her father would forever live on Manaslu. The dead remained. It was the hard truth of climbing 8000-meter peaks.

But if Alison's body suddenly appeared somewhere on these slopes, perhaps wedged into a rock, would she try to bring the body down, despite every argument against it?

Ambivalence skittered on the edge of Lindsey's mind.

"We keep going," Ty said quietly. "Fabrizio, you all can climb with us and on the way back down we can discuss options about Sal's body."

"No, we won't hold you up," he replied. "I am not certain what we should do. You should go. We will radio you with our decision."

Lindsey sensed that Elena was likely too upset to climb. The other two climbers—Vincenzo and Bruno—all nodded and agreed with Fabrizio.

"Then we go," Fiske announced.

Without further conversation, everyone dispersed. Lindsey returned to her tent to collect her gear. Ty stopped and kneeled in the entranceway.

"You okay?"

She nodded, filled with shock and sadness. She focused on checking the contents of her pack.

"How do you feel?" he asked. "Any headaches? Nausea?"

"No, I'm good."

"Promise you'll tell me if that changes."

His stony gaze held her eyes, then he wavered and she saw a flash of concern.

"How do *you* feel?" she asked.

"I know the signs. I'm not the strong, silent type. I'll tell you."

"You better. Because sometimes you are the strong, silent type."

He leaned in and gave her a quick, hard kiss. As he pulled away, she grabbed his jacket and brought him back to her. She didn't want to think that it so easily could have been him instead of Sal. Closing her eyes, she let her hunger loose on Galloway's mouth, and he returned the gesture with just as much urgency.

When he finally pulled back, he said, "Should I tell the others to go on without us?"

"It's a thought."

His lips curved into a ghost of smile.

"A rain check, then?" she asked, not wanting to let go of this moment with him.

"As soon as we return to Base Camp."

The warm promise in his eyes filled her with hope, because they all knew they were living on borrowed time.

Within a half hour, they left the spirit of Sal behind, and Lindsey joined the line of climbers as they began the push to Camp Four.

∼

LOSING SAL SEEMED TO LOWER EVERYONE'S SPIRITS, AND THE LACK OF fixed ropes delayed them further. Lindsey planted a bamboo wand about every forty-five feet. It might be the only way to find the trail if they had to descend in a white-out.

The day wore on, first sunny, then cloudy and windy. It was impossible to talk. With so much time to her own thoughts, Lindsey's mind oscillated between two things: Sal and Ty. Death and sex. She had just enough humor to add taxes to the mix.

Moving one foot and then the other, she stopped for a breath, a shallow, unfulfilling endeavor. Then she took another step and struggled to fill her lungs. The air was so thin that it was as if she were trying to breathe through a straw.

Ty was ahead of her, a speck of color moving in a white background, and to distract herself she imagined his lithe, muscular, and very naked body against hers.

She liked the way he moved—exacting and strong—entirely in command of himself. If he truly wanted her to accompany him to the South Pole, she would find a way to go. She didn't want K2 to be the end of her time with him.

She stopped and steadied herself, her thoughts swirling, refusing to stay put. Maybe she needed to stop thinking about Ty and pay attention to where she was.

First things first.

Climb K2.

Then go to the South Pole.

By late afternoon, visibility had deteriorated, and Lindsey's entire world had narrowed to the three feet of barely-discernable steep trail before her.

Their progress had been slow. Not just slow. Turtle slow. Glacial-movement slow.

From her position, Lindsey didn't see Ty until he had descended upon her. He pulled his neck gaiter down just enough to talk.

"This isn't working," he said. "It's too difficult to see. We're heading back to Three."

Lindsey nodded, but disappointment swept over her. She fought the urge to sit down and give up.

Maybe she could grab a short rest.

In fact, a nap sounded really nice.

"C'mon, Linds."

Tyler's loud admonition jolted her out of her stupor. She gave him a nod to indicate she understood.

There were no fixed ropes since this area was nothing more than a giant snowy shoulder. She was roped to her team and she remained between Ty and Ditch during the descent, a slow and laborious task. Beck, JJ, Artie, and Fiske came down with them, following the wands that she had planted.

It was dark when at last they reached Camp Three. Completely spent, Lindsey looked forward to resting with a cup of hot chocolate. She tried not to think about Sal's body, cold and stiff, lying somewhere on the ledge. The other Italians had likely moved him outside so no one would have to bunk with him.

Lindsey's tent was glowing. Someone was inside.

Damn. Her shoulders sagged in defeat. When she unzipped her home at Camp Three, she wasn't surprised to find Elena in residence.

"What are you doing here?" She set her pack down, removed her crampons, then crawled inside and secured the entrance.

"We couldn't decide what to do," Elena said. "The others are here too. It got late, so we must stay here again tonight."

Lindsey invaded the small enclosure—*my tent*, she reminded herself—and removed her mittens and helmet. Elena had scooted aside, dusting snow from her sleeping bag and grabbing her things as Lindsey made little effort to be polite.

"My stove is on," Elena finally said, a huff in her voice.

A glance to the back vestibule confirmed that an open flame was going, a flap open for venting, and immediately Lindsey's mood lowered to a less heated level. The last thing they needed was for the nylon material to catch fire.

"Why are you here?" Lindsey's tone had become more reasonable, which she supposed was a good thing. She waved her hand around to indicate the inside of the tent.

"Sal ...," Elena's voice broke, then she seemed to shake it off. "I could not stay in my tent with him. You were gone. You know I would do the same for you."

Hardly.

"Why did you return?" Elena added.

"It was a whiteout up there, and our progress was too slow. We had to come back."

Lindsey pulled off her liners and rubbed her scalp, enjoying the sensation. "Will you go down tomorrow?"

"We will ascend."

Lindsey stopped itching and looked at Elena. "Are you sure?"

"No, but we have come so far."

Shadows slanted across Elena's face, and a sliver of unwanted compassion tugged at Lindsey. First David, now this. While she could foresee a friendship with Shaw in her future, she all but snarled at the idea that she and Elena might become friends.

Lindsey sighed and said honestly, "I'm really sorry about Sal."

"Thank you." Elena pulled her sleeping bag tighter around her shoulders. "We cannot give up. Sal would not want that."

Lindsey couldn't disagree. But had that very thought been on Alison's mind when she'd stormed away from David and their tent for the summit? Was this the first of many bad decisions Elena was about to make? Should Lindsey talk her out of it?

She had to try.

"Elena, you have to be willing to let it go. Sometimes summits just don't happen. It's not worth your life."

"I know, but we are on K2. It is the biggest prize in mountaineering, even more than Everest. We cannot give up now."

Lindsey understood. The dragon always lay in wait, coiled and desperate, wanting glory. And the beast didn't like to surrender. It did everything to avoid the bitter pill of failure.

Climbing mountains, especially ones like K2, was tackled only by the truly obsessed. Or a special kind of masochist, as her mother had once said during a rare moment of anger after losing her husband.

Lindsey bore no illusions that she was a full-fledged member of this club as much as any of the other climbers here. The dragon had made certain the fire in her blood never died, that she would yearn for this life despite everything she had lost. Her father. Her sister.

But at the end of the day, climbing was filled with the big questions: What are you made of? How much courage do you possess? How far can you keep going when physically and mentally hanging on by your fingernails?

Such trials had become a necessary part of Lindsey's life. Hadn't they?

Elena offered some of her boiling water for hot chocolate, and Lindsey gratefully accepted. She sipped the drink after firing up her own stove to melt more snow for a noodle packet of soup. She would need to continue making water for the next few hours to replenish her water bottles.

The tent unzipped and Lindsey immediately recognized Ty beneath his hood and face mask.

He stopped short when his gaze landed on her houseguest. "Hi, Elena," he said. "I just realized the Italians are here." He crowded inside and zipped the flap shut.

"They're planning to go up tomorrow," Lindsey said, happy to see him now that she was feeling better, indulging a long look at his handsome face and five-o'clock shadow.

Ty's eyes looked extra blue in the dim light of the headlamp still glowing from Lindsey's helmet beside her. She wished they were alone.

"Are you ladies okay?" he asked.

Elena nodded.

"We'll head out at three a.m." His gaze lingered on Lindsey.

"I'll set my watch." She gave him a smile of regret. They couldn't very well kick Elena out of the tent to grab a few moments of privacy.

"All right, I'll see you both in the morning." He turned to leave.

"Oh wait, I almost forgot." He handed Lindsey a packet of cookies. "I thought you might like these."

"Thanks." She took his offering, smashed as it was. "I was trying to figure out dessert for this evening."

He flashed a devilish grin, and Lindsey's heart did a few jumping jacks in her chest.

He left, and Lindsey became aware that Elena had witnessed her mooning over Galloway.

"Is he the one?" Elena asked, tucking herself back into her sleeping bag, her dark hair shooting out of the hat she wore to cover her ears.

"What do you mean?"

"The one you are shacking up with on this trip."

Lindsey wasn't sure how to respond. Elena wasn't a good friend, a girlfriend to confide in about men, so her inclination was not to discuss it. But stuck in the intimacy of a small tent at 24,000 feet on a mountain in a snowstorm made it difficult to avoid the woman.

When Lindsey didn't answer, Elena continued, "I knew someone climbing in the Dolomites a few years ago. A sudden storm came in and trapped many. My friend told me about Tyler Galloway. He said the American rescued three men up high. He is a strong man. A good one. If you don't bunk with him, then I might."

A flash of jealousy burned hot in Lindsey's chest. "I'm shacking up with him," she said clearly and succinctly.

Elena laughed. "Now, was that so hard to admit?"

Lindsey shook her head, trying hard to find something to like about the woman.

"I do not know why we never got along," Elena said. "There are so few women in the mountains. We get all the male attention, but it gets lonely."

There was no point in rehashing the business on Cerro Torre and the accusations Elena had flung at Lindsey and Alison. They were stuck in this tent together; arguing wouldn't make the time pass any faster.

Still, Lindsey nursed the idea of asking David to switch tents with her. That way she could spend the night with Ty. But that would leave David with Elena, and that didn't seem fair.

"You always had Alison," Elena continued. "You never needed any female friends. I was sorry when I heard that she had died. I am sure this must be hard for you."

"Why do you feel the need to attack other women climbers?" So much for letting bygones be bygones.

"What do you mean? I do not do that."

Ignoring her response, Lindsey plowed on. "Can you honestly say you've been on an expedition where you didn't sleep with another climber?"

Elena's face blanched.

Lindsey immediately regretted the harsh words. The past was the past as far as Cerro Torre was concerned, and as for Elena's sex life, it wasn't any of Lindsey's business. Unless, of course, the woman went after Galloway.

"It's no crime to have a boyfriend," Elena said.

"No. Were you and Sal ...."

Elena shook her head. "Just friends." Tears sprang to her eyes. "I know. Hard to believe. He was more like a brother. I cannot believe he is gone. I know I should have done something, I should have seen that he was acting strange. I should have insisted that he go down."

Lindsey remained silent. She had played such mind games when Shoop had died on Kangchenjunga, and she still ruminated about Alison's death, over and over until her head hurt.

"Maybe I have had too many boyfriends," Elena said, tears spilling more freely. "But I am not like you or Alison. You are good climbers. I have heard from many that you both are some of the best." She paused. "I have always worried that I am not good enough."

Is that why Elena attached herself to a male climber at every chance?

"Elena, you don't need a man to get you up a mountain. If your skills aren't where they need to be, then change them. Work harder, pay attention, train better. All you need is a determination to solve your own problems, to find the best route, but the biggest thing is to change the idea in your mind that you're not good enough to be on the mountain."

Elena stared at her, as if she hadn't heard such words before.

Lindsey wanted to add that Elena had likely hijacked her own progress in skills and technical expertise by relying too much on the men she climbed with. But it wasn't Lindsey's job to turn Elena into a world-class mountaineer, nor to give the woman a pep talk.

She needed to stop, anyway, before the messenger was shot. Elena would likely not appreciate the spotlight on her psyche. Lindsey sure as hell didn't.

They filled their water bottles then settled into their sleeping bags for what was certain to be a sleepless night.

CHAPTER 18

Tyler arose at 2 a.m. after his beeping watch woke him from a shallow slumber. He snapped on his headlamp lying nearby, casting eerie shadows on the tent wall.

The howling wind violently flexed the nylon fabric in heaving fits, and Tyler's lips were so cold he could hardly move them. He brought his hands—covered in mittens—to his cheeks and blew in them to warm up his face.

David sat up but said nothing. Talking took too much effort.

Ty pushed back the sleeping bag he had crammed himself into, dislodging a sheet of ice crystals from its surface, and adjusted the fleece hat on his head.

Would they continue to have a weather window? He'd spoken to Brynn last night on the radio, and she'd reported that they should be good for the next two days.

They really needed to get to Camp Four.

Was it already the third day of them being this high?

David unzipped the tent door and a blast of arctic air slammed into Ty. While David scooped hard, crunchy snow into a pan, Ty burrowed his face into his sleeping bag to stay warm. A quick glance outside revealed a clear sky of twinkling stars. A good sign.

But damn, it was freaking cold.

They huddled back in their tent.

When David urinated into a designated skull-and-cross pee bottle, Ty looked away, trying to give him some semblance of privacy. Although when it was Ty's turn, he really didn't care if David looked or not. They were living like frat boys, sporting what felt like monstrous hangovers from oxygen deprivation, but without the benefit of partying and hot girls.

Except there was one captivating girl in the vicinity.

He would care even less about his appearance if Lindsey weren't here. Such were the pros and cons of having women on the team, but he hardly regretted bringing her.

He'd had one night with her, and that was enough to make him question his bachelorhood. Lindsey Coulson wasn't a drive-by.

After some time, David announced in a low monotone, "Water's ready."

Ty grabbed a baggy filled with oatmeal, powdered milk, and protein powder from his pack and added it. He also broke off a piece of frozen butter and popped it into the gloppy concoction. Once cooked, he and David ate it directly from the pot, although with no appetite and a tinge of nausea, Ty found it a chore and had to force it down.

"This stuff is as awful as what one of my foster moms used to make," David said.

"How many homes did you live in?"

"Five or six, I think. Enough to know not to get too attached."

"Are you still in contact with any of them?"

David nodded. "The last one. The husband and wife's kids were grown and gone, so they took the strays no one else wanted. I was pretty shut down but determined to make my way in the world, so I wasn't a troublemaker. As long as I kept my head down, did my chores and homework, they didn't hassle me. The guy was the one who turned me onto climbing. And it changed my life."

"And look at you now." Ty glanced around their lodging. "Living the glamorous life. We must be nuts to do this."

David laughed, a rarity, and Ty was glad to see it.

"It's not for everyone, that's for sure."

Ty sighed. "I really want a cup of coffee. And not the stuff at Base Camp, although Habibe doesn't do a bad job, but a steaming cup that doesn't need cream or sugar because it's so good all on its own, made from fresh grinds and purified water."

"Stop. Now you're just being cruel."

They sat in silence, Ty imagining the perfect cup of joe, and it appeared David's thoughts were the same if the moonstruck look on his face was any indication.

"Is there a woman?" Ty asked.

"What do you mean?"

"It's been two years since you lost Alison. Is there anyone in your life?"

David handed the oatmeal to Ty. "No. Not like that."

Ty scraped the remainder of the food from the metal container and finished it off. "I get it. But at some point, you've got to move on. Maybe coming here was good for you. Maybe for Lindsey, too. Hell, I'm starting to sound like a psychologist."

David opened the tent and broke more hard snow with his ice axe. He put it into the pan and set it back on the stove, closing the tent flap again. "If you were, you'd have a field day dealing with the slick egos of mountain climbers. You could make a fortune hanging out a shingle at Base Camp. But the truth is, there aren't many women out there like a Coulson." David leveled his gaze at Ty. "But I think you've figured that out for yourself."

"Now who's a shrink?"

∿

Suited up for climbing, Lindsey crawled out of her tent and gasped from the shock of the cold air as it hit her face, but thankfully the wind had died down.

She swung her headlamp back to the entrance. "See you at Camp Four," she said to Elena, who was nowhere near ready to go up or down the mountain.

And with hope we won't have to share a tent again.

Ty and David stood nearby at the ready, the glow of their head-lamps illuminating them, so she gave a wave and Ty returned the gesture.

As she slung her pack around her shoulders, Lindsey took in the valley below. A full moon had risen, bathing the land in a soft glow and reflecting off the endless array of snow-capped peaks.

The curvature of the earth was visible.

Incredible.

Awe-inspiring.

And peaceful.

A greater purpose filled her, despite the obvious insignificance of her presence on K2. Perhaps there was no outward value in scaling mountains, but the interior change she experienced from her accomplishments was monumental.

Two climbers approached. Ditch and Packer.

"We're so damned lucky," Packer said, hidden beneath his coat and helmet and hood and goggles.

Lindsey nodded, since her face was also bundled behind fabric to stay warm.

"It sure beats the office," Ditch said.

"It's an office with a view," Packer said. "You ready for the bigtime, Lindsey?"

"You know it."

Packer moved past her. "Last one up buys the beer."

THROUGH THE THREE HOURS OF DARKNESS AND THEN FINALLY DAYLIGHT, Ty moved upward. It was slow-going through deep snow, so each member of the team took turns breaking trail.

Avalanche hovered in Ty's mind. If the day stayed clear, and they were in these conditions by afternoon, the sun hitting the slopes could loosen it. It didn't help that occasionally he could feel the slope settling beneath him. His heartrate accelerated each time he felt a shift, wondering if the entire slab would give way. He thought to stop and check for avalanche conditions, but the truth was, they had no alternative but to cross the area as quickly as they could.

But speed was difficult. The heavy snow slowed their progress, and the thin air drained their energy. The had entered the death zone, the area above 24,000 feet, where the body was getting so little oxygen that it was in the process of deteriorating. With every second that passed, they were dying. Without question, they needed to spend as little time as possible at this altitude.

When they stopped briefly for a lunch break, all Ty could get down was an energy gel packet. He thought it was strawberry-banana but couldn't tell. Along with the others, he forced himself to drink copious amounts of water, but not so much that he would have to urinate anytime soon. Packer sucked down two gel packets and a candy bar.

"Don't stuff yourself," Ditch said.

"I've hit puberty," Packer answered. "I need the calories."

Lindsey nibbled on an energy bar, while David and Ditch didn't eat at all, just drinking from their thermoses.

Ditch, Packer, and David began to head up—all roped together—while Ty stayed back with Lindsey. As they prepared to continue, Beck came upon them.

"You want to rope with us?" Ty asked.

Beck simply nodded, not bothering to expend the effort to speak. Ty tied onto Beck who tied onto Lindsey.

Slogging through the snow, Ty was grateful they followed the others, since it offered a somewhat clear path, although he was still knee-deep, and sometimes waist-deep, on the pathway. The cloud cover dispersed, and blessed sunshine bathed them in a sliver of warmth that lifted his spirits.

He used a breathing technique he knew to be beneficial at such high altitudes—pursing his lips, he inhaled deeply, then exhaled forcefully as if he were blowing up a balloon. A doctor had told him once that it improved gas exchange in the lungs, as well as preventing fluid buildup. Ty also climbed with a stiff-looking gait that helped prevent too much strain on the calf and thigh muscles, which left unchecked could progress to uncontrollable twitching.

A glance behind him showed Beck working his way slowly up about twenty feet below, and beyond him was Lindsey in her blue climbing suit.

He checked his altimeter—*24,900 feet.*

They weren't far from Camp Four.

The snow shifted beneath him.

Abruptly he stopped moving and looked up. Two climbers were descending. The Italians? Maybe Vincenzo and Bruno? How had the two of them gotten ahead? When they had left Camp Three, there had been no sign of them. He had assumed they were still asleep.

The slope settled and moved again.

Shit.

Whoever it was above them, they were triggering this.

Ty started digging vigorously into the snow with his ice axe. He needed to find an anchor. He needed to find ice, so that his axe could get a firm grip. Lindsey and Beck's lives could depend on it.

The slope started to slide.

Shit! Shit! Shit!

He threw himself down and flung both axes against the mountain, praying for them to catch.

A wave of snow rolled over him. He kicked the points of his crampons trying to gain purchase as his axes dragged against the icy slope. He slowed, then suddenly stopped, but the shift in the rope connecting him to Beck and Lindsey told him they hadn't arrested. Holding tight, he bore down, hoping he could hold them.

A low, guttural yell escaped him as the rope jerked taut, knocking the breath from him. He gripped the axe handles so hard that his fingers throbbed.

But he held fast.

He remained in this position, waiting for the rope to go slack, shaking from the cold and the fear coursing through him.

He gasped for breath, for each goddamned breath, his pressure breathing shot to hell.

At least he wasn't buried.

The rope pulled at him. He gritted his teeth and held tight.

Goddammit.

He wouldn't be able to hold on much longer.

Straining, he yelled again, but his hands slipped from the axe handles. As he fell, the leashes connecting them to his harness yanked the axes from their anchors, and he tumbled backwards.

CHAPTER 19

Lindsey was spread like a spider against the mountain, anchored by her axes above her and her crampons below. She had survived the initial avalanche and managed to arrest, but then the rope above her went slack.

Oh no!

Ty and Beck were falling. Clumps of snow rained down, forcing her to tuck her chin so her helmet could protect her head.

She didn't dare move lest she weaken her position.

Please let me hold them. Please. PLEASE.

She sensed more than saw the tumble of one body and then the other, and she braced for impact.

The sharp yank dislodged her with a jolt, and she immediately threw her right axe back into the slope and clenched her leg muscles, forcing her crampons into the ice so she wouldn't slide far.

She stopped.

Okay. She sucked in a breath. *Okay.*

"Lindsey!" It was Beck, somewhere below her.

"Yeah." But her quiet response didn't travel far; she feared raising her voice might blow her right off the mountain.

"Don't move! Ty's in a crevasse!"

She closed her eyes for a second, then yelled, "Are you secure?"

No answer. She waited.

"Okay," Beck said.

She was on a sixty-degree slope, and snow from the avalanche had settled around her. Stepping down just enough to give slack in the rope that connected her to Beck, she carefully turned to sit facing away from the mountain, digging her crampons into the slope to hold her.

Pulling off her pack, she hooked it to a carabiner on her harness so it wouldn't slide away.

"Is Ty okay?" she yelled. "I need a few minutes to set an anchor."

"He's talking."

That's good.

With her ice axe, she dug a T-trench beside her. Beneath the snow was hard ice, and she struggled to get the depth she wanted. When it was as good as it was going to be, she grabbed a sling and attached it to her axe, then placed it into the trench, the sling faced downward toward Ty and the crevasse. With her gloved hand, she packed snow back into the trench to cover the axe as much as possible.

From her pack, she retrieved a mini-traction device, clipped it onto the rope and then onto the sling. Very slowly, she shifted the weight from her to the new anchor, wanting to avoid a shock load which would likely pop the axe right from the mountain.

It held. Thank God.

She attached a prusik and used it to belay herself down to Beck. When she came to him, he'd installed an ice screw and had added Ty's weight to it. With this double-backup now in place, she nodded at Beck, who yelled down to Ty.

"We're set! You can ascend!"

Lindsey watched the slope below, trying to determine where Ty had disappeared. If he couldn't haul himself out, she and Beck would need to rig a pulley system like the one she'd used to rescue Brynn, but it was more difficult considering the angle of the slope and the altitude, which naturally made them weaker.

When Ty's head appeared, she gingerly moved closer to him, carefully checking for any ice bridges that could collapse into another crack in the mountain. Ty crawled out, grunting as he used his ascender to climb the rope, and collapsed onto his back.

Not caring about Beck's presence, Lindsey kissed Galloway, grateful that he was alive.

~

LINDSEY SAT ON A LEDGE THAT SHE HAD HASTILY DUG WITH THE HELP OF Beck. They huddled together beside Ty, a stove between them melting snow, trying to get past the shock of what had just happened.

"I don't understand," she said, beginning to shiver, both from the cold and from nerves. "Who was above?"

"It was Vincenzo and Bruno," Ty said. "They must have left before us this morning."

"Why would they leave Fabrizio and Elena behind?"

Beck shrugged. "Who knows. Maybe they didn't want to wait. Losing Sal has messed with their heads."

"Do you know what happened to them?" she asked, concerned.

Ty rested a hand on her back. With so many layers between them, she could hardly feel it but appreciated the gesture, nonetheless. "Once we regroup, we'll figure it out," he said. "We need to get something hot inside you."

Her teeth were chattering. "I'm sorry. By all accounts, you should be the one we're worried about."

"It was all you, Lindsey," Beck said. "You held us. You set the anchor. We wouldn't be here if it wasn't for you." He grinned. "Let me make you some soup."

She nodded, waiting for the buzz of anxiety to abate. Her heart pounded and her limbs felt like noodles.

Steadying herself, she glanced at the two men. "Well, you two are pretty skinny, so it wasn't too hard."

They both laughed.

"Do you wanna go down?" Ty asked her.

Despite everything, resolve filled her. "No. We should keep going."

Beck's face broke into his signature big grin as he leaned over the stove. "I like her, Ty. If you don't marry her, I think I will."

AS THEY REORIENTED AND PREPARED TO SET OUT, IT DIDN'T TAKE LONG FOR Ty to realize just how far they had fallen.

Too far to make it to Camp Four today.

"We need to backtrack to Three," Ty said. "I lost a bunch of gear."

"Like what?" Lindsey asked.

"My bivy sack and a coil of rope."

"Maybe they fell right into Camp Three," Beck said, his tone equal measures of amusement and sarcasm.

Ty pulled out the radio. "We can only hope, but I'm pretty sure we're off-route." He switched it on. "Brynn? You there? Over."

"Tyler. It's good to hear your voice." Her words crackled.

"Lindsey, Beck, and I had some problems, so we're headed back to Camp Three. Over."

"Copy that. I'll relay your position to the others. Many are at Camp Four—Packer, Ditch, and David; Fabrizio and Elena; the three Germans; and JJ, Artie, and Lindsey's boyfriend, Anders Fiske. Over."

"You're hilarious. How's the weather? Over."

"You're running out of time. You need to summit tomorrow. Over."

Ty gave a resigned nod. "Yeah. Copy that. I'll check in again at eight p.m. Over."

"Be safe, brother dear. Love you. Over and out."

Ty switched off the radio. With no discussion, they descended to Camp Three.

When they arrived, Beck went to his own tent, and if there was any silver lining to the day's events, it was that Ty could finally share accommodations with Lindsey.

As they unloaded their packs and fired up the stove, Bruno and Vincenzo called to them from outside, so Ty unzipped the entrance.

Bruno leaned down, his eyes bloodshot and ice clinging to his dark brows and eyelashes. "We are very sorry for the avalanche."

Ty wasn't feeling very congenial. "Yeah, well, shit happens." He was beginning to think they shouldn't climb below *any* of the Italians.

"Fabrizio and Elena are going for a summit tomorrow," Bruno continued, "but we are done."

"Really?" Lindsey asked. "What about Sal?"

Bruno's sad expression said it all. "We are done," he reiterated.

Sal's body sat ten yards away, but Ty didn't bother to argue with the men. They all knew that Sal wouldn't be leaving. There was no reason to pretend otherwise. It was clear the two Italians had lost their will to continue, and in such a state, the best they could do was concentrate on getting themselves off the mountain.

They said their farewells and Ty went to work preparing ramen noodles, while Lindsey sorted through his pack to determine if anything else was damaged. She removed a stove smashed beyond repair.

"I think there's an extra one around here somewhere," she said.

"Let's try to zip the sleeping bags together."

She chuckled. "You faced death in that crevasse, so naturally you're looking to get in my pants."

"Only if you'll let me."

She worked on the sleeping bags while he finished making their dinner. They ate, and then cocooned themselves together, the shared body warmth welcome. He gathered her against him, enjoying the unexpected time alone.

"Thank you for holding the belay," he said quietly. "I owe you one."

She moved just enough to bring her lips to his. "Don't think I won't collect, Galloway."

It had been a hell of a day, and he didn't want to think any more about what could have happened. He focused his attention on Lindsey's mouth, nibbling and devouring, exploring the taste of her. It had been four days since they'd made love in her tent, and it felt far longer.

They had both removed their climbing suits but still wore thermal layers. He cupped her buttocks with his hands and pressed her closer, his body aching to have her completely naked.

"It's good to know it's all working," she said, referring to the fact that he was rock hard. "Or have you been popping Viagra?"

"No. It's just you."

"We could try."

He sighed against her neck. "I can't believe I'm saying this, but it seems like a bad oxygen choice."

She laughed. "Do you want to strap on our regulators and hook up an O2 tank?"

"That would make things interesting."

"It would be like having sex on Mars."

He tucked her against him, tangling his legs with hers for warmth. "I think we've solved it."

"What's that?"

"How life began. The Martians couldn't keep their hands off each other."

~

THE NOISY CLAMOR OF THE STREETS OF KATHMANDU OVERWHELMED Lindsey. In a daze, she followed behind Alison as they passed vendors selling prayer wheels, puppets, pottery items, expensive singing bowls, vibrant artwork featuring Buddha deities, and colorful pashmina scarves, all while trying to stay clear of the rickshaws whizzing by.

Earlier that day, they had returned from their Manaslu summit, conquering their first 8000-meter peak, a pilgrimage based on the death of their father. It had been six weeks of isolation from the world, and Lindsey wasn't sure if she wanted to cry because the epic endeavor was now over and successful, or because she missed the crushing intimacy of living in a tent, alone, her world and obligations narrowed to basic things like waking, eating, waiting, and sleeping.

Despite Manaslu's reputation as avalanche-central, it was a simple life.

A life her father had loved. Craved. Been addicted to.

She would have stayed in the modest hotel room she and Alison were sharing and slept away the accumulation of bone-deep exhaustion, except for the obsession in locating hot, fresh, and definitely not freeze-dried food.

Shoop, their guide, mentor, and friend, had taken leave of them to head home, but Alison said she wanted time to explore the capital of Nepal. And where Alison went, Lindsey followed.

Oddly enough, Manaslu winked in the distance. Not many Himalayan peaks could be seen from the hustle and bustle of Kathmandu, and certainly not the prize of them all—Mount Everest. Lindsey tugged on her sister's arm, bringing her to a halt, pointing at the object of their accomplishment. The one mountain that would forever haunt the Coulson legacy.

"Hey, Dad," Alison said, an ethereal smile on a face that looked remarkably good after the rigors of high-altitude climbing for weeks.

A glance in the mirror before they had left the hotel told Lindsey that shedding twenty pounds during the expedition hadn't done her any favors—dark circles shadowed her eyes and the gaunt protrusion of her cheeks made her appear that death was waiting just around the corner for her.

Alison resumed her march and Lindsey struggled to keep up as her sister cut into a cafe. After greetings of *namaste* they were seated and ordered quickly.

Once they had their drinks—two cold glasses of a local Nepal lager—Alison raised her glass and they toasted.

"We did it," Alison said. "What next?"

Lindsey savored the beer. "Home. Rest. And getting back into the routine of my research."

"But we need to strike while we're hot. I was thinking that we could pop over to Cho Oyu."

Nearly choking on her drink, she set the glass down. "Now?"

Alison gave an excited nod.

"You're crazy," Lindsey said. "And I'm completely wiped. I just wanna go home. I wanna see Mom. And how would you pay for it?"

Alison drummed her fingers on the table, her green eyes, so light as to be almost gray, sparkling with intensity. "Are you sure you don't want to try? I could scrape together the money. We're already acclimated. We could speed climb it."

A server arrived with their meal, the traditional Nepali staple of *daal bhat*. Lindsey inhaled the tangy aroma of garlic, ginger, and coriander wafting from the lentils, and her stomach grumbled in anticipation. She started spooning the mixture over the accompanying white rice.

"I think we should become professional climbers," Alison said. "We could get sponsorship."

Lindsey's only focus was eating and washing back the simple cuisine with intermittent slugs of her beer. It was quite possibly the best meal she had ever had.

Finally, she nodded. "All right, we can try to up our game, but let's plan for next year." Before Alison cut her off, she quickly added, "I'm not like you. Manaslu drained my batteries. I need time to recharge."

"Fine." Alison made fast work of her food. "I'll start planning as soon as we get back to the States. Next year, we should do the double-knockout of Everest and Lhotse."

The beer loosened Lindsey's melancholy, and she began to catch some of Alison's fervor. The dragon was now reclining and stretching like a contented cat, purring to its master, *Keep climbing.* Lhotse was Everest's twin sister. Scaling both in one season was very doable.

Lindsey awoke to howling wind, reminding her where she was: K2. A layer of ice crystals coated the sleeping bag and the stark cold air froze her exposed face. Ty dozed beside her. She turned to him and burrowed close, relieved that she wasn't alone.

Later, she dragged her eyes open a second time as Ty moved about. "Good morning," he said. "Sleep good?"

"I wish," she mumbled.

Ty fired up the stove and began the twenty-minute process of melting snow into water.

She sat up. "When this is over, can we go to Tahiti? Would you teach me to surf?" She had decided during her restless tossing after her dream of Alison that living in a bungalow with Galloway and wearing hardly any clothing would be the perfect antidote after the hell of K2.

"Sick of climbing already? But we're having such a good time." But he gave a nod. "I'd love to teach you to surf. It's a date."

"That's right. We've never had a real date."

"I don't make noodles for just any girl."

"So, you're saying this trip is one long extended date?"

"It was my plan all along, you know, to lure you into the Karakoram so we could be alone, and I could woo you."

He brought his lips to hers and lingered, then returned to tending the stove. He prepared oatmeal and a full bag of butter for their breakfast. When he made tea, she found a piece of biscotti in her pack and offered him half. They dunked it into the shared lukewarm beverage. Despite the fancy breakfast, the meal was tasteless, and Lindsey ate more out of habit than hunger.

They dressed, packed up, and left the tent. Amidst the blowing wind and swirling fog, they dismantled their shelter and tied it onto Ty's pack. Beck joined them and soon they were ready to begin their upward climb.

By mid-afternoon, with clouds blanketing the mountain, they reached Camp Four at 25,500 feet. Several tents greeted them, yellow and red dots contrasting starkly against the white terrain.

But Galloway didn't stop and instead moved farther up the ridge. Beck left them to find his own team and all Lindsey could do was continue to follow Ty. When she spied another set of tents just below where the snow slope steepened, she understood why their team had pitched camp in a different spot. It would lessen their time to reach the summit, buying them possibly an hour or more. At this altitude, it could mean the difference between descending in daylight or darkness.

Ditch greeted them. "Glad you made it. We were worried when we heard what happened." He hugged Ty and then Lindsey.

"We decided to take the scenic route," Ty said. "Anybody on the summit today?"

Ditch nodded. "The Poles topped out. They're on their way down now." He paused. "David went with them."

The news irritated Lindsey, but she could hardly blame Shaw. She and Ty were a day late getting to Camp Four. Still, he had accused her of being a maverick and then had pulled a stunt like that.

"Each man to himself," Ty said. "That's what I'd proposed in the beginning."

"True," Ditch replied. "But it's regretful that he won't be here to help us break trail tomorrow."

"Is that why you stayed back?" Lindsey asked, surprised.

"I did want to wait for you both. But Packer has been struggling with a cough."

His loyalty warmed Lindsey's heart, but would she have done the same? They were so close to the summit that she could all but sniff it. Summit fever. It was a real thing.

She needed to forgive David for wanting this mountain done once and for all.

"It's going to be crowded tomorrow," Ditch continued. "The Germans, Beck and his team, and Elena and Fabrizio are all in position."

"Is that why you left the neighborhood?" Ty asked, indicating the tents a hundred yards down on the Shoulder.

"It'll give us a head start."

Ditch helped Ty and Lindsey dig out a platform for Lindsey's tent. Once it was up and her stuff inside, she went to see Packer while Ditch and Ty discussed options for tomorrow's summit bid.

She peeked inside the tent Packer was sharing with Ditch. "Hey, how are you doing?"

Sitting upright with a fleece hat pulled low on his forehead, he sipped liquid from a pan. "You're late."

"It's good to see you too."

"Dammit, woman. You've got to stop following me." His raspy voice vibrated like a rattlesnake.

"You didn't think you could get away from me so easily, did you?" she chided, her voice soft.

A coughing fit wracked him, and Lindsey moved to sit beside him. "That sounds rough," she said gently.

He shook his head. "Just a little tickle. I plan to get that summit tomorrow. Try and keep up, sweetheart."

Despite her worry, she smiled. "Are you sleeping on O2?"

He sighed. She knew the answer was no. She also knew that he ought to, if he hoped to maintain any strength to climb tomorrow. In truth, he should go down, but she doubted he would consider that option.

"You should," she said quietly.

"Quit henpecking me. You should save it for Galloway. If a guy's getting sex then he deserves it."

So much for her and Ty keeping their relationship a secret. She looked at Packer expectantly.

He laughed. "We all knew it was coming. It was a matter of time. Not that he wasn't looking at you like half the guys in camp, but he was the only one you looked at that way."

"You're going to make me blush."

"Nah. He's the good sort, and so are you. I expect to be invited to the wedding."

"You're very confident in a mountain romance."

He lay down, pulling his sleeping bag around him. "I'm a hopeless romantic."

Her lips curled into a smile. "Yes, you are. Get some rest. Maybe I'll bring you some dinner later."

"I'll take a philly cheesesteak and a side of fries with lots of ketchup." He closed his eyes.

∽

TY CRAWLED INTO LINDSEY'S TENT. HER HEADLAMP LIT THE ENCLOSURE while the wind roared outside like a jet engine.

"How do you feel?" Ty asked.

With her climbing suit pushed to her waist, she hovered over her stove like a mother crooning to her baby. "Sore. You?"

"Ready to go."

She smirked at his innuendo, her brown eyes sparkling. A hat hugged her head and blond hair fanned her shoulders. She looked more bewitching than she had a right to, considering everything they'd been through the past few days.

Darkness had descended. He zipped the tent closed, pretending that it offered them protection from the wrath of K2. It was an illusion, he knew, but the mind needed such comforts to keep from going mad.

"We can go for it," she said, raising an eyebrow in his direction. "Right here, right now. I'll even let you keep your climbing suit on." She dropped a tea bag into the semi-boiling water.

He pulled off his mittens, then rubbed his hands together and blew on them. "Very tempting, Coulson."

"But ...."

"To be honest, it seems like too much work. Said no man, ever. Except Tyler Galloway on K2. Twice."

"I wonder if I should take it personally."

"Are you kidding? You're the hottest girl I've ever shagged."

Lindsey's face scrunched in disgust. She poured the tea into a cup and handed it to him. "If you want me to cook you a gourmet meal of split pea soup, you're gonna have to sweet-talk me better than that." Then she added, "Ditch mentioned something about a job."

Ditch was chatting about Ty's life choices with Lindsey? So much for his cautionary lecture about romances on expedition.

He smiled. "Yeah. I've been offered editor-in-chief at Mountaineer Magazine."

"Congratulations. Will you take it?"

He sipped the hot beverage, enjoying the warmth. "Maybe. Probably. I don't know. I'm guessing you work regular hours in the lab. Do you think I can handle the monotony?"

She added more snow chunks from a baggy she had stashed beside her. "I hate to break it to you but climbing the same mountain over and over for weeks on end is very monotonous. So, yes, you can do it."

"Thanks for the pep talk." He shared the tea with her.

"You're the Lost Boy who found his way," she said, taking the cup. "An unknown path is hardly a deterrent for you."

"All roads lead somewhere, don't they?"

She frowned. "But you were a child. Don't you think you were lucky?"

"I don't believe in luck."

"How can you say that? In the mountains, anything can happen."

Ty rummaged around in his pack until he found a gray-colored pullover and pulled it out. "I believe in cause and effect." He unzipped his climbing suit and freed his arms from the sleeves, then slipped the garment over his head, adding a layer of warmth. "And back then, my reptile brain took over."

"Survival instincts?"

"Don't you believe in them?"

Lindsey handed the tea back to him. "There was something Ingerman told me that day I argued with David in the mess tent."

When she didn't continue, Ty prompted her. "What's that?"

"As David and Freddy were descending, he saw a figure in the scope above the Bottleneck."

Tyler didn't move. "Jesus," he uttered.

"Did he really see her? Maybe it was a mirage. Even he's not sure." She raised her eyes to his. "He never told David. He never told anyone, he said."

"There wasn't anything that could've been done," Tyler said, his tone somber. "You know that, right?"

She nodded. "At first I was angry. If he and Freddy could have found her, then maybe she'd be alive."

"Don't play the blame game, Linds. You know we've all signed up for this. It could happen to any of us."

"Cause and effect?" she asked, arching an eyebrow.

"If you stay in your house your whole life, then naturally the chance of a young death is reduced. If you climb big-ass mountains, you've increased possible outcomes, especially those that involve untimely endings."

"I had no idea that a cold-hearted climber lurked inside you." She checked her slowly melting pot of ice.

"I didn't mean it that way." He waited until she looked at him again. "I sure as hell don't want to lose another Coulson on this mountain."

Her gaze softened. "Duly noted." She scooped the cup from his hand and downed the remainder of the tea. "Have you ever lost someone close to you?"

"Yeah," he replied, resting his arms on bent knees. "When I was seventeen, a couple of guys I hung out with at the University of Washington were later killed in a fall in the Tetons. I hadn't seen them in a while, but it really hit me when I found out."

"I'm sorry." She extended a leg—still covered in her climbing suit —alongside him so that she touched him. "You were in college when you were seventeen?"

"I was. My mother said I was gifted. I've never chosen to disagree with her."

"Cold-hearted and humble. What did you study?"

"Journalism. But climbing and generally goofing around outside was a strong second." He dropped a hand onto her leg and gave a squeeze. "The other friend I lost was during an ascent on Dhaulagiri. That was a tough one. Marcus and I frequently climbed together. An avalanche pulled the fixed ropes and him with it. We never found him."

"Marcus Hammond?"

"Yes."

Lindsey nodded, becoming quiet. "We crossed paths a few times. I didn't know you two were so close. I'm sorry about him too."

She emptied a packet of dry soup into her pot of water, stirring the contents with a spoon.

"Sometimes this thing we do is really fucked," he said.

"Then why do it?"

"If you ask my mother, she'll tell you I was hyperactive and always looking for something to challenge myself. But the simple answer is that I like it. How many people get to see the places we've seen or do the things we've done?"

She shut off the stove to let the food cool before they ate it, which wouldn't take long as the temperature plummeted.

"Tell me a memory of you and Alison," he said, threading his fingers with hers.

"Before Moonlight Buttress, we knew we needed more experience with crack climbing, so we trained hard in the gym then headed to Indian Creek."

Ty nodded with approval. "Some of the best crack climbing in Utah, or anywhere for that matter."

"The best, yes, but also the hardest. Crack climbing isn't intuitive at all, and I struggled the whole time. After a week, I was ready to call it. But Alison was always the taskmaster, and she said we'd do one more—Six Star Crack."

"It's a gorgeous splitter."

"I'm guessing you sent it on your first try."

"I did, but it was challenging. It's easier for you girls, you know."

"Why's that?"

He lifted her hand in his. "Your fingers are smaller. I had a hell of a time jamming my hands in. How'd you do?"

"Everything finally came together. I hit my stride and scrambled all the way to the top. I'm glad that Alison insisted we try one more. She was good about that—pushing past fears, pushing past boundaries. But I always worried that one day she would push too far."

And she had. The unspoken words hung in the air.

Ty pulled her toward him and kissed her. To lighten the mood, he said, "Did I ever tell you about the time I shit my pants on a crag in Zion?"

"You're disgusting."

"You're telling me you never had a bathroom crisis dangling off a rope?"

She nibbled at his lower lip. "Of course, but I'm a lady and would never speak of such things."

"Hello," said a voice in the distance.

They both pulled on their climbing suits and scooted out of the tent.

The Poles appeared—Piotr, Janusz, and Lech—and then David.

"How was it?" Ty asked.

"Cold and windy," David replied. "I'm sure our trail will be blown over by tomorrow. Make sure you start early."

"It took us eighteen hours," Piotr said.

"The summit is magnificent," Janusz said.

"Congratulations." Ty gave each man a fist bump.

"Did you fix any ropes?" Lindsey asked.

"We did through the first part of the Bottleneck," David said, "but stopped because it was taking too long, and we were running out of line."

"We are very tired," Piotr said. "No more chitchat."

As the three Polish men trudged on toward their tents lower on the Shoulder, Lindsey climbed back into her tent.

With David's headlamp shining in Ty's face, he could barely make out Shaw's features, but the shadows revealed a deep fatigue lining his eyes and mouth. "I'm sorry I didn't wait for you all," he said. "But I'd already been high for so long. I wasn't sure how much longer I could remain strong."

"I understand. I'm glad you bagged it. Now go rest. You deserve it."

"I'm getting the feeling that I'm solo in the tent tonight."

"Yeah, I'm bunking with Lindsey."

"I don't blame you. It'll make it easier for me to sleep in." He pushed his headlamp upward so that he could look directly at Ty. "Stay safe up there."

"Always," Ty said. "We'll see you back at Base."

David moved off to find his tent, and Ty returned to Lindsey. They ate the soup straight from the pan, although Ty stopped after a few bites when his stomach started to rebel.

Later, as they settled into their sleeping bags, their boots stuffed at the bottom to keep them as warm as possible, Lindsey asked, "Do you think David found peace at the summit?"

"I hope so."

~

At 11:00 p.m., Ty's watch alarm sounded. Lindsey awoke from an unsatisfying sleep—she felt as if she hadn't slept at all—and slowly tried to get her bearings.

Ty was sitting upright, still encapsulated in his sleeping bag, and she thought she must be in Utah with some handsome climber.

But it was so damned cold.

K2.

Now she remembered. She was on one of the most inhospitable mountains in the world. And today, she would try to reach the summit. Her stomach clenched, a combination of nerves and fear. With well-honed practice, she pushed it aside. Long ago, after that revelatory talk with Alison, Lindsey had learned to wait while the inevitable unease moved through her body. It was only a slight apprehension—a good sign. Anything stronger would take valuable energy to process, and she needed to conserve as much as she could.

Without talking, she and Ty switched on headlamps and began the laborious process of preparing to tackle the mountain. For a while, as the wind flexed and flattened the sides of the tent, Lindsey simply sat trying to untangle her thoughts and clear the cobwebs from her mind.

She needed to eat, but her lack of appetite inspired little enthusiasm for it.

Ty partially unzipped the tent door for ventilation and lit the stove. Cold air funneled inside, and Lindsey buried her face into the edge of her sleeping bag. He had brought in two baggies of ice already, so he emptied one into a pan and set it atop the stove.

Lindsey wriggled her wrist free and looked at her watch—11:30 p.m. By the time they exited the tent it was 1:35 a.m. It had taken that long to eat a bit of granola, take care of bathroom necessities, don their down climbing suits and harnesses, stuff feet into boots and over-boots, pull on balaclavas and hat, helmets, mittens, and finally strap on crampons. Time behaved like the current of a river, flowing so swiftly that it was impossible to grab hold of it, to plan with any certainty how long anything would take.

Everyone carried packs whittled down to necessities for summit day. She filled a bottle with a warm energy drink and stashed it in a pocket against her body to keep it from freezing. She decided to ditch the O2 and breathing apparatus to reduce weight, but left a small camera, a few gel packs for sustenance, a 125-foot thin nylon rope and additional climbing gear. Ty and Ditch both carried radios.

The wind gusted but the sky was clear, with the universe laid bare above them, thousands of stars rolled out like a sparkly carpet. The glow of snow-capped mountains extended across the floor of the earth below them.

They were alone as they left, but some of the tents lower on the Shoulder were glowing, so the other teams—the Americans and Fiske, the Germans, and what was left of the Italian team—were at least awake.

Lindsey considered where she stood. Only a tiny fraction of humans had ever set foot at this exact spot. How many? A hundred? Maybe two hundred?

Lindsey took a breath, struggling to inhale deeply, but it was a shallow effort.

Do the dead still exist, somewhere?

Religion had never offered Lindsey solace. It had always been the wild, remote places that connected her to the idea of a bigger picture, to the ineffable nature of life.

Robbie. Shoop. Alison.

Slowly, Lindsey's anger over losing them thawed ever so slightly.

Maybe one day, it would disappear altogether.

She forgave them for wanting to be in the mountains as much as she did. She forgave them for dying.

"You ready?" Ty pinned her with his headlamp.

She nodded.

Time to climb.

CHAPTER 20

In the darkness, Tyler began the long haul to the summit. He was roped to Lindsey behind him, and Ditch was roped to Packer, farther back. There would be crevasses and this would offer protection, however they decided not to connect all four together. If one fell, the ripple effect could pluck each climber off the slope.

It was slow-going. Ty took a step then stopped to inhale, then another, then another. He began to count to pass the time. The higher he went, the more seconds between each step. He counted to thirteen between the last two steps. The wind blew down on them, and his hands and feet ached from the cold. But if the aching stopped, he needed to worry about frostbite, so he tried to embrace the pain.

As they approached the mouth of the Bottleneck, Ty could just make out the narrow gulley above them under the light of a full moon. Only about one hundred feet across, it was a forty to fifty-degree slope comprised of snow and rock. Above it large ice seracs loomed overhead, presenting a very real menace and a serious concern. Should one break off, the consequences could be dire.

Ty began kicking steps into the firm snow as spindrift coated him with ice crystals. With careful and steady movements, facing into the mountain and using his ice axes and crampons, he and Lindsey did a diagonal crossing.

Near the top of the Bottleneck, the snow conditions worsened. Ty encountered first soft, deep powder, and then a breakable ice crust, and then soft powder again. It took all his concentration to stay focused and alert. He and Lindsey alternated leading, and they settled into this pattern for nearly two hours. Packer and Ditch were too far behind to take a turn breaking trail.

The movement of climbing finally began to create body heat, and Ty became less cold and found a better rhythm with his progress. If all went well, they would summit by this afternoon, maybe sooner. Then they could be back at Camp Four by tonight. If the weather held, they could be at Base Camp by tomorrow night. The thought filled him with purpose and resolve.

At the top of the Bottleneck, just before entering a leftward traverse, which Ty knew to be the most difficult part of the summit route, he and Lindsey stopped to wait for Ditch and Packer. Ty drank water from his thermos and squeezed a chocolate gel pack into his mouth, while Lindsey sipped from her water bottle. Then Ty took out his camera and snapped a few photos, but it was still hazy as dawn approached.

"Packer is struggling," Lindsey finally said.

"I noticed." But he didn't voice aloud what he knew needed to be done, and that was to have Packer turn around.

When Ditch was about thirty yards away, Ty mustered enough energy to yell down to him.

"What's the story?" he asked.

The wind had died, offering an eerie silence.

"Packer's done," Ditch responded.

"I am not." But Packer's reply was weak, his voice barely audible. He slumped where he stood, hanging onto the mountain by his axe.

"Can he go on his own?" Lindsey yelled.

Ditch's reply was succinct. "No."

Ty trusted his mentor's assessment. Packer shouldn't have come up at all, but it was difficult to be so near the summit and throw in the towel. Still, it annoyed Ty that the man's stubbornness would likely cost Ty the summit.

"I'll return with him," Ditch added.

With a certain amount of regret, Ty shook his head. "No. It'll be me."

Lindsey snapped her gaze to him.

He lowered his voice and said to her, "It's my team. My responsibility. You go to the top with Ditch."

"No."

"Yes," he countered. "If I can get him down quickly, then I'll turn around."

Lindsey didn't answer. They both knew that might not be possible. In all likelihood, Ty was giving up the summit.

"We can all go down," Lindsey said. "We can summit tomorrow."

"No. We've got a semi-good weather window." He'd spied lenticular clouds on some of the other surrounding peaks, and that usually meant something was coming. There was a good chance that tomorrow was a no-go. "Don't waste it."

Despite layers of clothing and gear, Lindsey's body language conveyed a distinct ambivalence.

"It's okay, Linds," he said. "I trust Ditch with my life, so I trust him with *your* life. I want you both to have this."

Her nod conveyed reluctance.

"Anchor yourself," he said. "I'm going to unrope and downclimb to Packer."

It took an hour to make the partner switch. Tiny dots of light moved near Camp Four, indicating that the other teams were heading up. If Ty could get Packer back through the Bottleneck, he might be able to rejoin the summit bid with Beck, JJ, and Artie.

"C'mon," Ty said, beginning the descent.

"This mountain is an ass-killer," Packer replied, his throat raspy. "I've decided I hate its guts. And I can't believe you're letting Ditch steal your girlfriend. You're a mensch."

"I've got your back."

"And I've never taken it for granted."

The emotion in the man's voice was apparent, and his gratitude was a balm to the disappointment hanging over Ty. As he looked to the rising sun that crept upward from the horizon over China, he bolstered himself with a phrase his dad often used.

The day isn't over yet.

~

Lindsey didn't like leaving Ty and Packer, but she put it behind her and reoriented her focus to what lay ahead.

She and Ditch came to a fixed rope. This was the 100-foot rope that the Poles had placed yesterday, but it was very loose. It was attached with only two ice screws, one on either end. If one of them fell near the center, they would yo-yo for a bit, possibly pulling one of the anchors.

Ditch stood ahead of her. "I don't like this."

She didn't either. "But it does offer some protection."

"All right. Clip in. But climb like you aren't. A fixed line should never make you complacent."

They hooked themselves to the rope and used it like a handrail. Moving along the traverse proved to be sketchy, and it was all Lindsey could do to make sure she didn't fall. Kicking in the toe of her boots, she struggled to get her crampons to gain any purchase on the crunchy snow that barely covered the steep rocky face.

Finally, as the sun was rising, they passed through the traverse and started up a long diagonal ramp that led to the summit snowfield.

As Lindsey moved to take the lead, Ditch said, "We're about a thousand feet from the summit. Maybe five or six hours to go."

She smiled. "Try and keep up."

"You've been hanging around Packer too long."

For the first time in weeks, optimism filled her. The snowfield wasn't very technical.

The summit of K2 was within reach.

~

Tyler finally arrived at the start of the Bottleneck with Packer, but the route was logjammed with climbers. They would have to wait until it was clear. Earlier they had gotten Brynn on the radio and she'd been able to relay a message through Beck to have David meet Ty at the bottom of the Bottleneck. If all went well, Ty estimated this could happen by 10 a.m.

Two hours later, all the climbers had passed by—Beck, JJ, Artie, and Fiske; the four Germans—Wolfgang, Karl, Frieder, and Volker; and Fabrizio and Elena. Beck confirmed that he'd spoken with David.

Packer could move under his own effort, but it was painstakingly slow as they downclimbed. When they finally met up with David, he was hunched over and gasping for breath.

"I've got him." David held on to Packer, keeping him upright. "Go on," he said to Ty. "Get back up there."

Ty hesitated.

"It's your call, but the clock is ticking," David added.

Packer glanced back at Ty. "Only those who will risk going too far can possibly find out how far one can go."

Ty was impressed that Packer got the words out without succumbing to a coughing attack.

"That sounds a little too deep for you," David said to the shorter man.

Packer gave a phlegm-filled chuckle. "It's T.S. Eliot, you asshole. Sometimes I *do* read. Bag that K2 bitch, Galloway, and don't take no for an answer."

David grunted as he shifted his hold on Packer. "And there's the bastard I know."

Ty looked back up the route he'd just descended. "I'm gonna go." He needed to go as light as possible, so he shed his pack. "You can leave this here. I'll get it on the way down."

He retrieved two full water bottles, spare mittens, a camera, and his headlamp, and stuffed everything into his climbing suit. He looped a fifty-foot rope across his body, then handed his radio to David.

"Take it," Ty said. "You might need it more. Ditch has one, and I'll likely catch Beck and his crew."

David took the radio with a nod. "If I can get Packer to Camp Three, I'm going to move."

"Do what you have to. We'll catch up."

A slight cloud cover was beginning to form. With little fanfare, Ty turned and began climbing back up.

With the other teams having moved through the route, he didn't struggle breaking trail, which helped his speed.

Around noon, he met up with Wolfgang and Karl, who were downclimbing.

Wolfgang removed his oxygen mask. "We are turning around." He spit his words out past a hoarse voice.

Ty didn't ask why.

"Elena and Fabrizio." Wolfgang tilted his head behind him. "They are struggling. We tried to say come down. You should tell them."

"Okay." But Ty had no desire to counsel other climbers. They could do whatever the hell they wanted.

At the top of the traverse he came across the two Italians.

Fabrizio silently acknowledged him. "I am done. I am going down."

Elena looked at Ty. "Can I climb with you?"

Tyler shrugged and moved past her. "Suit yourself."

But she couldn't keep up, and Ty had no patience to slow his pace for her, since his late start could ultimately bite him in the ass.

Leaving her behind, clouds soon began to swirl around him, and his visibility was reduced to several feet in front of and behind him. He nearly tripped over JJ on the summit snowfield, and soon passed him. Then he reached Beck and Artie.

He told them of the two Germans turning back, as well as Fabrizio.

"And Fiske?" Beck asked.

Ty drank from his water bottle, then said, "I haven't seen him."

"Shit." Beck shook his head. "He was with us in the Bottleneck, then we lost him in all the cloud cover."

Ty stowed his bottle into a pocket and zipped it closed. "He must've turned back," he said.

"But you would've seen him," Beck said. "Is there someone behind you?"

"Elena. She's determined, I'll give her that. And so is Fiske. Maybe he passed you?"

Beck laughed. "Jesus, you think? I must be losing it."

"Maybe he has magic fairy dust and flew to the summit," Ty said, unable to keep the sarcasm from his voice. If there was one thing marring his perfect summit day, it was having to share it with that "King of the Mountain" asshat.

Ty glanced toward the summit, currently obscured from their view with the thick fog enveloping them. "Have you seen Lindsey and Ditch?"

"No," Artie answered. "They're probably reaching the summit now."

"You boys ready?" Ty asked.

Beck waved him on. "You lead, we'll follow."

Ty began his final push to the top of K2.

LINDSEY SCANNED THE HORIZON. CLOUDS ENGULFED THE MOUNTAIN below, but above, where she and Ditch inched along, it was clear. Endless blue sky and a strange calm accompanied them as the pinnacle of K2 beckoned.

She was leading, moving slowly but steadily in a rhythm she had been practicing for the past six hours, getting closer to achieving what had seemed impossible for so long.

But didn't the path through the *impossible* hold the key to everything important in life? Passion and purpose? The whole reason for being human?

She took a final step and reached the top. As she sucked in breath after breath, Ditch came beside her.

"Congratulations," he said, checking his watch. "Three-thirty p.m. Not too bad."

Lindsey grinned and gave him a hug, then stepped back to take in the view. A sea of white fluffy clouds blanketed the earth, an array of mountain peaks rising to the heavens.

Nanga Parbat, the "naked mountain" and the ninth-highest in the world, drew her eye in the distance. In her euphoric state, she vowed to climb it one day. Closer were the tips of Broad Peak and Gasherbrum II, keepers of the entrance to K2. When trekking in, it wasn't until reaching the crossroad of two mighty glaciers at a place called Concordia that these two 8000'ers signaled the sharp left turn that revealed the mistress they guarded—K2 herself, resplendent in all her savage glory.

The clouds hid everything else, from the Kunlun Mountains—one of the longest mountain chains in Asia—to the view into China, but Lindsey could hardly be disappointed. She and Ditch shared their success in a hallowed silence.

Lindsey felt a connection to something higher, to nature at its extreme, to the very universe itself. She had stood atop other mountains but never had she before experienced such a divine awareness.

"I wish you were here, Al."

Shifting out of her reverie, there were housekeeping chores to attend to. She retrieved her camera, and she and Ditch took turns photographing each other, and then snapped a photo together.

Ditch pulled out the radio and tried to reach Ty.

"This isn't Ty, it's David. He left his radio with me when he headed up this morning, over."

"Copy that," Ditch said. "Lindsey and I are at the summit."

"Congratulations."

"How's Packer?"

"We're still at Four. I gave him some dex and bought us some time, but I need your help in getting him down. Over."

"We copy. See you later."

"Safe journey. David out."

Ditch shut off the radio. He didn't say it, but if Packer needed dexamethasone, a type of steroid, then his cough had most likely turned into pulmonary edema. He needed to descend as soon as possible.

"Time to go," she said.

"I agree."

Where was Ty? The cloud cover that had seemed so serene and peaceful now gave her pause. Something was brewing below them.

They hastily hydrated, and Lindsey turned away when Ditch needed to perform a toilet function, but they were soon putting the summit in their rearview mirror. They almost immediately ran into Frieder and Volker, filling Lindsey with disappointment that it wasn't Ty.

With little discussion, they passed the two men, but soon another climber emerged from the clouds.

Ty.

She would have run to him if she could have.

Ditch reached him first, but it took several more minutes before Lindsey caught up.

"How did you move so fast?" she asked.

"Tyler's a gifted climber," Ditch said.

"I tried my damnedest to catch you," Tyler said. "I'm proud of you, Linds."

She settled for the fist bump he offered, but what she really wanted was a kiss. Giving a nod toward Ditch, she said, "Thanks for loaning me your secret weapon."

"I won't share Ditch with just anyone." Ty grinned, and she welcomed the shot of warmth it sent to her very cold toes.

"Enough talk," Ditch cut in. "Get your ass up there, and then get back down. David needs help with Packer."

"Edema?" Ty asked, concern in his voice.

Ditch nodded.

"I'll catch you at the Bottleneck," Ty said, and left them.

Reluctantly, Lindsey continued her descent, and she and Ditch were soon plunged into the cloud cover where thick heavy snowflakes greeted them.

Hurry, Ty.
This weather was shit.

Ty hadn't expected to reach the summit of K2 alone, but as he stood on the second highest point on earth, he marveled that he had it all to himself. With no radio, he couldn't let Brynn know that he was okay, but with hope Ditch would relay the news to her.

He was gratified that most of his team had succeeded. This vocation—this crazy hobby—was always a gamble, no matter how well the climbers prepared.

And while he would have liked nothing more than to be here with Ditch and Lindsey, he was content that he had achieved his goal.

He sat down to enjoy the spoils of his victory—the view. It was hard to believe, but he was at the same altitude that most commercial airlines flew.

He hoped his dad would be proud. The larger-than-life Big Jim Galloway, who plowed through life always with a purpose, was ever a source of inspiration. And frustration. It was tough growing up in the shadow of such a man. Is that why Tyler couldn't commit to a desk job? Would it stifle his drive to live outside-the-box? Because God knew that in order to keep up with his old man, he needed to ingest rocket fuel and plenty of it.

How did his mom put up with living with that kind of high-intensity lifestyle?

She'd been a climber in her younger days, but although she had aspired to Everest and other 8,000-meter peaks, she had never fulfilled that dream. She'd always said that having her children was her best adventure, and she'd been happy to give up her vagabond ways to raise Alec, Ty, and Brynn.

Children. The thought had never much crossed Ty's mind. Until now.

As he stood atop this remote earth outpost, a new drive began to emerge, and it had everything to do with Lindsey.

Maybe coming here had never been about the mountain.

The urge to catch up to Lindsey and Ditch filled him, as well as wanting to get Packer safely back to Base Camp. Without looking back, he left the summit.

He had K2 in the bag, but in descending he was going toward something more important than conquering an unrelenting and harsh peak.

Fate? Maybe.

But living on rocket fuel was unsustainable, and it had taken a stubborn and brooding blond-haired woman to make him see it.

～

LINDSEY TRUDGED DOWN THE SUMMIT SNOWFIELD, MANAGING TO FOLLOW what remained of the trail. They'd passed Beck, Artie, and JJ, and now a dark form materialized.

Elena.

She wasn't moving, so Lindsey gave her a nudge, and the woman opened her eyes. Surprisingly, she had been asleep.

"Elena, get up. We're going down."

She didn't acknowledge Lindsey but stared at nothing.

When Ditch reached them, Lindsey said, "She's in bad shape."

"What a fucking surprise," he said, his voice dripping with contempt, shocking Lindsey with its fervor. The older man had been nothing but cool, calm, and collected during the last four weeks.

But she agreed with him. Dragging Elena off the mountain held little appeal.

"Let's see if we can rouse her," Lindsey said.

They began to talk to her as best they could, considering the heavy snowfall, the lack of oxygen, and the enormous effort to speak at all. Elena began to respond, so Ditch squeezed the contents of a gel pack into her mouth and Lindsey forced her to swallow several swigs of her energy drink.

Finally, a tiny spark of life ignited in the woman's eyes.

"Can you climb?" Lindsey asked.

"I need to go to the summit," Elena croaked out.

"It's over, Elena," Lindsey said. "The weather is turning. If you keep climbing, you'll never get off this mountain."

Lindsey and Ditch pulled Elena to her feet. Unroped, they put Elena between them and headed down with Ditch in the lead, but it was like leading an old lady off the mountain.

This would take time. Time they really didn't have.

DURING TY'S DESCENT, THE WEATHER HAD WORSENED. HE DROPPED INTO dark clouds and now heavy snowfall blanketed him. At one point, he stopped, and Beck, JJ, and Artie caught up to him following their own summit. In the darkness, they now huddled together. It was 6:30 p.m. and the sun had finally set.

"Do we go on?" Beck asked.

"You want to bivouac?" JJ asked, his long beard crusted with ice. "That's a terrible idea, and you know it."

Beck shook his head. "But we could go off course."

The afterglow of leaving the summit had quickly faded for Ty, and not just because of the weather. A bad feeling had been building over the past two hours. "Can you get on the radio?" he asked Beck. "Make sure everyone is okay?"

He managed to get Brynn down in Base Camp.

"No word from Fiske," she replied to Beck's inquiry about his AWOL teammate.

And while it was cause for concern, Ty was more worried about Lindsey and Ditch.

Beck held the radio close to his mouth. "What about Elena, over?"

"Ditch called about forty-five minutes ago. He and Lindsey were guiding Rossi down. They're hoping for some aid. Have you found them? Over."

"That's a negative. We're still above the Bottleneck. Weather is bad. Over."

"Look, I've talked to Ingerman, who talked to your weather guy."

Brynn's voice crackled with static. "This storm isn't going to break tomorrow. You need to get off the summit. Now."

"Copy that. We'll check back in a few hours."

"Be safe. Tell Tyler that if he's going to walk, then it better be toward something. Brynn out."

"That's it then," Ty said. "We go. Ditch and Lindsey need our help."

"What about BFE?" Beck asked.

"What?"

"Big Fucking Ego Fiske. What if he's in trouble too?"

"We can't stay here, Beck," Artie said. "No one has seen him, which means he probably turned back early on and is now too humiliated to show his face. I'm not gonna comb the mountain for that idiot and risk my life in the process."

"He's right," Ty said. "We go to the Bottleneck. And we rope together, to avoid getting off course."

"You lead us, Galloway," Beck said. "You've got the best sense of direction. You're the Lost Boy."

"I appreciate your faith in me." While his pathfinding skills weren't always a certainty, he generally made a habit of looking behind him regularly during his ascents to commit to memory the landmarks on the way down.

But it was dark, and snowing, and none of them had wanded the route. A big mistake. But no point dwelling on what-ifs. When he was that lost boy, it hadn't occurred to him to stop. It also hadn't occurred to him that he would be forever lost.

They roped together and continued their descent.

AFTER NEARLY TWO HOURS OF MAKING HIS WAY DOWN, TY WAS CERTAIN HE had found the top of the Bottleneck. A rumble not long ago had been unmistakably an avalanche, and the alarm bells were still ringing loudly in his ears. Beck had called Brynn again, and she told them that Ditch had radioed David about the Germans possibly getting caught in the Bottleneck. She didn't know about Lindsey or Elena, but Ty knew that Ditch wouldn't have left the women, so they were likely together.

Beck, JJ, and Artie had taken turns leading, and now Ty was in front. As he neared where he thought the short, fixed line began, the hunched form of a climber hanging on the steep slope materialized.

"Lindsey!" he yelled.

But as he got closer, he realized it was Elena Rossi. She was secured to an ice screw and didn't stir, a rope leading away from her.

"Lindsey!"

A shadow flickered in his headlamp.

It was her.

He smiled, relieved, only to be filled with panic when a loud snap cracked through the air.

He scrambled forward on the steep slope, but he wasn't fast enough, and Elena blocked his way. The blast of snow knocked him back and he started sliding until the rope attaching him to Beck and the others yanked tight, stopping him. He kicked in his crampons and tried to breathe.

As the puffs of snow settled, he frantically scanned the spot where he had just seen Lindsey.

She had to be there. He climbed quickly to her last known position. Nothing.

No!

This couldn't be happening.

K2 can't take another fucking Coulson!

Filled with rage, he slammed his axe into the ice and screamed her name in anguish.

CHAPTER 21

"Why didn't you tell me, Al?"

Lindsey sat on a snowy slope as the setting sun cast the giant shadow of K2 across the valley below.

Alison, wearing gray snow pants, a powder-blue jacket, and goggles pushed atop her brown hair, took a seat beside her.

"Tell you what?" Alison asked.

Together, they gazed at the magnificent view.

"That K2 was so difficult," Lindsey said.

"But I thought you knew. The dragon lives here."

"I can't seem to escape him."

"Not a him. A her." Alison smiled. "It's said in the Buddhist tradition that a bounty hunter was trying to rid the world of evil, so he tracked down a bunch of sisters who needed reforming. One patrolled Everest, another Shishapangma, and another Kangchenjunga. But the last daughter was the most difficult. She climbed atop her turquoise dragon and fled to K2. The bounty hunter chased her and finally convinced her to change her ways, but she hasn't fully reformed. She and her dragon still crave the taste of human flesh."

Lindsey's eyes snapped open, sharp pain slicing through her shoulder, and she sucked in a lungful of thin air.

She hung by her right arm on the side of an icy slope, her feet dangling against nothing.

The serac.

The Bottleneck had released another piece, and the resulting avalanche had slammed into her.

I'm dead.

And if not, she would be soon enough.

She kicked her feet into the mountain, but only her left boot caught. Her flailing right foot had no crampon. Trembling, she looked to her left, barely moving her head. Her headlamp was dead or gone altogether. She lifted her left hand, clad only in a thin black liner. The mitten was gone.

I'm in a shitload of trouble.

Stop. Work the problem.

She touched her head and felt her helmet. Intact.

Her eyes burned. Her goggles dangled near her chin. Maybe they weren't broken.

Her pack?

Her left hand fumbled but found a strap. Good.

The snowfall had stopped but clouds still blanketed the night sky. Straining, she was barely able to make out the terrain.

She was on a sheer face ... somewhere.

Which way?

She shifted and white-hot pain shot through her shoulder. Shivering, she dragged her gaze to her right arm, stretched above her. The tether to the ice axe had twisted around her wrist, and somehow the axe had gotten itself embedded into the mountain, arresting her fall.

Sweet Jesus. That was some serious luck.

And Ty didn't believe in luck. She couldn't wait to tell him.

Now what?

She kicked her left foot a tiny bit higher to relieve the strain on her arm.

"Son-of-a-bitch." She dragged out the word, the guttural response assuring her that she was indeed still alive. Remembering the vision just before she awoke, she said, "If you really are here, Al, then I could sure use your help."

But the only answer was the whistle of a biting-cold wind.

Bracing herself, she yanked her left foot out, gritting her teeth as her full weight was put on her right arm, then punched a step even higher than the last one. Grunting, she used that leg as leverage and pushed herself onto it, releasing the strain on her right arm.

Dizzy with pain, she paused, but she could move her arm, however slightly.

Maybe not broken. Dislocated? Did it matter? She'd never make it off this slope.

Would she freeze or fall to her death?

Hanging her head, stark loneliness consumed her.

I'm so sorry, Mom.

Tyler.

Hadn't she seen him right before she was blown off the Bottleneck? Maybe he would look for her. A tiny flame of hope burned in her chest.

Her gaze settled on a lone ice screw attached to her climbing harness. Her left hand was becoming more and more frozen. She didn't have much time.

She didn't want to accidentally drop the screw, so she left it attached to her harness and pressed it into the slope near her hip. It was difficult to gain purchase and it slipped when she tried to start rotating it. She worked at it over and over until finally it caught. Lifting the built-in handle out, she quickly rotated it into the ice, then hooked herself to it with a sling.

At least she had an anchor in case she fell.

She needed to get into her pack, but her right arm blocked the ability to get it off her back. She would need to let go of the axe.

Slowly, she leaned back on the sling, testing its strength, and groaned from the pain in her shoulder, but the anchor held.

The safety loop of the axe was wrapped around her right wrist so tightly that she realized she was losing feeling in her fingers. Gritting her teeth, she tried to jiggle her wrist free and almost blacked out, forced to wait for the pain to dissipate before she could regain even a sliver of focus.

Searching her harness, she located a multi-tool. She would have to unclip it.

Steady.

One, two, three.

She unhooked it with her left hand, going less by feel, since her fingers were numb, and more by forced movement. She stretched her left arm overhead and positioned the cutting edge of the tool against the narrowest part of the leash, sawing at the nylon until it gave way. Unsure if she would retain consciousness, she quickly clipped the tool back on her harness, and then wiggled her right arm free.

She screamed as the sling took all her weight, and her right arm was freed.

Gasping, she dangled on the anchor, reeling from the pain. When the haze lifted enough that she could think again, she unclipped her pack and removed it from her right shoulder and then flipped it around to the front of her body. She fumbled for a carabiner on her harness and clipped it onto a loop on the pack.

With one hand, it was difficult making her way into the main pouch, but eventually she located a spare mitten and her extra crampons. And extra goggles; the ones jammed around her chin were busted. Unfortunately, she didn't have another ice axe and would have to make do with only one. Her trekking poles were also gone.

She had no idea how long it took to retrieve the items she needed, and then to secure the crampon onto her right foot while dangling from her anchor, get her left hand into a mitten, and replace her pack on her back. It also took a long time to tie herself onto the ice screw with her extra rope.

She located another screw in her pack and clipped it onto her harness for easier access. She would use it only if she had to. With her right arm immobile, she would need to leave her original anchor in place. Eventually she would get too far away from it, but at least the rope would offer some protection, although the farther she got from the anchor, the worse a fall would be.

She was so tired; all she wanted to do was close her eyes and sleep. Shaking herself awake, she opened her eyes.

I can do this.

How far had she fallen? Was she above or below Camp Four? Either way, moving to the right should bring her to the Abruzzi Route. If she was lucky, she might step right into Camp Four, where a tent and food would be waiting.

I can do this, she chanted in her head. *I'm not gonna die up here.*

With her right arm resting limply against her body, she kicked her right foot into the slope, then with her left hand she shifted the axe to the right, and then she moved her left foot. It was a movement of one or two inches.

How long would she have to do this?

How long *could* she do this?

~

Ty yelled until his throat froze and his lungs were spent.

He hadn't moved from where he had slid, and now he had to accept that Lindsey was gone. There was no way she could have survived.

Bewildered and catatonic, he couldn't move. Beck and JJ hauled him up.

"Get it together, Ty," Beck said.

He stared at them, unable to speak.

Lindsey.

This wasn't how it was supposed to go.

He'd been so careful in his pursuit of her. Why? He'd known all along that she was different, that her presence in his life wasn't like any other woman he had known. He'd told himself he was just glad to have a competent climber on the team, but the truth was he'd been flattered when she'd approached him, even a little in awe of having her on the expedition.

He had admired her for a long time. As he and Ditch had ironed out all the expedition logistics in the last six months, his mind had frequently been on her. He had even contrived ways to visit Berkeley so he could see her again, but he'd always backed off, not wanting to seem obvious. Or desperate.

He should have visited her. He should have taken whatever opportunity they might have had together and enjoyed every last minute of it.

Because now she was gone.

There was no getting that time back.

He knew the risks of climbing, and especially climbing *this* mountain, but he'd never truly believed that he would lose anyone. He was a fool.

And now Lindsey was dead.

But what if she's not?

His mind whipped into a frenzy.

"I need to look for her," he said.

"Tyler." Beck's voice was somber and filled with compassion.

"You don't know that she's dead." Ty looked past Beck. "How much rope do you have?" he asked JJ, his brain soaring back to life.

"About fifty feet." But JJ's tone was as reluctant as Beck's. Ty ignored it.

"We have to get Elena down, as well as ourselves," Beck cut in, his voice stern. "Looking for Lindsey makes no sense."

"I'm not asking you to go. All I'm asking for is some rope."

Beck looked behind him. "Guys, help me out here."

"He's right," JJ said, agreeing with Beck. Then he said to Ty, "You're risking your own life going after her. And she ...."

He didn't finish, but Ty knew what he wanted to say. Her body was likely mangled beyond recognition. He had only seen a climber fall to his death once, and it had been gruesome—an arm twisted unnaturally and snapped at the elbow, a smashed skull with part of the brain exposed.

Ty swallowed back the bile rising in his throat. "I have to know," he said.

"Then I'm going with you," JJ said, then added with little modesty,

"I'm the strongest of any of us at the moment. Beck, can you and Artie handle Elena?"

"This is bullshit," Beck said, his voice clipped. "I'm not gonna lose both of you over this. She really meant that much to you?" The question bordered on derision.

"Yes." Ty's voice broke.

"I'm sorry to be an asshole about it, but she's dead, Galloway. You don't have to die, too," Beck pleaded.

"We're wasting time," Ty snapped. "Radio Brynn and tell her what's going on. Find out who can help us. See if the Germans are still around. Hell, maybe the Poles can come back up. Have her call David and find out where Ditch is."

"I only have one fucking radio," Beck said. "How am I supposed to talk to you and JJ?"

"Send up smoke signals," JJ said, already retrieving rope from his pack.

"You both are fucking certifiable, and it's pissing me off."

JJ moved past Beck. "Let's get this rope off Elena. We can use it to rappel. Artie, once we go, can you untie it from the ice screw and release it to us? It'll give us one more go with it to get lower."

"Goddammit," Beck yelled. "Artie, speak up, will you?"

"We're all adults here," Artie said. "They can choose their own path. I'll help you get Elena down."

Beck swore again but then held up his hand. "Wait," he said to Ty. He pulled out his radio and got Brynn on the line. He told her everything that was happening, as best they knew it.

"My God," she said, when she heard about Lindsey. "How's Ty?"

But to Beck's credit, he didn't go crying to her over Ty's decision.

"He's okay, Brynnie. But he and JJ are going down to do a search. Can you please contact whomever you can find and tell them to check the areas near Camp Four? Time is critical."

"I copy that." Then she added, "He just can't stay where he should, can he?"

"Restless bastard," Beck muttered, but Ty realized he hadn't said it directly to Brynn.

"Tell him that I love him. Tell him he'd better come back. Over."

"Copy that." Beck turned off the radio and handed it to Ty. "Take it. You're gonna need it more than us. But there's not much juice left, so use it sparingly."

Ty tucked it into a pocket in his climbing suit. "Thanks."

Beck glared at him. "Try not to break your sister's heart. I'll never forgive your sorry ass if you die."

Ty's mind was only on Lindsey, and the slim chance that she might still be alive. He would have to comfort Beck and his hissy-fit later.

FOG HAD SET IN AND LINDSEY COULDN'T SEE BEYOND HER HAND. A CHECK on her watch revealed that for two hours she had been moving horizontally like an inchworm on a nearly ninety-degree slope. Exhaustion pressed on her, trying to convince her to stop, to give up, to just die already, but over and over she shoved it aside in a fury of anger that offered the benefit of briefly injecting her body with heat.

Never had she concentrated so fully while climbing, no doubt burning twice the number of calories from not only the physical exertion but also the mental concentration it took to contain the pain of her shoulder in an iron-clad box in her mind.

There was no room for despair.

She might die—and the continued rumble of ice fall did nothing to calm her nerves—but she sure as hell wouldn't make it easy for the dragon.

Suddenly, in the dim glow of clouds that were backlit by the moon, she spied a snow-covered platform. With excitement, she moved toward it only to reach the end of her rope, its tautness holding her back.

Shit. You couldn't have been just a few meters longer?

It wasn't easy untying herself from it—at one point, she had held onto the dangling safety cord of the axe with her teeth—but once she was free, she watched it fall away into the abyss with deep regret.

She continued her inchworm pace, aware that one wrong move

and she would be toast. When she made it to the ledge, it wasn't a pretty sight as she twisted and grunted her way onto it.

As soon as she felt relatively safe, she lay on her stomach as her body succumbed to violent shaking, igniting the pain in her shoulder. She screamed in agony.

"Who's there?" The words floated to her, barely audible.

She quieted, her ragged breath echoing in her ears.

"Is there someone there?" came the bodiless voice.

It sounded like Fiske.

With effort, she pushed to her knees. She strained to see through an opening in the fog and spied the outline of a person huddled in a notch about ten feet away.

She stood and stumbled over to him, then dropped to her knees again.

"Fiske!"

He lifted his gaze to her, his head bobbing as if he were drunk.

Opening her mouth to speak had instantly frozen her tongue, so she clamped her mouth shut and spoke as if she were practicing ventriloquism. "How did you get here?"

He ignored the question and asked, "Are you a dream?"

"No." She slumped beside him, drained of energy. "Are you hurt?"

"It's nothing."

Whatever. She sucked in a breath and the dry air raked her already parched throat.

She pushed her goggles up to see better, but quickly put them back when the cold blasted her eyes.

"I need rope," he said. "Give me your rope."

Even in delirium, he was still a pompous ass. She glanced back from where she'd come, thinking of the line she'd been forced to cut and release to the wind.

"Sorry, no rope," she said. *Not that I'd have handed it over to you.*

One thought pressed on her—something needed to be done about her useless right arm. And she'd be damned if she'd ask Fiske for help.

If it was dislocated, couldn't she pop it back into place? Isn't that what Ditch had done for Aldo?

"Are you anchored?" she asked.

"No."

"Well, shit, Fiske. Let me do it for you."

Fumbling at her harness, she found the lone ice screw still in her possession. One-handed, she drove it into the mountainside near the man's shoulder, located a carabiner on his harness, and hooked him in.

When he said nothing, she didn't bother to hide her irritation, adding, "You're welcome." Then she attached herself to the protection as well.

Uncertain how to proceed with her arm, she took the most obvious approach. She wrapped the end of a sling around her right wrist, then tucked the other end around her boot. Hunched over, she hesitated, fear pooling in her stomach.

Don't be a wuss. Just do it.

"What did you say to me?" she snapped at Fiske.

"Nothing."

She frowned. "Alison?"

"Your sister? Have you snapped?"

If she had, she would never admit it to him.

She stood, yanking her arm hard, and screamed. She gasped as the pain ripped through her shoulder, and she slumped to the ground. Had she made it worse?

Closing her eyes, she lost consciousness.

Ty stopped downclimbing and listened. In the swirling fog, he couldn't see JJ, but he could hear the pings of his ice axes. They had been climbing separately for several hours, not roped together because they had little of it left.

They had been methodically searching the slopes below the Bottleneck for any sign of Lindsey. He knew it was a longshot, but still he kept working his way down this godforsaken monolith of ice and death.

But now he waited, sensing something. Was it Lindsey? Was she close?

His intuition was soon proved wrong. As if a god was plucking the strings of some giant cello, Ty listened in horror as the sound echoed and ricocheted, growing louder and faster.

The glacier above was calving again.

The noise continued, creating a zigzag of fractures in the ice, and Ty frantically tried to decide whether to move right or left, since the wrong choice could prove fatal.

He wanted to yell to JJ to take cover, but there was no time. He could only hope that Moses' divine intervention would hold.

In the end, Ty remained where he was, the inability to decide becoming his decision.

Chunks of ice began raining down. Ty tucked his head to avoid a direct hit to the face, and he held tight to the mountain with his axes and crampons.

The rumbling grew, and a piece of ice the size of a refrigerator tumbled so close to Ty that the edge sliced through the shoulder of his climbing suit. He held fast as the deadly avalanche exploded off rocks and boulders below, throwing up a blast of snow.

A bellow grew in his gut and a roar left his mouth.

And then nothing.

With his ears ringing, he opened his eyes. The avalanche was over. He breathed in. He breathed out. And he shook.

"Galloway?" JJ's voice carried over from Ty's right side.

"I'm here," Ty replied, but his response was weak.

"We need to get off this fucking mountain."

Yeah. They did.

Ty sagged in defeat, grief pressing on him.

Lindsey.

He would never see her again.

CHAPTER 22

"Linc."

Lindsey opened her eyes. The white slopes sparkled in the bright sunlight. Alison sat on the ledge with her. Lindsey straightened her back and lifted her right arm. It didn't hurt. Nice.

"When did the weather get better?" Lindsey asked.

Rather than answering, Alison said, "It's a beautiful day, isn't it?"

Lindsey sensed that something didn't feel right, but she was so happy to see Al again that she decided against delving into it.

"I want to talk to you about David," Alison said, her lips rosy and her cheeks flush with life. "I need you to tell him that it's time he moved on."

"Did you really not want children?"

"I didn't. I knew it deep in my heart, and he didn't believe me. I assumed we would live a life climbing the mountains of the world."

"There's more to living than that."

"That's not what Dad wanted."

Lindsey squinted. She wore no goggles or sunglasses, but the sunlight was tolerable. "Have you seen him?"

"Yes. He's very sorry for hurting Mom, but he lived doing what he loved. It's enough for him."

Lindsey shook her head. "It still hurts. Losing Dad blew our lives apart. Losing you did it again."

"That's why you have to go back. Don't leave Mom alone. And the jacket is in the back of her closet."

Lindsey was greeted by darkness and cold and loneliness, the warmth of her encounter with Alison fading quickly.

She was anchored on the side of K2, and she could barely move.

I'm frozen, and I'm dying.

She turned her head, just barely, to see if Fiske was still there. He was motionless beside her. She looked back to the sky, stars intermittently peeking out between the cloud cover.

Dawn had to be close. Didn't it?

Could she wait that long?

With effort, she moved her right arm. There was a dull ache in the shoulder, but the limb was more functional than it had been. She would take the small victory.

What now?

She and Fiske had no rope. No idea of their location. No hope that anyone would come looking for them. Tyler would assume she had died in that avalanche.

But what of Fiske? Had he managed to tell someone that he'd fallen? Would they be looking for him?

Was he her last and final hope?

The ass becomes the savior.

"Fiske." Her voice was barely audible. She tried again, louder. "Fiske."

No response.

She forced herself to twist toward him, the movement stiff and excruciating but at least it generated a little heat, and she envisioned her sluggish blood flowing a bit faster.

I'm not dead yet.

Lifting her left arm, feeling as if it carried an anvil, she bumped him with her hand. Her body rebelled, stiff and sore and so cold.

She continued to push at him, and just as she decided he might be dead—an oddly impassionate conclusion in her mind—he moved.

Not dead. She wasn't sure if she was happy or disappointed, since it occurred to her that she could take his ice axe to replace the one she'd lost.

"Fiske. Wake up. We can't sleep anymore. We won't wake up next time."

He stirred.

"Is there anyone looking for you?" she asked, her voice hoarse.

"I do not know."

"Who were you climbing with?"

"My team was a bunch of fools, so I climbed alone."

Great. No one would be looking for him. Maybe they were even celebrating his disappearance. She could hardly blame them, but it did mean that she would have to save herself.

"Can you climb?" she asked.

"Are you fucking crazy?" He slurred his words, the swear word sounding unnatural with his accent.

Maybe I am.

"I'm not staying here," she said. "If I can get to Camp Four, I'll tell whoever I can that you're here."

"You would leave me?"

In a heartbeat. Moral obligations be damned.

She stood—no easy feat—and started pumping her arms and legs to get the circulation going. "If you want to give up, that's your business."

"You know the way?"

The clouds parted and she looked to the sky. The Summer Triangle was visible. In and of itself, it didn't show the way, but she determined they were to the west of the Abruzzi. The knowledge boosted her confidence and fueled her resolve.

"Yes," she said.

She secured her pack and cleared all the safety gear, since they might need it. Stepping over Fiske, she left the ledge and began her inchworm technique again with only three points of contact on the mountain, but luckily her right arm was more mobile, and the slope wasn't nearly as vertical as before.

Fiske could follow her or not.

~

TYLER CLIMBED OFF THE STEEP SLOPE AND FELL TO HIS KNEES, HIS BODY
desperate for oxygen and his heart heavy. Nearby, JJ also slumped
forward. They had finally made it off the precarious slope they had
been traversing for the past several hours.

There had been no sign of Lindsey.

Grief spurred a wave of nausea, and Ty waited for his stomach to
mutiny. But he had nothing to expel. He hadn't eaten in well over
eighteen hours, and his mouth was so dry and parched that he was no
doubt dangerously close to dehydration.

Dejected and sickened, he pushed to his feet and followed JJ to
Camp Four, locating the tents that Beck and his team had set up. He
didn't have the strength to go farther up the shoulder to find David,
Ditch, and Packer, if they even remained. He had no idea.

Beck came to meet them, bolstering Ty with a shoulder under his
arm. "It's damned good to see you both. Did you find anything?"

JJ shook his head. Ty didn't have the energy to talk about it.

"Dawn is coming," Beck said, guiding Ty toward a tent.

JJ sat down to remove his crampons, and Beck helped Ty do the
same.

"Rest for a bit," Beck said. "We're descending at first light."

"What about Ditch?" Ty asked.

"I don't know. There's a glow up higher, so they're in their tents.
You can wait for them, but I don't think you should. Do you have my
radio?"

Ty nodded. "It's dead."

"I'll see if I can dig up some batteries, but it's so fucking cold that
nothing is working. We've got Elena here, but she's in bad shape. We
need to go down. *You* need to go down, Galloway."

Ty crawled into the tent and lay down beside JJ. Later, Beck
brought them both hot soup in a bottle. Ty sipped it, but nausea roiled

in his gut. A few times he went to the tent entrance and hung his head outside, but nothing came up.

His body wasn't releasing anything—not food, not grief.

Tyler wanted the pain to stop, but he knew it was only just beginning.

How could he descend and leave Lindsey here?

~

AT DAWN, TY AWOKE. SLEEPING HAD OFFERED A SMALL REPRIEVE FROM the void that his mind had become, but now the previous day came rushing back.

He sat up and switched on his headlamp, pushing the white-hot grief back. He couldn't afford to break down. Not yet.

Beck leaned his head into their tent. "How're you both?"

JJ stirred and pushed upright, scratching his mess of hair. "We're all right," he said, but his somber tone spoke volumes.

"I managed to talk to David on the radio," Beck said. "Yesterday when Ditch was descending with Lindsey and Elena, the Germans got into trouble. When the first block of ice came down, they got tangled in the fixed rope. It took Ditch two hours to free them. That's why he never made it back to the women."

Ty didn't say anything. If Ditch had gone back, he'd probably be dead, too.

"I'm really sorry, Ty," Beck said. "Somehow we've lost Fiske. He's MIA."

"You haven't heard anything?" JJ asked.

"Maybe he was caught in one of the avalanches as well."

Ty didn't care about the Norwegian, but they couldn't leave him behind if there was some chance he was alive. "Are you sure?" Ty asked.

Beck paused. "No. The only plausible conclusion is that he fell, or the mountain pushed him off. Either way, it's unlikely he's alive." Beck glanced behind him. "The sky is clear. We really can't stay here any longer. We need to descend. Fiske knew the risks. May his sorry ass rest in peace."

"I'll wait for Ditch and the others," Ty said.

"Shit," Beck muttered under his breath. "I'm all for being a team player, Galloway, but it's gonna take time to get Elena down. We can't waste a second."

"I understand, but I'm not leaving my team to save my own ass. I'll wait and help them with Packer." Ty looked at Beck. "You didn't mention anything, but I'm assuming he's not any better."

Beck grimaced. "All right, it's true. He's in bad shape." Beck flicked his gaze to JJ. "You going with us?"

JJ nodded, and Beck left.

JJ rested a hand on Ty's shoulder. "You did all you could. Sometimes shit just happens. She was a good climber that had the bad luck of being in the wrong place at the wrong time."

"Thanks for your help in looking for her," Ty said, his voice strained. "I appreciate it."

"Beck only becomes a rotten bastard for those he loves. And he loves you."

Ty gave a half-hearted smirk. "I know."

"We're done here. K2 has kicked us to the curb. It's time to go home."

Home. Ty thought about Lindsey's mom. How in God's name would he break the news to her?

JJ clapped Ty on the shoulder. "You can get through this," he said, his voice calm and quiet. "Just take it one step at a time."

Ty tried to take a deep breath, to somehow flush out even a tiny bit of the agony, but everything hurt. He had a feeling everything would hurt for a very long time.

~

As a pink hue began creeping up from the horizon, Ty helped Beck and his team break down their tents and gear at Camp Four. Later, when he met up with Ditch and David, they carried Packer between them, the seriousness of the man's condition sinking in.

Packer slid to the ground and slumped over to rest, panting for breath. David and Ditch's faces, etched with stern and stoic resolve, nearly broke Ty.

"This stupid, fucking mountain," Packer said, staring at the blowing snow surrounding him. A coughing fit wracked his body, and he sounded like a barking sea lion. When he finally caught his breath again, he said, "Tell me she went fast. Tell me it was painless."

Ty said nothing.

They all knew it hadn't been painless.

If they didn't get Packer off the mountain—and quickly—he would die too. And Ty didn't want to lose anyone else. With little emotion, he said, "Let's get going."

CHAPTER 23

In the afternoon, Lindsey came upon debris and trash at what was left of Camp Four. Where was everyone? She glanced around, but there was no sign of habitation. Just her and Fiske, the last human she would choose to be stranded with.

The fire that had propelled her off that ledge was dying swiftly as hope dwindled. They were alone. No one was here. She strained to look upward to where her team had pitched their camp before starting their summit bid and saw nothing but a field of white.

She was so damned thirsty. She had avoided putting any snow in her mouth because she'd been so cold all through the night that she couldn't afford wasting any bodily energy to melt it.

Screw it.

Getting up here had warmed her, her fingers and toes painfully coming back from the brink of frostbite.

Dropping to her knees, she began scooping snow into her mouth, frantic to hydrate her body. Somewhere behind her, Fiske was doing the same.

At last, she stopped. What if someone had left a stove behind? She pushed to her feet and began to search for anything useful that might have been discarded.

She spied a tent, or what was left of one, about twenty feet away.

The wind had ripped it apart. A search among the remnants of nylon and poles revealed a wrapper with Italian wording. The tent had likely been Elena's, or one of the woman's teammates.

Was Elena even alive?

Lindsey paused, briefly closing her eyes. Her head pounded, and the urge to curl up in this ramshackle shelter and sleep swept over her.

Just a few hours. Then she'd be fresh and ready to start down the mountain.

No.

She rubbed her temples, the mitten chafing her wind and cold-burned skin. She struggled to remember what day it was, but it eluded her. She struggled to remember how long she'd been this high on K2. She couldn't. She struggled to determine how long it had been since all the other climbers had descended, essentially abandoning her. No fucking clue.

You're not above the Bottleneck, like I was.

Al?

I was trapped. You're not.

Alison ....

Okay. She needed to descend. The sun was shining, so she needed to go now. There was no telling when bad weather would return.

Lindsey searched the debris again. She discovered a broken stove and an empty propane canister. Useless. And disappointing. An empty oxygen bottle was also useless to her, but there was a sleeping bag and a ski pole. Not useless.

She fantasized that she held a huge glass of ice water, and she nearly wept from imagining the cool fluid flowing down her throat like a waterfall, but she had no moisture to produce even one tear.

She spied a baggy. Pulling it free from the snow, it revealed itself to be one of Ty's butter bags. He must have given one to Elena. A spurt of jealousy bloomed in her chest, and the ridiculousness of it made her laugh, the sound dry and humorless.

She ripped it open and started gnawing at it like a popsicle, but her mouth was so dry and the butter so rich, even in its frozen state, that she almost immediately felt sick.

Fiske.

She'd give it to him. Another humorless chuckle echoed in her head, and she wasn't certain if it was her or Alison.

Because of course her sister was with her right now.

Her gaze snagged on another wrapper, a Kendal mint cake. She grabbed it and tore it open. It was rock-hard but she nibbled on a corner and the minty flavor, along with the sugar, started to revive her.

She tucked it into her sleeve, scooped up the sleeping bag and ski pole, and returned to where Fiske was lying on his side, sleeping.

She nudged him with her boot. He moved.

Not dead. Again.

"I found food." She tossed the baggy at him.

In a daze, Fiske sat up and removed the frozen piece of butter. "Lard?"

Lindsey shrugged, and said, "We can't stay here. We need to descend."

He broke off a tiny piece of butter and moved it around in his mouth with a look of disgust.

"My tent is over that way." He spat out the contents of his mouth and handed her the bag. "I just need to find it."

"No. Everyone's gone. I can only assume they all think we're dead. No one is coming back. If we don't go now, they'll all leave Base Camp and we will surely never leave this mountain alive."

Exactly what had happened to Alison.

"You are wrong." Fiske rolled onto his back. "They will come back. I am going to wait. I just need to rest a little bit more, and then I will find my tent. I have food and a stove. I can make tea and eat. You will see."

She grabbed her pack and pulled out the Dexedrine, then tossed it at him. "Take this. You need it." It would jumpstart his system. She wasn't going to drag him off the mountain.

She set to work stuffing the sleeping bag into the main pouch of her pack. Once that was done, she pulled out the empty water bottle from a pocket in her climbing suit and began shoving snow into it, the pieces hard and chunky, but she didn't stop until it was full. Then she put it back into the pocket where it would stay close to her body. With luck, what little heat she could generate might melt it, at least some of it. She found another empty bottle in Fiske's gear and did the same, then shoved it at him.

"Put this somewhere warm," she said. "Stand up. We need to go. Now."

Between here and Camp Three, there were no fixed lines. Both she and Fiske only had one axe each and no rope to offer even a smidge of protection. Hoping she wouldn't regret it, she shoved the ski pole at him.

"Use this to get to Camp Three," she said. "After that, we can use the fixed lines."

"I don't need a fucking ski pole. Or drugs. I'm not taking orders from a woman."

Why am I trying to help this asshole?

And she had been close to sharing her mint cake. Biting back a retort, she moved past him.

Hadn't she done her moral obligation by now? If he had been stuck here with the Germans, they would have abandoned him on that ledge, just as they had dispassionately refused to help with Elena. But hadn't Fiske's own team left him?

He had no one to blame but himself.

Only then did she notice that it was late in the day, and the wind had picked up considerably. Clouds were rolling in like ocean waves.

The fucking karma of the universe.

She turned back to Fiske, and said through gritted teeth, "You'd better hurry!"

It was late afternoon and the mountain above had become socked in. Ty and his team had just arrived at Camp Two when David turned on the radio, having kept it off to preserve the battery.

"Brynn, this is David, over."

"I'm here," she answered. "Thank God. Are you all right? Is Tyler with you?"

"Yes. We've got Packer. He's not doing well. Can you pull the first aid gear in the back of the mess tent and have supplies ready, over?"

"Yes."

"Can you also get Juneid to radio the military? Packer's gonna need evac to the hospital in Skardu. He's showing signs of pulmonary edema and some frostbite. Over."

"I'll tell him. Where are you? Over."

"We're in Camp Two. We're gonna take a short rest and continue down. What's the status on your end? Over."

"The Poles are assembling now and will come back up to meet you, probably Camp One. Over."

"Appreciated. Tell them Beck, Artie, and JJ are ahead of us with Elena. Not sure of her status, but she's in bad shape, too. Over."

"Copy that. I'll relay the message. David, I need to tell you something. Can Tyler hear me?"

David flicked his gaze to Ty. "Yes," he replied to her.

Ty made sure that Packer was secure where he sat, then stepped over to David, who handed him the radio.

"Brynn, it's Ty."

Ditch moved closer, and together the three of them listened intently to the radio that Ty held in front of him.

"A few hours ago the clouds parted, and we saw something on the scope near Camp Four," she said. "Over."

"Sonovabitch," David muttered.

The back of Ty's neck prickled. "What did you see?" he asked. "Over."

"Two figures moving."

Ty stilled. His pulse hammered in his head, making him dizzy. "Who?"

"We couldn't tell. But the only two climbers not accounted for are Fiske and Lindsey."

She's alive.

Ty tried to suppress the hope blasting through him, in case it wasn't true, but already his mind was racing to what needed to be done.

"Tyler," Brynn's static-filled voice interrupted his thoughts. "We're not entirely sure what we saw. Weather's coming in. High winds." He could hear the panic in her voice. "I don't want you going back up, but I don't want Lindsey to be stranded, if it's really her. I don't know what to do. Over."

"You did the right thing in telling us. How long until the Poles get here? Over."

"I don't know," she answered. "Two hours? They're exhausted. You're exhausted. I'm just not sure this is a good idea."

"I know. Give us a minute."

Ty looked at David, then Ditch, their eyes barely visible behind their goggles.

"I can get Packer down," Ditch said.

"You're not going to talk me out of this?" Ty asked.

"Even if I tried, I know it wouldn't matter." Ditch's lips spread into a ghost of a smile. "David?"

The question hung in the air.

"I couldn't save Alison," he said. "I won't make the same mistake again. I'm going."

The three of them quickly divided up what gear and food they had. The tents were still standing at Camp Two, so Ditch would let Packer rest for two hours so he could brew water. With hope, by then the Poles would be close enough to aid in getting Packer back to Base Camp.

"You bring her back," Ditch said, when Ty was ready. "Fiske, on the other hand, is a different story."

Ty released the barest hint of a laugh, the first one since they had gone for the summit—yesterday. It seemed so long ago.

As he and David began a rapid ascent, fueled for now by adrenaline, his heart pounded with joy.

Stay alive, Lindsey. I'm coming.

CHAPTER 24

The wind blasted Lindsey as she struggled to crawl toward the top of the Black Pyramid. She hoped she was in the right place. In the dark, she couldn't be certain of her direction. The wands she had planted days ago had proven helpful in getting to Camp Three, but there was no such guidance now.

Upon arriving at Camp Three, a fresh avalanche had buried any tents that might have remained. Even if she and Fiske had wanted to stay, it wasn't safe. There was nothing to do but keep going.

The hellish conditions, however, frightened her.

She couldn't bivouac in this wind with only a sleeping bag, which she'd be forced to share with Fiske, a reality that not even the threat of death could tempt her to do.

Damned if I do, damned if I don't.

The monsoon weather was a statement, loud and clear—K2 was telling them to get the hell off her mountain. The dragon was done with humans playing on her flanks.

With her odds of survival dropping quickly, all Lindsey could do was push on, trying to ignore the obvious truth.

She was dying.

She'd been dying from the moment she had arrived at Base Camp.

On her hands and knees, she searched frantically for the rope.

Maybe she was fooling herself. Maybe she should give up. Is this what it had been like for Alison? For Shoop? For her father?

She looked behind her. Where was Fiske?

Returning to her task, she located several lines leading off the rocky escarpment and into the abyss. She needed to choose wisely, as if she were picking out the holy grail, otherwise she'd fall just like Elena had the day she'd slammed into Lindsey.

Grabbing a rope, Lindsey tugged, repeating the process, trying to determine how secure each one was.

A slap of wind knocked her over. Scrambling, she hooked her rappelling device to the last rope she'd had hold of, just as she was slammed against rock-hard ice, her harness yanking tight. Her quick thinking had kept her from flying off the mountain. Fiske rolled toward her.

She flung the trekking pole toward him that he'd rejected earlier.

"Grab it!"

But the wind had hold of him, and he had no anchor. Tumbling, he flailed in desperation to grasp her lifeline, but he slid right past her.

He was gone.

Just like that.

She heaved herself in his direction, searching for any sign of him. If he'd managed to grab a ledge, a protruding rock, something ... anything. But snow blasted around her, obscuring her vision, and in the pit of her stomach she felt the horror of what she couldn't see.

Fiske was gone. And if he wasn't dead already, he was about to be, his body falling and bouncing off the slopes. Not survivable.

Despair rose in her chest.

Did Fiske deserve to die? Had it been her fault?

Did it even matter?

She was near to death now, so close that she could feel the icy tentacles rooting around her. She had been a fool to come here. Alison had been a fool, too.

As she lay on the ground, the maelstrom of K2's wrath whipping around her, the anguish gave way to calm.

"Tyler," she whispered. "I'm sorry."

Something shoved at her, pushing her onto her back. A shrouded figure leaned over her.

"Lindsey! I've got you!"

⁓

TY CUPPED THE BACK OF LINDSEY'S HEAD AND ANGLED HIS WATER BOTTLE to pour hot liquid into her mouth. She sputtered, so he eased back.

Unbelievably, he and David had found her clinging to the mountain above the Pyramid, in shock. He hadn't wanted to move her, but Camp Three was unlivable, and they had tents and modest supplies at Two. So he and David had spent the last three harrowing hours getting her down one of the most challenging spots on K2.

All three of them crammed together inside a tent, using their weight to keep it anchored from the gale-force winds. He prayed the shelter would hold. They had Lindsey tucked into a sleeping bag, trying to warm her.

"Fiske," Lindsey said, her voice hoarse.

Ty cupped her cheek with one hand and shook his head, saying as gently as he could, "No."

"My fault." Her voice rose in panic.

"Shhh." He pushed her back. "Don't move, Linds. It wasn't your fault. We saw him as we were coming up to you. You tried to grab him, but he should've been hooked to the fixed line. There wasn't anything you could've done. It wasn't your fault," he repeated.

"He was such an asshole, but I did everything I could not to leave him up there," she said in a rush and a dry sob.

Ty kissed her forehead. She was alive! It was all that mattered.

David handed him a cup filled with soup.

"Try some of this," Ty said, holding the container while she took a drink.

She lay back. "I can't believe you found me. Everyone had left the mountain. I thought I was alone."

"Brynn and the others in Base Camp saw you on the scope," David said.

Lindsey shifted her gaze to him, and Ty was glad to see a spark of awareness in her eyes. She wasn't as far gone as he'd feared.

"We would never have left you," David added, his cheeks sunken and his eyes lined with fatigue.

Would Lindsey tell David that it was very likely that he *had* left Alison on the mountain, however unintentional? Ingerman could have been wrong—he had been ill on that trip, just as he'd been on this one. It wouldn't serve anyone to rehash all the what-ifs, because it would never bring Alison Coulson back.

Ty had no doubt that David suffered, would always suffer, over the death of Alison. Just as Ty would have if they hadn't been able to rescue Lindsey.

"Thank you," Lindsey said to David, her eyes filled with gratitude.

As she consumed more soup, her energy level started to rise, and she told them what the last twenty-four hours had been like for her. The recounting was unbelievable, from her surviving the serac break and ensuing avalanche to her incredible feat of traversing a steep, icy face in the dark with only one axe and an injured shoulder. Then she had found Fiske, and she'd been forced to maneuver him and herself to safety.

The drive she had exhibited and her will to survive were both humbling and impressive.

"I don't know how you did it," Ty said to her. "As soon as the sun rises, we'll get you down to Base Camp."

"How's Packer?" she asked.

"Not good," David replied. "As soon as the weather breaks, we're going to evac him. We'll do the same with you."

"I don't want to be any trouble."

David scoffed. "You've been nothing but."

"David," Lindsey said, her voice edged with an urgency. "I saw her."

Ty stilled, as did David.

"I know I sound crazy, but I saw Alison. I talked to her. In fact, I'm pretty sure she helped me get off the mountain."

In many of the stories that Ty had heard over the years of climbers hallucinating at high altitudes, the imaginary interaction had often been detrimental to the climber. In extreme cases, the climber was instructed to throw him or herself off the side of a cliff to expedite their descent, or remove items of clothing, such as boots and mittens, which only served to hasten their death.

That Lindsey had somehow spoken with the dead and lived to tell about it was yet another testament to her grit under extreme pressure. That, and luck. She'd been right. Luck was always an ingredient to the success or failure in the wilderness.

"She wanted you to know that she forgives you," Lindsey said to David. "That it's time to move on."

David gave a nod, swallowing convulsively.

Lindsey added, "It's not your fault either for leaving her."

David wiped at his eyes. "I'm so sorry I didn't save her."

"I know," Lindsey replied. "I forgive you, too."

David hunched over, his shoulders shaking, and Ty reached an arm around him.

Together, the three of them waited for the dawn of a new day.

CHAPTER 25

S kardu *Combined Military Hospital*
      Pakistan
August 15

THE DAYS BLURRED TOGETHER FOR LINDSEY. TYLER AND DAVID HAD
helped her get off the mountain with ropes and belays and her own
power, but the gaps in her memory left her unsettled. One thing she
knew for certain—she had been on the edge of death. K2 had been
ready to claim her as one of its own, just as it had taken Alison.

Upon her arrival at Base Camp, Ditch had set up a makeshift ER in
the mess tent, caring for Lindsey, Packer, and Elena, plugging IV's into
them, administering pain meds and steroids, and trying to keep their
spirits high until a military transport could make it into the
Karakoram.

She had a vague memory of Ty, David, Ditch, and Beck carrying
her in a stretcher to the helicopter, a large bird flying lazy circles above
her. *I foiled you on this one, Charon. You're not getting my soul yet.*

Tyler had rarely left her side, or so she was told later by Packer, her
touchstone at the hospital, since hanging out with Elena had been low
on her to-do list. After the three of them had been helicoptered out of

the Karakoram, Ty, Ditch, David, and Brynn had remained to collect gear—some still on the mountain—and break down all the camps. Then they had trekked for ten days with over a hundred Balti porters back to Skardu.

Every day since, Lindsey could think of nothing she wanted more than to see Galloway.

Was she in love with him? Or was she just grateful that he'd come back up the mountain to save her?

You saved yourself.

Those had been Ditch's words. Much of that time in the medical mess tent was vague, but she'd remembered that. *You can't dwell on what happened to Fiske.*

Easier said than done. Guilt weighed on her, worsened by having to field questions—mostly by phone—from reporters since she had begun feeling better. She'd already told the story of Anders Fiske's death at least a dozen times.

She'd experienced this after losing Shoop, but Alison must have handled the brunt of those inquiries because Lindsey couldn't remember it being this difficult. Is this what it had been like after David had lost Alison? It was hell to go through, and a special level of hell to recount it over and over, and she hadn't even liked Fiske. David had been in love with Alison. The aftermath of that expedition must have been brutal for him.

Lindsey sat in a private sitting area and enjoyed the sun-bathed view of Skardu outside the window. The nurses had begun letting her leave her bed for short periods each day, and she usually came here, the solitude a balm to her soul. The town was in a broad valley carved by glaciation and was the gateway to the Karakorams. It merited a much longer stay and not from a wheelchair. Maybe she would return.

The door opened and Packer was wheeled in by a nurse. "Good morning, superstar." Despite lingering dark circles under his eyes and a pallor to his skin, he was slowly coming back to life.

The press had dubbed her fight to survive on the icy slopes of K2 as nothing short of a miracle, and despite the death of Fiske—and

Salvatore Gallo—they had been focusing on her fearless efforts to save not only herself but the Norwegian.

Too little, too late.

She found nothing heroic in her story. People had died. And she had lived. The simple truth was that she had barely managed to skirt the ever-present element of bad luck.

The nurse parked Packer beside Lindsey's wheelchair and left.

"I see you've put on your prettiest hospital gown to greet the gang," he said, his voice still wheezy during his recovery from pulmonary edema.

She gave a wistful smile. "I wish." She lifted her bandaged left hand, which had suffered from frostbite. Medication kept the excruciating pain under control, along with the recovery of her right shoulder and its torn ligaments. "It's impossible to do my hair." Adding to her lack of grooming, her complexion was peeling and her lips were chapped, although looking far better than the cracked skin from ten days ago. She was a sight, but there wasn't much she could do about it.

Packer leaned forward. "You look beautiful."

"Illness has made you sentimental."

He sank back in his chair. "I suppose."

The door opened and Ty entered, his tall frame gaunt beneath an olive-green fleece and black trail pants. He looked scrubbed clean and freshly-shaven, and Lindsey's mouth spread into a grin as far as her healing lips would allow. David, Ditch, and Brynn followed.

Ty came up behind Packer and gave his shoulder a friendly squeeze, but his attention shifted quickly to her, his gaze intense. "Sorry we're late."

Tears welled in Lindsey's eyes. Ty leaned over and gently cupped her cheek. Without breaking a beat, he kissed her and she sighed into it.

"I missed you," she whispered.

With a palm on either side of her face, creating a barrier to give them privacy, he said in a low voice, "I'm so glad to see you."

He kissed her again, gently, then used his thumbs to wipe the tears streaming down her face.

"All right, all right," Ditch said. "Let the rest of us see her, Ty."

He was forced back, and Ditch gave her a kiss on the cheek. "He's been a bear without you."

More tears. Lindsey couldn't hold them back.

"Aww," Brynn said. "Don't cry." She gave Lindsey a hug, doing all the work, and held her close for a moment. "I'm so happy you're okay."

"You did my share of the work of breaking camp," Lindsey said between sobs. "Thank you. I'm indebted to you."

Brynn stepped back to give David room, and said, "You can pay me back by going on an adventure with me one day. Just the girls."

Lindsey laughed. "Deal."

David bent over and kissed the same cheek that Ditch had. "How are you?"

"Humbled. Grateful."

David nodded, his gaze hooded. "How's the frostbite?"

Ty finished talking to Packer and pulled a chair over to sit beside Lindsey. He reached over and gently clasped her right hand where it was tucked against her abdomen because of the bandaging on her shoulder. The others also grabbed seats from a nearby table and made a circle around the two wheelchairs.

"The doctor is optimistic." She glanced down at her feet, also frost-bitten, both also loosely bandaged to protect the skin and muscles. "He doesn't think I'll lose any fingers or toes. I should be able to fly home in another week."

Ty squeezed her hand. "I'll stay and go with you."

"What about the magazine job?" she asked.

"I'm gonna take it, and they've agreed to wait until I can get back, but there's a condition. They want me to write a full-length feature about our trip. I'm sure you've been inundated by news outlets, but I can field those requests now."

"Ha, that's sneaky, Galloway," Packer cut in. "You're demanding an exclusive."

"Are you her agent now?" Ditch asked, his tone dry.

"I could be." Packer winked at her. "Don't be swayed by his animal magnetism, sweetheart."

Ty cast an annoyed look at the man before turning back to her. "You can think about it. By the way." He reached into the satchel he'd set by his chair and pulled out the journal she had kept of her climbing life with Alison. "I made sure I got this from your tent." He carefully set it on her lap. "I didn't want anything to happen to it."

"Thank you," she said, her voice thick with emotion. Regrouping, she asked, "Did everyone get out of Base Camp okay?"

"Yes," Ditch answered. "We spent several days clearing the high camps with help from the Poles and Beck and the others. Even the Germans joined in. I'm guessing they felt thankful for my help at the Bottleneck, and perhaps a little guilty over their lack of empathy in helping us with Elena. Speaking of, how is she?"

Lindsey gave a nod toward the door. "Just down the hall. You could pop in and say hello."

"I'll pass."

"She seems to have amnesia about what occurred up there," Packer cut in. "But don't worry, I read her the riot act for not saying *grazie*. And since I was as much a burden as she was, I want you all to know that when we get stateside, there's a steak dinner with your name on it."

"Don't go overboard," Ditch said. "Your wallet might break when you crack it open for the first time."

Packer chuckled, then became uncharacteristically serious, looking at each of them in turn. "Thank you. I wouldn't be here without you."

They sat in silence, the room filled with gratitude, friendship. Camaraderie.

Lindsey wouldn't hesitate to climb with any one of them again.

Ditch handed Packer a mint cake. "I saved one for you."

The gesture made the man cry, which he quickly pushed aside. "So where to next?" he asked, attempting to shift the somber mood.

"I've already told Ty," Ditch said, "but I've decided to retire from the big mountains."

Packer stopped and stared. "You're walking away from Everest?"

Ditch nodded. "I think my luck is running thin, and I'd like to live to a ripe old age. I made it to the top of K2, with the esteemed Lindsey Coulson, no less." His gaze glittered as his eyes met hers, warming her with the unspoken praise. "I'd say I'm going out on top."

"It was an honor to climb with you, Ditch," she said.

"The pleasure was mine. Only one thing would get me back on an icy slope, and that's if you ever needed me."

"Thanks, but I hope never to be in that position again."

"I'm looking forward to beer and pizza and a good long sleep," David said.

"I may just like you yet, Shaw," Packer said.

"Don't be too hasty. The jury's still out on you."

"What's left of the fourteeners club for you?" asked Packer.

"I've got my eye on Cho Oyu for next year."

"If you need a pack mule, keep me in mind."

David nodded. "I may just do that. But what about K2 for you? You comin' back?"

Packer sighed. "It'll probably gnaw at me like a cockroach. I suppose I'll have to team up with Elena. Perhaps we'll have a love connection, kinda like Ty and Lindsey, and head to the K2 summit together."

Ditch grimaced. "You really want to get back on that mountain with her?"

Packer's eyes widened with a feigned innocence. "For sex? Yes. I'm a lush. I fully admit it."

Everyone laughed.

"What about you, Brynn?" Packer asked. "You ready to actually climb?"

"No," she replied, her brown hair pulled back in a ponytail. "I'll leave you all to it. I'm looking forward to lower elevations."

"Didn't you just get an email about going to Bolivia?" Ty asked.

She nodded.

"La Paz sits at nearly 12,000 feet," he said. "But after being at K2 Base, that'll hardly bother you."

"Hmmm. Maybe. I think I've had enough adventure for now."

"You can never have enough adventure," Packer exclaimed.

"Let me recover from this trip first," Brynn said. "What are your plans, Lindsey?"

"Get back to work."

"Well, I hope that Ty will bring you around to visit, seeing as how you both will be near each other with him staying in San Francisco for his new job and you in Berkeley." Brynn threw a look at her brother. "You should meet our parents."

"I'd like that." Lindsey looked at Ty to gauge his reaction.

"I was planning to invite you. I just didn't want to scare you away. Too much Galloway can be overwhelming."

Lindsey smiled. "I think I can handle it."

"I don't doubt it." His gaze was filled with warmth, and something more, causing her stomach to somersault, thankfully not with nausea. Instead, anticipation and even a sense of hope beckoned.

Her life had been filled with pivot points: her father's death when she was a child, her first climb while in high school that ignited a passion in her soul, climbing Manaslu and finally understanding how much of Robbie Coulson she carried in her DNA, the devastation of losing Alison and the wasteland her life had become because of it, and now Ty Galloway. These moments had been filled with the highest highs and the lowest lows, but one thing had been constant—there had been no turning back once the pivot occurred, not unlike the activation of a jumping gene. No restart, no inkling of how she could return to the girl she'd been before the change. But unlike all the others, Ty was different.

Ty was a dragon slayer.

"Why do we do it?" Packer muttered under his breath.

Everyone went silent again.

"I think Messner says it well," Ditch said. "He couldn't recollect the soft beds and good meals of his life, but rather the days he'd spent in the wilderness, cold and hungry. That's what marked him."

"Yeah, yeah. I've heard it all before," Packer said. "We're all made of the same stuff—the rocks, the plants, the animals. We're all imbued with spirit." He stopped abruptly when he realized everyone was staring at him. "That's the point of life, or so I've heard," he murmured.

"There's a philosopher inside you yet," Ty accused, his tone soft.

He scoffed but said with affection, "I've been stuck with Lindsey too long. We might all be made from the same primordial soup, but some of us are more gluttons for punishment than others."

Ditch leaned back in his chair and crossed his arms. "Maybe we're unable to live in black and white. We need the Kodachrome."

"Evolution occurs in the chaos," Lindsey said. "Dormant genes spring to life at the edge."

"But it's a razor's edge, with death right on the other side," Ditch said. "It's not without risk, that's certain."

"To the victor go the spoils," Brynn said.

"It's all true," Ditch said, "but I've come to realize that adventure can be had anywhere. Becoming one with the land can be done closer to home, I'm thinking. The journey doesn't have to be at the expense of our lives." He looked at Ty. "That new job of yours, I think it will be good for you."

Ty smiled. "An adventure of the mundane. But will it impress my dad?"

"I can't answer that one," Ditch said. "But we'd all like you to stay alive, and I've no doubt that includes your father." His focus shifted to Lindsey. "We can't bring back those we've lost—Alison, your dad, even Anders Fiske—but we can acknowledge the deal that each of us has made when entering the mountains, whether we consciously agree to it or not: some of us won't survive."

The pain in Lindsey's chest was of a decidedly non-physical sort. Her heart was cracking open and happiness was reaching out to her. Al was gone, but Lindsey still had purpose, a reason to keep going. She didn't know how long she would have on this earth, but it was time to let go of her grief and live again.

"All right," Packer cut in. "I've got one question. Does anyone have any vodka?"

CHAPTER 26

San Francisco
     Mid-September

TY PULLED LINDSEY CLOSE, TUCKING HER NAKED BACKSIDE AGAINST HIM. She stirred, which stirred him in response. He began exploring her curves with his right hand to see what options were available in these pre-dawn hours.

"I'm still content from last night," she murmured.

He kissed his way along her injured shoulder, although it was nearly healed. "Then I'll just admire you."

She laughed softly and rolled to her back. "All right, you win. It's way too early but you're awfully good at wooing, did you know that?"

"I'm not sure what you're talking about." He brought his mouth to hers. "My one-handed siren."

"You don't seem to be complaining."

"Not for a second. I can be handsy for the both of us."

"Until you find that next siren."

"No mountain compares to you, Linds." He slanted his lips over hers and kissed her deeply, then kicked the covers back and settled atop her. "There are these mountains, however."

His mouth went to one of her breasts, and she gasped then sighed as he suckled. He gently pushed her left arm to the side so he wouldn't accidentally hurt the hand that was almost recovered from frostbite. He knew how much it meant to her to be able to climb again.

In the gray light of his apartment bedroom, he admired her gentle peaks and valleys, letting his mouth do most of the searching, and he couldn't resist a quick taste. He scooted down and kissed her stomach, his hands cupping her backside, then he indulged lower. She groaned and squirmed, but his hold kept her in place so he could have his fill. Her hips bucked, and the fingers of her good hand dug painfully into his hair, but he didn't care.

"Ty," she whispered, barely able to talk. "You better get up here."

As he shifted and braced himself over her, she kissed him, not hesitating to take the taste of herself from him. The acceptance was more arousing than he could have imagined. He teased entering her as long as either of them could stand it, and then in one motion she accepted him, fully, without hesitation, and the world was set right once again. Before he let his desire take him, he stopped and looked at her.

"Don't move," he whispered.

Her eyes opened. "What's wrong?"

"I just want to look at you."

Her eyes narrowed. "Is this from 'Out of Africa'?"

"It's a good scene."

"You're weirdly sentimental." Her legs tightened around him.

They both turned their head when a whine emitted from the side of the bed.

"Speaking of Meryl Streep," Lindsey said.

Ty's chocolate Lab rested her head on the edge of the bed as she watched them intently, her tail thwapping a relentless beat on the faux-hardwood floor.

"Muck, turn away, sweetheart." When the dog wouldn't budge, Ty said more forcefully, "Git." She dropped to the floor and feeling a little guilty, he added, "Just give me five minutes and then I'll take you for a run."

Lindsey's eyes widened. "Five?"

"Ten?"

She clenched around him. "I only need thirty seconds. Quit talking and finish what you started, Galloway."

She wrapped her arms around him and set their bodies into a steady rhythm, and Ty gladly followed her lead. He buried himself deep and gave everything he had.

~

LINDSEY STEPPED THROUGH THE FRONT DOOR OF THE MODEST TWO-bedroom home where she had lived through her teenage years. When her dad died, her mom had moved the short distance from Berkeley to Walnut Creek to take a job as an office manager at a large medical practice where she still worked today.

Ty had met Lainie a few weeks ago at Lindsey's apartment in Berkeley, but this was his first visit to her mom's house. Like many people before him, he'd remarked that mother and daughter looked like sisters.

Ty followed Lindsey into the living room decorated with a plush white sofa and a fancy Moroccan rug, and immediately took an interest in the framed photos lining the shelves. The simple décor reminded her that a visit from Muck might not go over well. Already she was thinking of the mutt like she might a child. And Lainie was now the unsuspecting grandmother.

Knowing it was too soon to inform Ty of her intense attachment to his dog—to him?—she glanced at the man in question, clad in an untucked button-down navy shirt, his hands jammed in his jean pockets.

Ty Galloway. Dragon slayer.

He was looking at the family pictures on display—Robbie Coulson in the mountains, an array of photos of Lindsey and Alison as wild and wooly young girls with messy hair, crooked teeth, and happy smiles, traipsing in the big wide outdoors.

Over his shoulder, he grinned at her. "You and Alison look like little dirtbags."

"It's in the Coulson DNA."

"Hello?" her mom's voice came from upstairs.

"Hi, it's us," Lindsey yelled.

Her mom appeared, her blond hair shorter than Lindsey's and pushed away from her face with a colorful headband. Despite the heartbreak that had sliced through her life, Lainie Kincaid-Coulson had remained fit, active, and optimistic, even if it was only sometimes for show.

Lindsey didn't know how her mom had kept going through the dark times after losing her husband and having to raise and care for two daughters on her own, how she had made it through the unbearable grief of losing her oldest daughter. Alison's tie to their dad—a man she had resembled in both appearance and in an intense personality—was now absolute.

Although she had seen her mom several times since returning from Pakistan, Lindsey hugged her tightly.

Lainie leaned back and fiddled with Lindsey's loose hair before turning to Ty and giving him a quick embrace.

"I thought we'd have a cookout if you're up for handling the grill," she said to him.

"I'd be happy to."

"Follow me to the kitchen." Lainie waved him along.

"I'm just gonna pop upstairs for a second," Lindsey said.

"Okay," her mom said. "Be careful with the steps."

She was mostly recovered from the frostbite, although her feet were still a little numb and tender, and she continued to baby her left hand. Although she had returned to the lab at Berkeley, she was doing mostly computer work until she could feel confident in her dexterity.

Reaching the landing, she headed for her mom's bedroom.

She had spent the last few weeks replaying the dreams and odd interactions she'd had with Alison while on K2. Had they simply been her imagination? Had oxygen deprivation played a part? In the days since the expedition had ended, her doubts over her ability to differentiate reality versus fantasy had grown.

And while she had told her mom broad details of the journey to conquer K2, she had kept Alison's ghostly involvement from the narrative for the same reason she had decided not to burden David with the knowledge that Alison still may have been alive when he had left the mountain two years ago. He deserved to move past the pain as much as her mom did.

Her mom's room was simple and elegant, with a full-sized bed covered in a nautical-themed quilt and a dresser with a lone photo of their family—Robbie, Lainie, Alison, and Lindsey—taken in Hawai'i so many years ago. Lindsey touched the glass with reverence before heading to the walk-in closet.

She flipped on the light, went straight to the back, methodically searching through each garment until she found it. The jacket. Her dad's jacket. Just where her sister had told her it would be.

A shiver ran through Lindsey. "Thanks, Al."

Like the caress of the wind, a voice whispered in her ear.

I love you, Linc.

THE END

If you enjoyed *Cold Horizon*, would you consider posting a review? Not only does this help other readers discover a book, but it also aids an author in pursuing promotional opportunities. My heartfelt thanks. ~ Kristy

~

Sign-up for Kristy's newsletter at kmccaffrey.com/PathwayNewsletter to receive Pathway series updates.

Read more about Ty and Lindsey in this short story

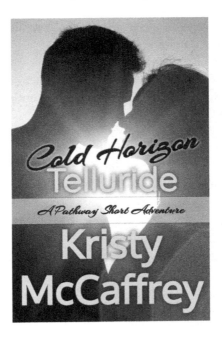

Lindsey Coulson has lost her edge. After surviving a harrowing descent of K2, the second highest mountain in the world, life back home has left her with serious doubts about continuing the dangerous life of a high-altitude mountain climber. When she accompanies her boyfriend, Ty Galloway, to a trade show in Telluride, Colorado, a chance encounter with a climber who knew her deceased dad—famed mountaineer Robbie Coulson—sets her on a different course.

Ty Galloway has settled into a nine-to-five routine with his new job as editor-in-chief of Mountaineer Magazine, but the monotony is already beginning to chafe. A weekend away with Lindsey at his parents' place seems like the perfect antidote, but when his mom and dad unexpectedly arrive, their presence puts a damper on his romantic plans. And they've got a few surprises in store for Ty.

(Includes appearances from Italian climber Elena Rossi and the irreverent mountaineer Dan Beck.)

Cold Horizon Telluride is part of The Pathway Short Adventure Series, a collection of short stories that offer continuing tales of the characters from the books.

Learn more about Cold Horizon Telluride
at
https://kmccaffrey.com/cold-horizon-telluride/

Women Who Have Reached the Summit of K2

Wanda Rutkiewicz (Polish) – 1986
Liliane Barrard (French) – 1986 *
Julie Tullis (British) – 1986 *
Chantal Mauduit (French) – 1992
Alison Hargreaves (British) – 1995 *
Edurne Pasabán (Spanish) – 2004 **
Nives Meroi (Italian) – 2006
Yuka Komatsu (Japanese) – 2006
Eun-Sun Oh (South Korean) – 2007
Cecilie Skog (Norwegian) – 2008 ***
Mi-Sun Go (South Korean) – 2008
Gerlinde Kaltenbrunner (Austrian) – 2011 ****
Maya Sherpa (Nepalese) – 2014
Dawa Yangzum Sherpa (Nepalese) – 2014
Pasang Lhamu Sherpa (Nepalese) – 2014
Luo Jing (Chinese) – 2014
Chris Jensen Burke (Australian) – 2014
Tamara Lunger (Italian) – 2014
Vanessa O'Brien (American) – 2017
Jing Xue (Chinese) – 2017
Gangaamaa Badamgarav (Mongolian) – 2018
Lisa Thompson (American) – 2018
Jianhong Li (Chinese) – 2018
Naoko Watanabe (Japanese) – 2018
Yuki Inayoshi (Japanese) – 2018
Viridiana Chavez (Mexican) – 2018
Sophie Lavaud (Swiss) – 2018

Died on descent
**First woman to complete all 14 8000-meter peaks,*
but only 13 without supplemental oxygen.

***Lost husband on descent
****First woman to complete all 14 8000-meter peaks
without supplemental oxygen.*

All 8000-meter Peaks in Descending Order

Mount Everest (8848 m)
K2 (8614 m)
Kangchenjunga (8586 m)
Lhotse (8516 m)
Makalu (8485 m)
Cho Oyu (8188 m)
Dhaulagiri (8167 m)
Manaslu (8163 m)
Nanga Parbat (8125 m)
Annapurna (8091 m)
Gasherbrum I (8080 m)
Broad Peak (8051 m)
Gasherbrum II (8035 m)
Shishapangma (8027 m)

GLOSSARY OF CLIMBING TERMS

Altitude Sickness: a condition caused by exposure to low amounts of oxygen at high elevations; can progress to high-altitude pulmonary edema or high-altitude cerebral edema, which if left untreated can lead to death.

Anchor: a belay / rappel point generally atop a pitch, marked by fixed protection (like bolts) or built using removable protection.

Ascender: a device for ascending a rope.

Bamboo Wand: a stick with a small flag on top used to mark paths over glaciers and snow fields.

Base Camp: the lowest camp on a mountain-climbing expedition.

Belay: to secure the rope while a partner climbs; belaying often involves the use of a 'belay device' that introduces friction into the system to help arrest a fall.

Bivouac (also Bivy): to spend the night out while approaching or climbing a multiday objective, or because of poor planning.

Bivy Sack: a small, lightweight nylon sleeve used as a standalone sleeping bag or to cover a sleeping bag for extra warmth.

Carabiner: a snap-link connecting the rope to some kind of protection.

Couloir: a steep gorge or gully on the side of a mountain.

Crampon: multipronged 'foot fangs' that clamp onto mountain boots for travel on hard snow and/or ice.

Crevasse: a deep crack in glacial ice, formed when a glacier spills over uneven terrain, causing the ice to split and fracture.

Death Zone: above 7000 meters, where mountaineers risk brain damage, edema, and death.

Dirtbag: connotes a climbing bum.

Edema: swelling caused by an excess of fluid in bodily tissues; high-altitude mountain climbers risk HAPE (high-altitude pulmonary edema) or HACE (high-altitude cerebral edema); both can lead to death. Treatment combines a swift descent to a lower elevation along with supplemental oxygen.

Fixed Line: skinny, static ropes left in place, often on expedition-style ascents, to facilitate wall or mountain travel.

Harness: a nylon waist belt plus leg-loop arrangement that attaches the climber to a rope and protection system.

Himalaya Range: a mountain range extending 1500 miles along the border between India and Tibet; contains ten of the fourteen 8000-meter peaks including Mt. Everest, the tallest mountain on earth.

Ice Axe: features an adze for chopping steps, a pick for sinking into snow and ice, and a spike for walking travel.

Ice Screw: a self-ratcheting, hollow, tubular screw placed in ice as an anchor or protection.

Jumar: a cam-action mechanical ascender, with handles, for climbing fixed lines.

K2: the second highest mountain on earth at 8,614 meters (28,251 feet) and the highest point of the Karakoram Range.

Karakoram Range: a mountain range spanning the borders of Pakistan, India, and China; contains four of the fourteen 8000-meter peaks including K2, the second-tallest mountain on earth.

Mt. Everest: the highest mountain on earth at 8,848 meters (29,029 feet) and located in the Himalayas.

Piton: a metal spike hammered into the rock as protection.

Prusik: a knot—and/or the 'prusik slings' used with this knot—used to ascend a fixed rope. 'Prusiking' was a precursor to 'jumaring.'

Rack: an over-the-shoulder gear sling and the protection clipped to it. The rack is key to traditional climbing.

Rappel: to descend a single or double line by sliding down the ropes with a belay / rappel device.

Send: to free-climb without falling; any successful ascent of a climb, wall, or mountain.

ACKNOWLEDGMENTS

I must give a resounding thank you to all the mountain and rock climbers who have told their stories in books, magazines, and on social media. It's this openness and willingness to share their experiences that allows someone like me to gain insight into the world they occupy. I studied the likes of Ed Viesturs, Jon Krakauer, Conrad Anker, the late Alex Lowe, Jennifer Lowe-Anker, Gerlinde Kaltenbrunner, Renan Ozturk, Jimmy Chin, Alex Honnold, Jennifer Jordan, Arlene Blum, Jim Curran, Kit DesLauriers, Heidi Howkins, Reinhold Messner, Jerzy Kukuczka, Sir Edmund Hillary, Tenzing Norgay, David Roberts, Cory Richards, Mark Jenkins, Melissa Arnot, Dave Hahn, Keith Ladzinski, Mike Horn, Peter Zuckerman, Amanda Padoan, Rick Ridgeway, Steph Davis, Lynn Hill, Sasha DiGiulian, Hilaree O'Neill, Emily Harrington, Maria Coffey, Graham Bowley, Jim Davidson, Kevin Vaughan, and many more dedicated and talented individuals.

My sincere thanks to author and dear friend Ann Charles for her support and advice during the writing of Cold Horizon, and her enthusiastic thumbs-up for the finished manuscript. A bow of gratitude to my beta readers—Michelle Davis, Denise Keef, Becky Humphreys, Vicki Huskey, Heather Chargualaf, Diane Garland, Corie Carson and Bob Dickerson—for reading the final draft quickly and offering excellent commentary and corrections that helped to strengthen the story.

Thank you to my editor, Mimi Munk. She's a gentle soul who handles literary babies—and the neurotic authors who birth them—with tender care and humor. And a second round of applause for Diane Garland. Not only does she beta read the final draft, but she also proofreads the final file before formatting. She also provides me with a worldkeeping service, meaning she keeps track of every detail in my story world and lets me know if I've got an error. Some mistakes are small, like inconsistent eye color for a character, but others are big, such as the misalignment of a backstory reference. She tackles the minutiae with the steadfastness of a mother and the heart of a warrior

And finally, I must thank my husband. He's the one who lives with me while I go through the five stages of novel writing: gleeful inspiration over an exciting topic, the joy of writing the first half of the story, frustration when the second half refuses to work on any level, despair that I may never finish the damned thing, and finally, depression when I type THE END. He read Cold Horizon, he loved it, and my heart became full again, bringing me back to gleeful inspiration so that I can begin the maddening process over again.

Read Brynn's story in ANCIENT WINDS
The Pathway Series Book 3

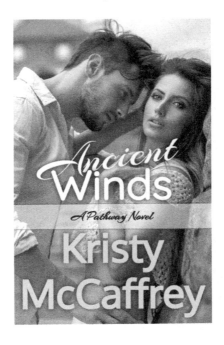

Brynn Galloway doesn't know it, but her academic career in archaeology is about to become a laughingstock. When a rare Sumerian artifact surfaces, her presence is requested in Bolivia, but nothing is as it seems. Soon, she's entangled in a desperate hunt not only for a valuable antiquity but also for answers to humanity that might stretch across time. And by her side is a sexy mercenary physicist with a maddening belief in space aliens.

Dr. Tristan Magee is in a bad mood. When his latest acquisition—an unusual and as yet untranslated Sumerian cuneiform tablet—is stolen right out from under him and spirited away to the Bolivian jungle, he'll do whatever it takes to get it back. Unfortunately, that includes partnering with a female archaeologist who proves to be the kind of distraction that brought down civilizations.

Learn more about Ancient Winds
at
https://kmccaffrey.com/ancient-winds/

ABOUT THE AUTHOR

Kristy McCaffrey has been writing since she was very young, but it wasn't until she was a stay-at-home mom that she considered becoming published. A fascination with science led her to earn two mechanical engineering degrees—she did her undergraduate work at Arizona State University and her graduate studies at the University of Pittsburgh—but storytelling has always been her passion. She writes both contemporary tales and award-winning historical western romances.

An Arizona native, Kristy and her husband reside in the desert where they frequently remove (rescue) rattlesnakes from their property, go for runs among the cactus, and plan trips to far-off places like the Orkney Islands or Machu Picchu. But mostly, she works 12-hour days and enjoys at-home date nights with her sweetheart, which usually include Will Ferrell movies and sci-fi flicks. Her four children have nearly all flown the nest, so she lavishes her maternal instincts on her chocolate Labrador, Lily, and Marley, an older yellow Labrador her family rescued in early 2018. Both dogs are frequently featured on her Instagram account.

"Try to love the questions themselves ..." – Rainer Maria Rilke

Connect with Kristy

Website: kmccaffrey.com

Newsletter: kmccaffrey.com/PathwayNewsletter

Facebook: facebook.com/AuthorKristyMcCaffrey

Twitter: twitter.com/McCaffreyKristy

Instagram: instagram.com/kristymccaffrey/

BookBub: bookbub.com/authors/kristy-mccaffrey

Made in the USA
Las Vegas, NV
28 November 2022

60562834R00174